TRINITY BLOOD

ILLUSTRATOR
KIYO KYUJO

AUTHOR
SUNAO YOSHIDA

CHARACTER DESIGN
THORES
SHIBAMOTO

VOLUME ONE

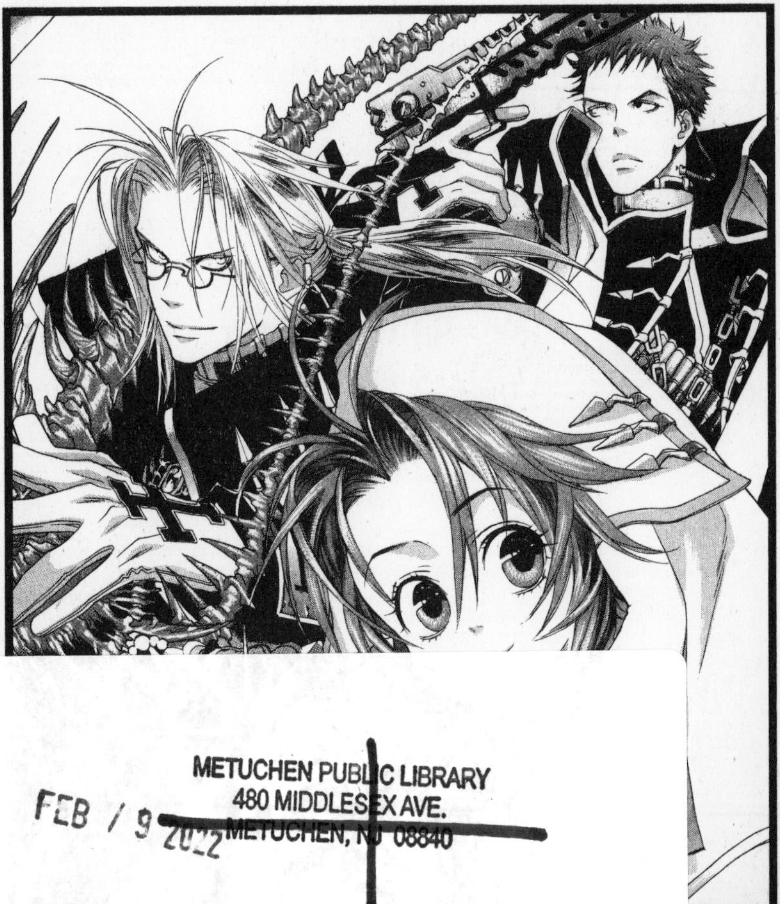

Trinity Blood Vol. 1
Illustrated by Kiyo Kyujo
Written by Sunao Yoshida

Translation - Beni Axia Conrad
English Adaptation - Christine Boylan
Associate Editor - Stephanie Duchin
Retouch and Lettering - Mike Estacio
Production Artist - Mike Estacio
Cover Design - James Lee

Editor - Lillian Diaz-Przybyl
Digital Imaging Manager - Chris Buford
Pre-Production Supervisor - Erika Terriquez
Art Director - Anne Marie Horne
Production Manager - Elisabeth Brizzi
Managing Editor - Vy Nguyen
VP of Production - Ron Klamert
Editor-in-Chief - Rob Tokar
Publisher - Mike Kiley
President and C.O.O. - John Parker
C.E.O. and Chief Creative Officer - Stuart Levy

(handwritten, right margin: YA-MANGA TRINITY BLOOD Vol. 1)

A  **TOKYOPOP** Manga

TOKYOPOP Inc.
5900 Wilshire Blvd. Suite 2000
Los Angeles, CA 90036

E-mail: info@TOKYOPOP.com
Come visit us online at www.TOKYOPOP.com

ISBN: 1-59816-674-3

First TOKYOPOP printing: November 2006
10 9 8 7 6 5 4 3
Printed in the USA

TRINITY BLOOD™

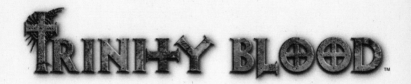

VOLUME 1

WRITTEN BY

SUNAO YOSHIDA

ILLUSTRATED BY

KIYO KYUJO

TOKYOPOP®

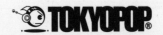

HAMBURG // LONDON // LOS ANGELES // TOKYO

CONTENTS

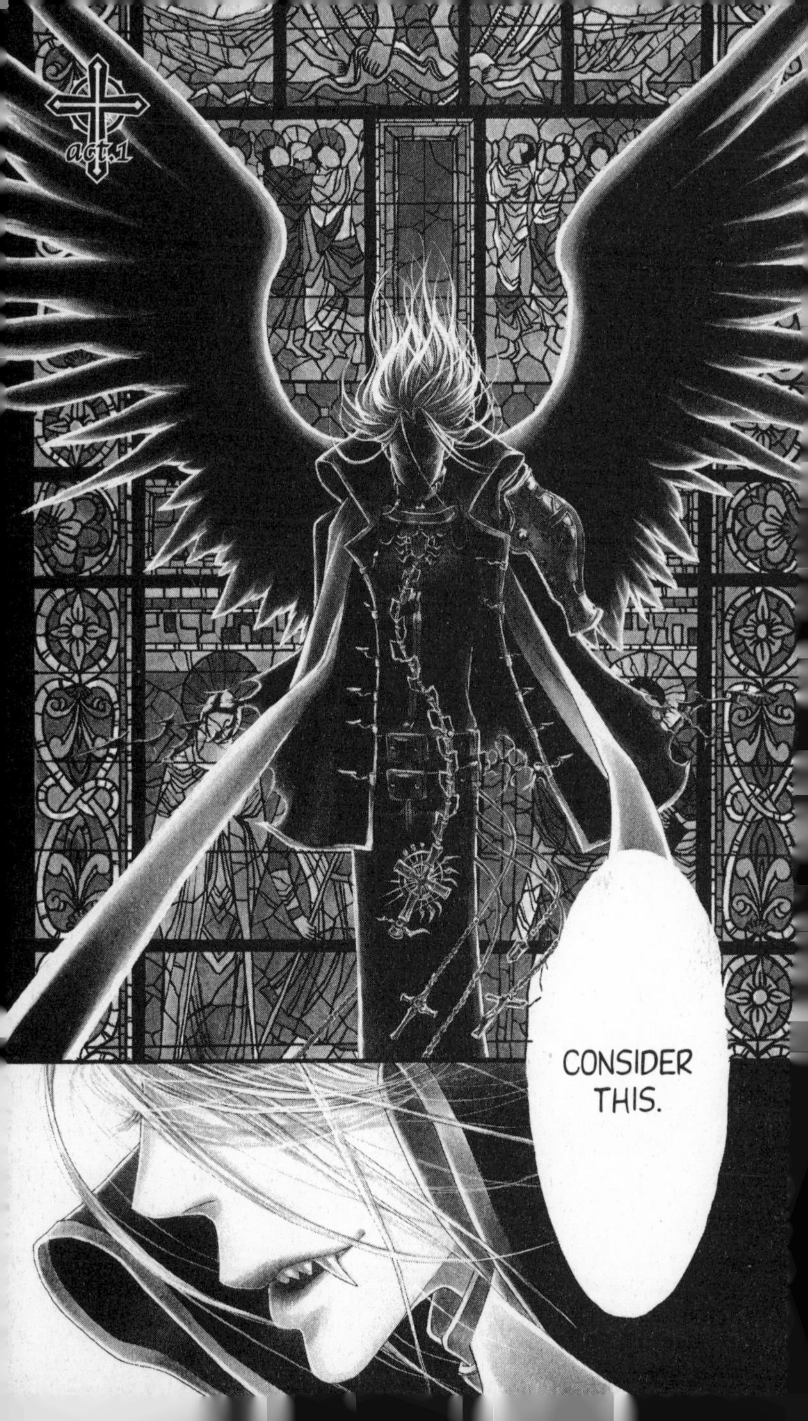
act.1
CONSIDER THIS.

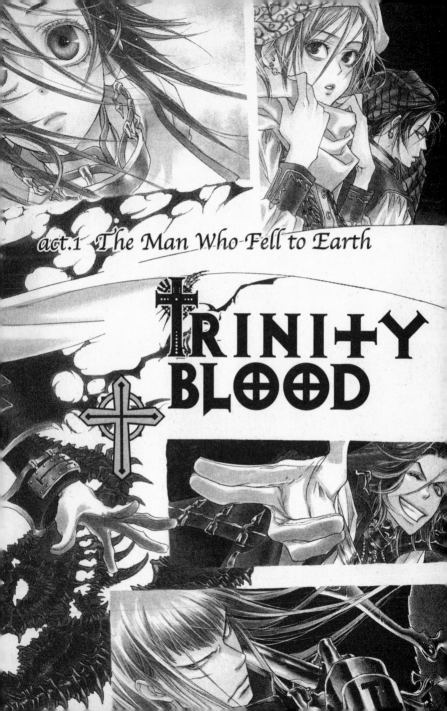

act.1 The Man Who Fell to Earth

TRINI†Y BLOOD

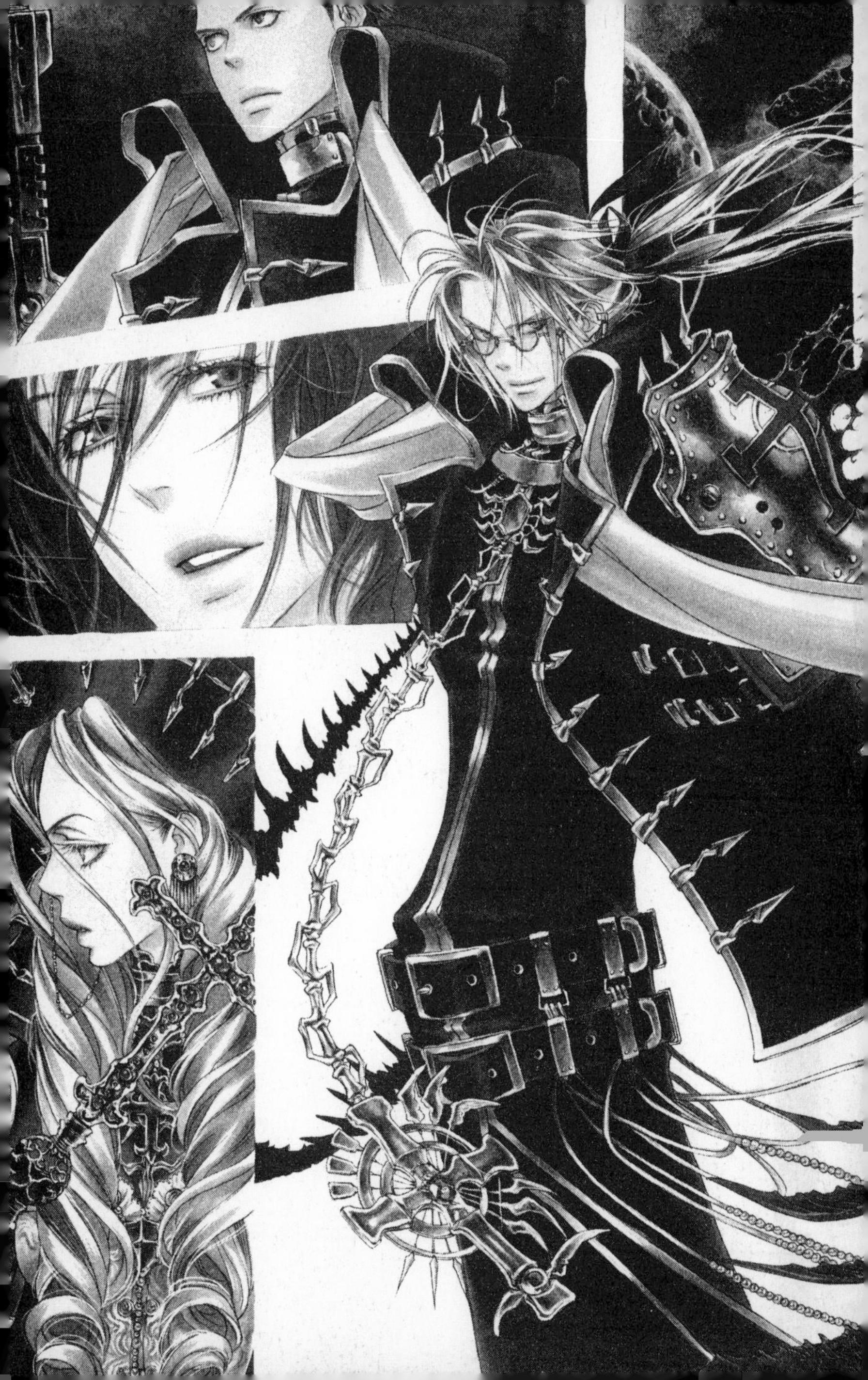

TRINITY BLOOD

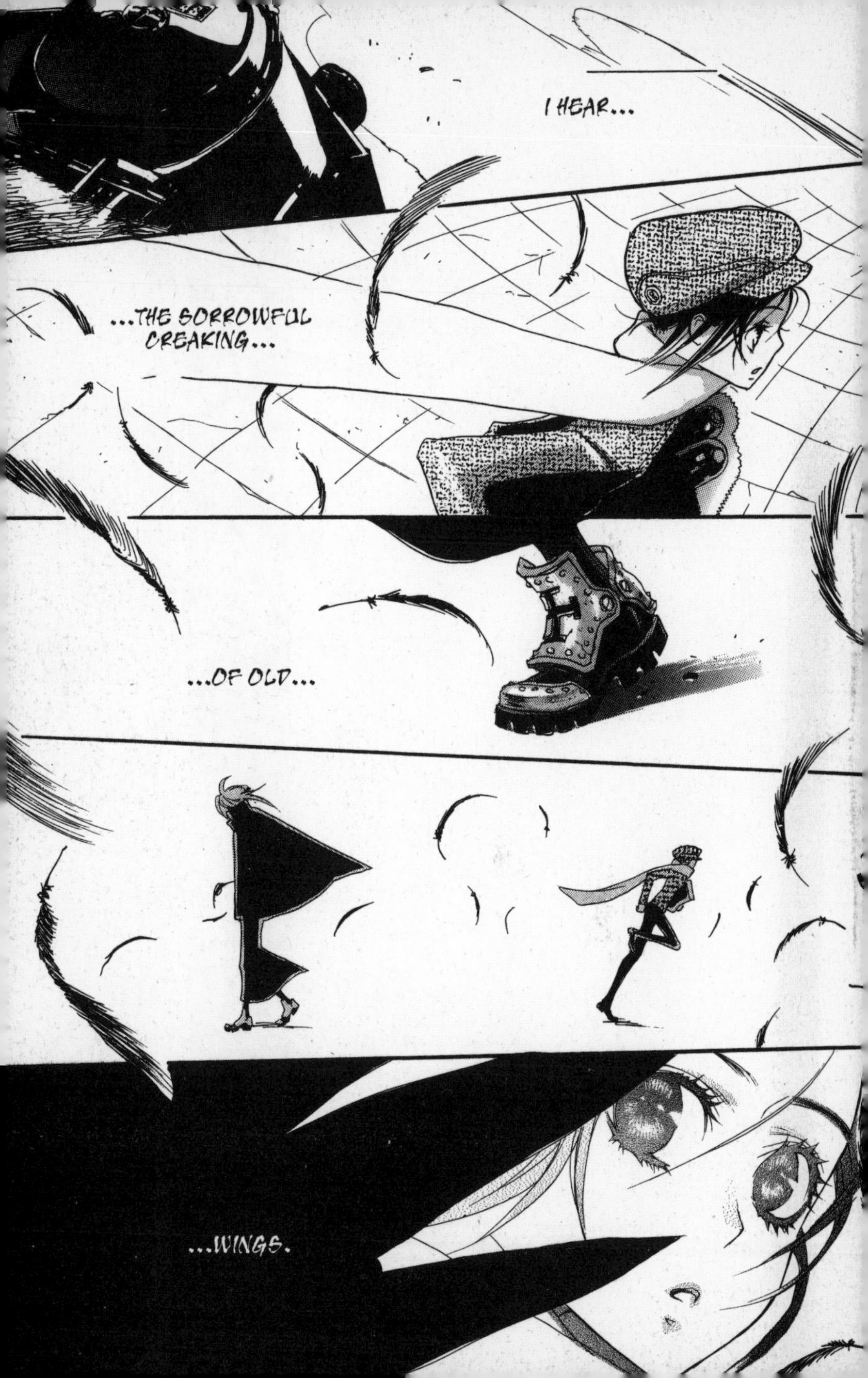
I HEAR...
...THE SORROWFUL CREAKING...
...OF OLD...
...WINGS.

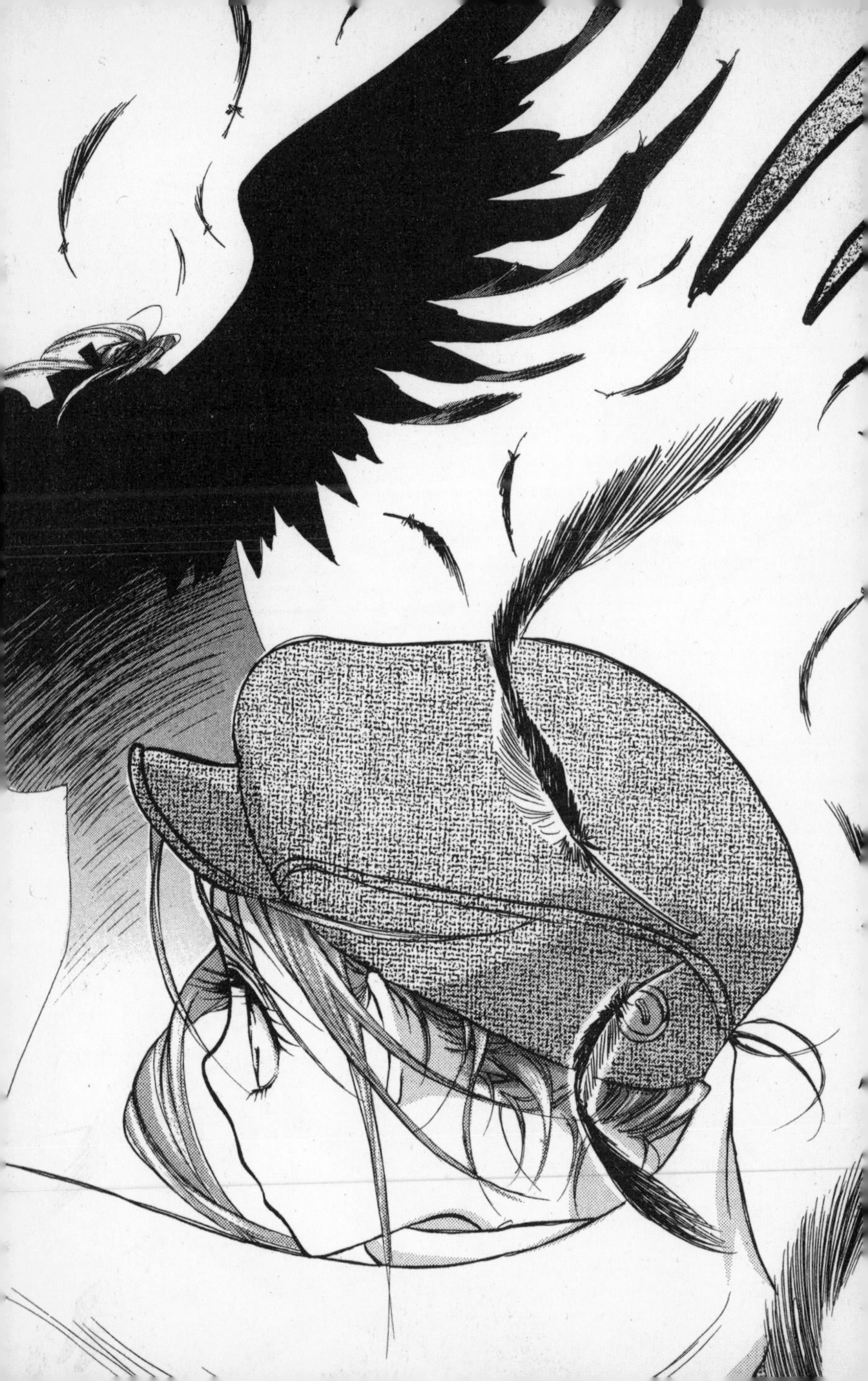

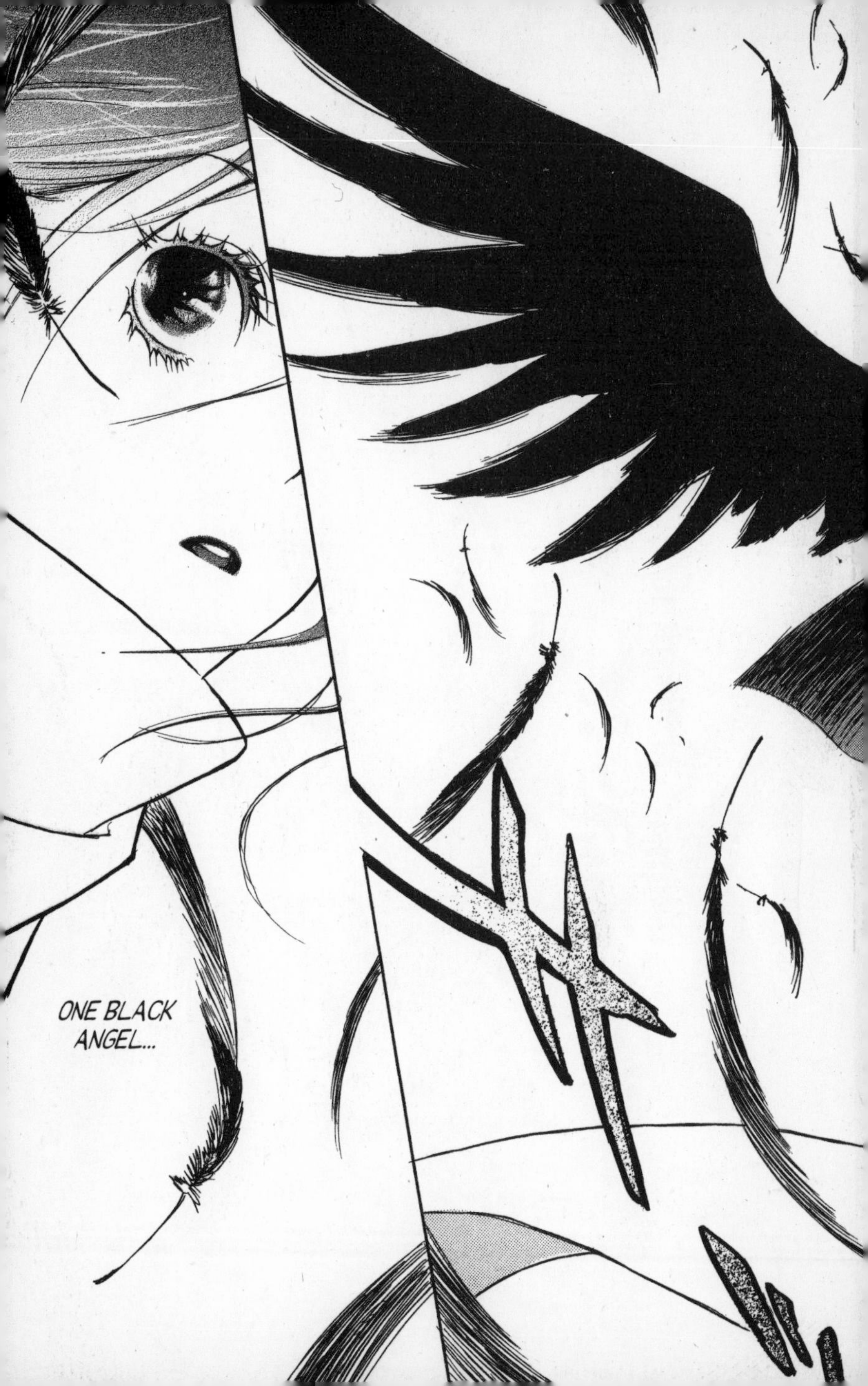
ONE BLACK ANGEL...

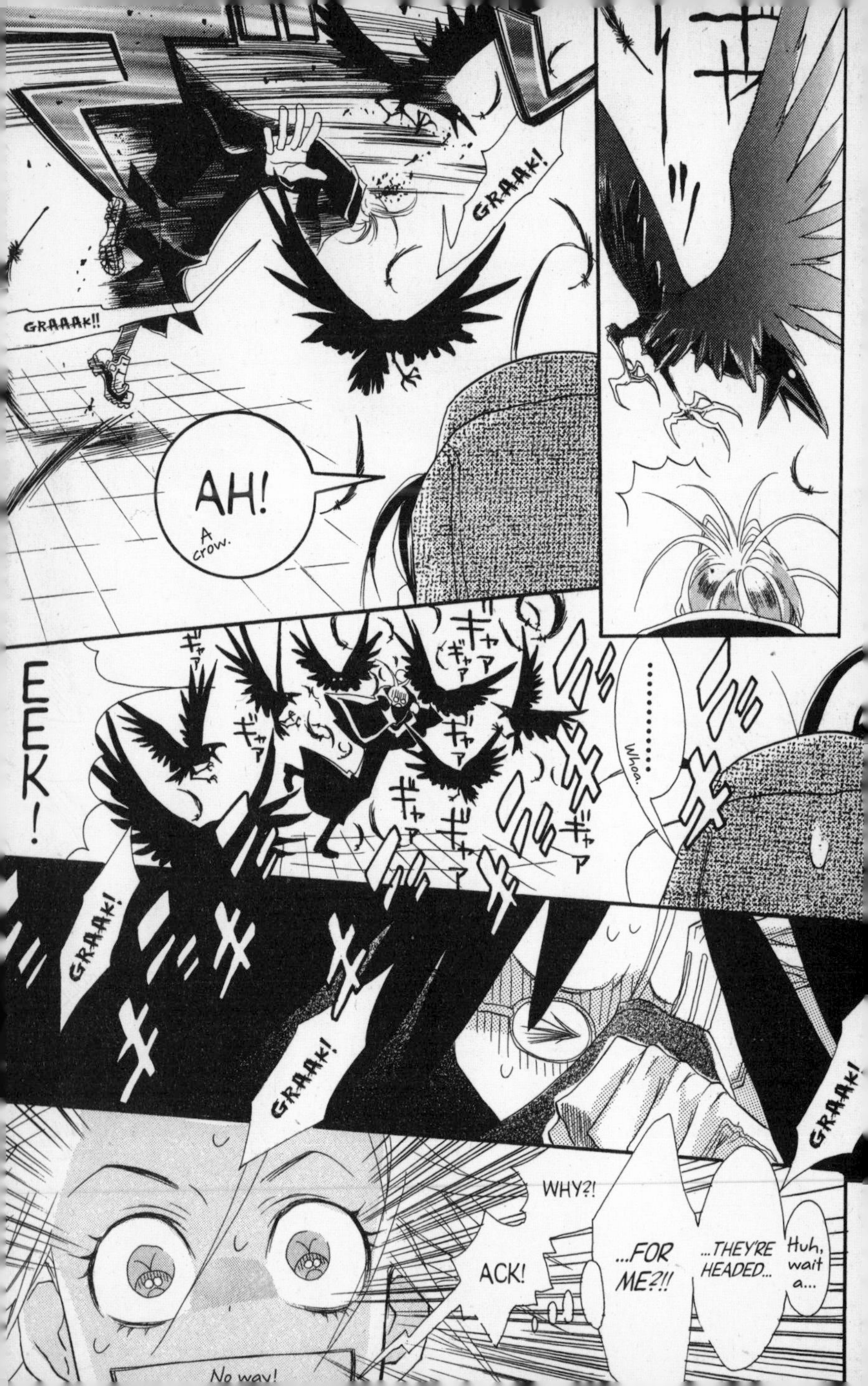
ギャ
GRAAK!
GRAAAK!!
AH!
A crow.
......Whoa.
ギャア
ギャア
EEK!
GRAAK!
GRAAK!
GRAAK!
Huh, wait a...
...THEY'RE HEADED...
...FOR ME?!!
ACK!
WHY?!
No way!

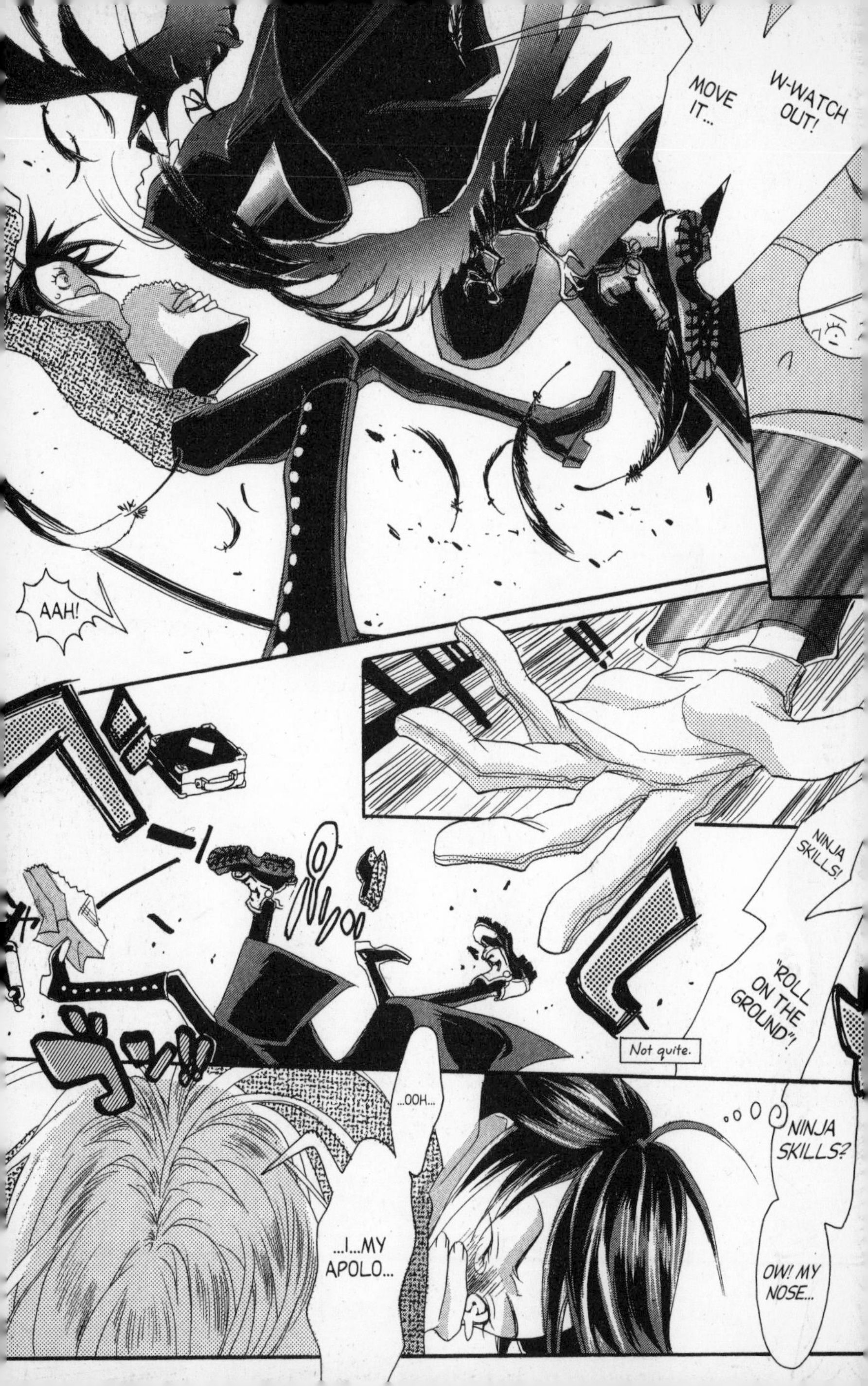
W-WATCH OUT!
MOVE IT...
AAH!
NINJA SKILLS!
"ROLL ON THE GROUND"!
Not quite.
NINJA SKILLS?
OW! MY NOSE...
...OOH...
...I...MY APOLO...

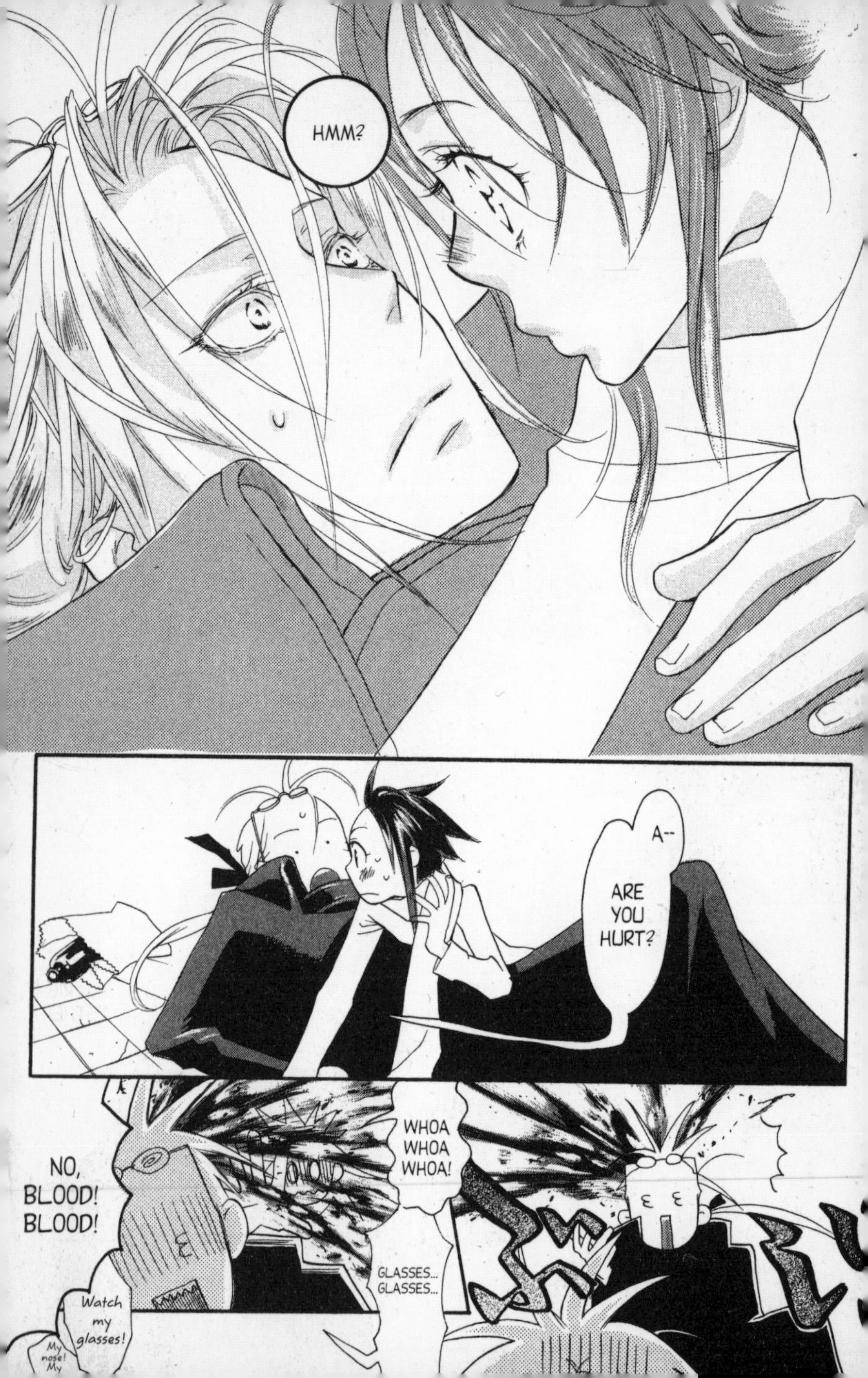
HMM?
A--
ARE YOU HURT?
WHOA WHOA WHOA!
NO, BLOOD! BLOOD!
GLASSES... GLASSES...
Watch my glasses!
My nose! My

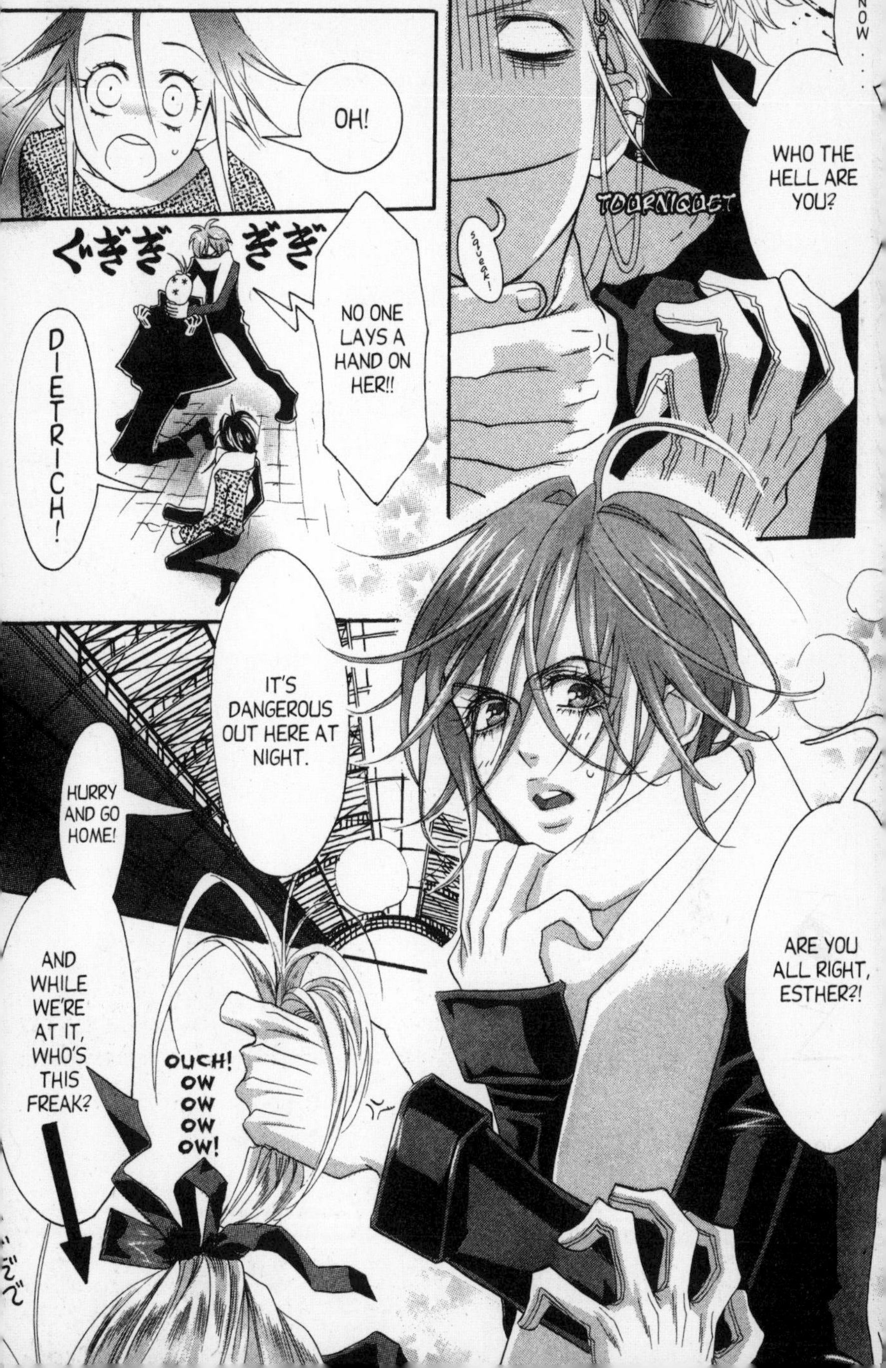
NOW . . .
WHO THE HELL ARE YOU?
TOURNIQUET
squeak!
OH!
ぐぎぎ ぎぎ
NO ONE LAYS A HAND ON HER!!
DIETRICH!
ARE YOU ALL RIGHT, ESTHER?!
IT'S DANGEROUS OUT HERE AT NIGHT.
HURRY AND GO HOME!
AND WHILE WE'RE AT IT, WHO'S THIS FREAK?
OUCH! OW OW OW OW!

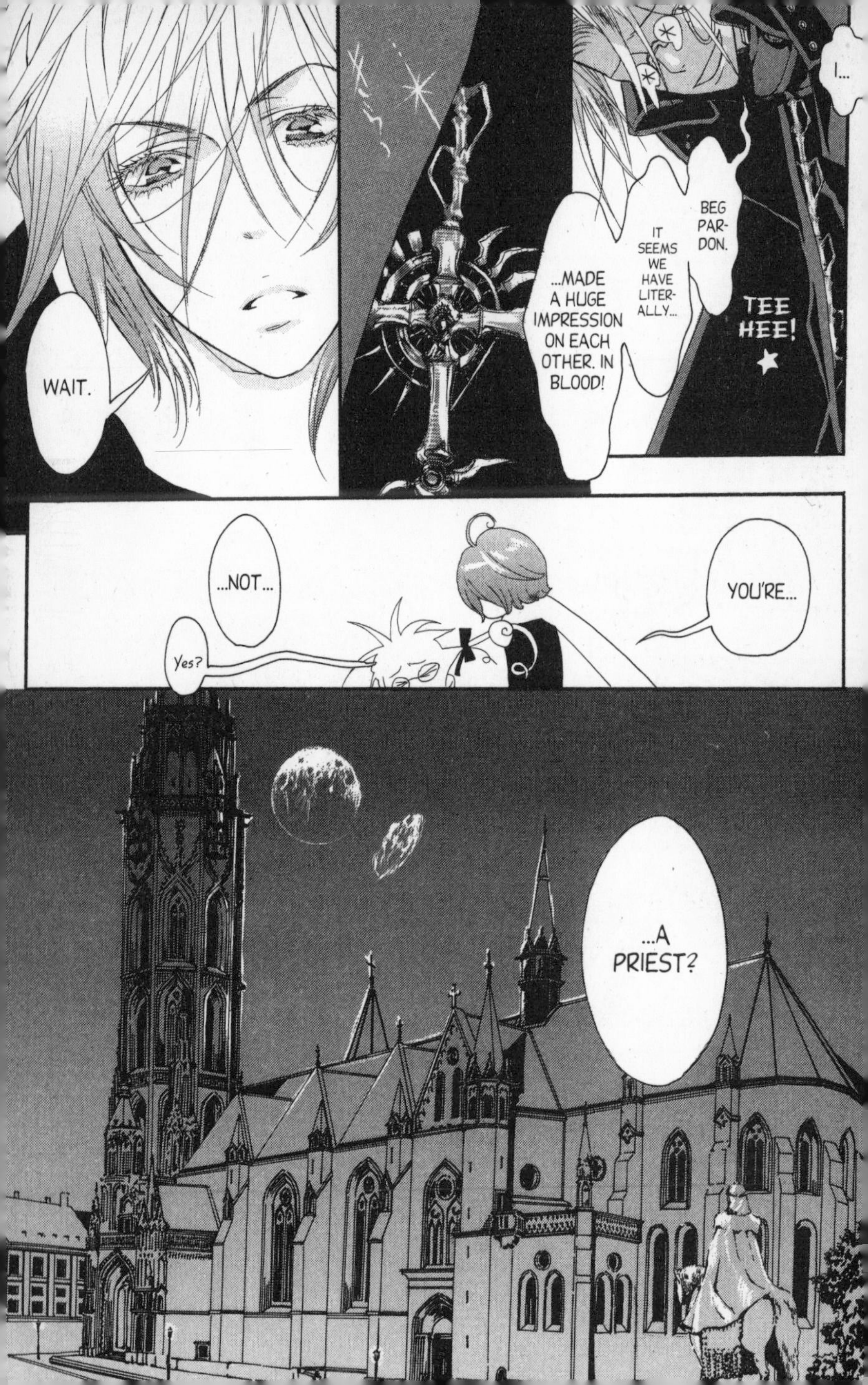
I...
BEG PARDON.
IT SEEMS WE HAVE LITERALLY...
TEE HEE!
...MADE A HUGE IMPRESSION ON EACH OTHER. IN BLOOD!
WAIT.
YOU'RE...
...NOT...
Yes?
...A PRIEST?

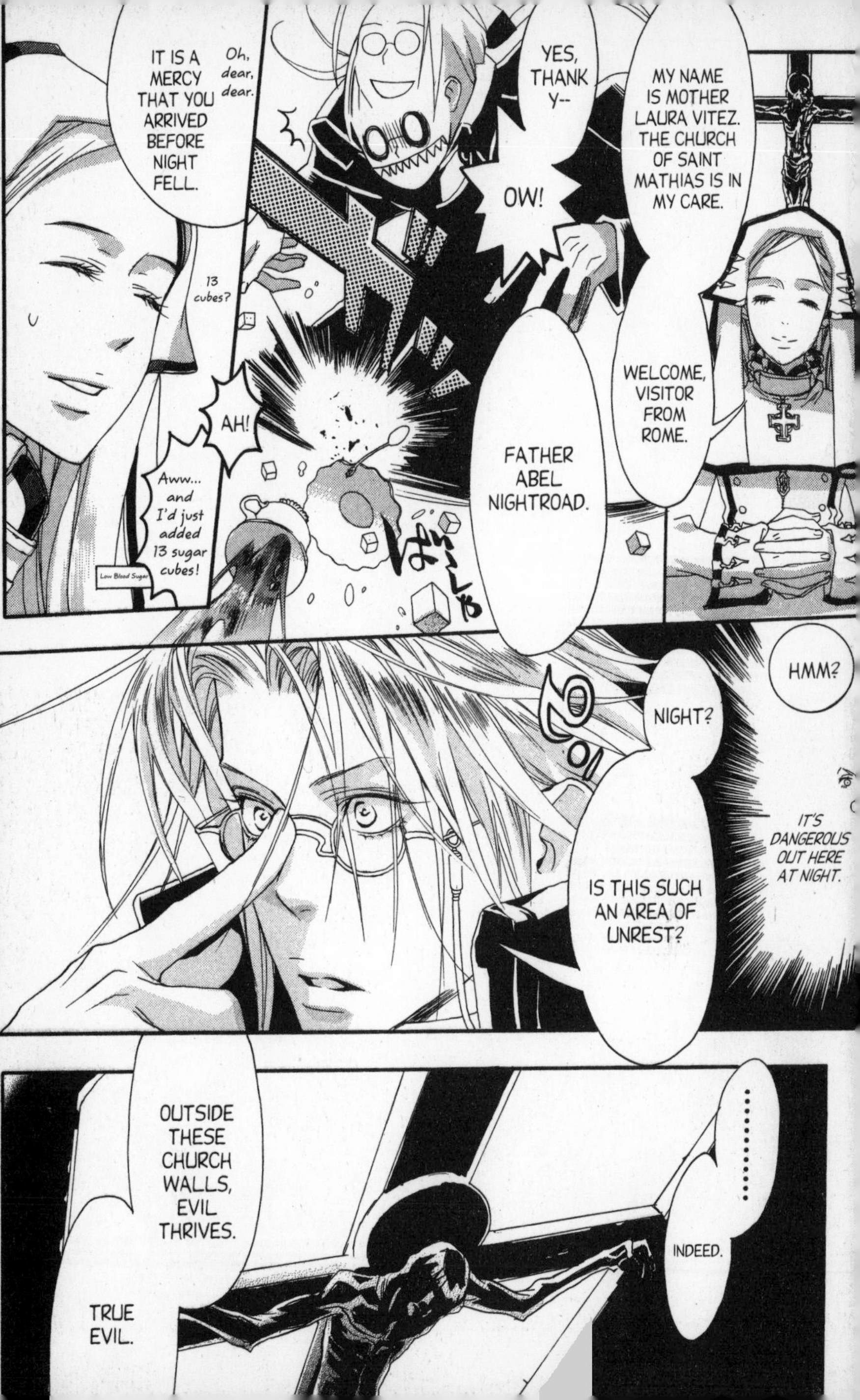

MY NAME IS MOTHER LAURA VITEZ. THE CHURCH OF SAINT MATHIAS IS IN MY CARE.
WELCOME, VISITOR FROM ROME.
FATHER ABEL NIGHTROAD.
YES, THANK Y--
OW!
IT IS A MERCY THAT YOU ARRIVED BEFORE NIGHT FELL.
Oh, dear, dear.
13 cubes?
AH!
Aww... and I'd just added 13 sugar cubes!
Low Blood Sugar
HMM?
NIGHT?
IT'S DANGEROUS OUT HERE AT NIGHT.
IS THIS SUCH AN AREA OF UNREST?
......
INDEED.
OUTSIDE THESE CHURCH WALLS, EVIL THRIVES.
TRUE EVIL.

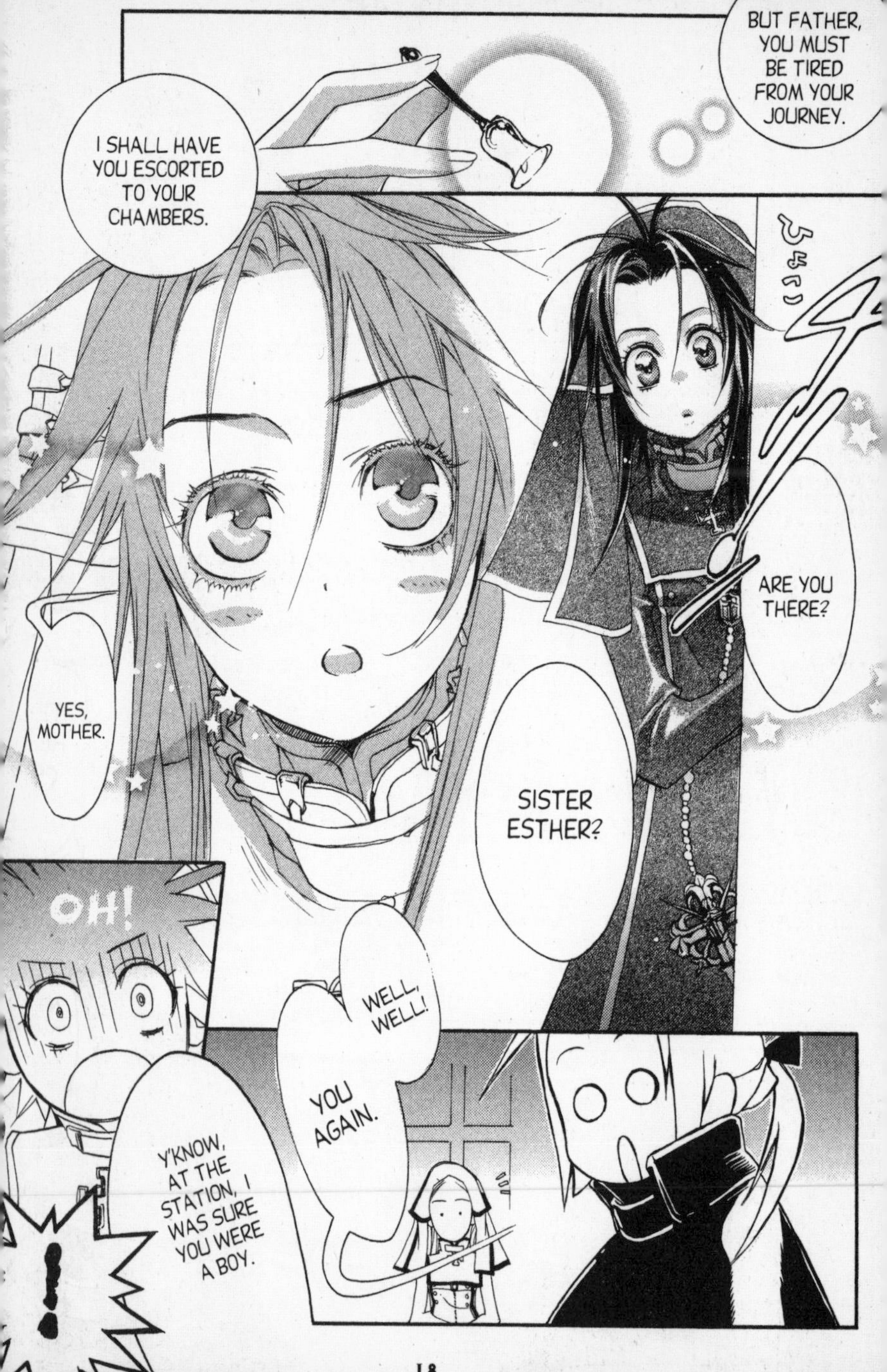
BUT FATHER, YOU MUST BE TIRED FROM YOUR JOURNEY.
I SHALL HAVE YOU ESCORTED TO YOUR CHAMBERS.
ぴょこ
ARE YOU THERE?
SISTER ESTHER?
YES, MOTHER.
WELL, WELL!
YOU AGAIN.
Y'KNOW, AT THE STATION, I WAS SURE YOU WERE A BOY.
OH!
!

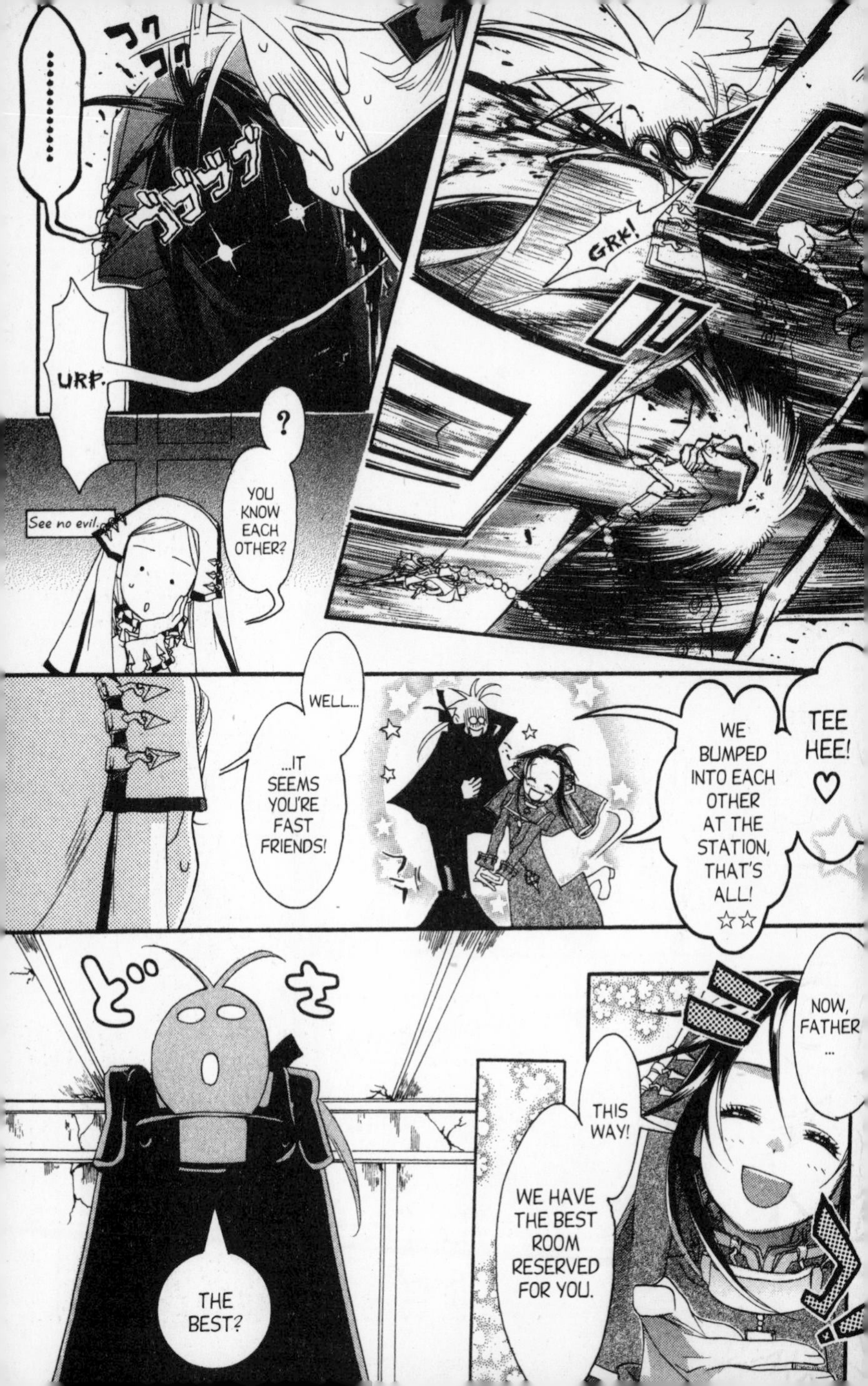
GRK!
ゴク ゴク
ヴヴヴヴ
......
URP.
?
YOU KNOW EACH OTHER?
See no evil.
TEE HEE! ♡
WE BUMPED INTO EACH OTHER AT THE STATION, THAT'S ALL! ☆☆
WELL...
...IT SEEMS YOU'RE FAST FRIENDS!
NOW, FATHER...
THIS WAY!
WE HAVE THE BEST ROOM RESERVED FOR YOU.
THE BEST?

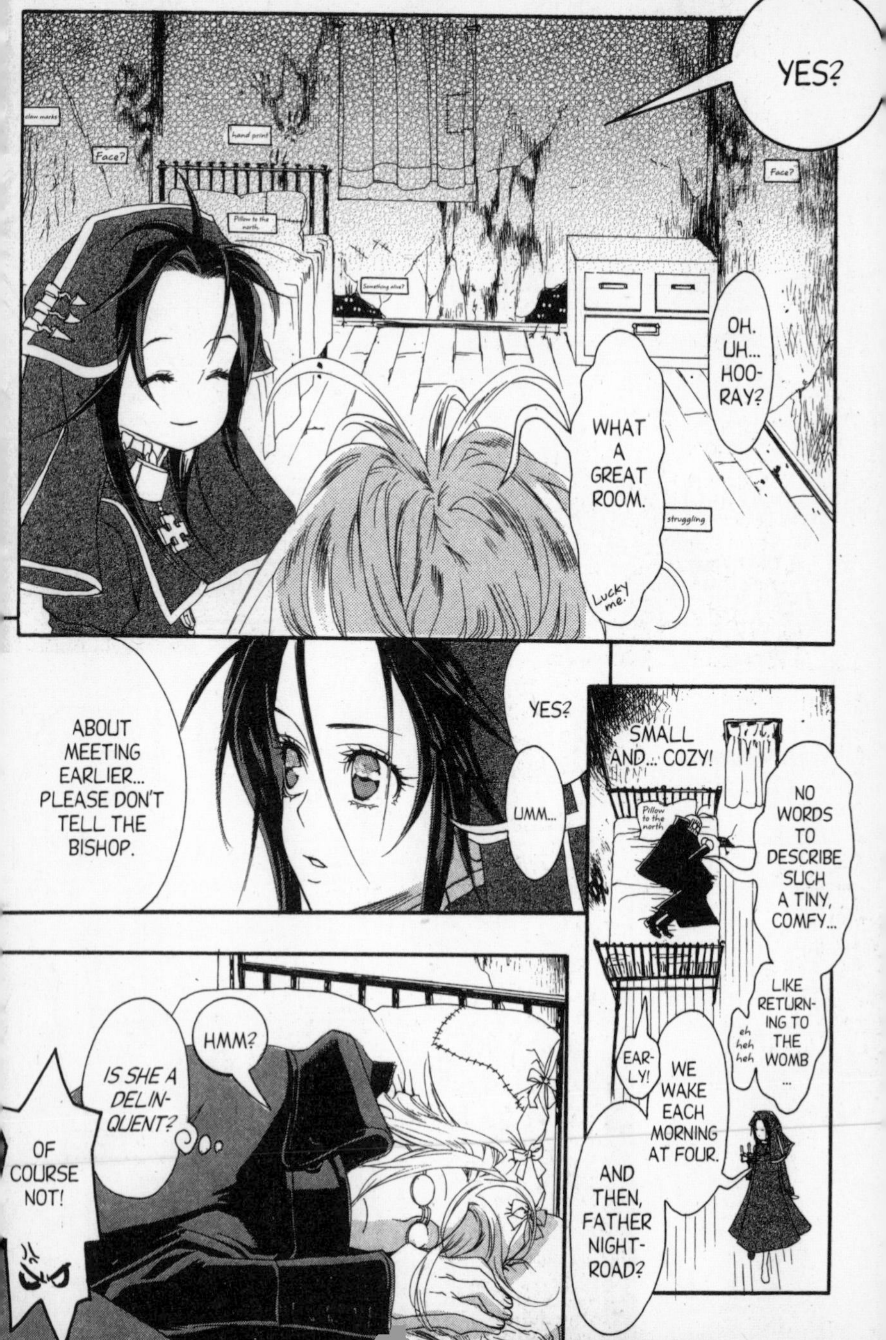
YES?
claw marks
hand print
Face?
Face?
Pillow to the north.
Something alive?
OH. UH... HOO-RAY?
WHAT A GREAT ROOM.
struggling
Lucky me.
SMALL AND... COZY!
Pillow to the north
NO WORDS TO DESCRIBE SUCH A TINY, COMFY...
LIKE RETURN-ING TO THE WOMB ...
eh heh heh
EAR-LY!
WE WAKE EACH MORNING AT FOUR.
AND THEN, FATHER NIGHT-ROAD?
YES?
UMM...
ABOUT MEETING EARLIER... PLEASE DON'T TELL THE BISHOP.
HMM?
IS SHE A DELIN-QUENT?
OF COURSE NOT!

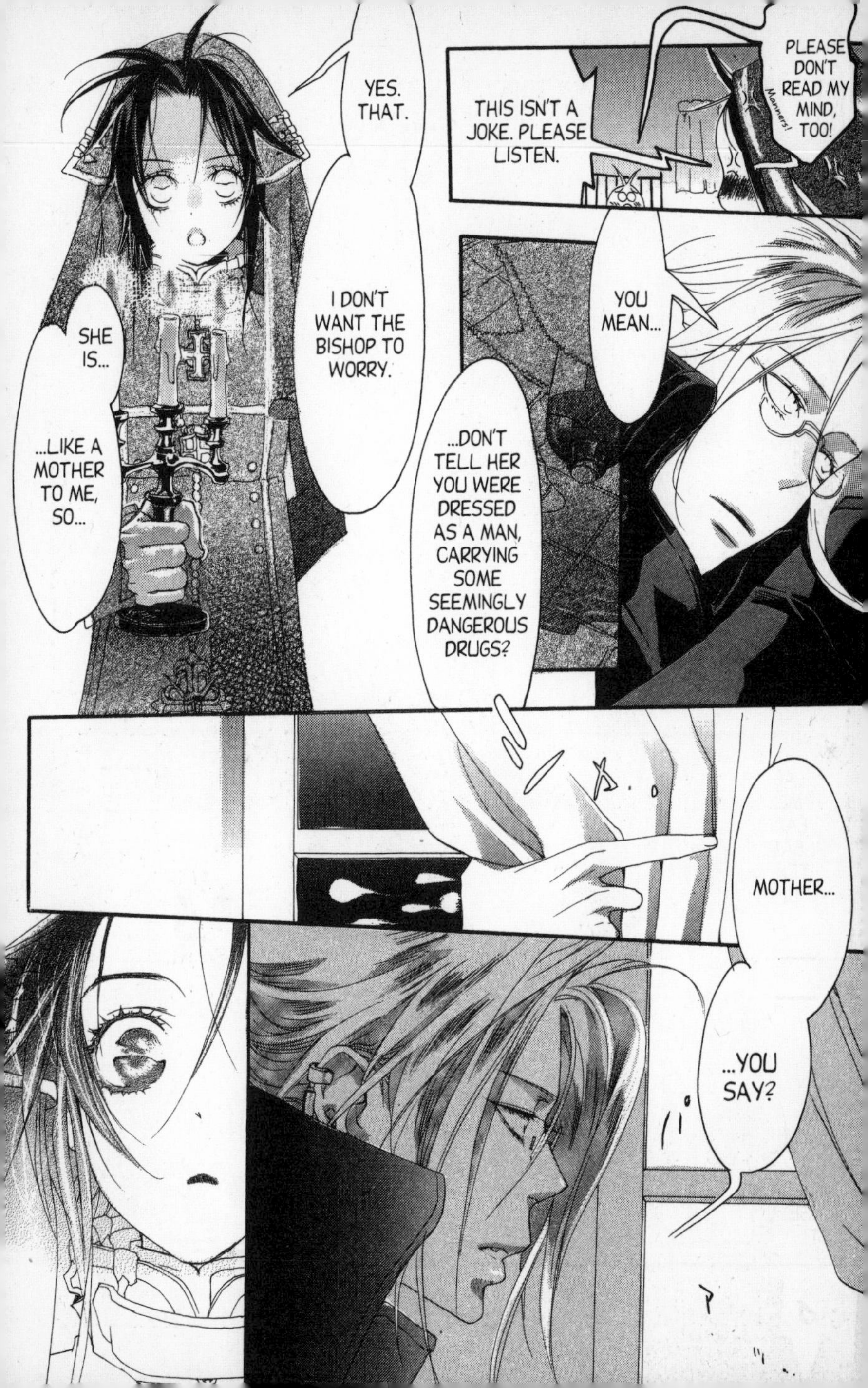

PLEASE DON'T READ MY MIND, TOO!
Manners!
THIS ISN'T A JOKE. PLEASE LISTEN.
YOU MEAN...
...DON'T TELL HER YOU WERE DRESSED AS A MAN, CARRYING SOME SEEMINGLY DANGEROUS DRUGS?
YES. THAT.
I DON'T WANT THE BISHOP TO WORRY.
SHE IS...
...LIKE A MOTHER TO ME, SO...
MOTHER...
...YOU SAY?

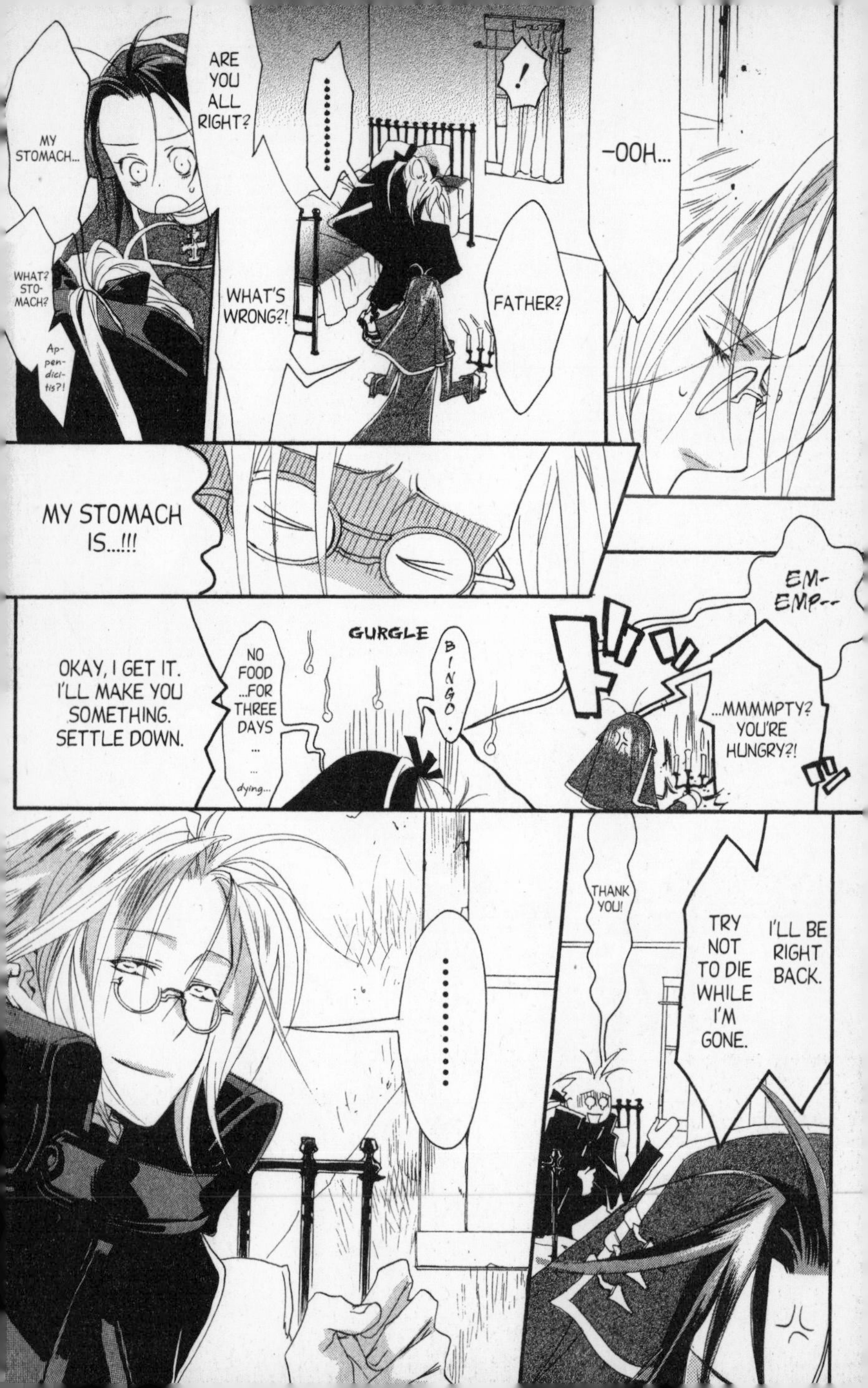
-OOH...
!
....
FATHER?
WHAT'S WRONG?!
ARE YOU ALL RIGHT?
MY STOMACH...
WHAT? STOMACH?
Ap-pen-dici-tis?!
MY STOMACH IS...!!!
EM- EMP--
...MMMMPTY? YOU'RE HUNGRY?!
BINGO.
GURGLE
NO FOOD ...FOR THREE DAYS ... ... dying...
OKAY, I GET IT. I'LL MAKE YOU SOMETHING. SETTLE DOWN.
I'LL BE RIGHT BACK.
TRY NOT TO DIE WHILE I'M GONE.
THANK YOU!
....

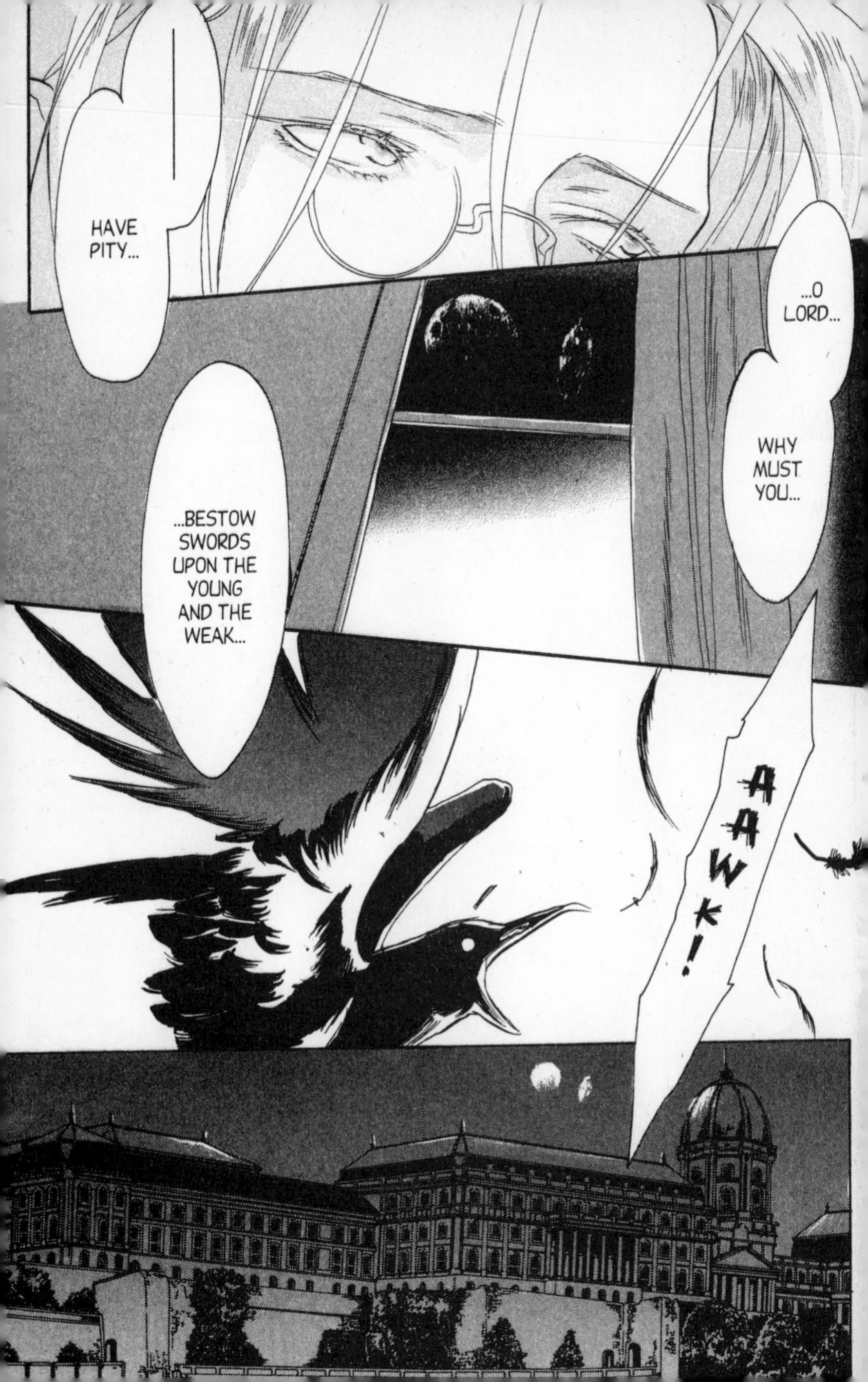
HAVE PITY...
...O LORD...
WHY MUST YOU...
...BESTOW SWORDS UPON THE YOUNG AND THE WEAK...
AAWK!

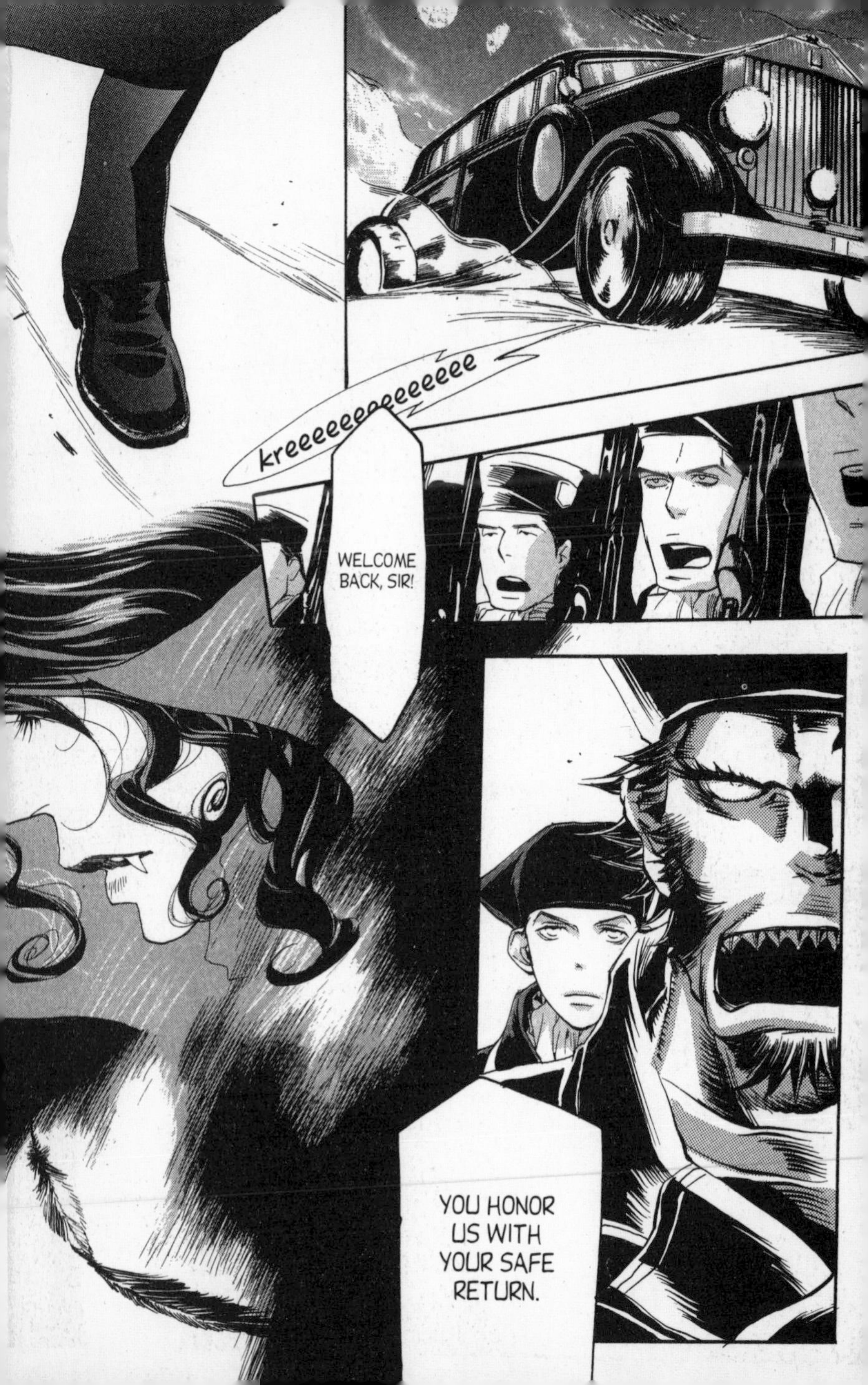
kreeeeeeeeeeeeee
WELCOME BACK, SIR!
YOU HONOR US WITH YOUR SAFE RETURN.

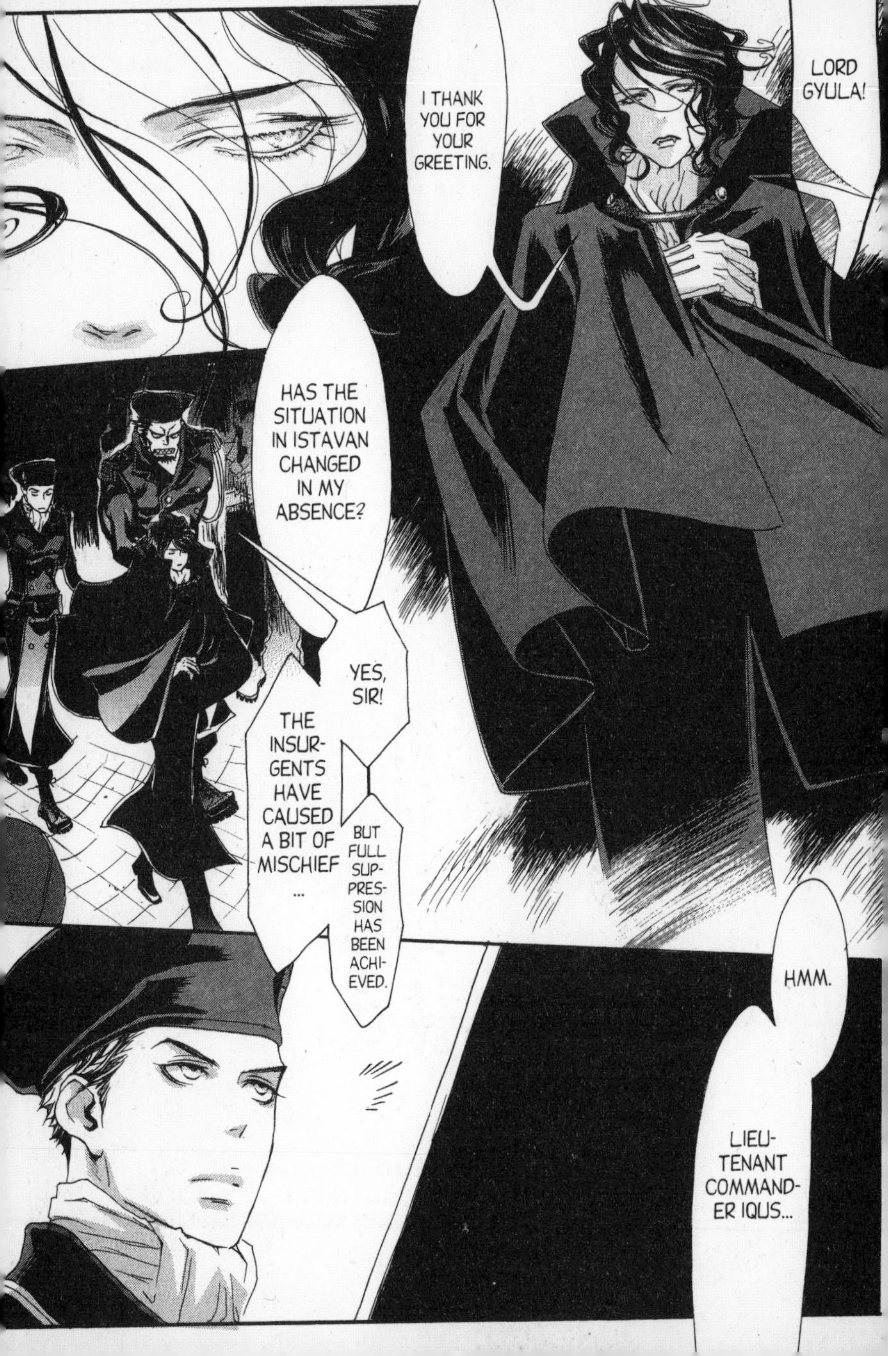
LORD GYULA!
I THANK YOU FOR YOUR GREETING.
HAS THE SITUATION IN ISTAVAN CHANGED IN MY ABSENCE?
YES, SIR!
THE INSURGENTS HAVE CAUSED A BIT OF MISCHIEF...
BUT FULL SUPPRESSION HAS BEEN ACHIEVED.
HMM.
LIEUTENANT COMMANDER IQUS...

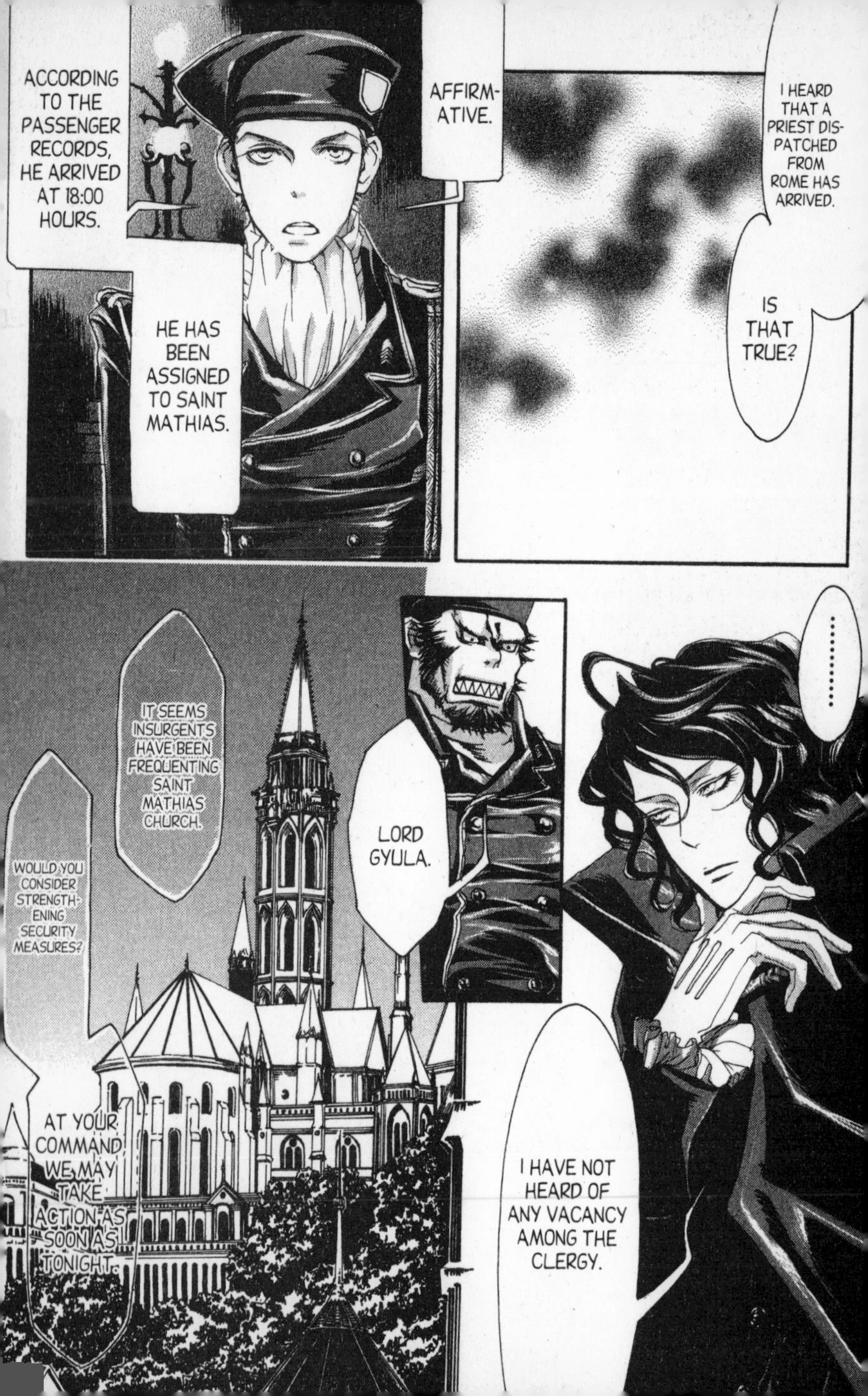
I HEARD THAT A PRIEST DIS-PATCHED FROM ROME HAS ARRIVED.
IS THAT TRUE?
AFFIRM-ATIVE.
ACCORDING TO THE PASSENGER RECORDS, HE ARRIVED AT 18:00 HOURS.
HE HAS BEEN ASSIGNED TO SAINT MATHIAS.
......
I HAVE NOT HEARD OF ANY VACANCY AMONG THE CLERGY.
LORD GYULA.
IT SEEMS INSURGENTS HAVE BEEN FREQUENTING SAINT MATHIAS CHURCH.
WOULD YOU CONSIDER STRENGTH-ENING SECURITY MEASURES?
AT YOUR COMMAND WE MAY TAKE ACTION AS SOON AS TONIGHT.

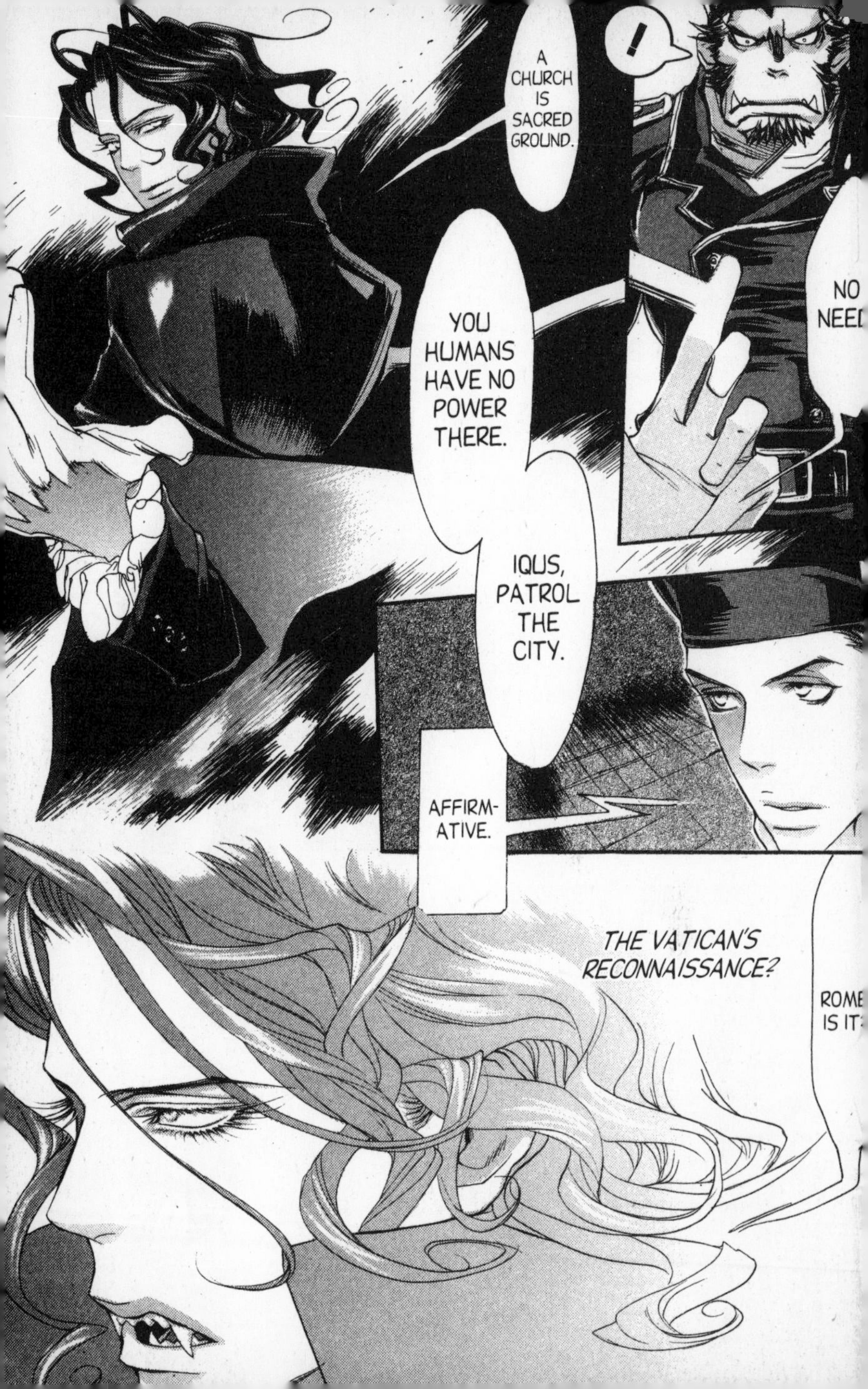
!
NO NEE
A CHURCH IS SACRED GROUND.
YOU HUMANS HAVE NO POWER THERE.
IQUS, PATROL THE CITY.
AFFIRM-ATIVE.
ROME IS IT
THE VATICAN'S RECONNAISSANCE?

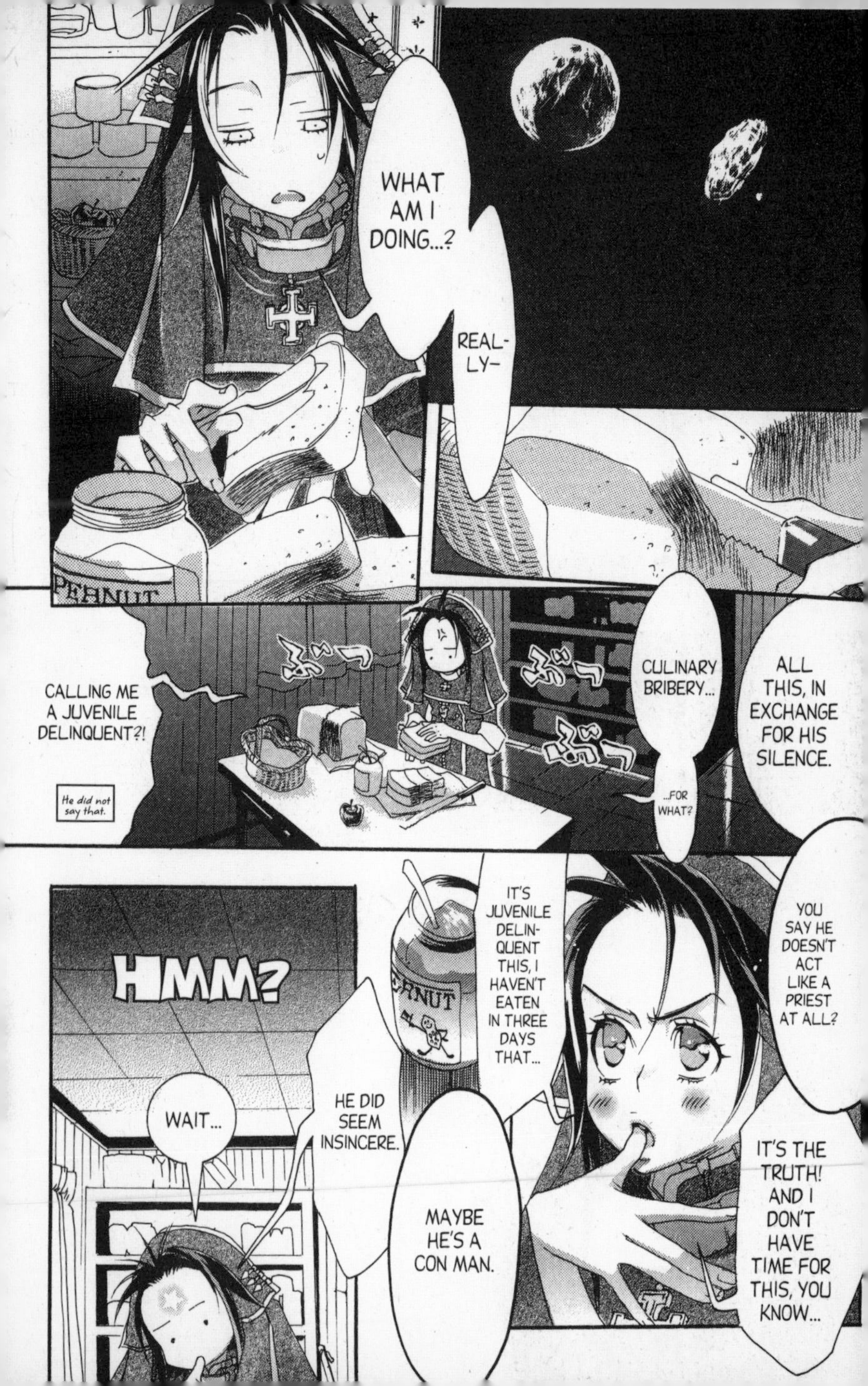
WHAT AM I DOING...?
REAL-LY-
PEANUT
ALL THIS, IN EXCHANGE FOR HIS SILENCE.
CULINARY BRIBERY...
...FOR WHAT?
CALLING ME A JUVENILE DELINQUENT?!
He did not say that.
YOU SAY HE DOESN'T ACT LIKE A PRIEST AT ALL?
IT'S JUVENILE DELIN-QUENT THIS, I HAVEN'T EATEN IN THREE DAYS THAT...
PEANUT
IT'S THE TRUTH! AND I DON'T HAVE TIME FOR THIS, YOU KNOW...
MAYBE HE'S A CON MAN.
HE DID SEEM INSINCERE.
HMM?
WAIT...

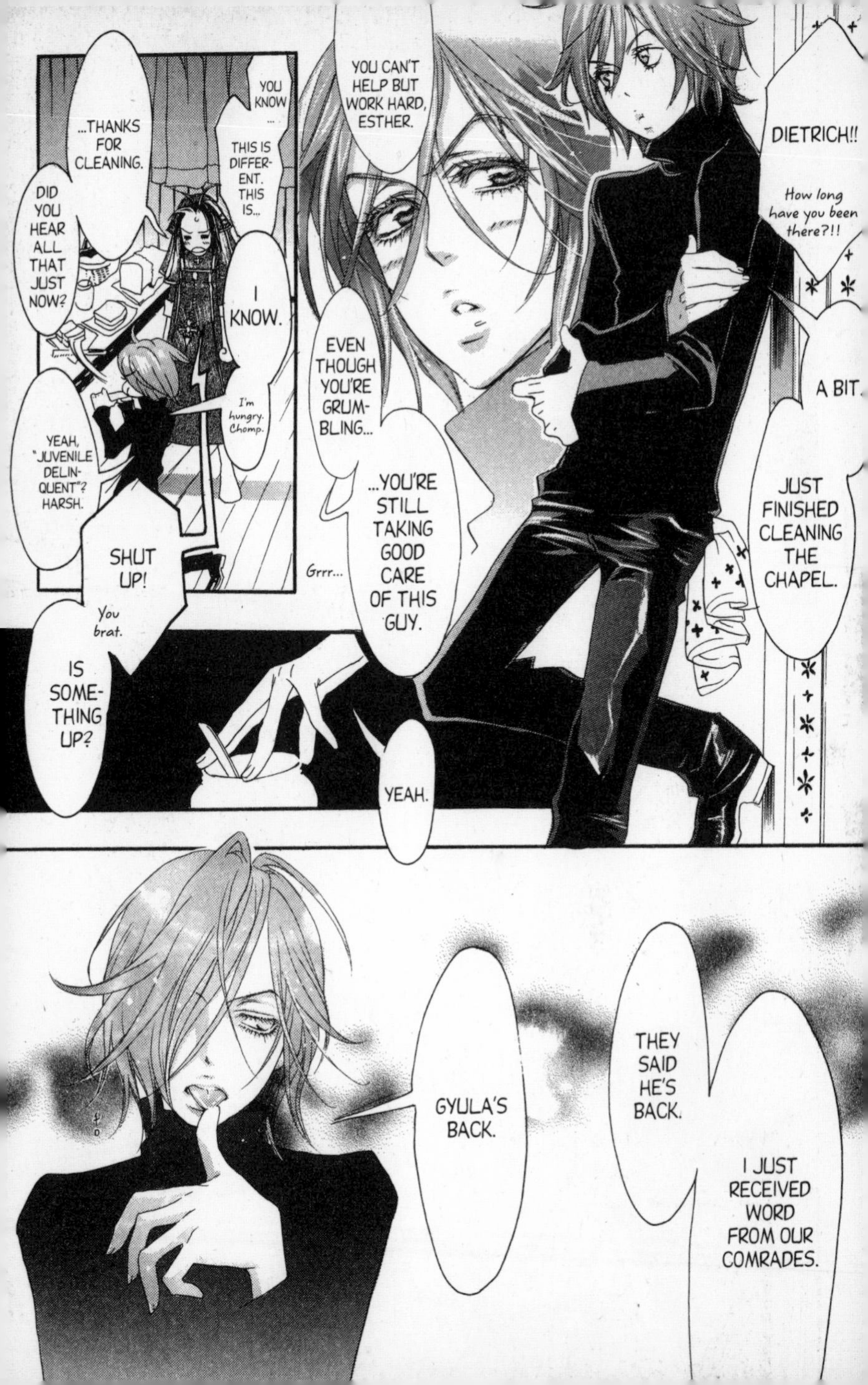
DIETRICH!!
How long have you been there?!!
A BIT.
JUST FINISHED CLEANING THE CHAPEL.
YOU CAN'T HELP BUT WORK HARD, ESTHER.
EVEN THOUGH YOU'RE GRUMBLING...
...YOU'RE STILL TAKING GOOD CARE OF THIS GUY.
Grrr...
YOU KNOW ...
THIS IS DIFFERENT. THIS IS...
...THANKS FOR CLEANING.
DID YOU HEAR ALL THAT JUST NOW?
I KNOW.
I'm hungry. Chomp.
YEAH, "JUVENILE DELINQUENT"? HARSH.
SHUT UP!
You brat.
IS SOMETHING UP?
YEAH.
I JUST RECEIVED WORD FROM OUR COMRADES.
THEY SAID HE'S BACK.
GYULA'S BACK.

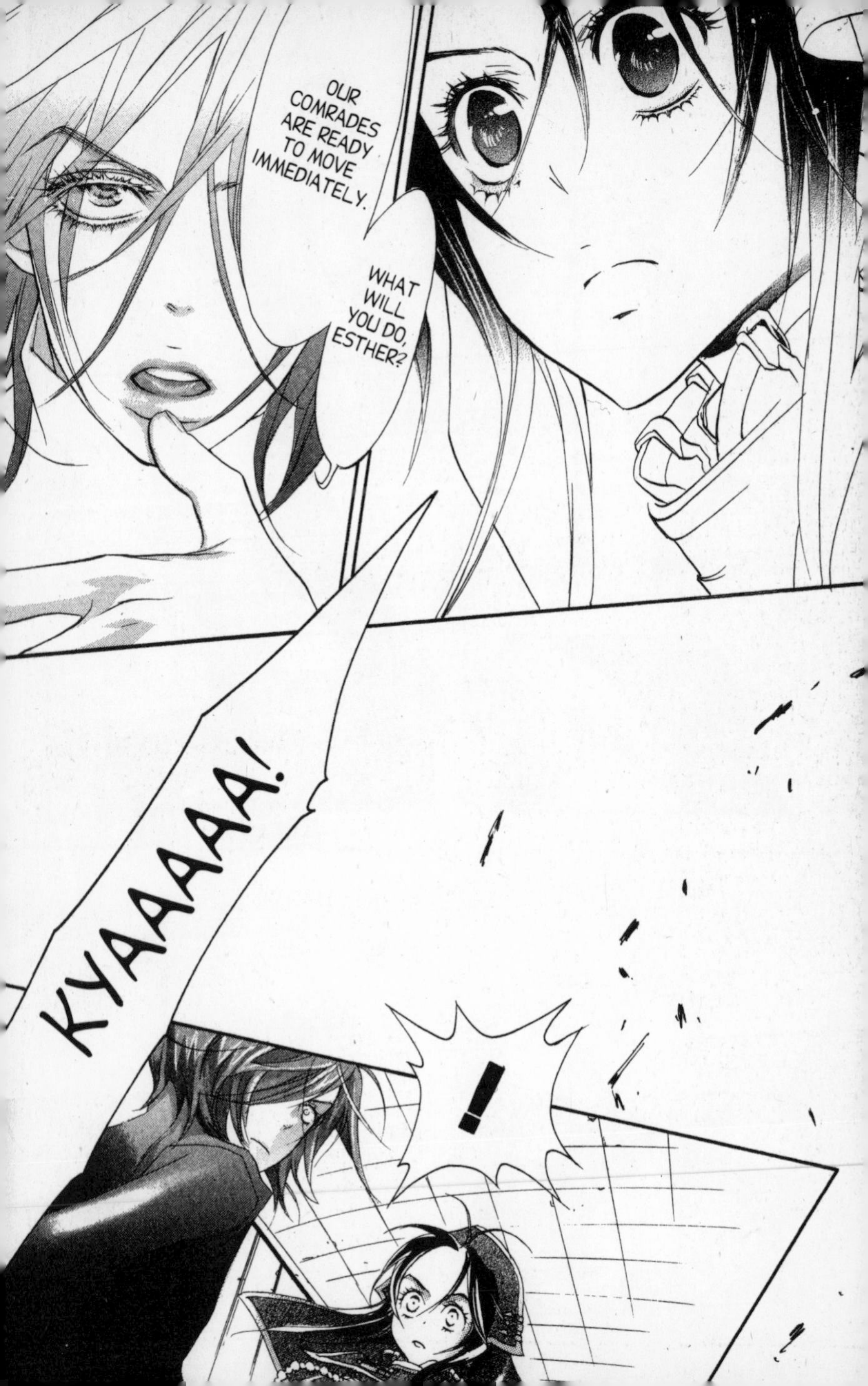
OUR COMRADES ARE READY TO MOVE IMMEDIATELY.
WHAT WILL YOU DO, ESTHER?
KYAAAAA!
!

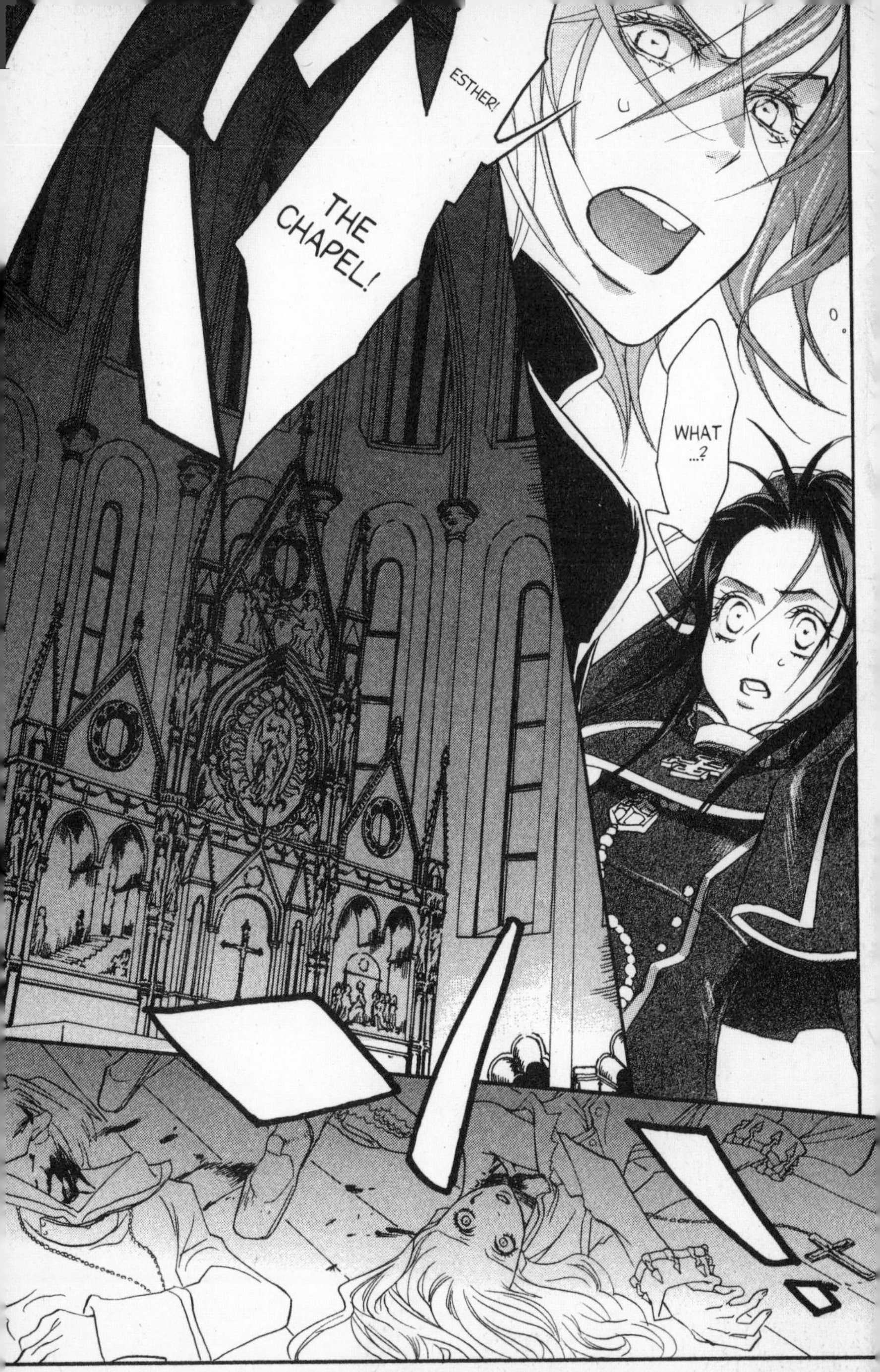
ESTHER!
THE CHAPEL!
WHAT ...?

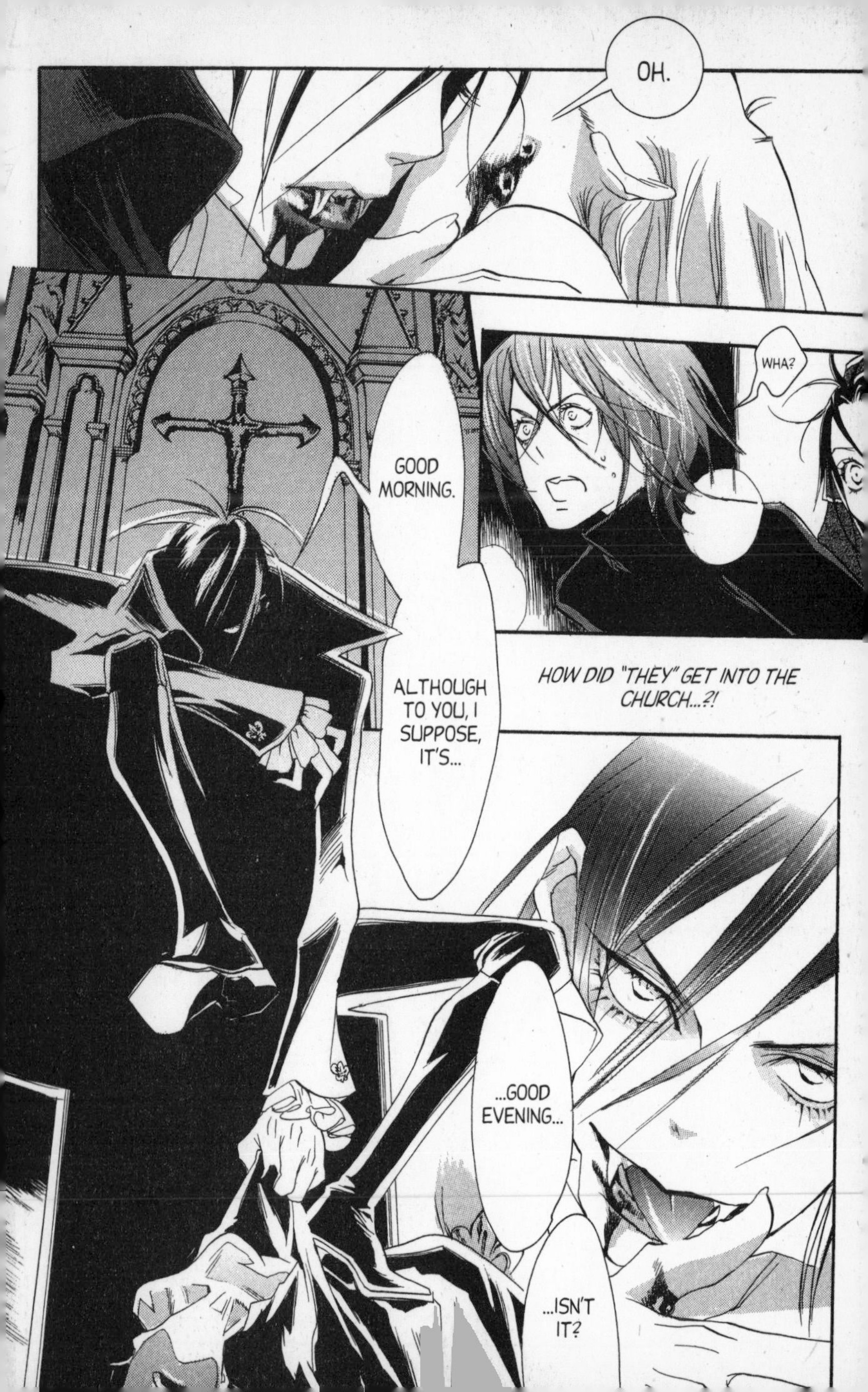
OH.
WHA?
GOOD MORNING.
ALTHOUGH TO YOU, I SUPPOSE, IT'S...
HOW DID "THEY" GET INTO THE CHURCH...?!
...GOOD EVENING...
...ISN'T IT?

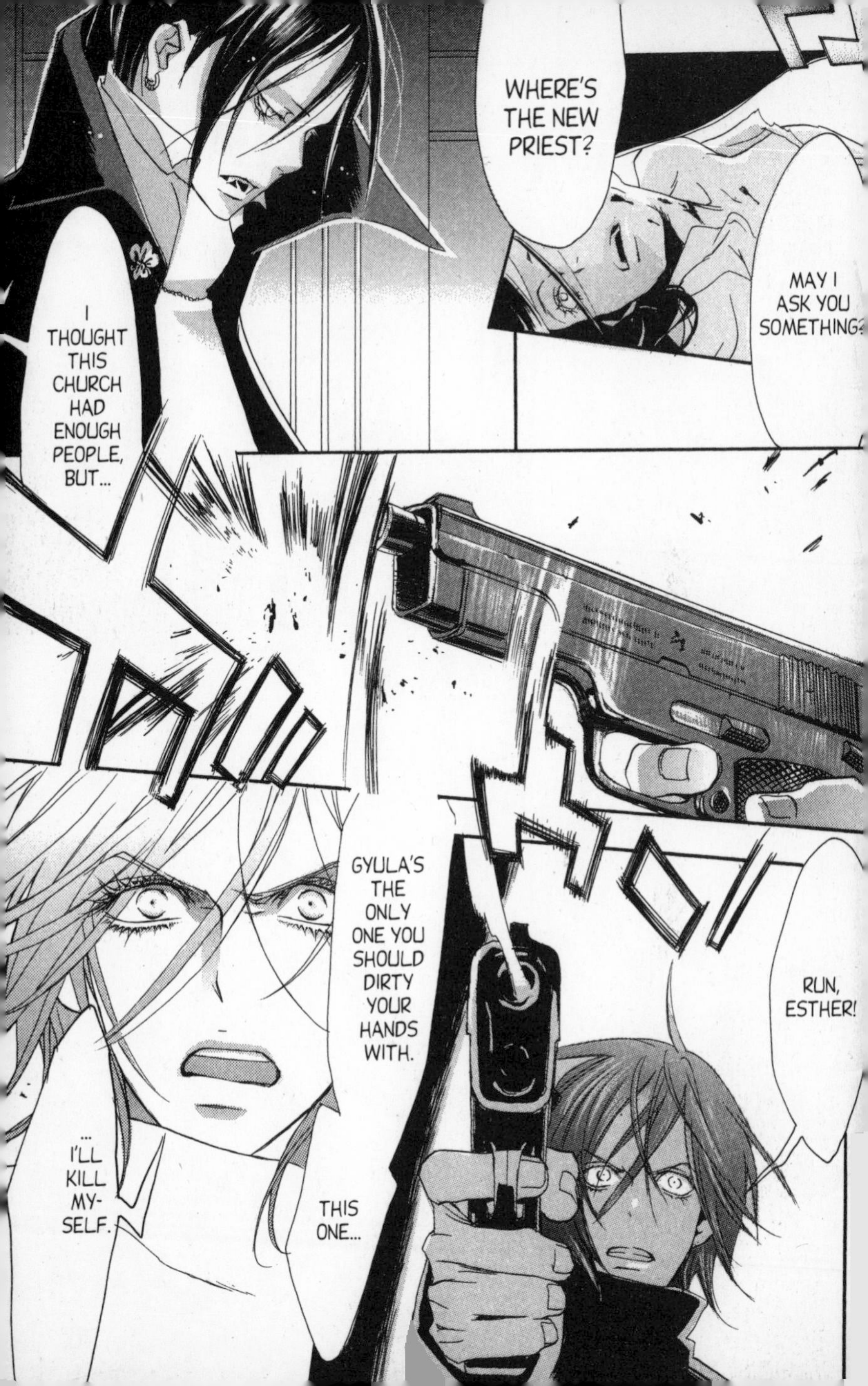
MAY I ASK YOU SOMETHING?
WHERE'S THE NEW PRIEST?
I THOUGHT THIS CHURCH HAD ENOUGH PEOPLE, BUT...
RUN, ESTHER!
GYULA'S THE ONLY ONE YOU SHOULD DIRTY YOUR HANDS WITH.
THIS ONE...
...I'LL KILL MY-SELF.

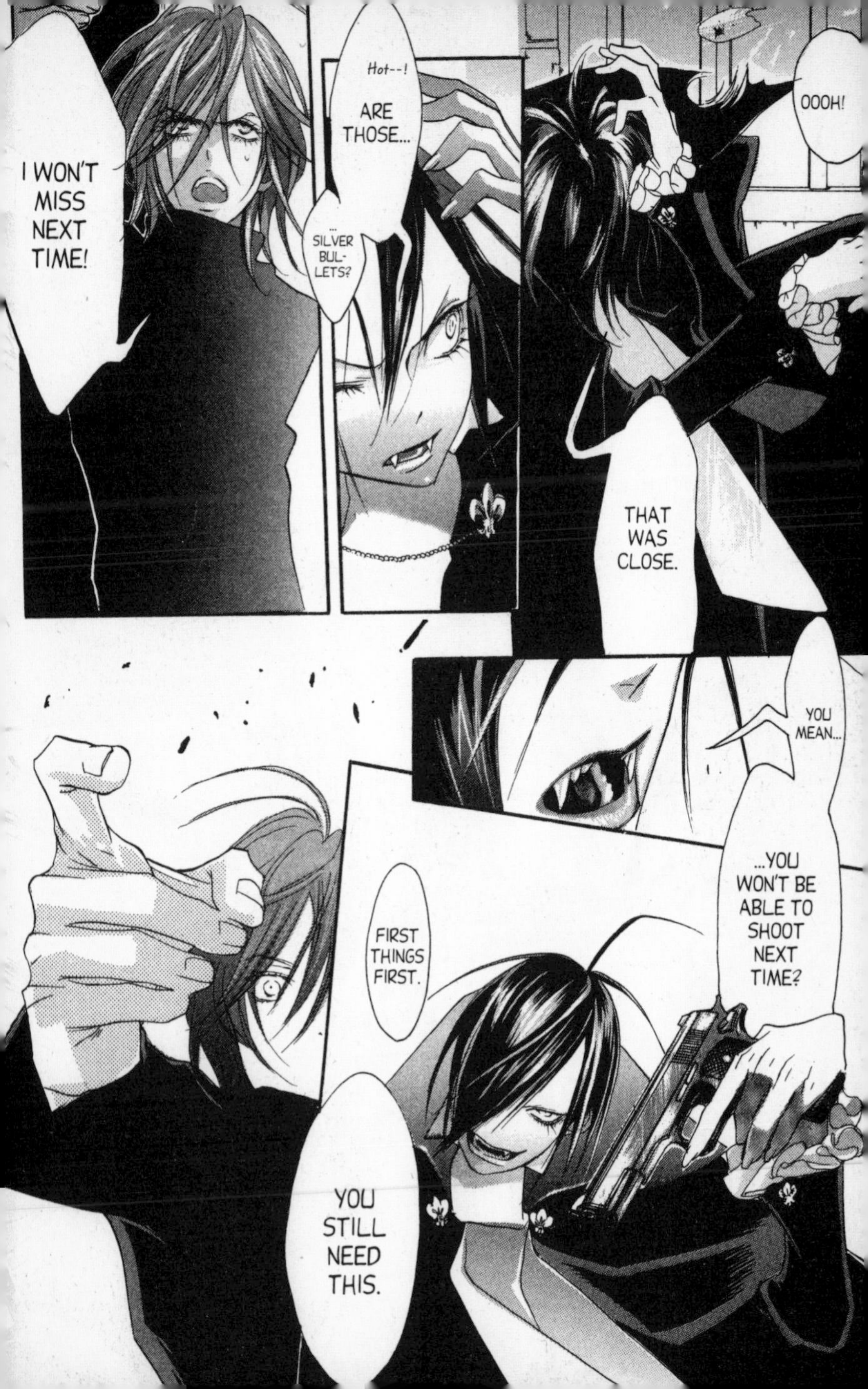

OOOH!
THAT WAS CLOSE.
Hot--!
ARE THOSE...
...SILVER BULLETS?
I WON'T MISS NEXT TIME!
YOU MEAN...
...YOU WON'T BE ABLE TO SHOOT NEXT TIME?
FIRST THINGS FIRST.
YOU STILL NEED THIS.

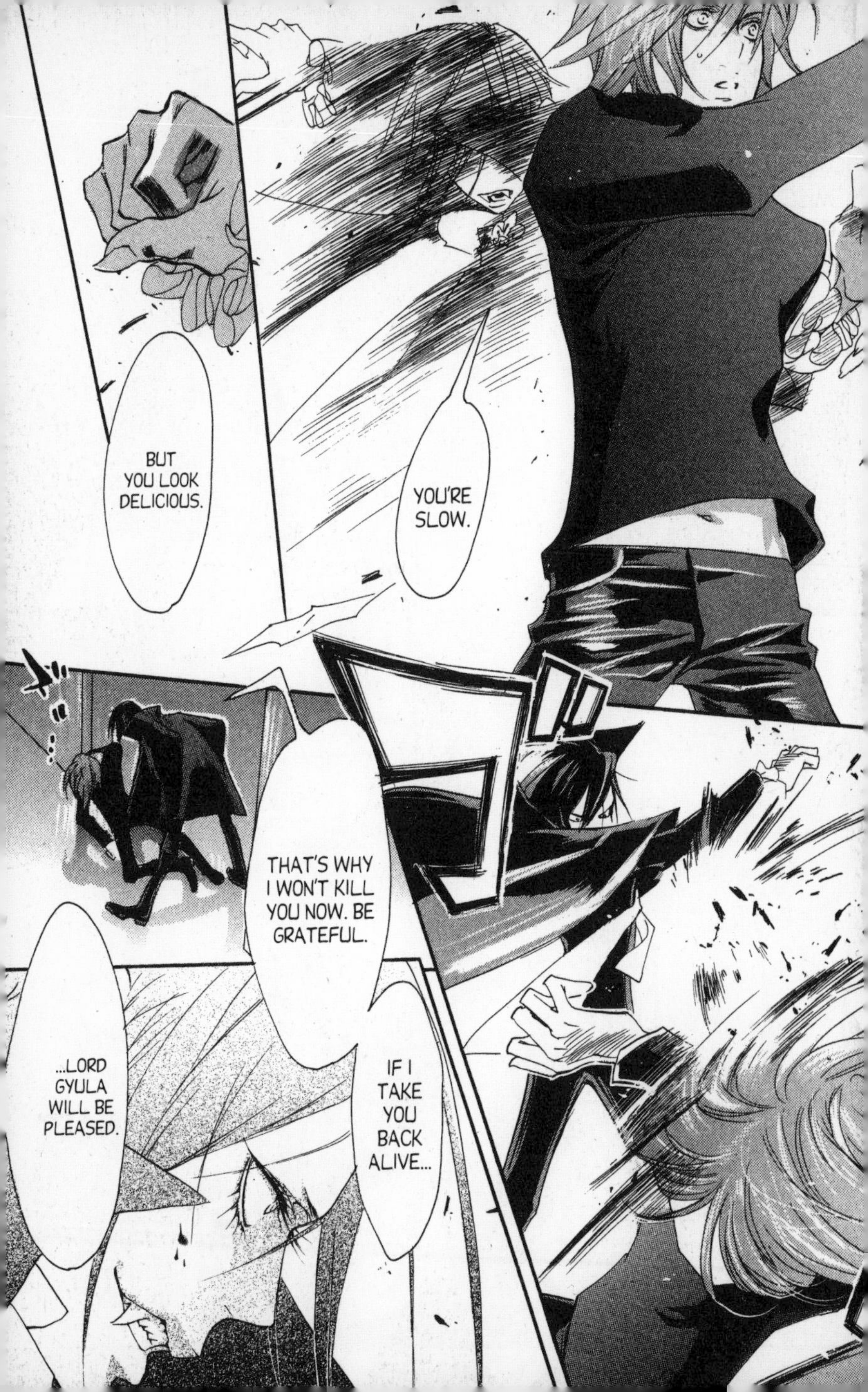
YOU'RE SLOW.
BUT YOU LOOK DELICIOUS.
THAT'S WHY I WON'T KILL YOU NOW. BE GRATEFUL.
IF I TAKE YOU BACK ALIVE...
...LORD GYULA WILL BE PLEASED.

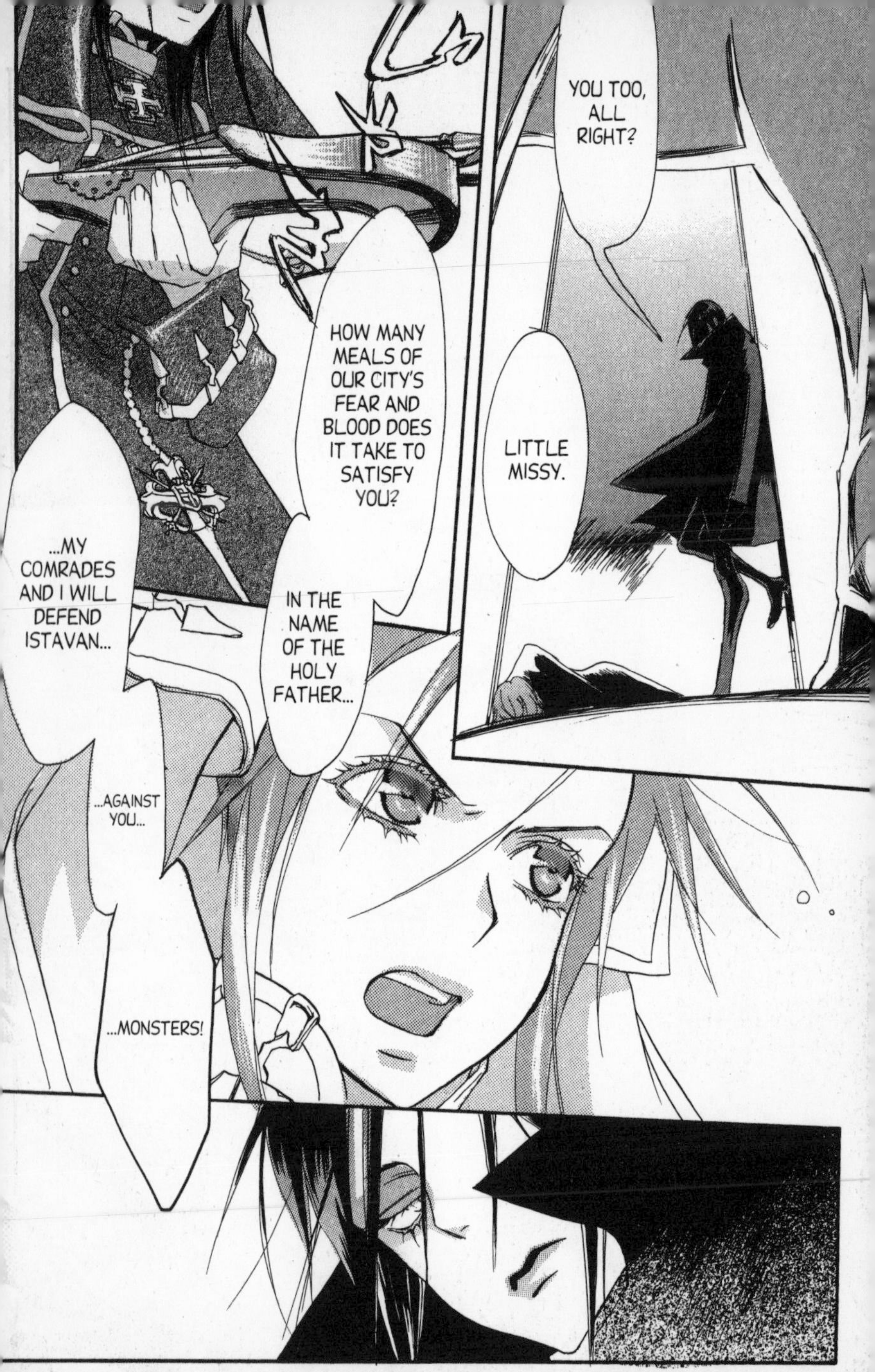
YOU TOO, ALL RIGHT?
LITTLE MISSY.
HOW MANY MEALS OF OUR CITY'S FEAR AND BLOOD DOES IT TAKE TO SATISFY YOU?
IN THE NAME OF THE HOLY FATHER...
...MY COMRADES AND I WILL DEFEND ISTAVAN...
...AGAINST YOU...
...MONSTERS!

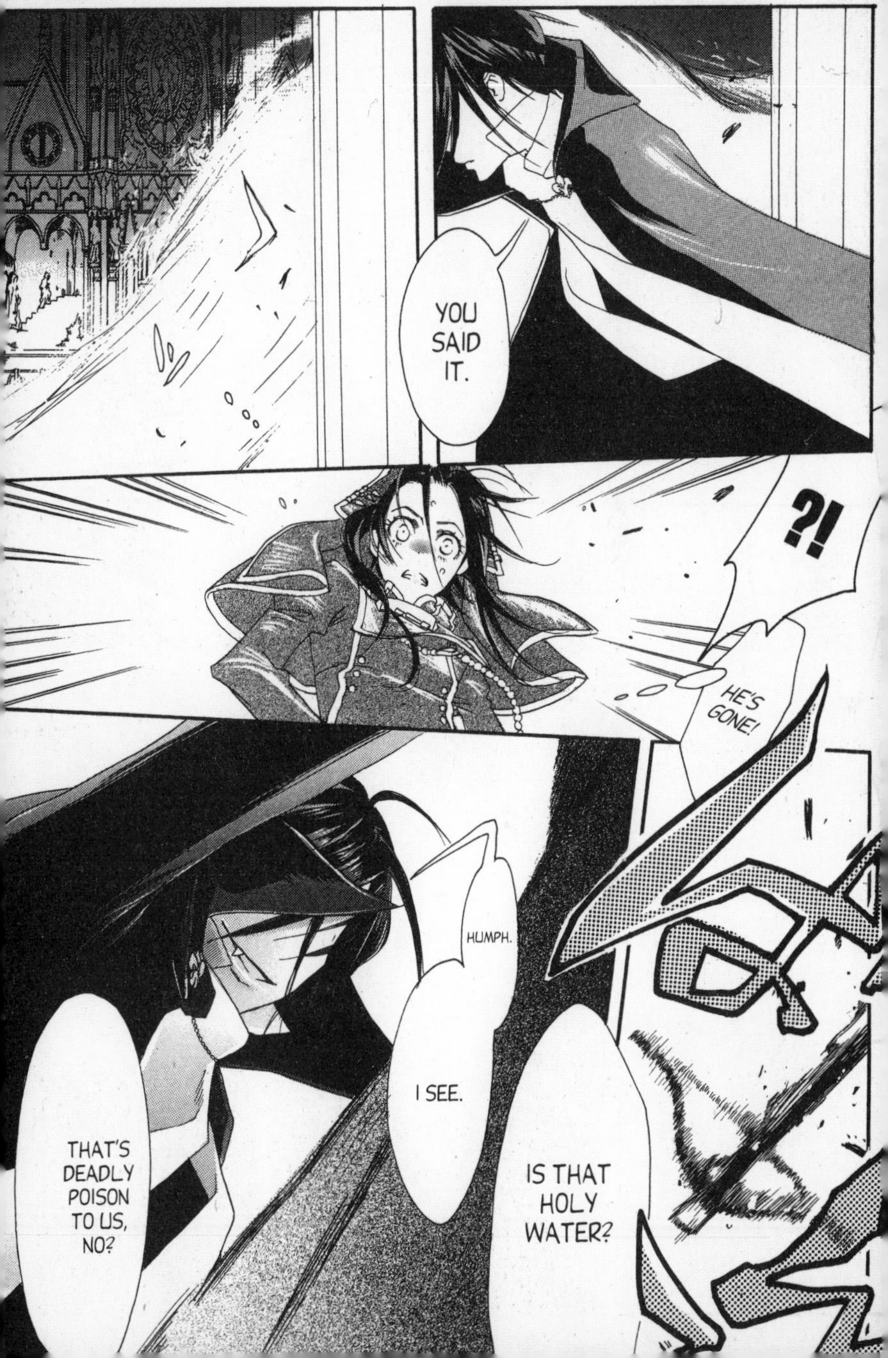
YOU SAID IT.
?!
HE'S GONE!
HUMPH.
IS THAT HOLY WATER?
I SEE.
THAT'S DEADLY POISON TO US, NO?

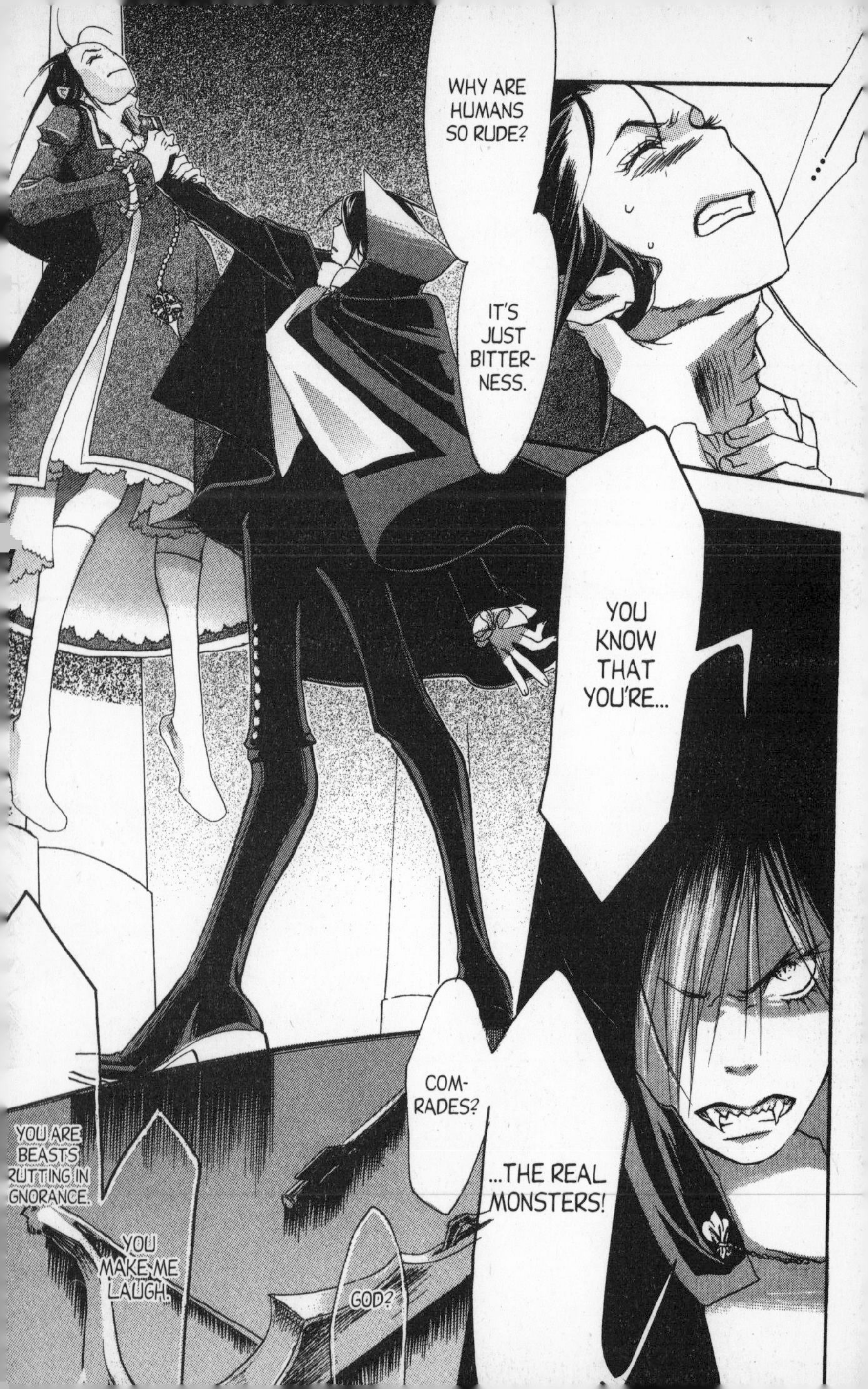
WHY ARE HUMANS SO RUDE?
IT'S JUST BITTER-NESS.
YOU KNOW THAT YOU'RE...
...THE REAL MONSTERS!
COM-RADES?
GOD?
YOU ARE BEASTS RUTTING IN GNORANCE.
YOU MAKE ME LAUGH.

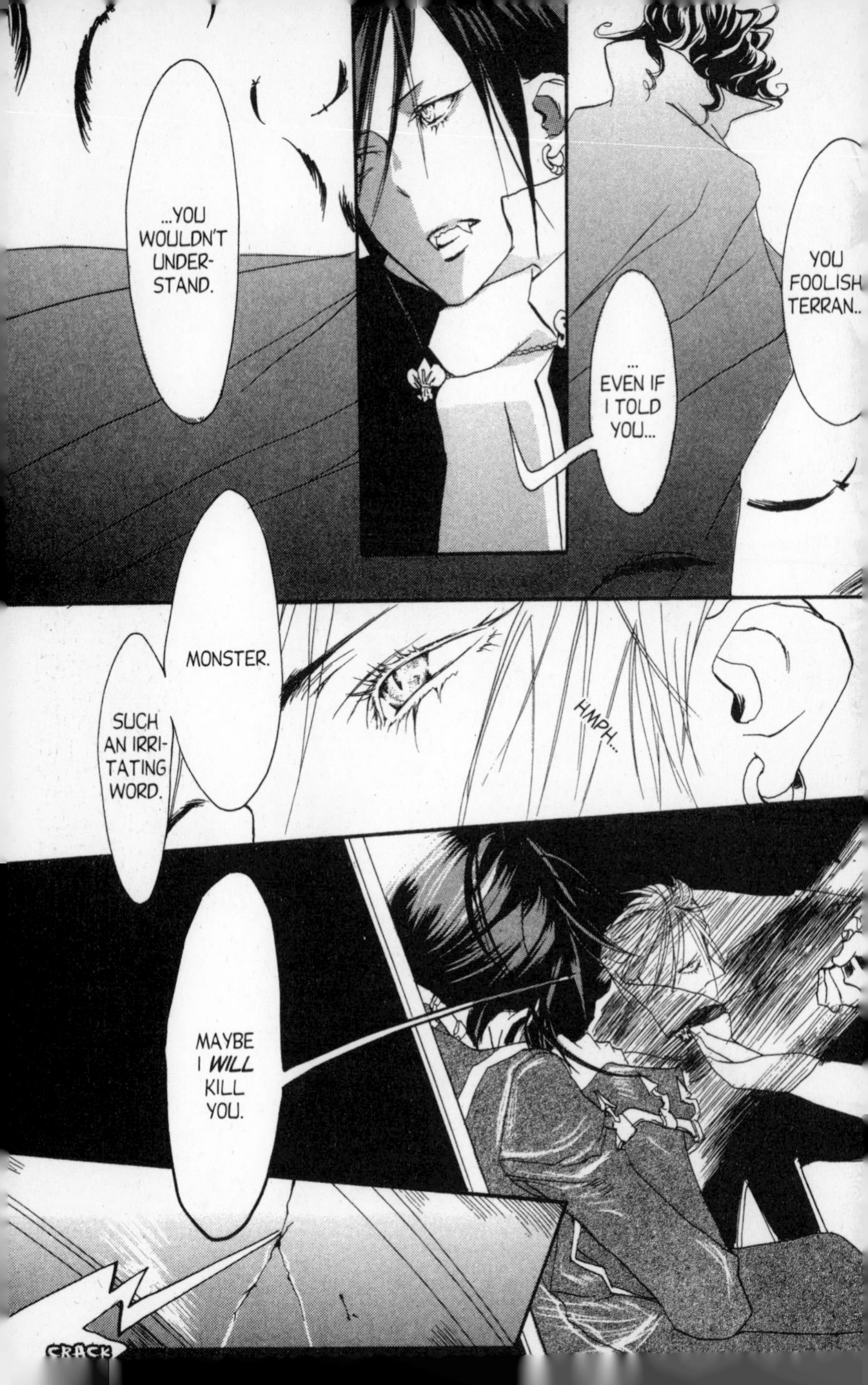
YOU FOOLISH TERRAN..
... EVEN IF I TOLD YOU...
...YOU WOULDN'T UNDER-STAND.
HMPH...
MONSTER.
SUCH AN IRRI-TATING WORD.
MAYBE I *WILL* KILL YOU.
CRACK

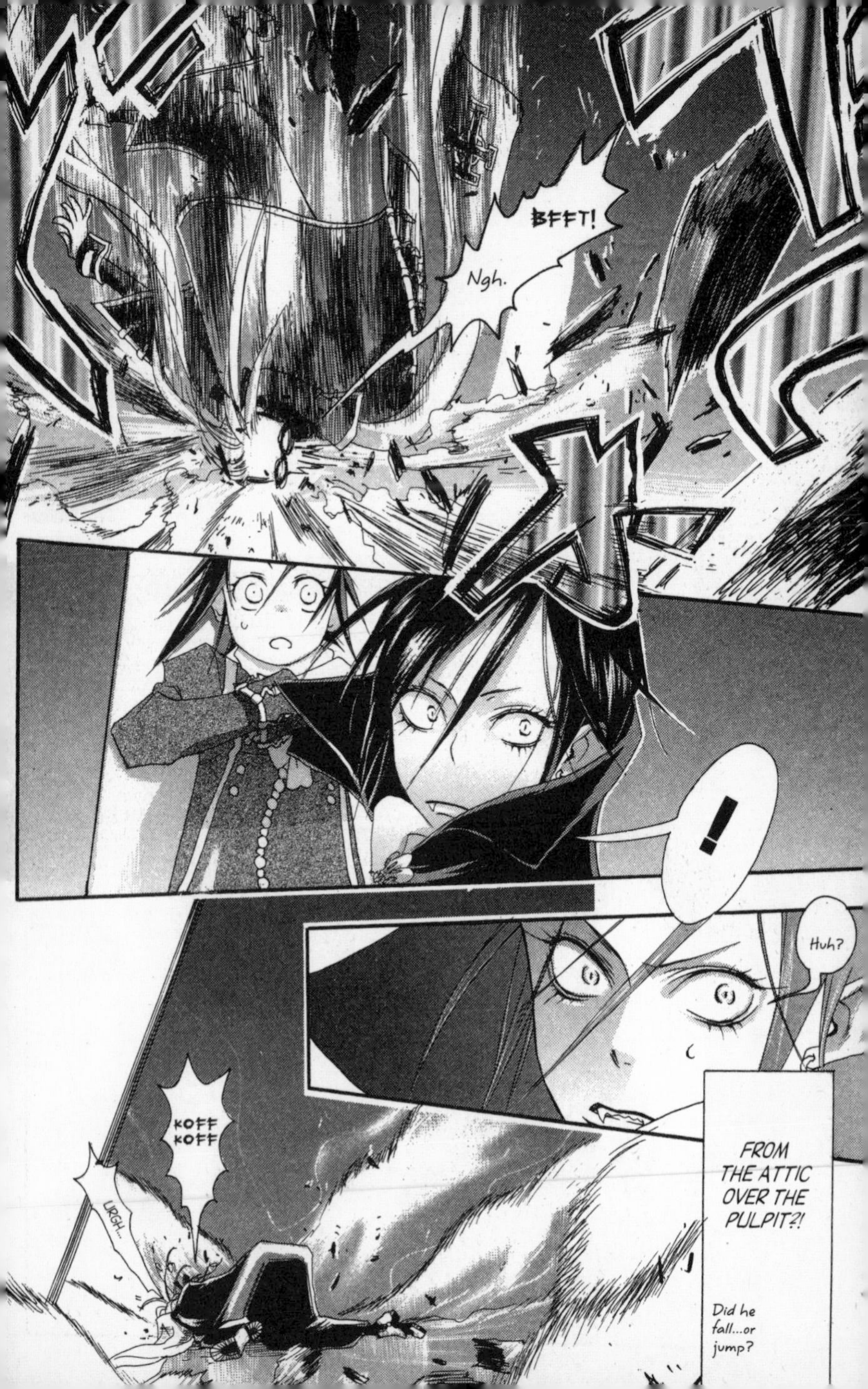
BFFT!
Ngh.
!
Huh?
FROM THE ATTIC OVER THE PULPIT?!
Did he fall...or jump?
KOFF KOFF
URGH...

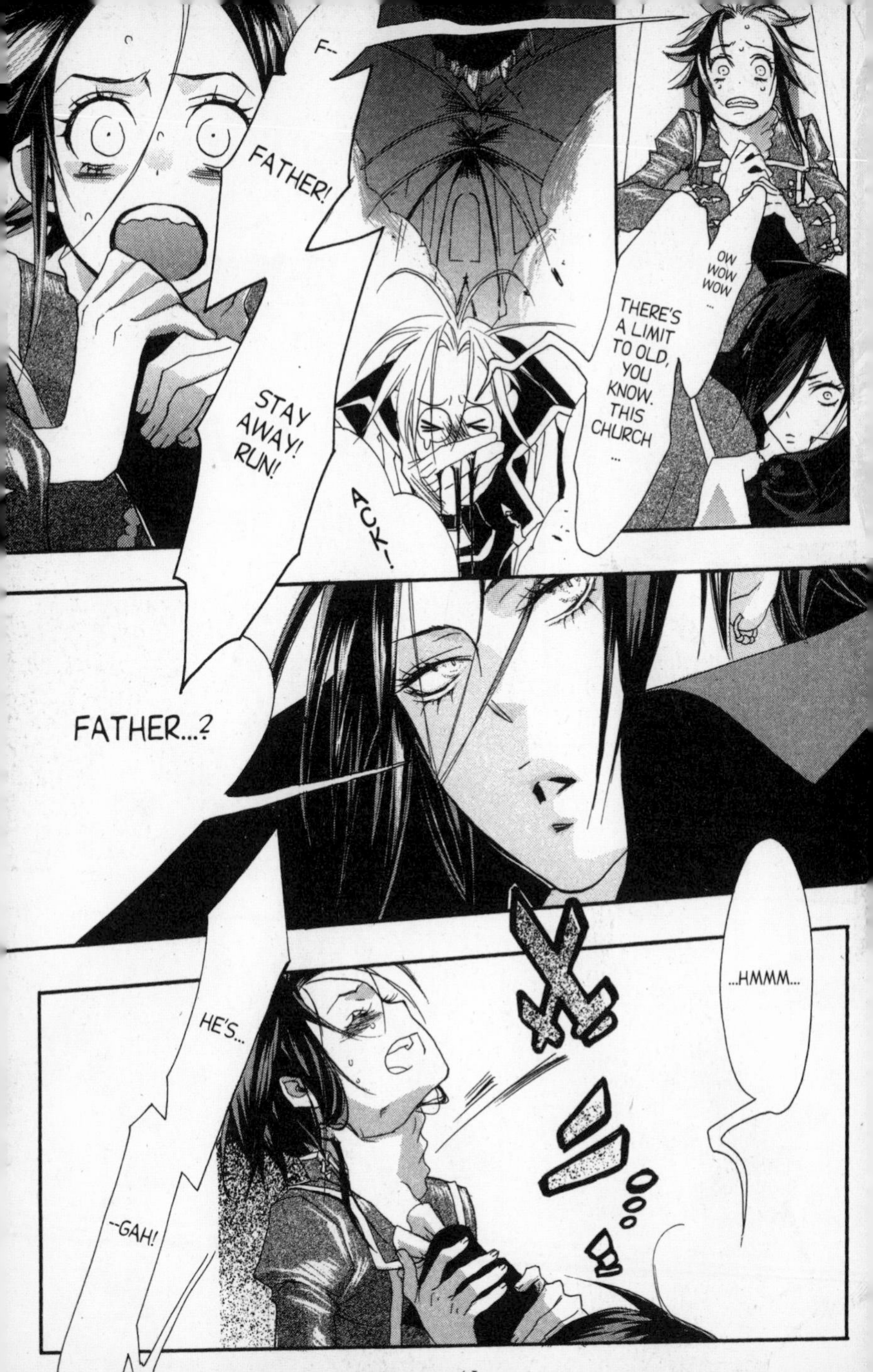
F-
FATHER!
ACK!
OW WOW WOW ...
THERE'S A LIMIT TO OLD, YOU KNOW. THIS CHURCH ...
STAY AWAY! RUN!
FATHER...?
...HMMM...
HE'S...
--GAH!

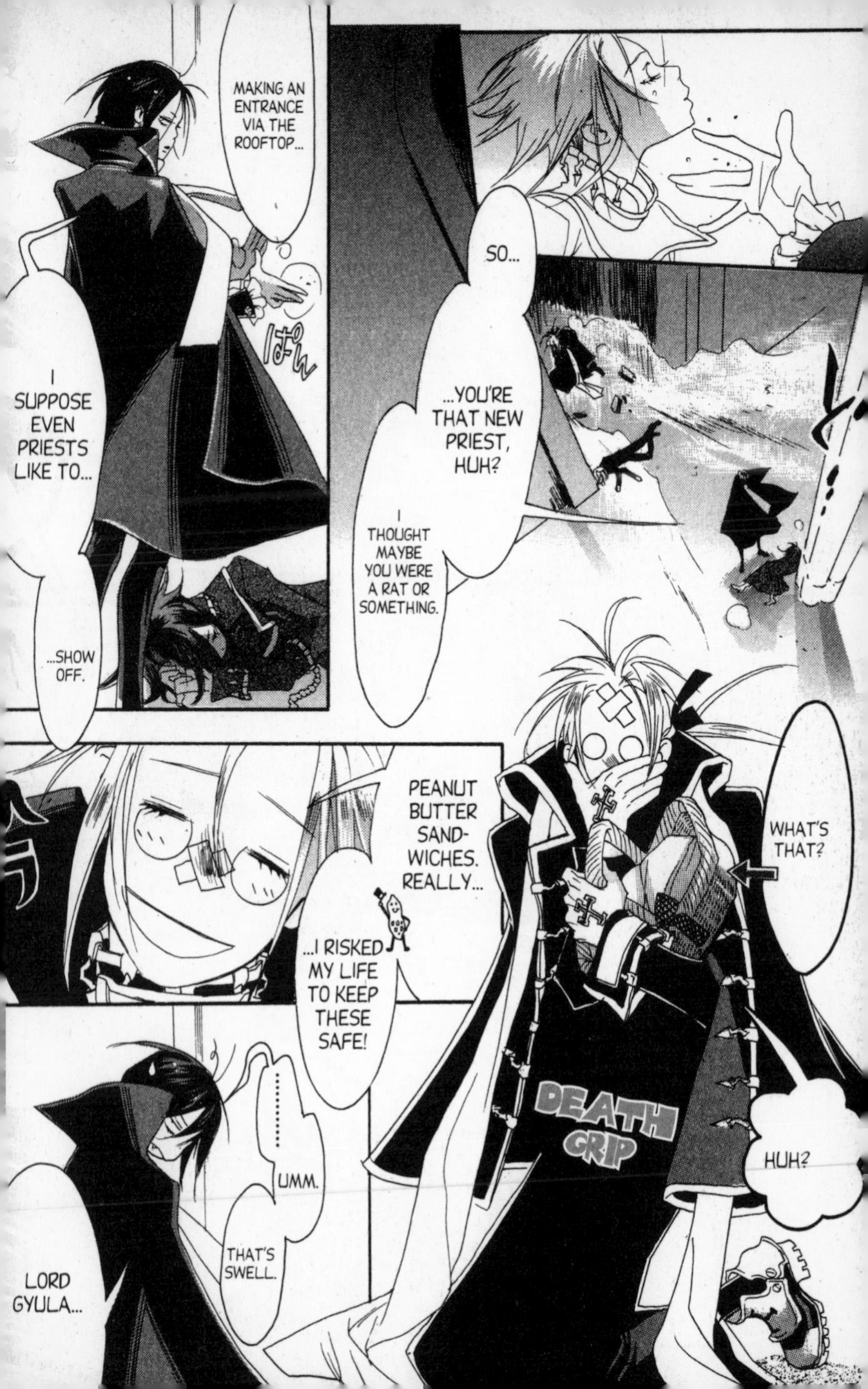
SO...
...YOU'RE THAT NEW PRIEST, HUH?
I THOUGHT MAYBE YOU WERE A RAT OR SOMETHING.
MAKING AN ENTRANCE VIA THE ROOFTOP...
ぱん
I SUPPOSE EVEN PRIESTS LIKE TO...
...SHOW OFF.
WHAT'S THAT?
HUH?
DEATH GRIP
PEANUT BUTTER SANDWICHES. REALLY...
...I RISKED MY LIFE TO KEEP THESE SAFE!
......
UMM.
THAT'S SWELL.
LORD GYULA...

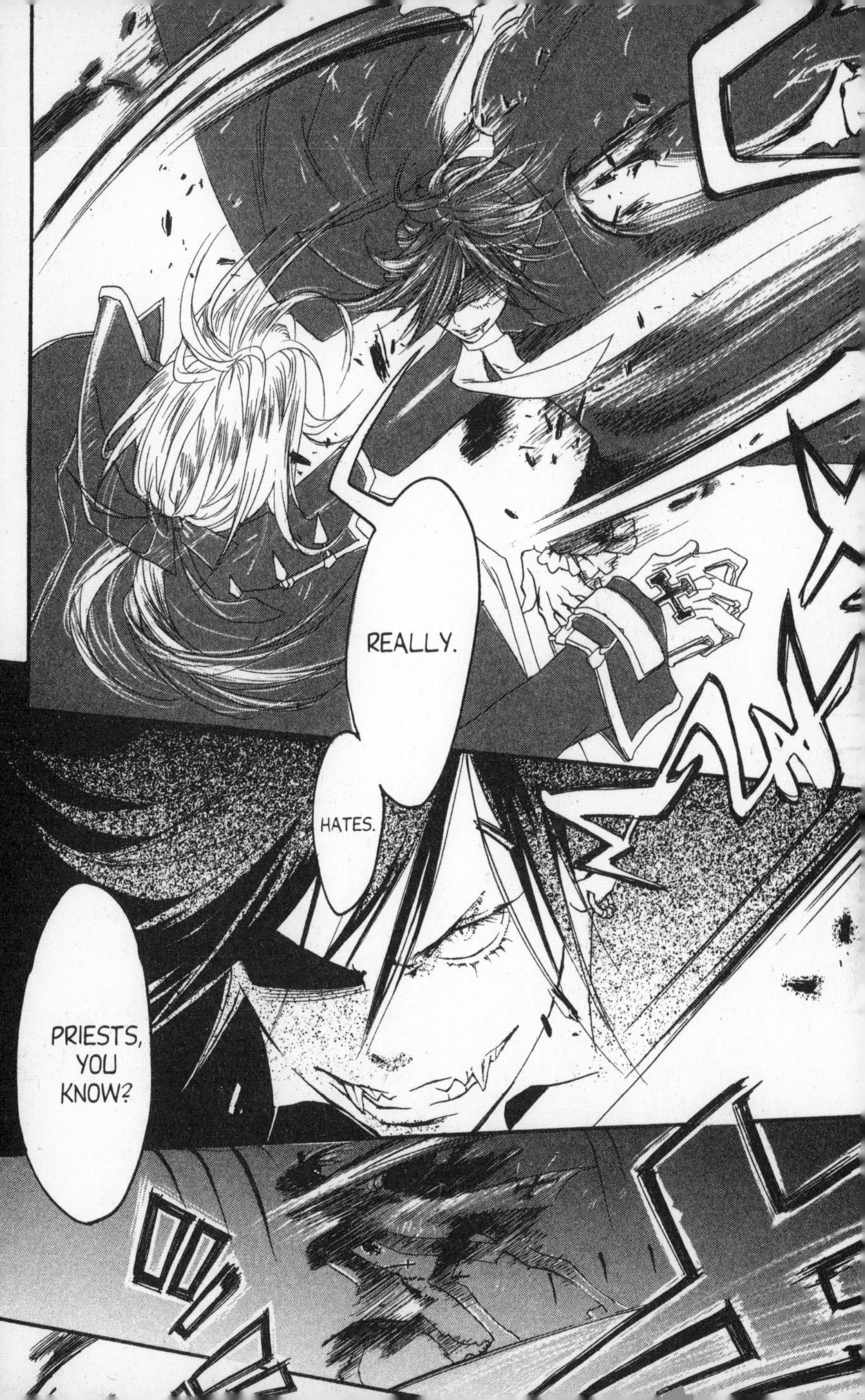
REALLY.
HATES.
PRIESTS, YOU KNOW?

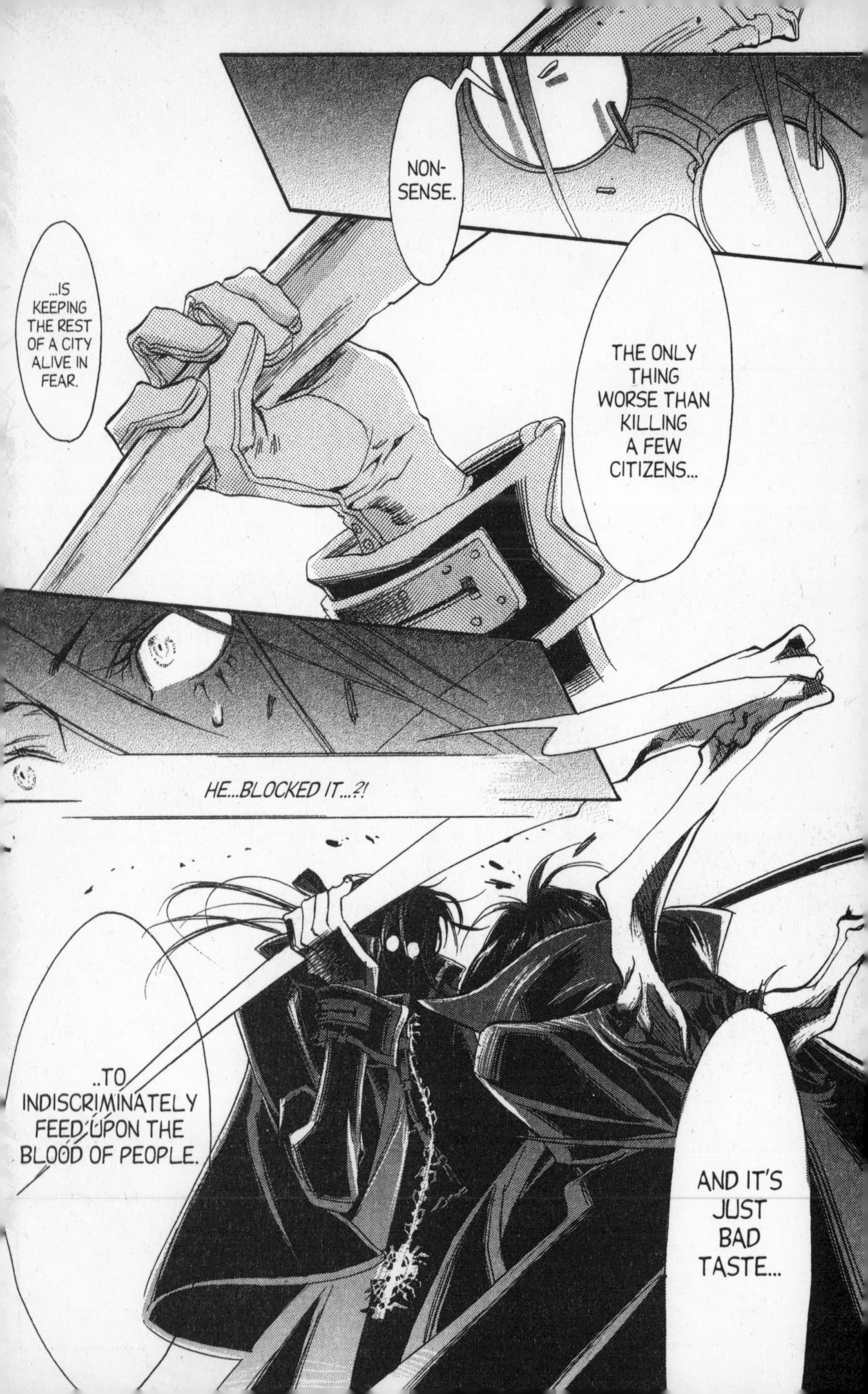
NON-SENSE.
THE ONLY THING WORSE THAN KILLING A FEW CITIZENS...
...IS KEEPING THE REST OF A CITY ALIVE IN FEAR.
HE...BLOCKED IT...?!
AND IT'S JUST BAD TASTE...
..TO INDISCRIMINATELY FEED UPON THE BLOOD OF PEOPLE.

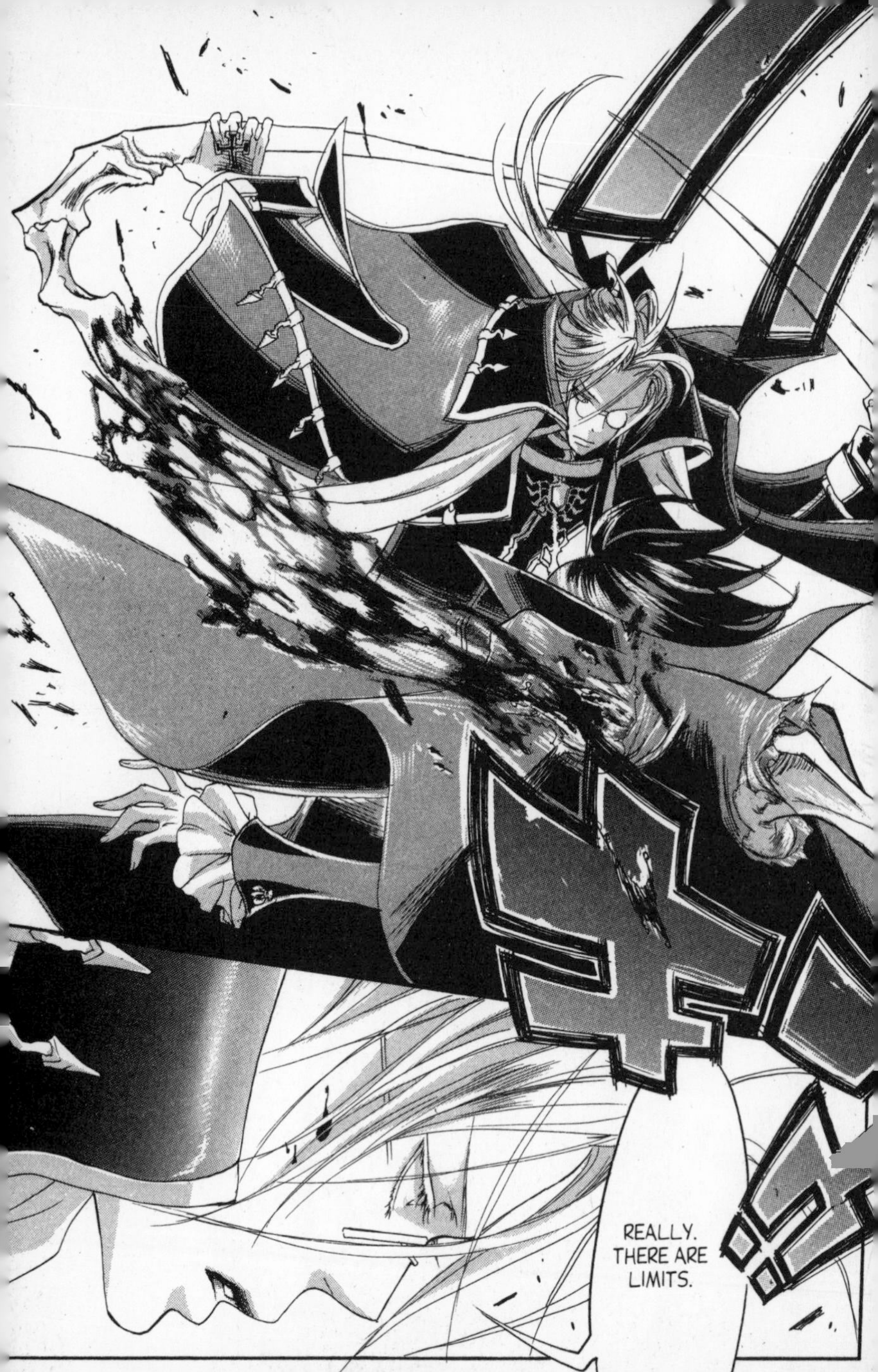
REALLY. THERE ARE LIMITS.

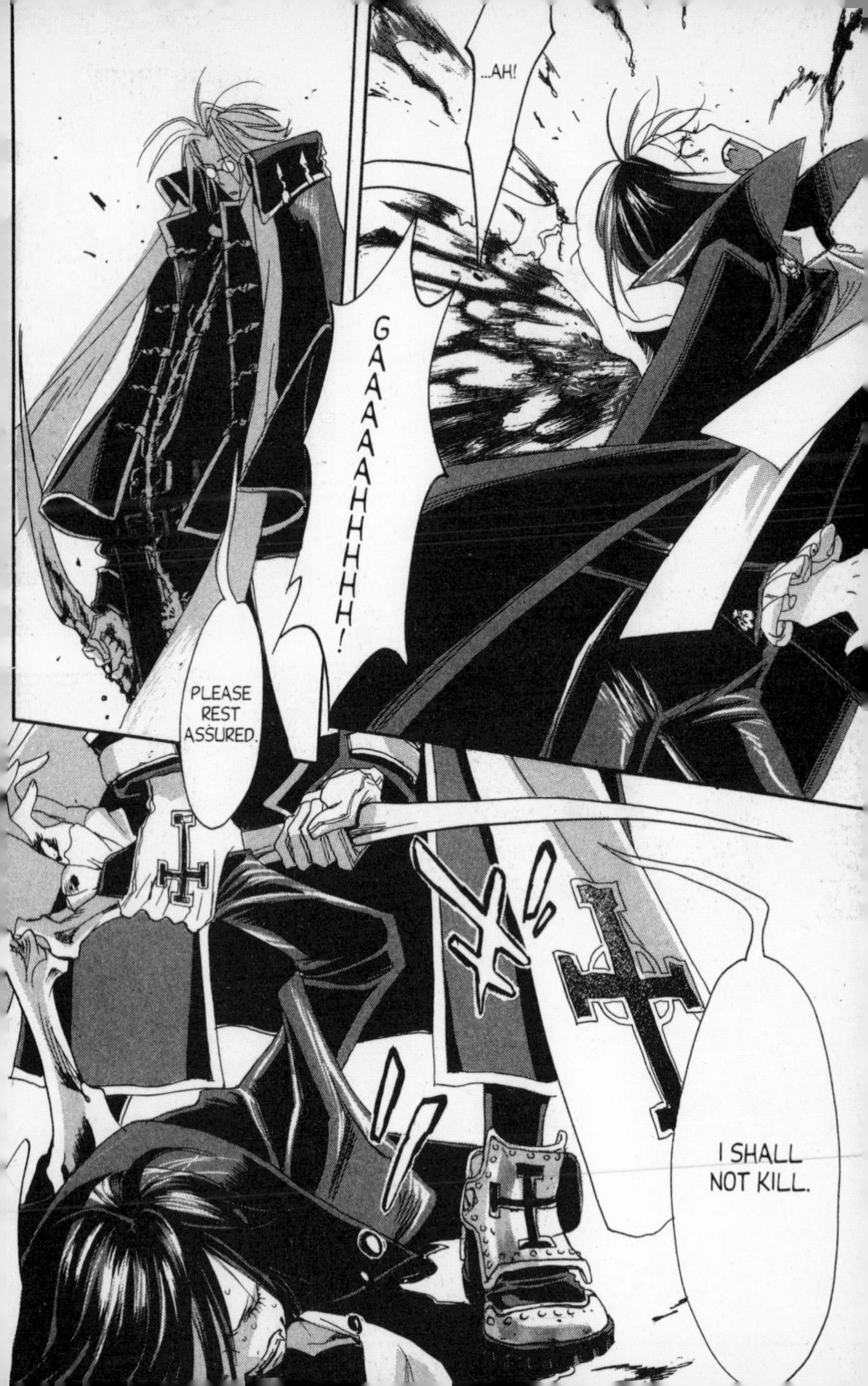
...AH!
GAAAAAHHHHH!
PLEASE REST ASSURED.
I SHALL NOT KILL.

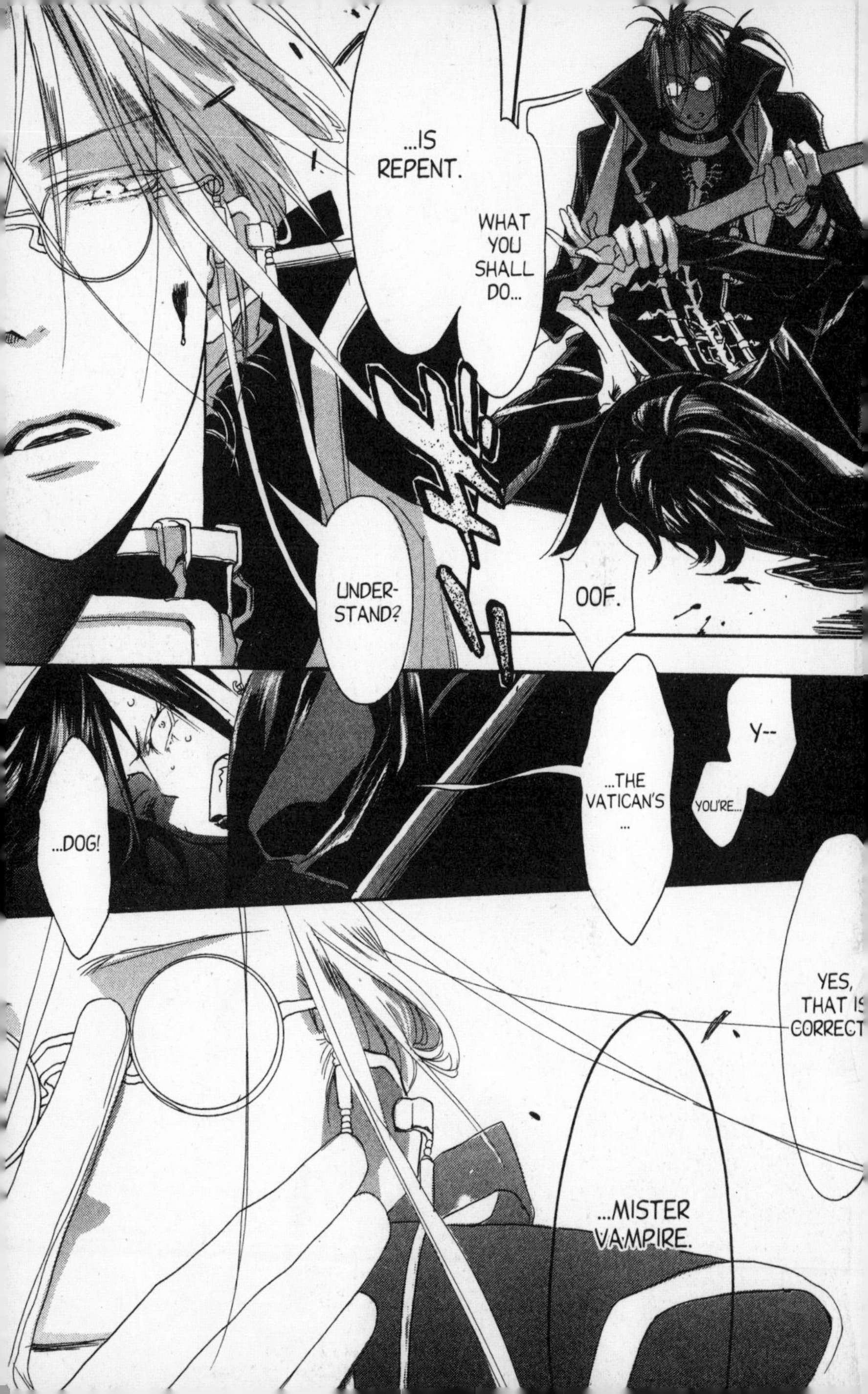

WHAT YOU SHALL DO...
...IS REPENT.
OOF.
UNDER-STAND?
Y--
YOU'RE...
...THE VATICAN'S ...
...DOG!
YES, THAT IS CORRECT
...MISTER VAMPIRE.

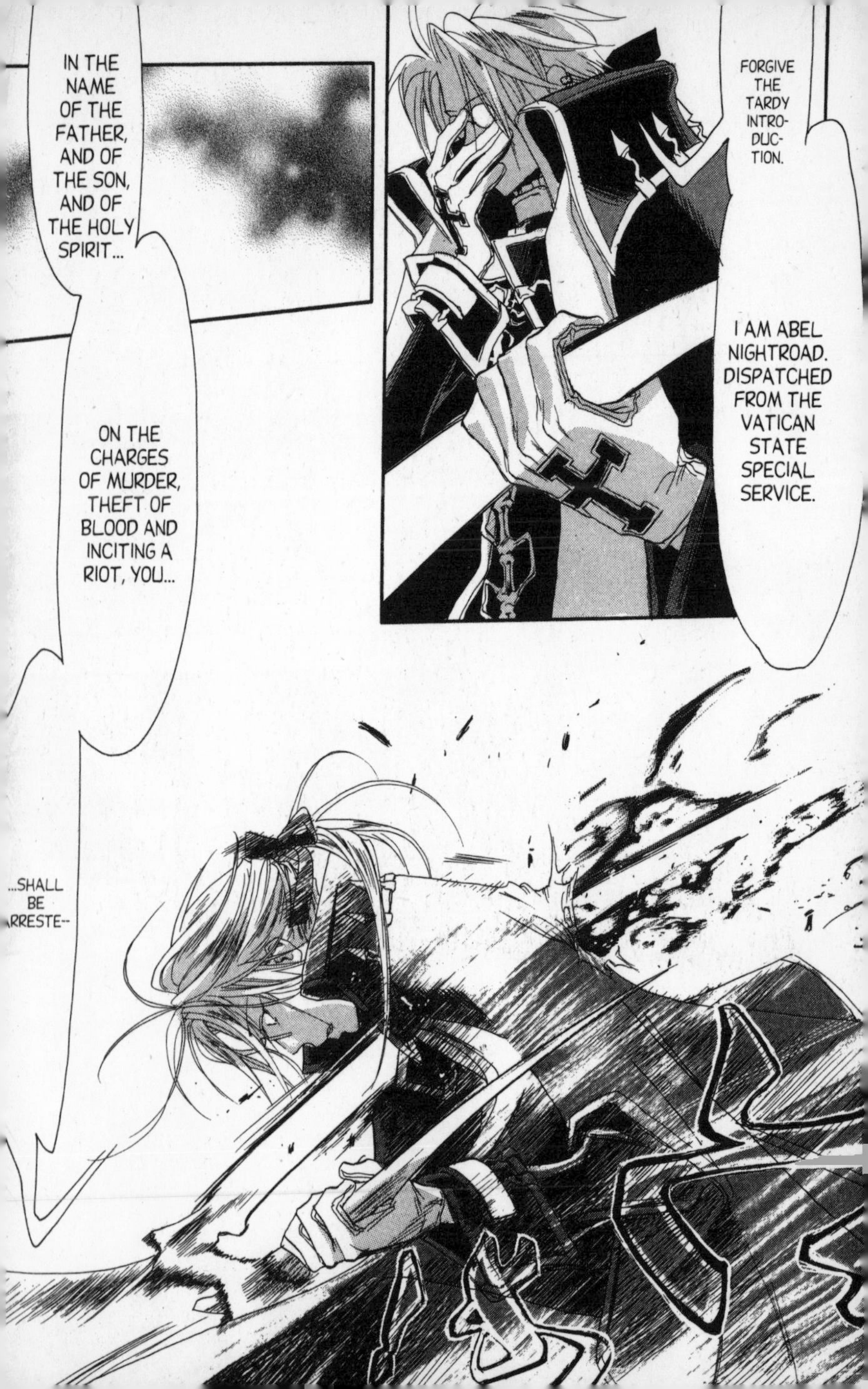
FORGIVE THE TARDY INTRO-DUC-TION.
I AM ABEL NIGHTROAD. DISPATCHED FROM THE VATICAN STATE SPECIAL SERVICE.
IN THE NAME OF THE FATHER, AND OF THE SON, AND OF THE HOLY SPIRIT...
ON THE CHARGES OF MURDER, THEFT OF BLOOD AND INCITING A RIOT, YOU...
...SHALL BE ARRESTE--

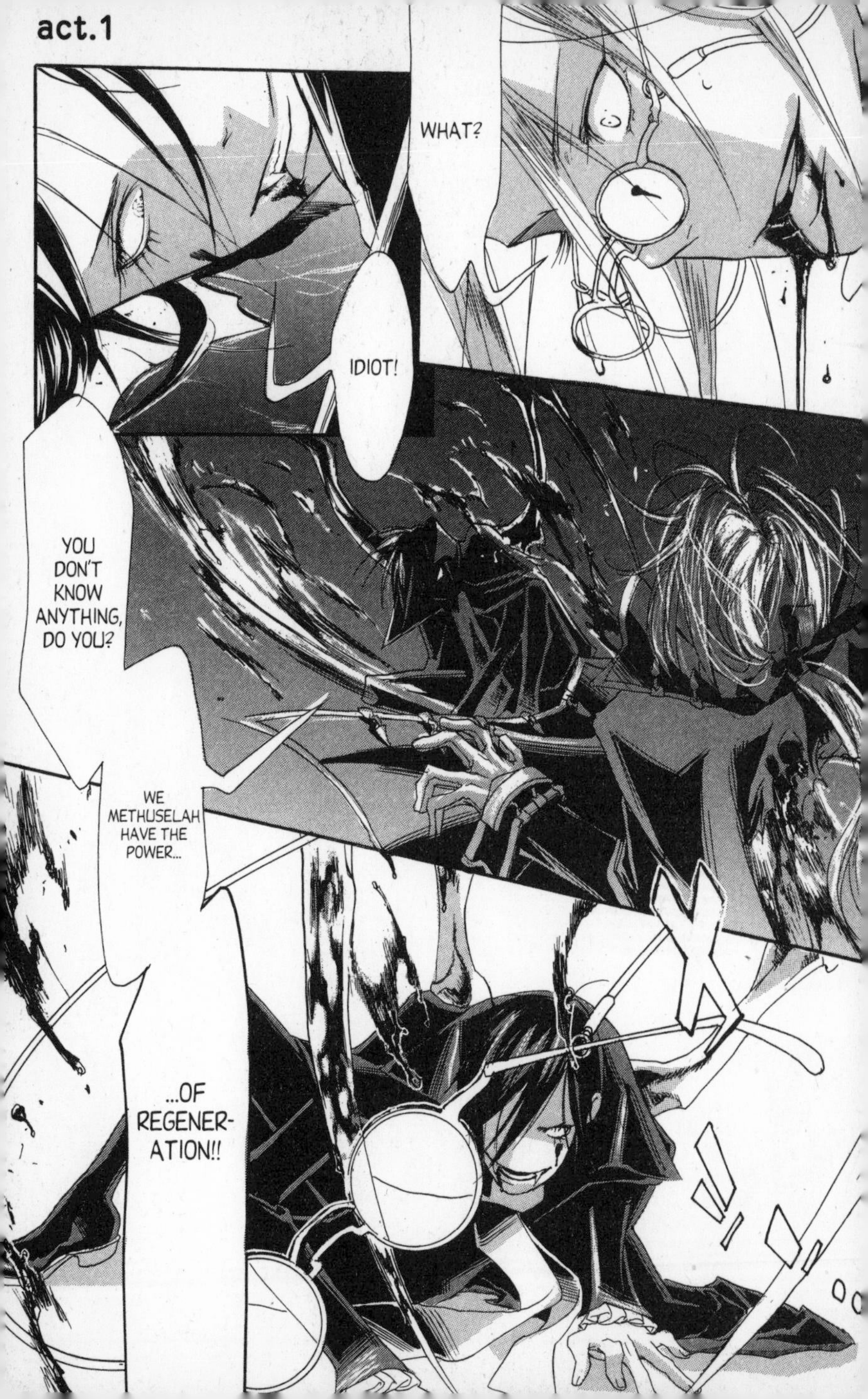
WHAT?
IDIOT!
YOU DON'T KNOW ANYTHING, DO YOU?
WE METHUSELAH HAVE THE POWER...
...OF REGENER-ATION!!

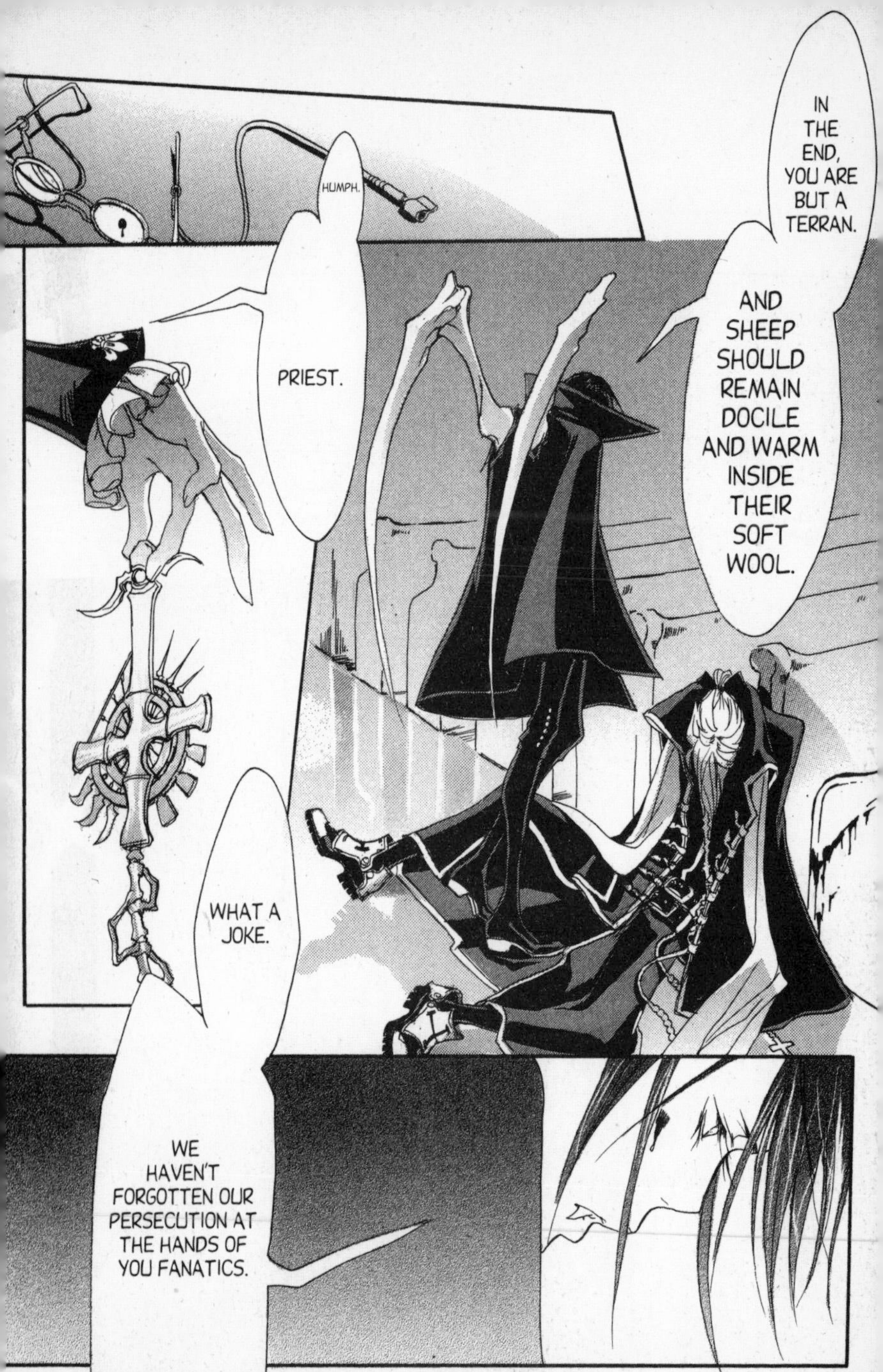
IN THE END, YOU ARE BUT A TERRAN.
AND SHEEP SHOULD REMAIN DOCILE AND WARM INSIDE THEIR SOFT WOOL.
HUMPH.
PRIEST.
WHAT A JOKE.
WE HAVEN'T FORGOTTEN OUR PERSECUTION AT THE HANDS OF YOU FANATICS.

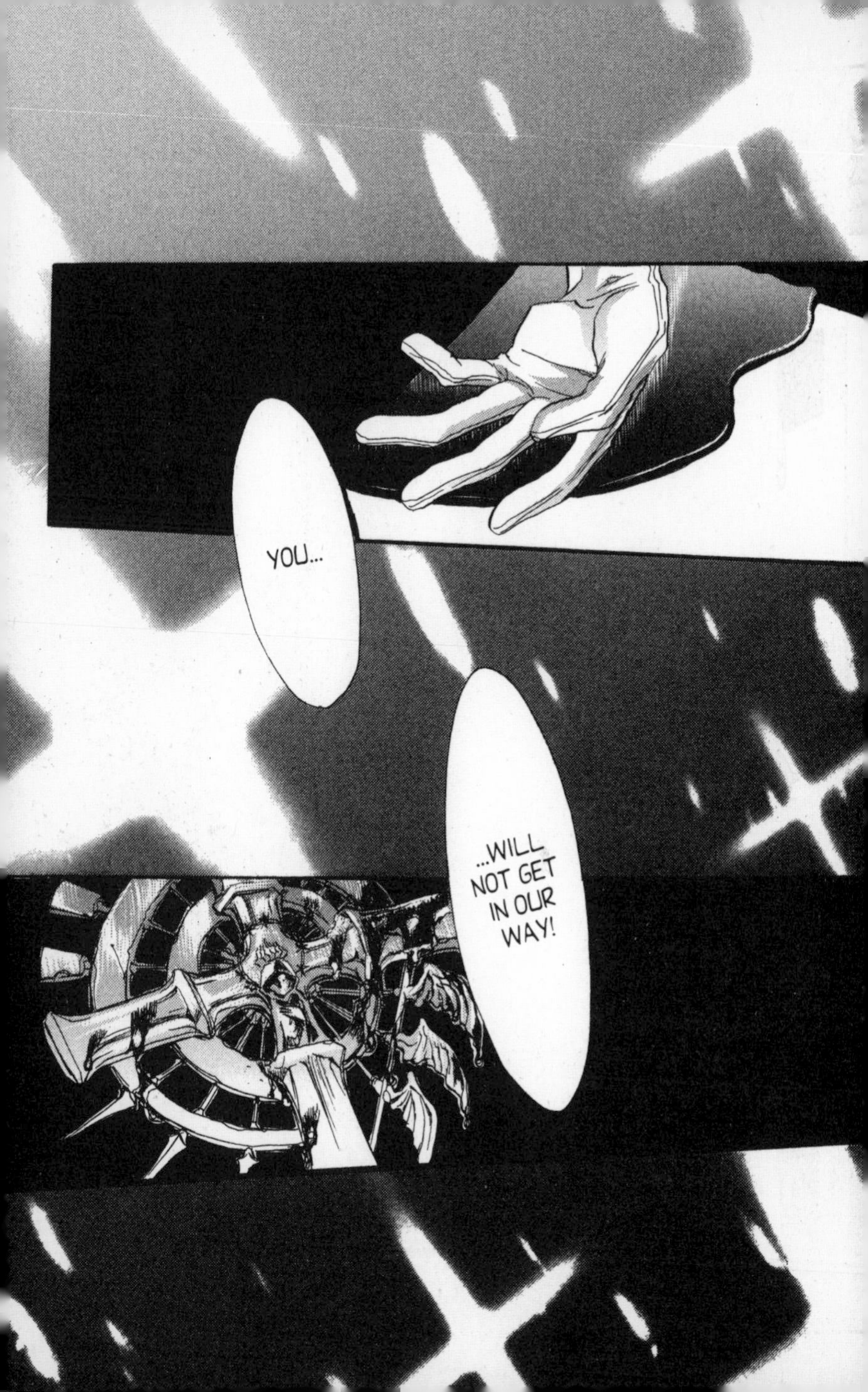
YOU...
...WILL NOT GET IN OUR WAY!

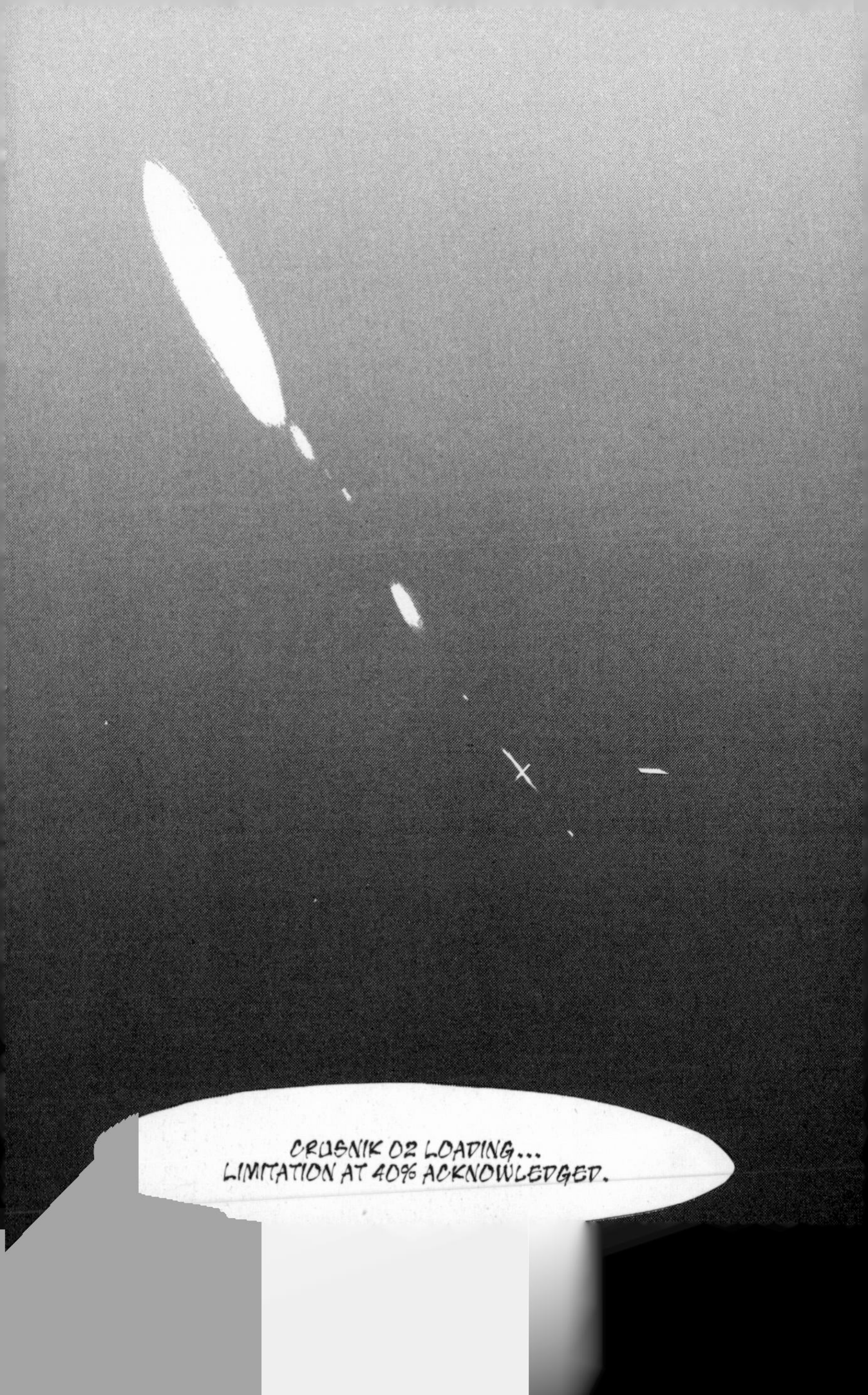
CRUSNIK 02 LOADING...
LIMITATION AT 40% ACKNOWLEDGED.

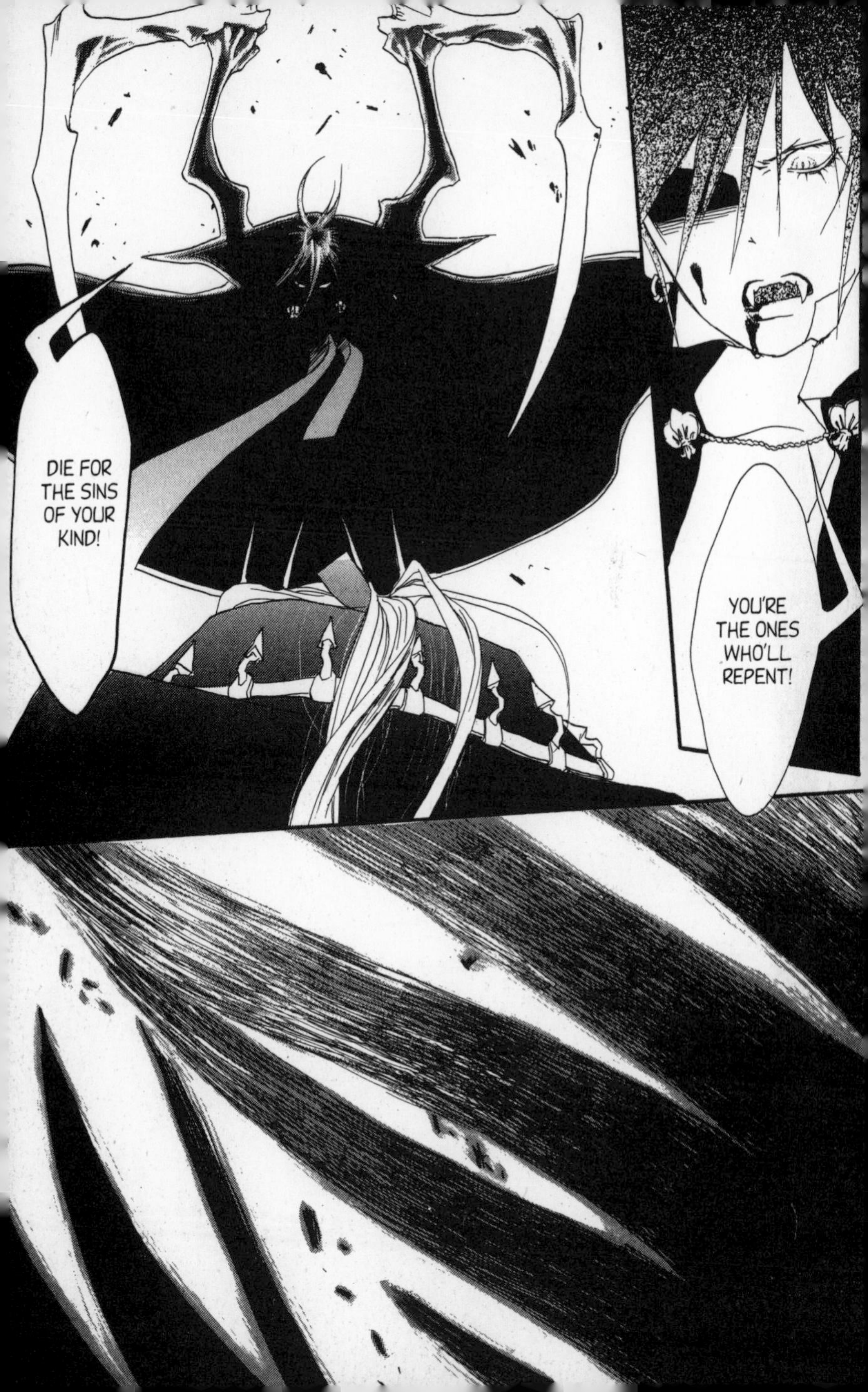
YOU'RE THE ONES WHO'LL REPENT!
DIE FOR THE SINS OF YOUR KIND!

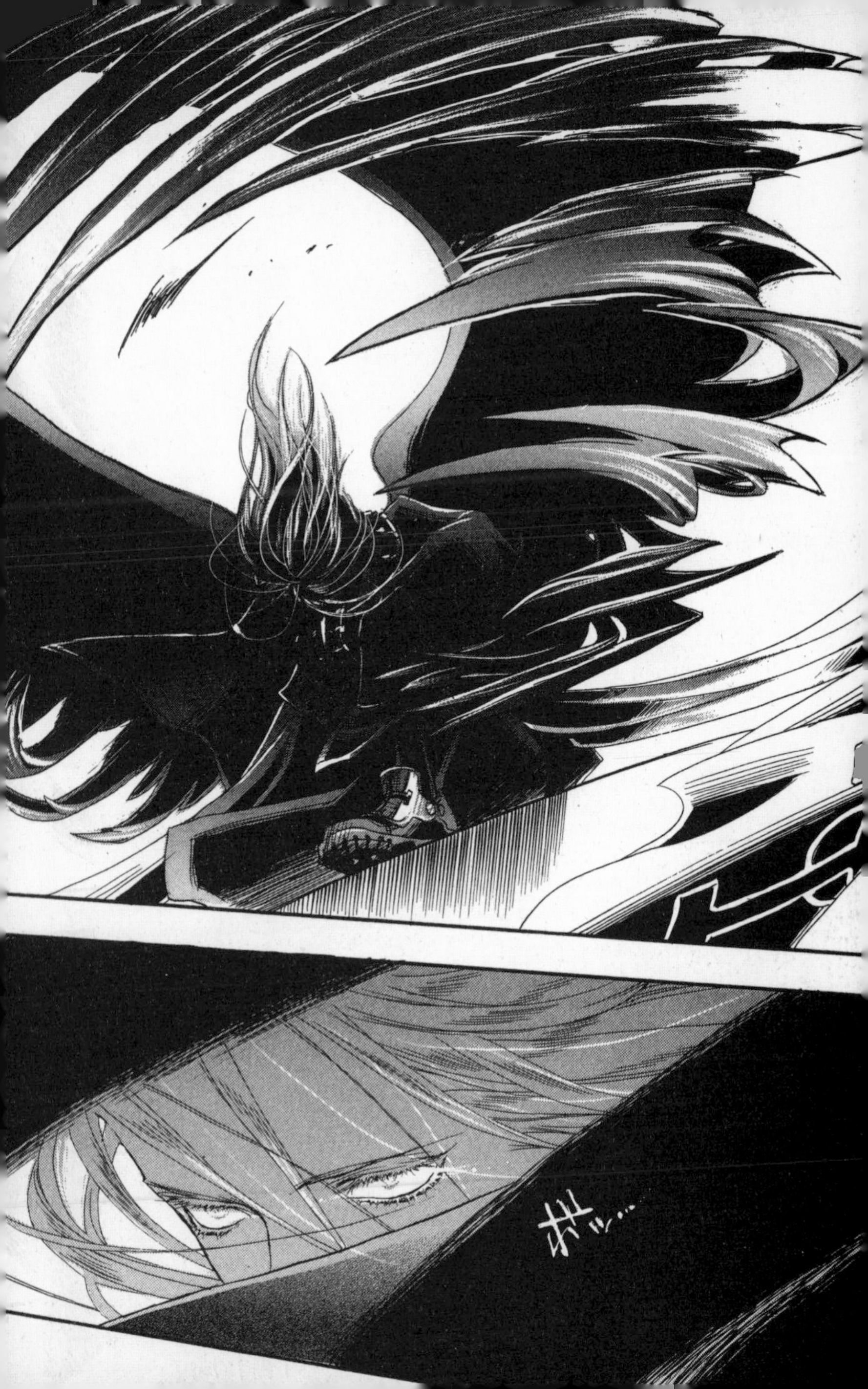
ボッ…

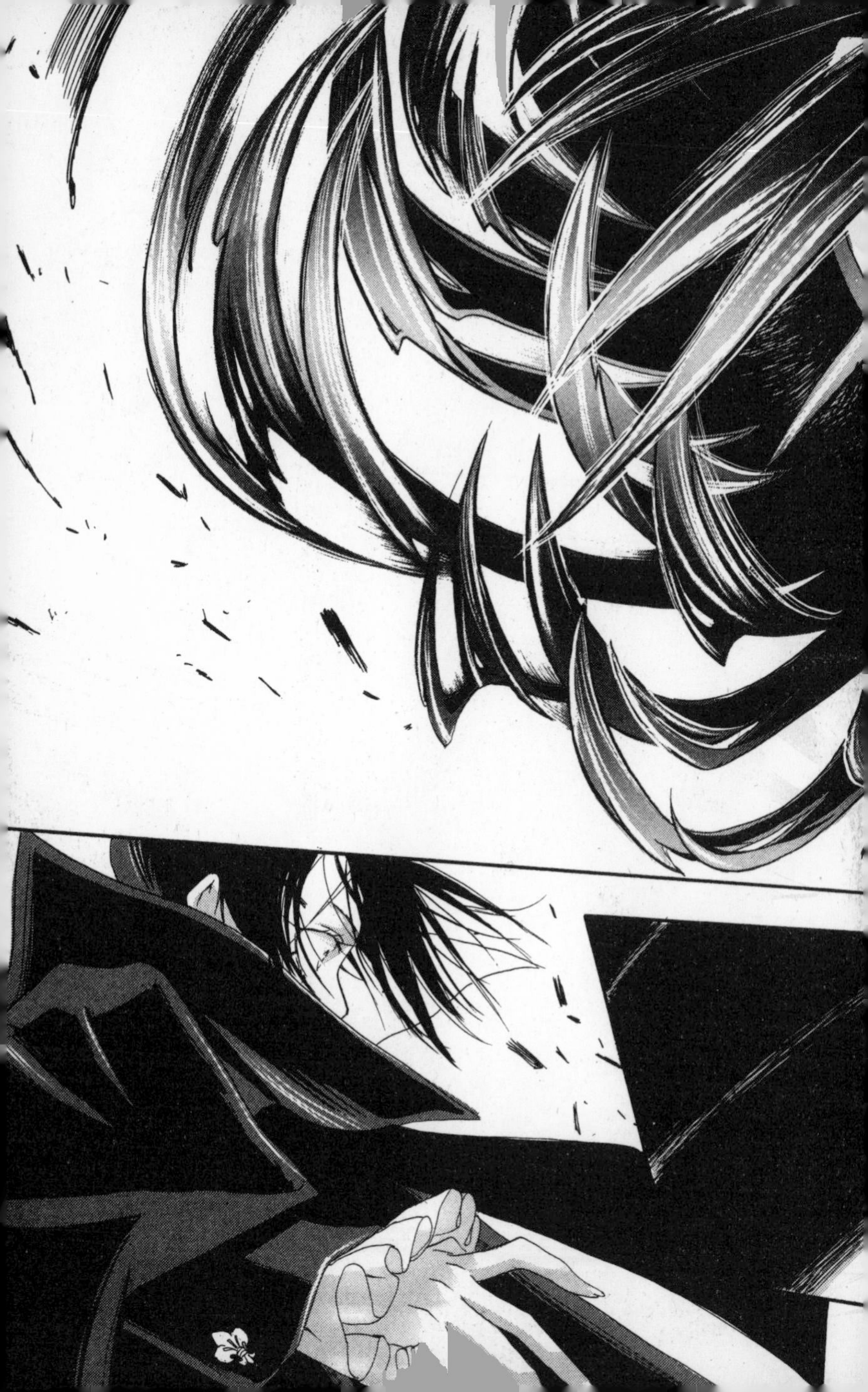

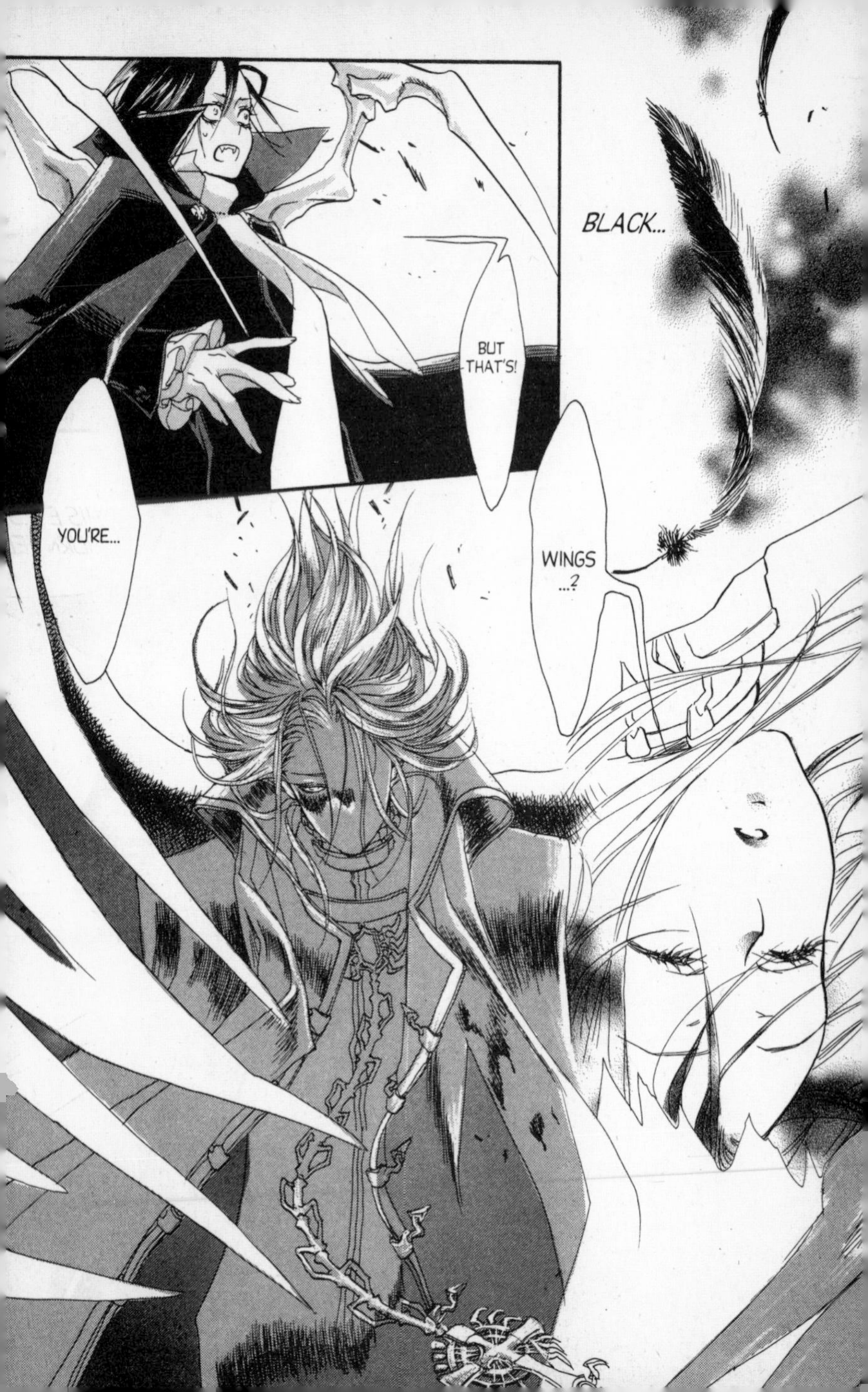
BLACK...
WINGS ...?
BUT THAT'S!
YOU'RE...

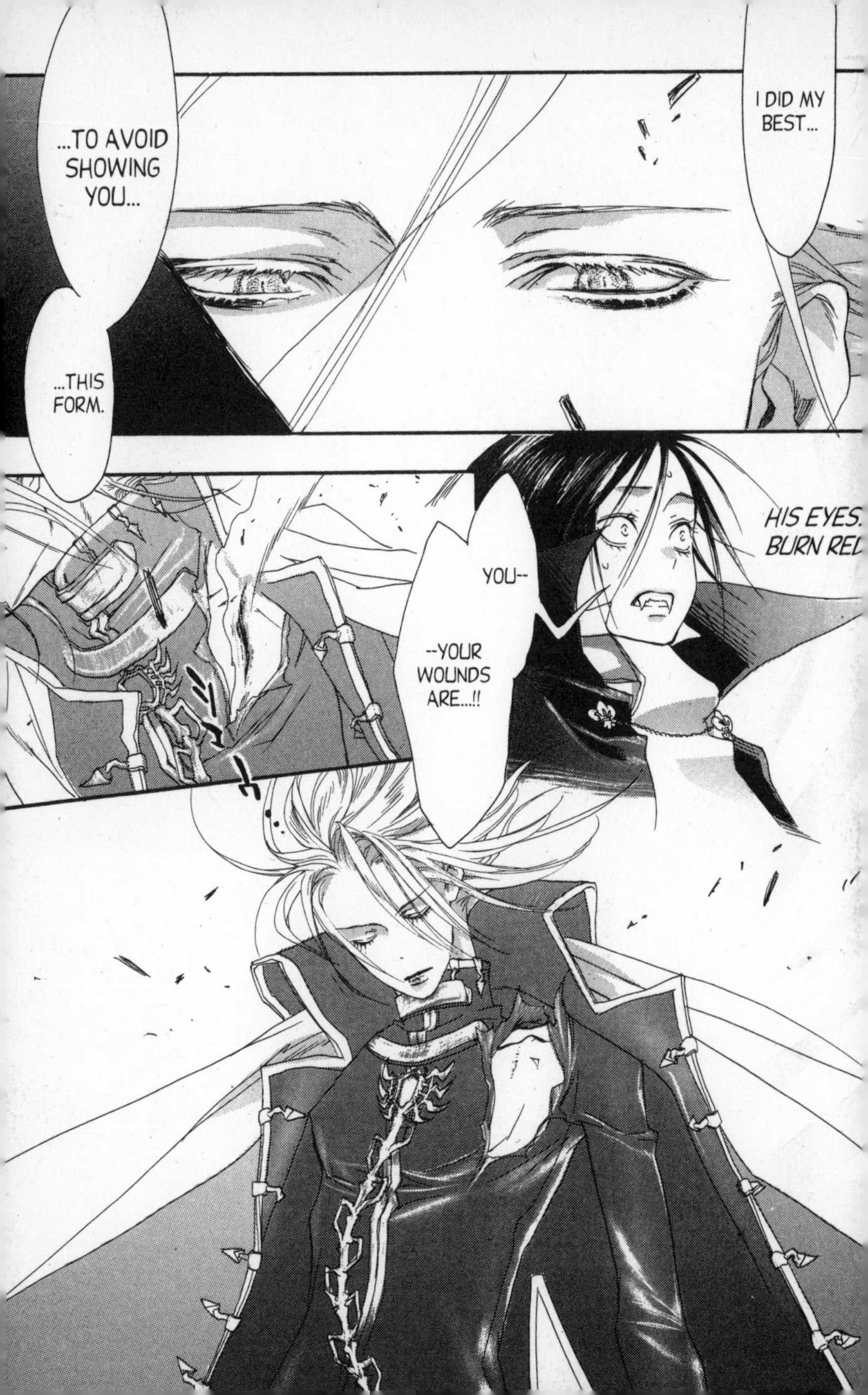
I DID MY BEST...
...TO AVOID SHOWING YOU...
...THIS FORM.
HIS EYES
BURN RE
YOU--
--YOUR WOUNDS ARE...!!

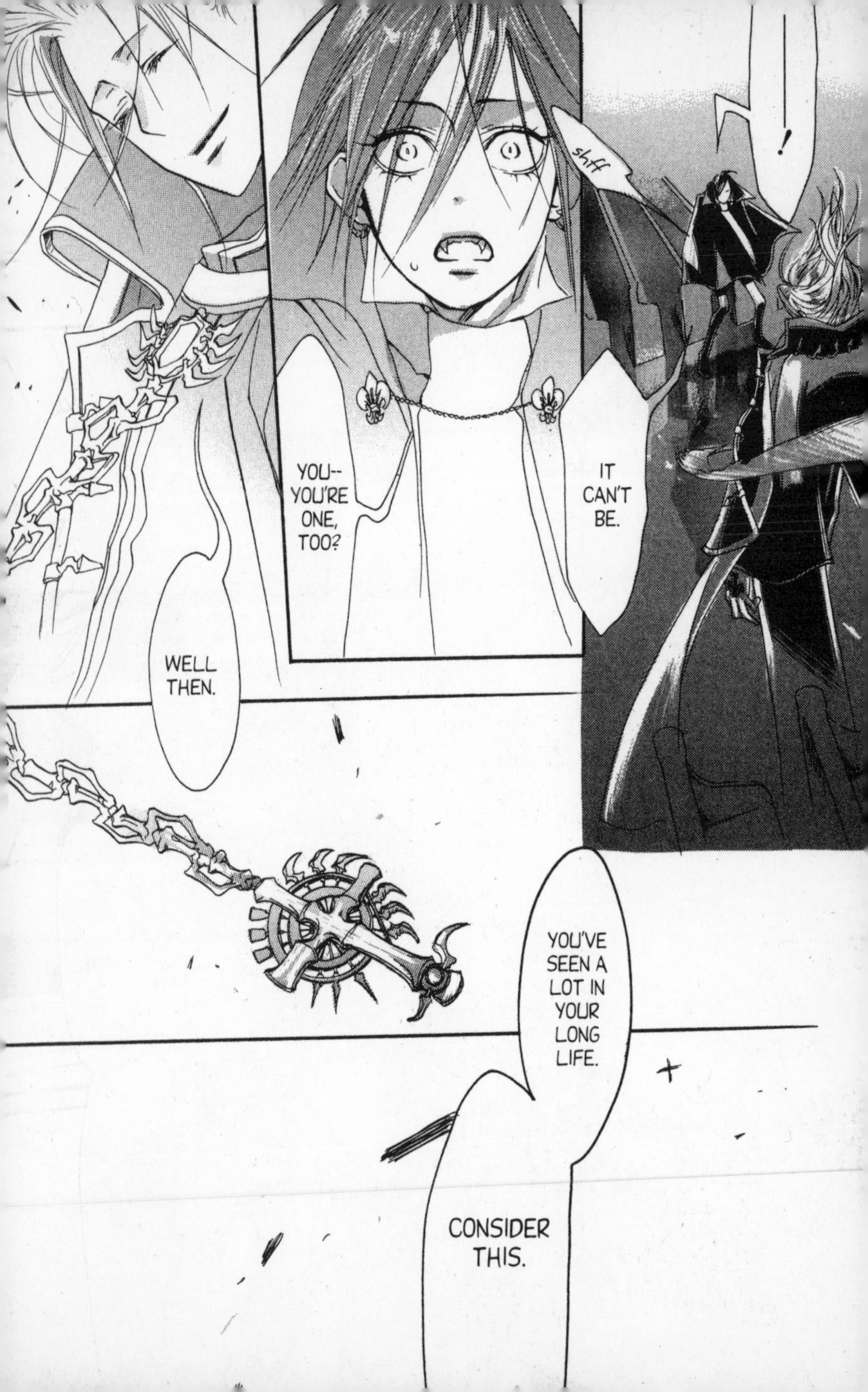
!
shff
IT CAN'T BE.
YOU-- YOU'RE ONE, TOO?
WELL THEN.
YOU'VE SEEN A LOT IN YOUR LONG LIFE.
CONSIDER THIS.

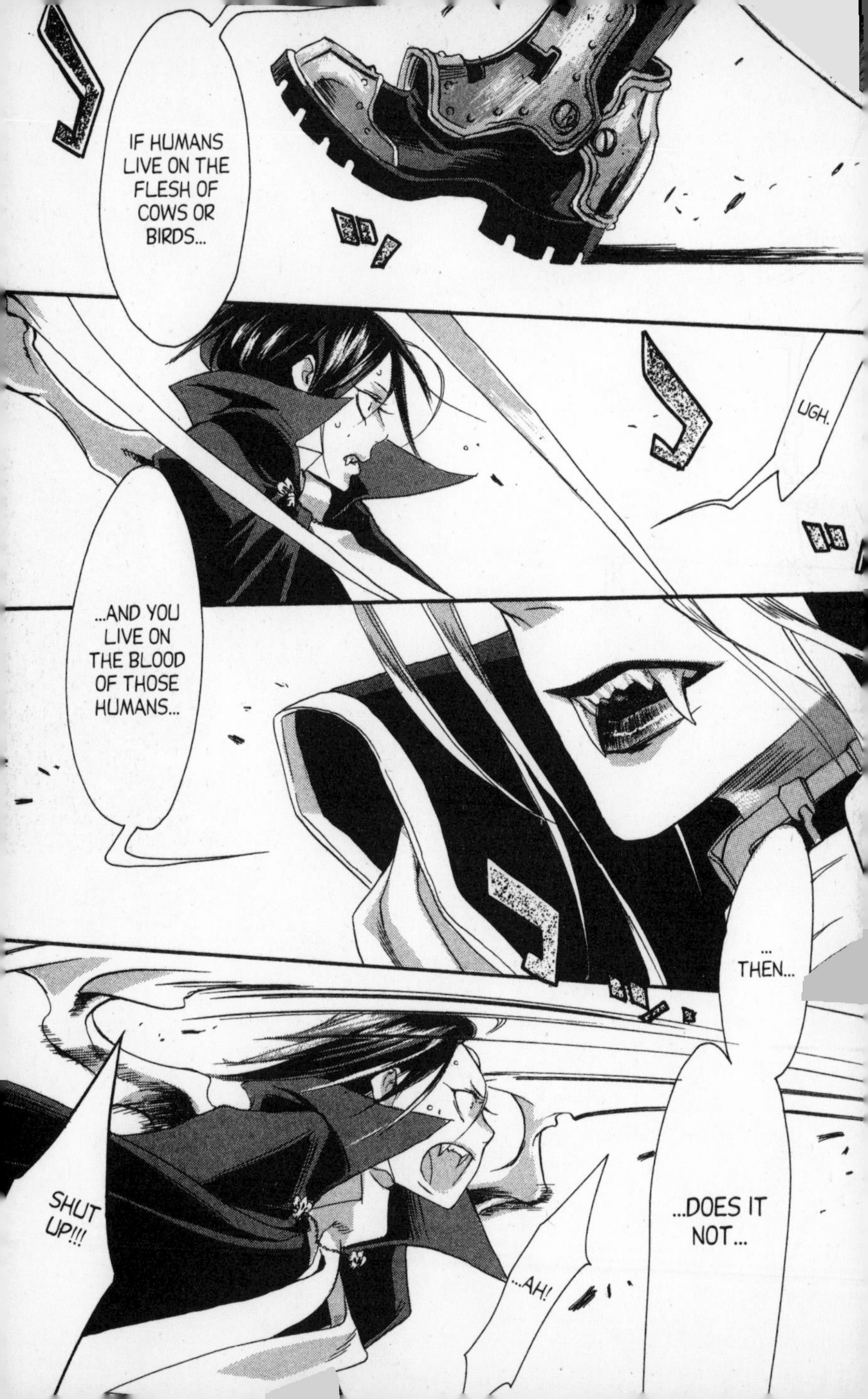
IF HUMANS LIVE ON THE FLESH OF COWS OR BIRDS...
UGH.
...AND YOU LIVE ON THE BLOOD OF THOSE HUMANS...
...THEN...
...DOES IT NOT...
...AH!
SHUT UP!!!

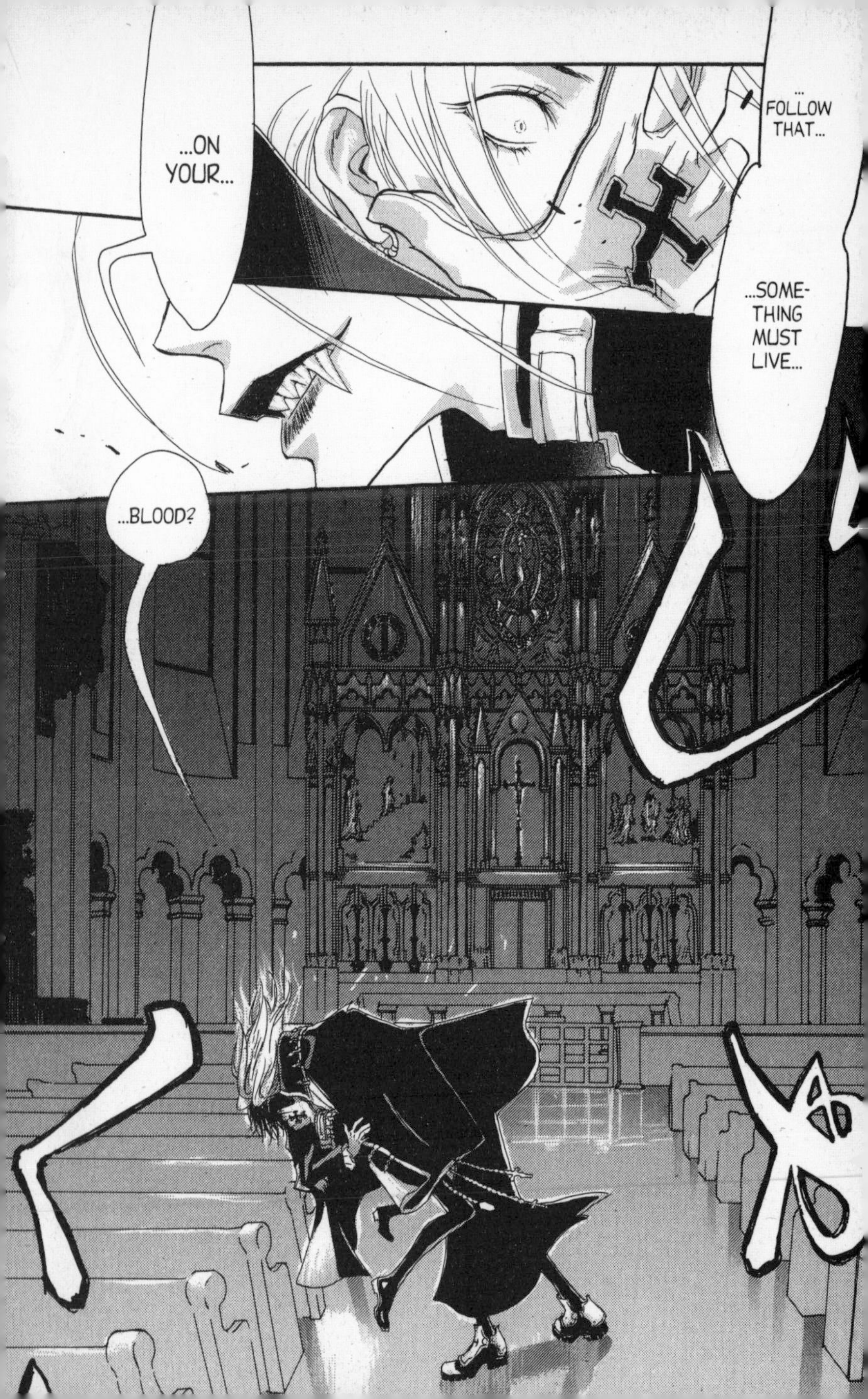
... FOLLOW THAT...
...SOME-THING MUST LIVE...
...ON YOUR...
...BLOOD?

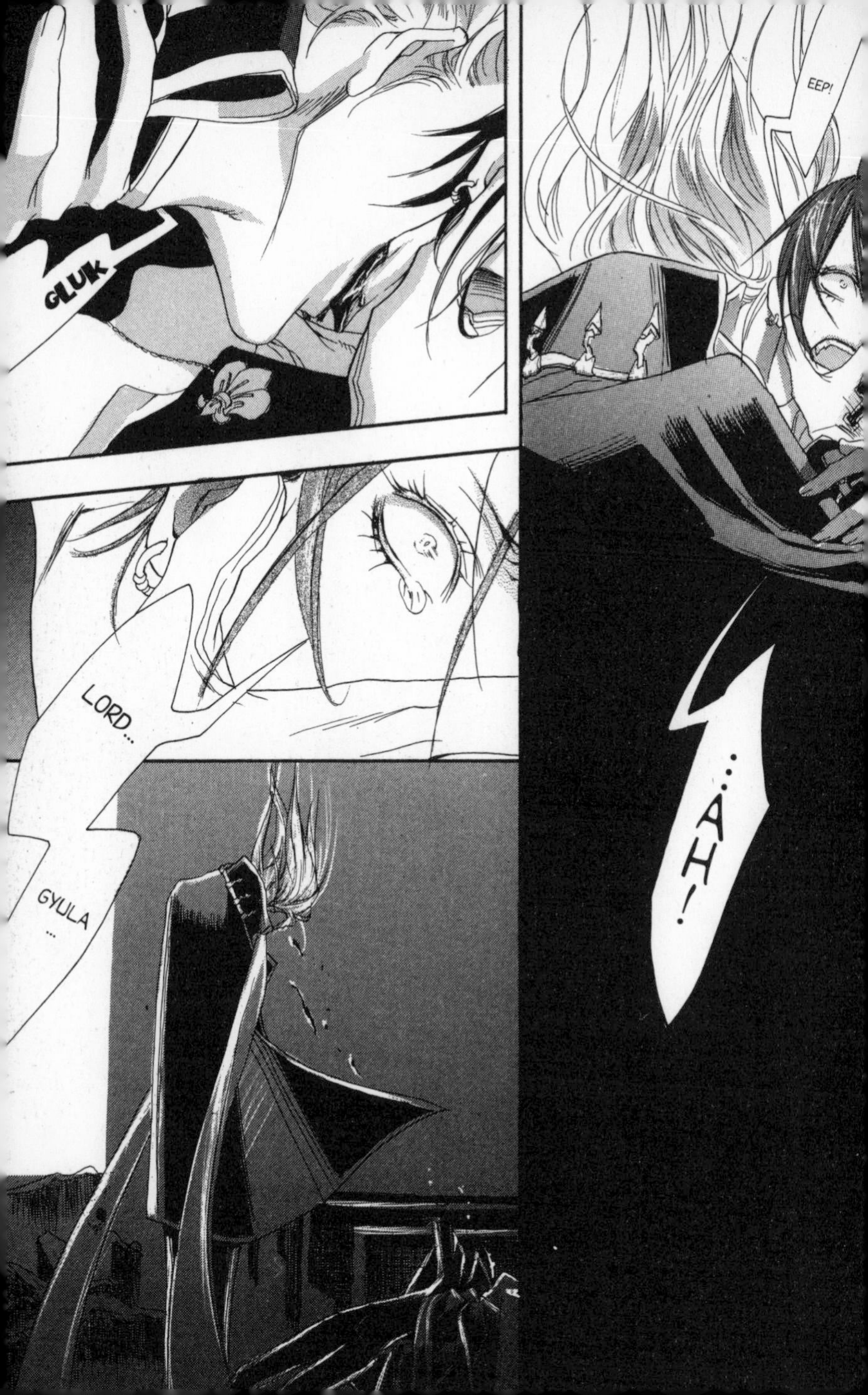
EEP!
...AH!
GLUK
LORD...
GYULA
...

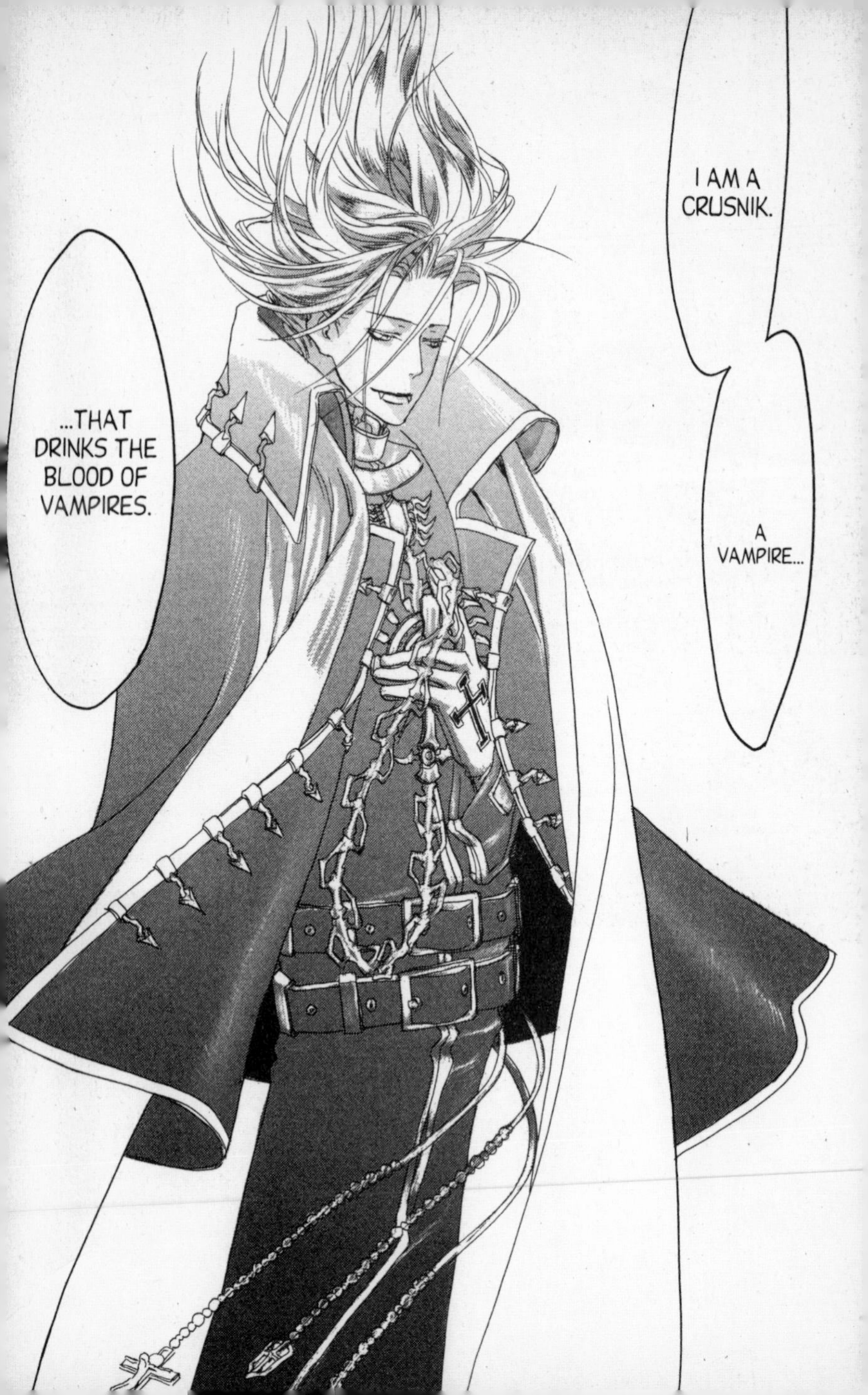
I AM A CRUSNIK.
A VAMPIRE...
...THAT DRINKS THE BLOOD OF VAMPIRES.

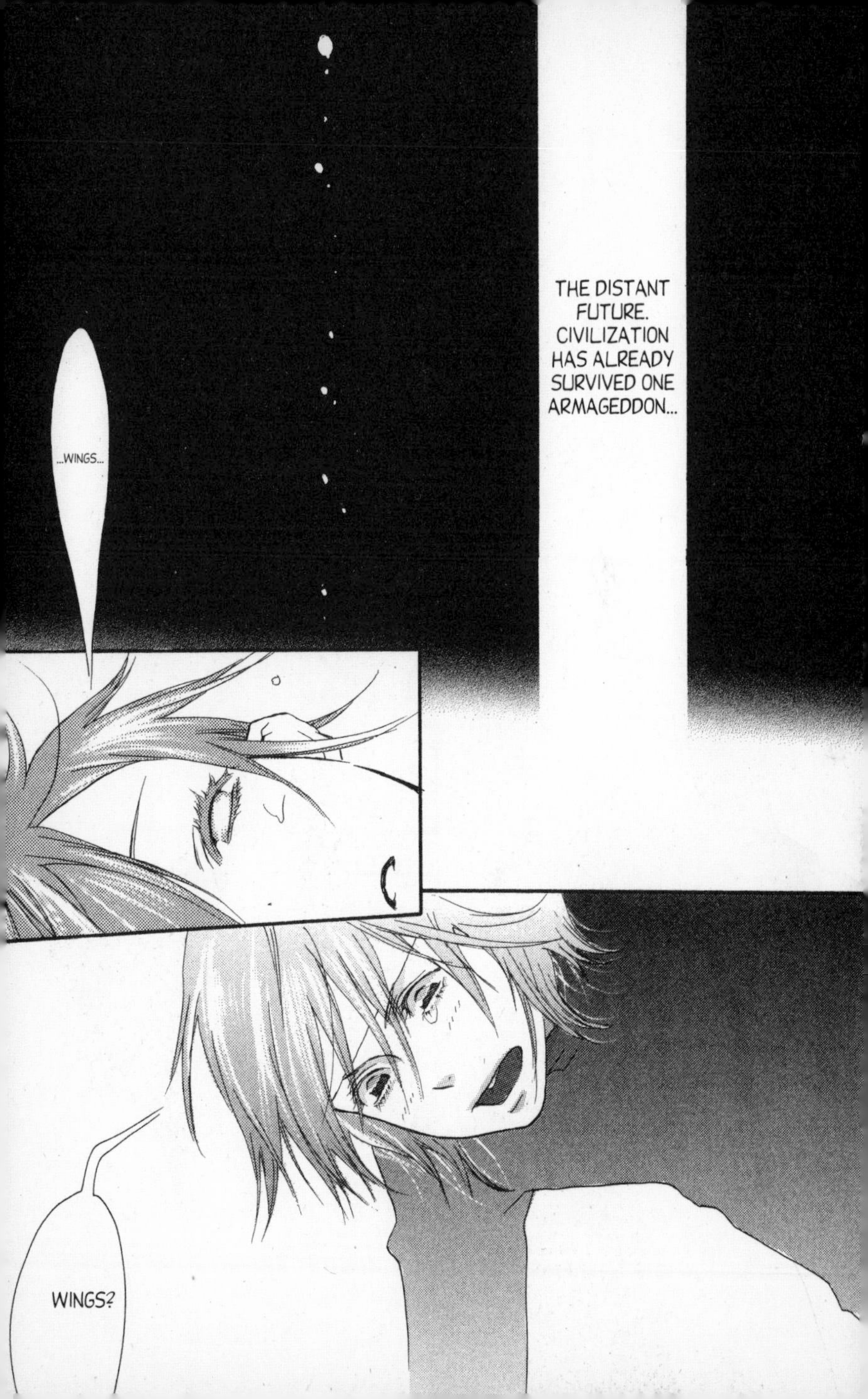
THE DISTANT FUTURE. CIVILIZATION HAS ALREADY SURVIVED ONE ARMAGEDDON...
...WINGS...
WINGS?

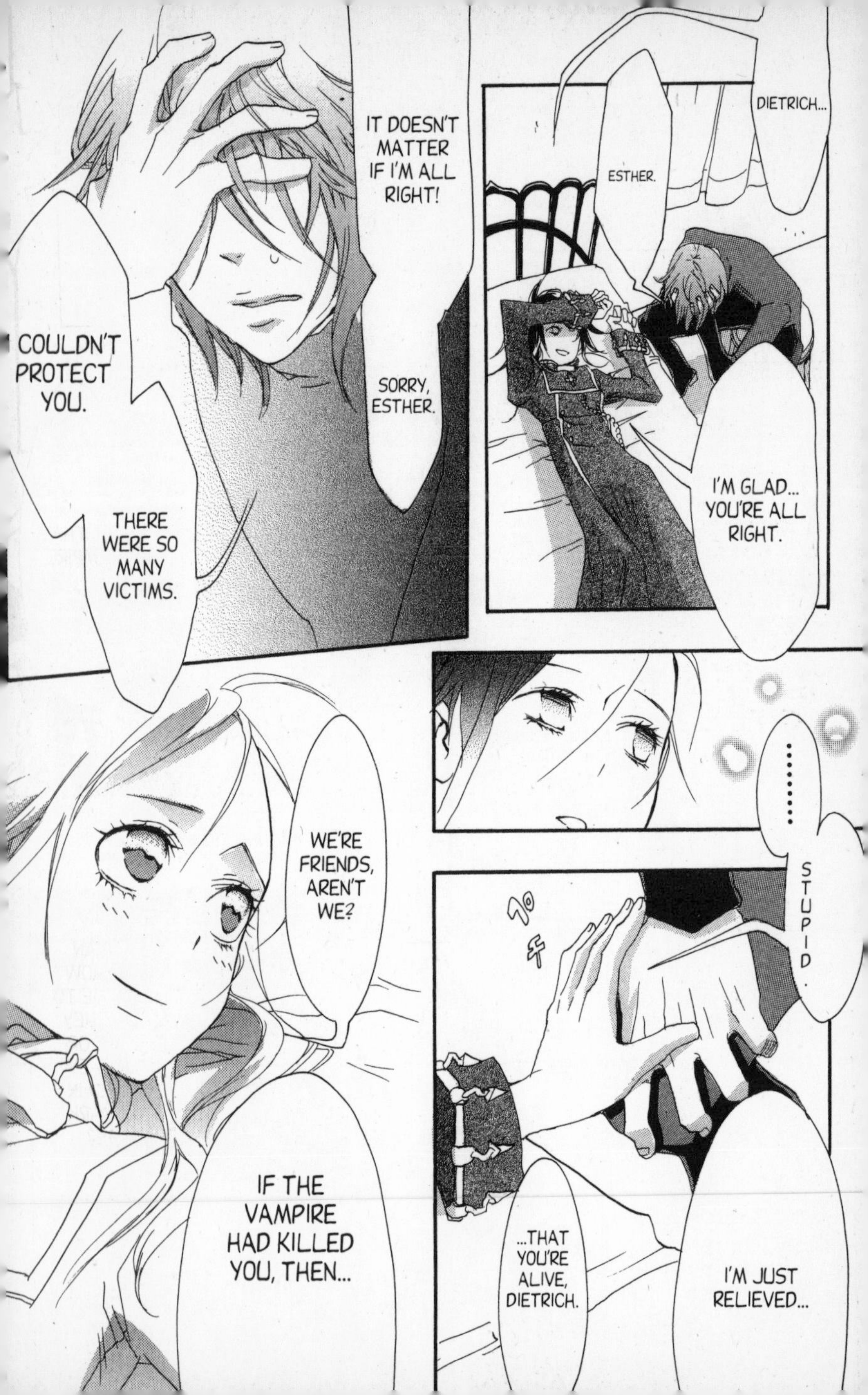
DIETRICH...
ESTHER.
...
I'M GLAD... YOU'RE ALL RIGHT.
IT DOESN'T MATTER IF I'M ALL RIGHT!
SORRY, ESTHER.
COULDN'T PROTECT YOU.
THERE WERE SO MANY VICTIMS.
......
STUPID.
I'M JUST RELIEVED...
...THAT YOU'RE ALIVE, DIETRICH.
WE'RE FRIENDS, AREN'T WE?
IF THE VAMPIRE HAD KILLED YOU, THEN...

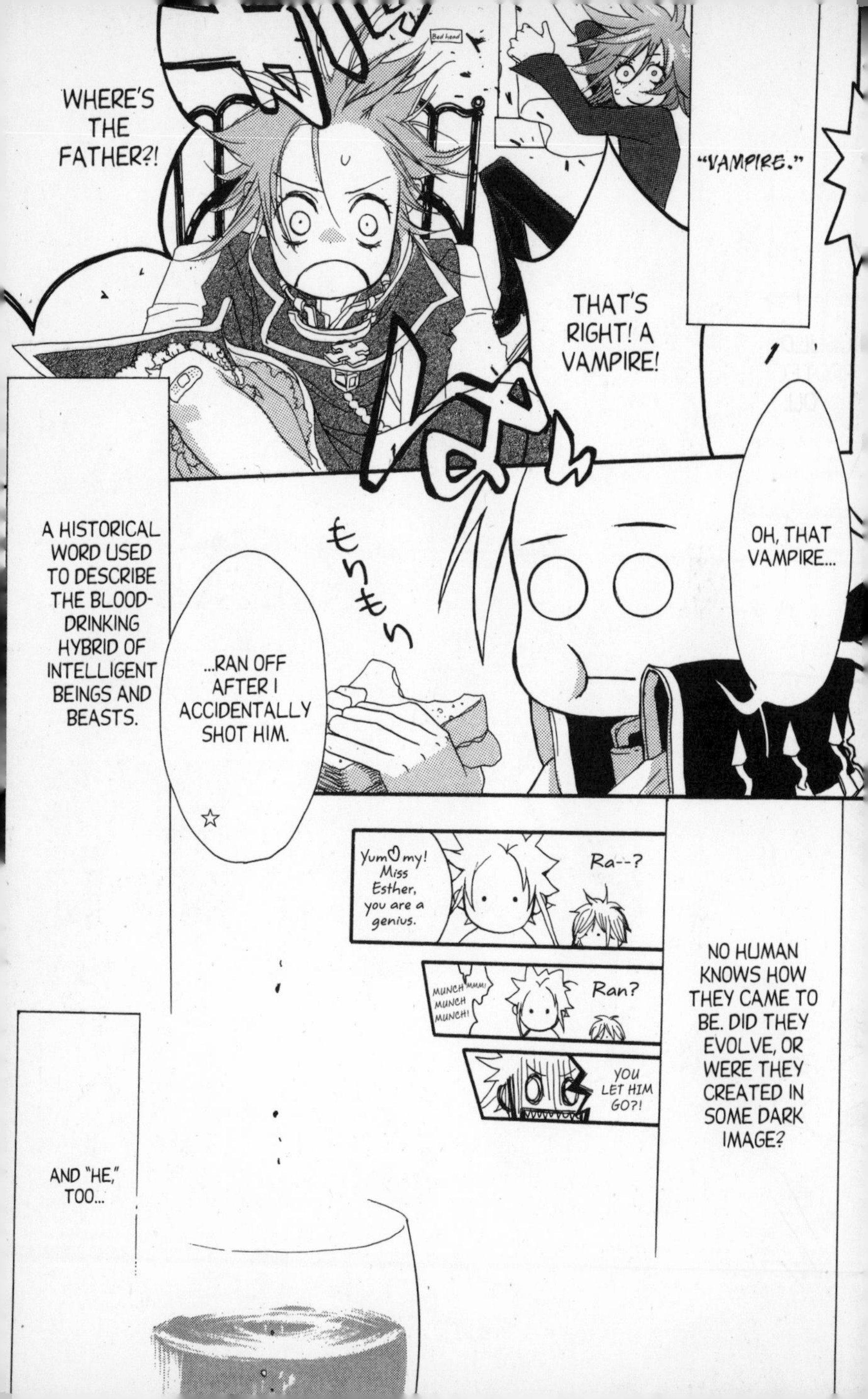
"VAMPIRE."
THAT'S RIGHT! A VAMPIRE!
Bed head
WHERE'S THE FATHER?!
OH, THAT VAMPIRE...
もりもり
...RAN OFF AFTER I ACCIDENTALLY SHOT HIM. ☆
A HISTORICAL WORD USED TO DESCRIBE THE BLOOD-DRINKING HYBRID OF INTELLIGENT BEINGS AND BEASTS.
NO HUMAN KNOWS HOW THEY CAME TO BE. DID THEY EVOLVE, OR WERE THEY CREATED IN SOME DARK IMAGE?
Ra--?
Yum♡my! Miss Esther, you are a genius.
Ran?
MMM! MUNCH MUNCH MUNCH!
YOU LET HIM GO?!
...
AND "HE," TOO...

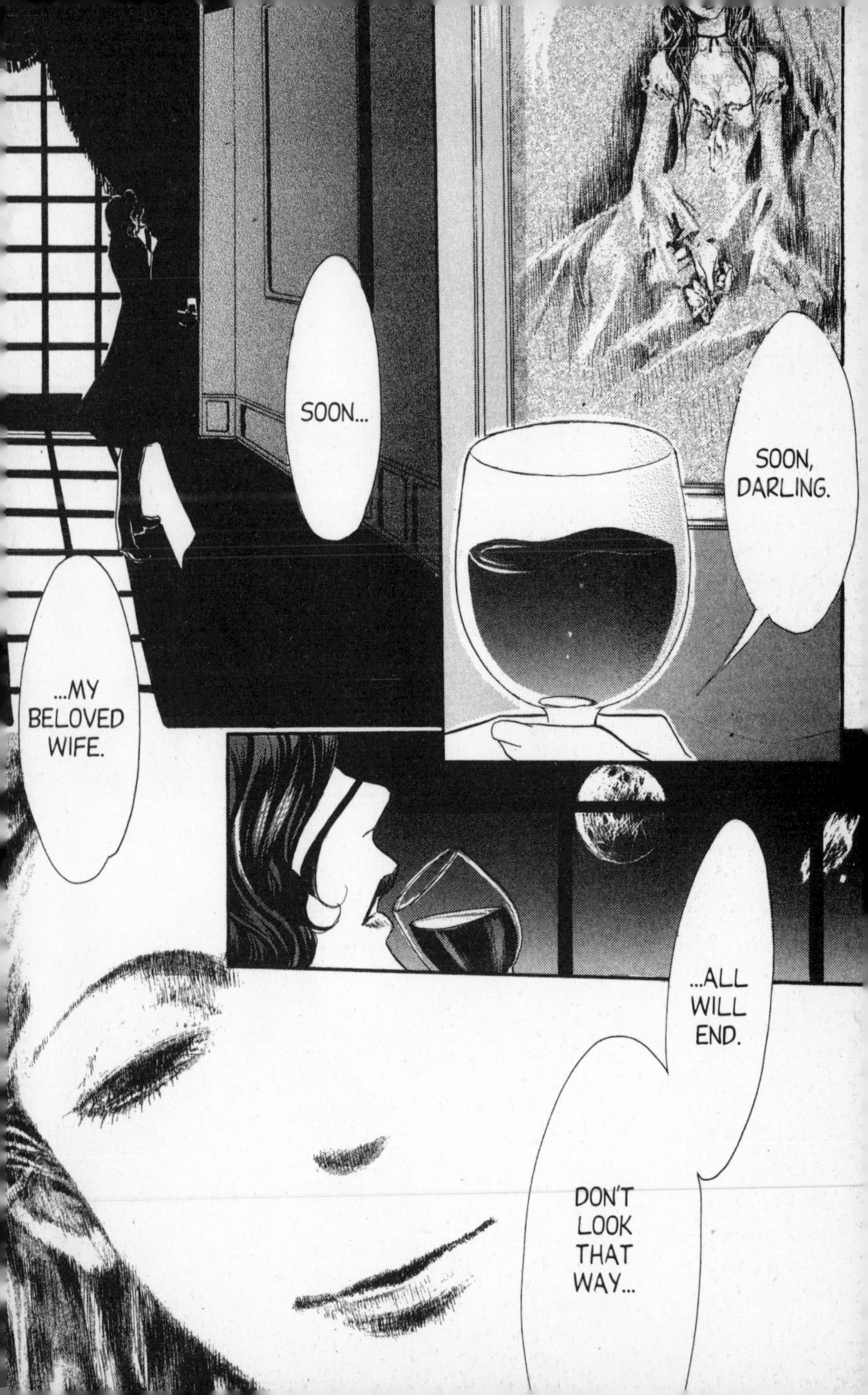
SOON, DARLING.
SOON...
...MY BELOVED WIFE.
...ALL WILL END.
DON'T LOOK THAT WAY...

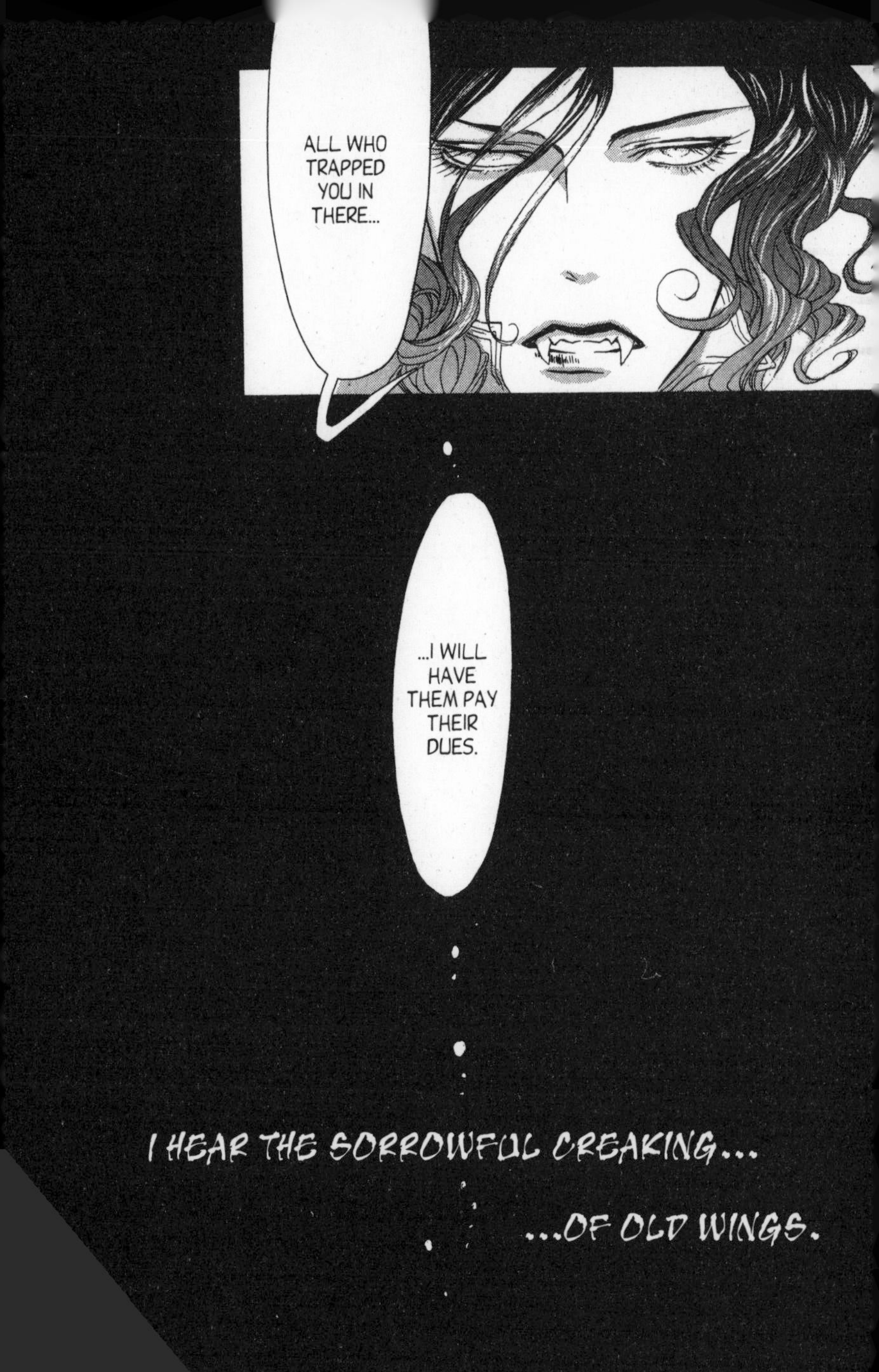
ALL WHO TRAPPED YOU IN THERE...
...I WILL HAVE THEM PAY THEIR DUES.
I HEAR THE SORROWFUL CREAKING...
...OF OLD WINGS.

★act 1 The Man Who Fell to Earth★ The End

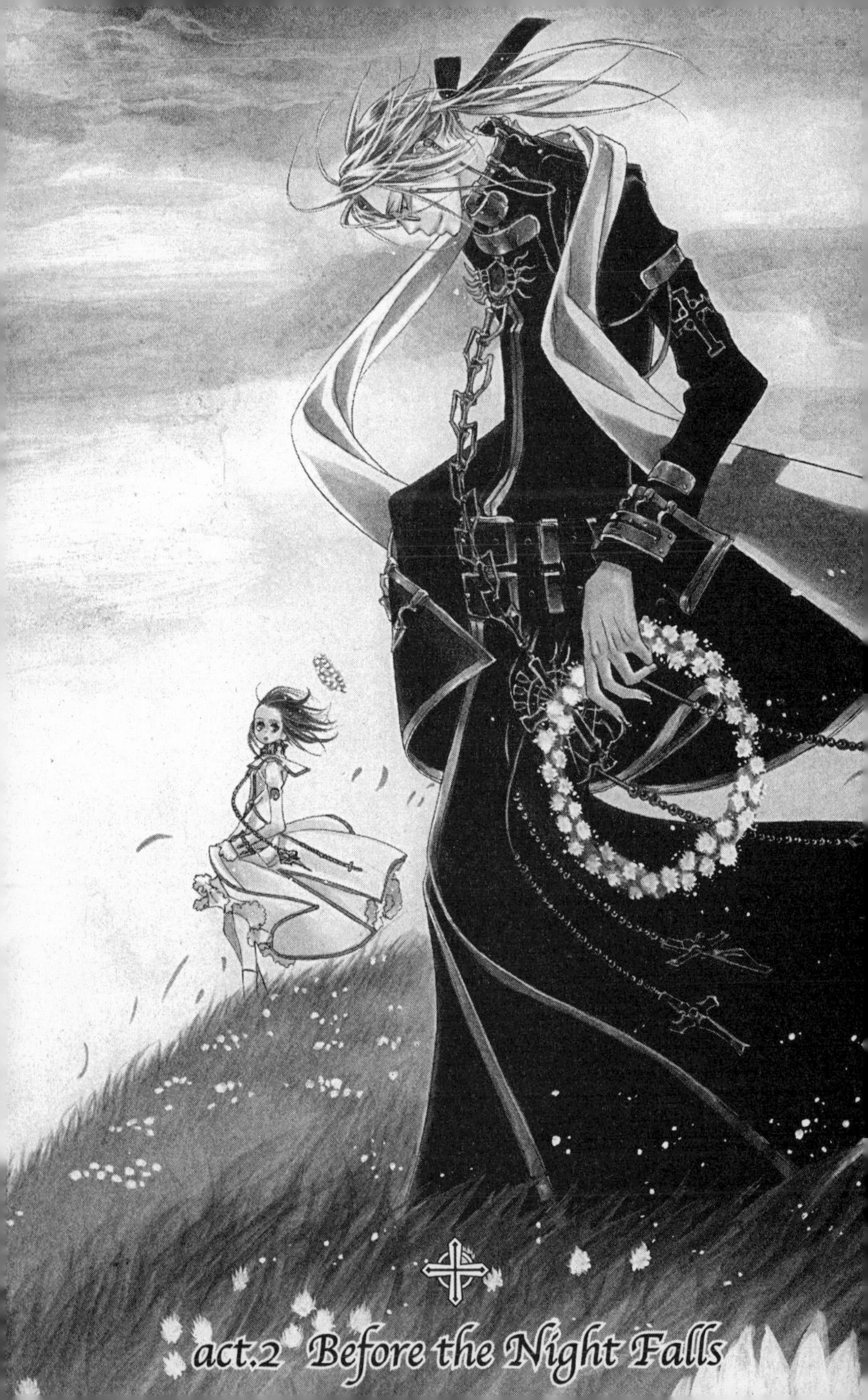

act.2 Before the Night Falls

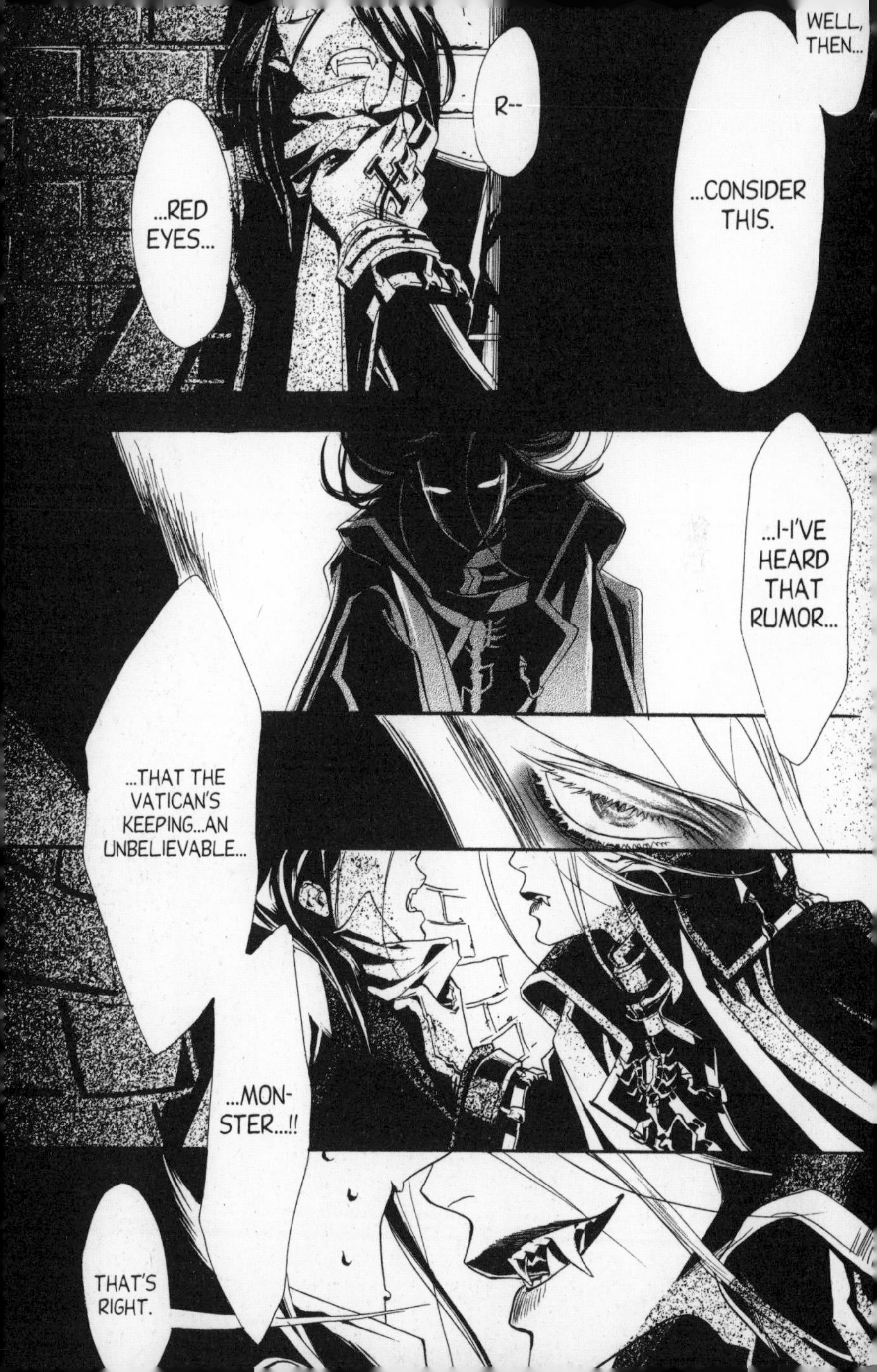

WELL, THEN...
...CONSIDER THIS.
R--
...RED EYES...
...I-I'VE HEARD THAT RUMOR...
...THAT THE VATICAN'S KEEPING...AN UNBELIEVABLE...
...MON-STER...!!
THAT'S RIGHT.

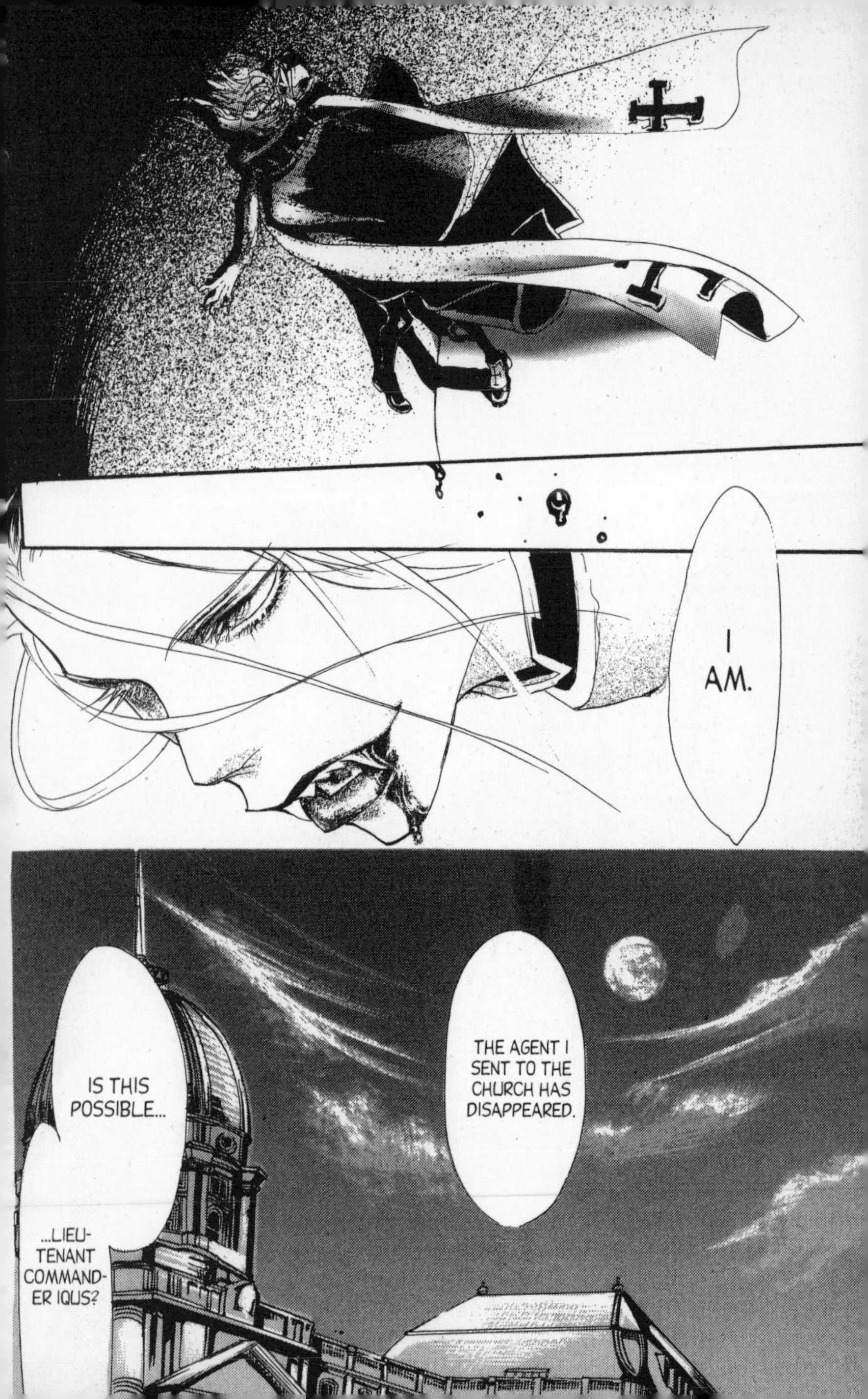
I AM.
THE AGENT I SENT TO THE CHURCH HAS DISAPPEARED.
IS THIS POSSIBLE...
...LIEU-TENANT COMMAND-ER IQUS?

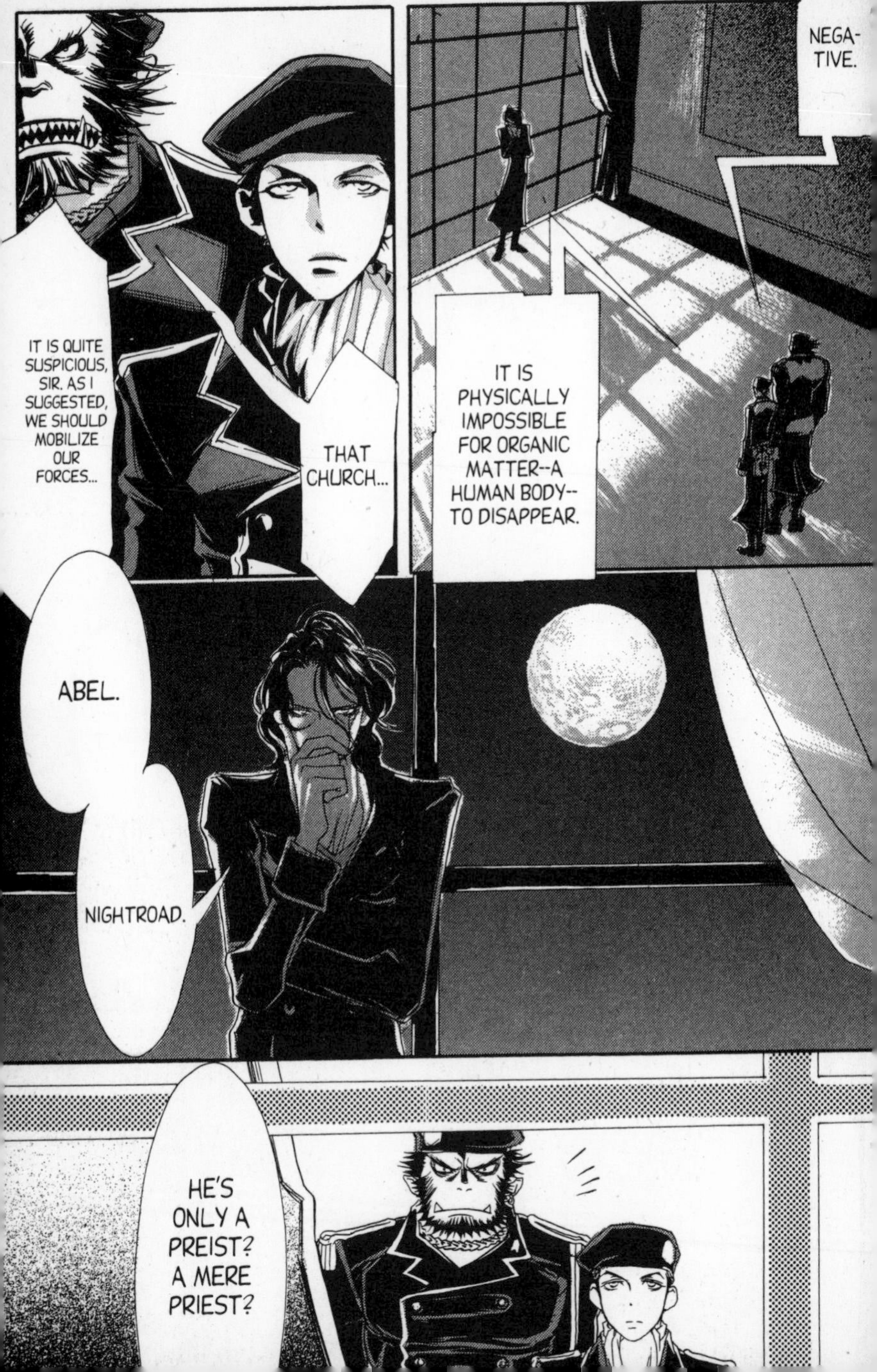
NEGA-TIVE.
IT IS PHYSICALLY IMPOSSIBLE FOR ORGANIC MATTER--A HUMAN BODY--TO DISAPPEAR.
THAT CHURCH...
IT IS QUITE SUSPICIOUS, SIR. AS I SUGGESTED, WE SHOULD MOBILIZE OUR FORCES...
ABEL.
NIGHTROAD.
HE'S ONLY A PREIST? A MERE PRIEST?

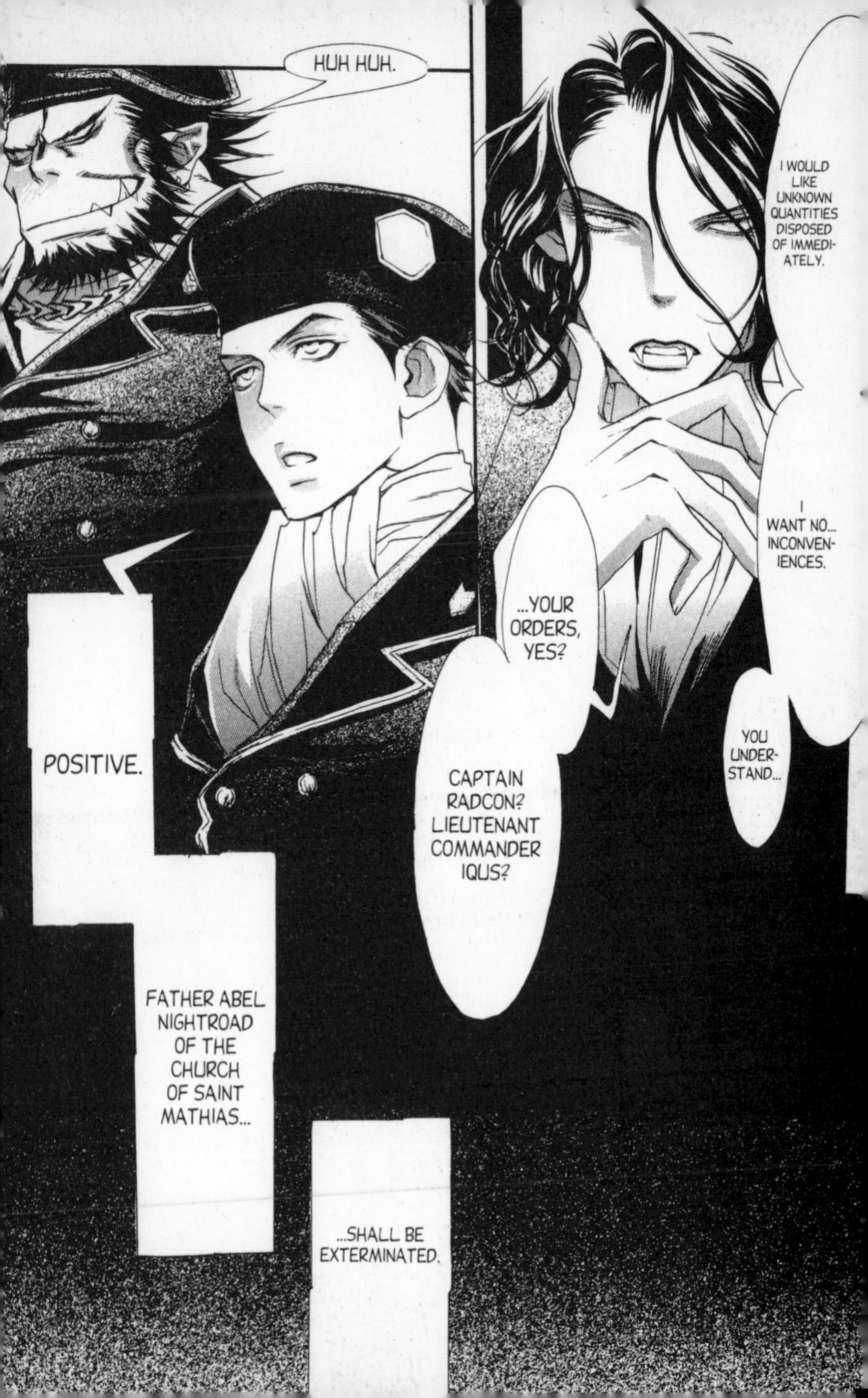
I WOULD LIKE UNKNOWN QUANTITIES DISPOSED OF IMMEDIATELY.
I WANT NO... INCONVENIENCES.
YOU UNDERSTAND...
...YOUR ORDERS, YES?
CAPTAIN RADCON? LIEUTENANT COMMANDER IQUS?
HUH HUH.
POSITIVE.
FATHER ABEL NIGHTROAD OF THE CHURCH OF SAINT MATHIAS...
...SHALL BE EXTERMINATED.

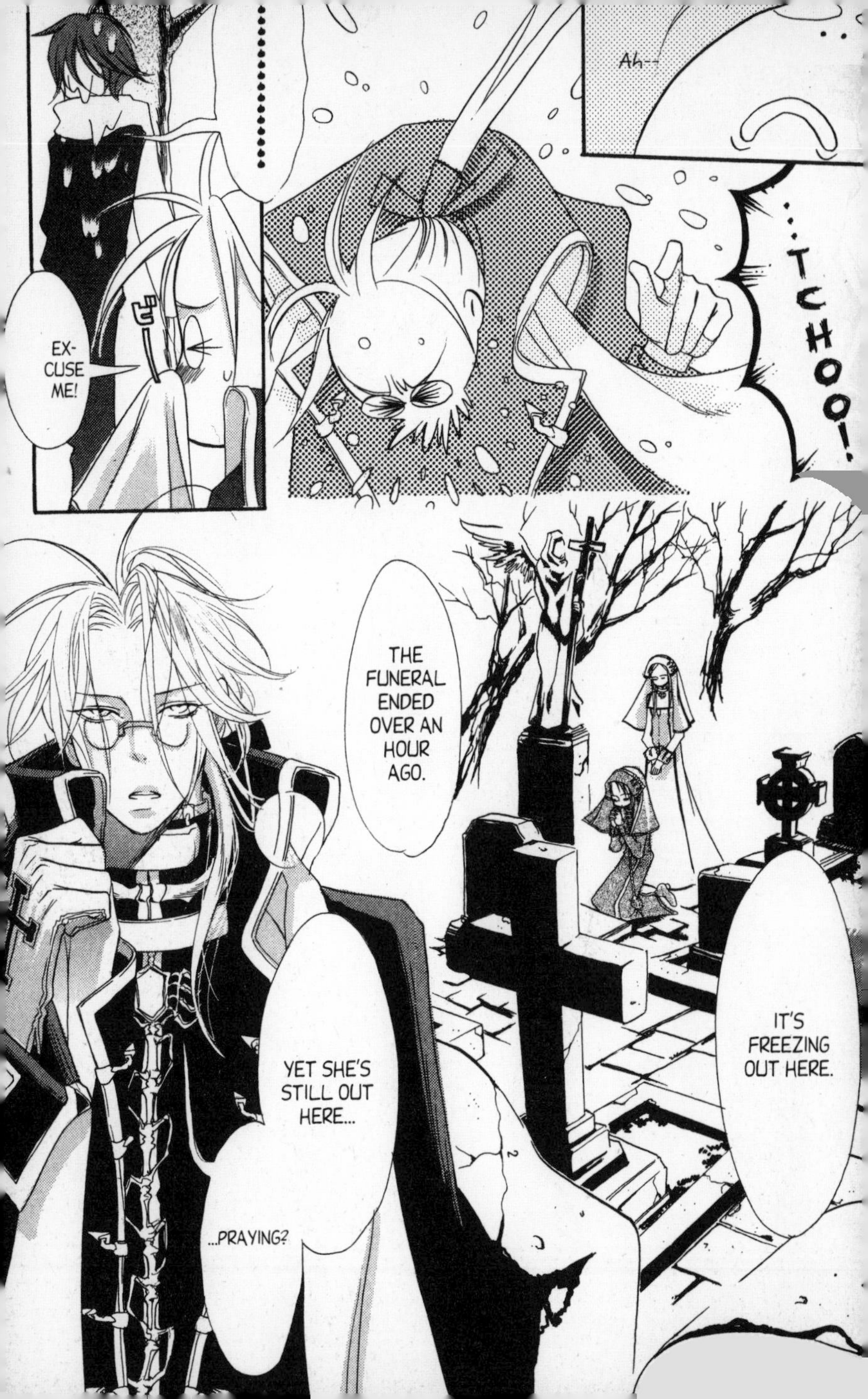

Ah--
...TCHOO!
EX-CUSE ME!
ビー
IT'S FREEZING OUT HERE.
THE FUNERAL ENDED OVER AN HOUR AGO.
YET SHE'S STILL OUT HERE...
...PRAYING?

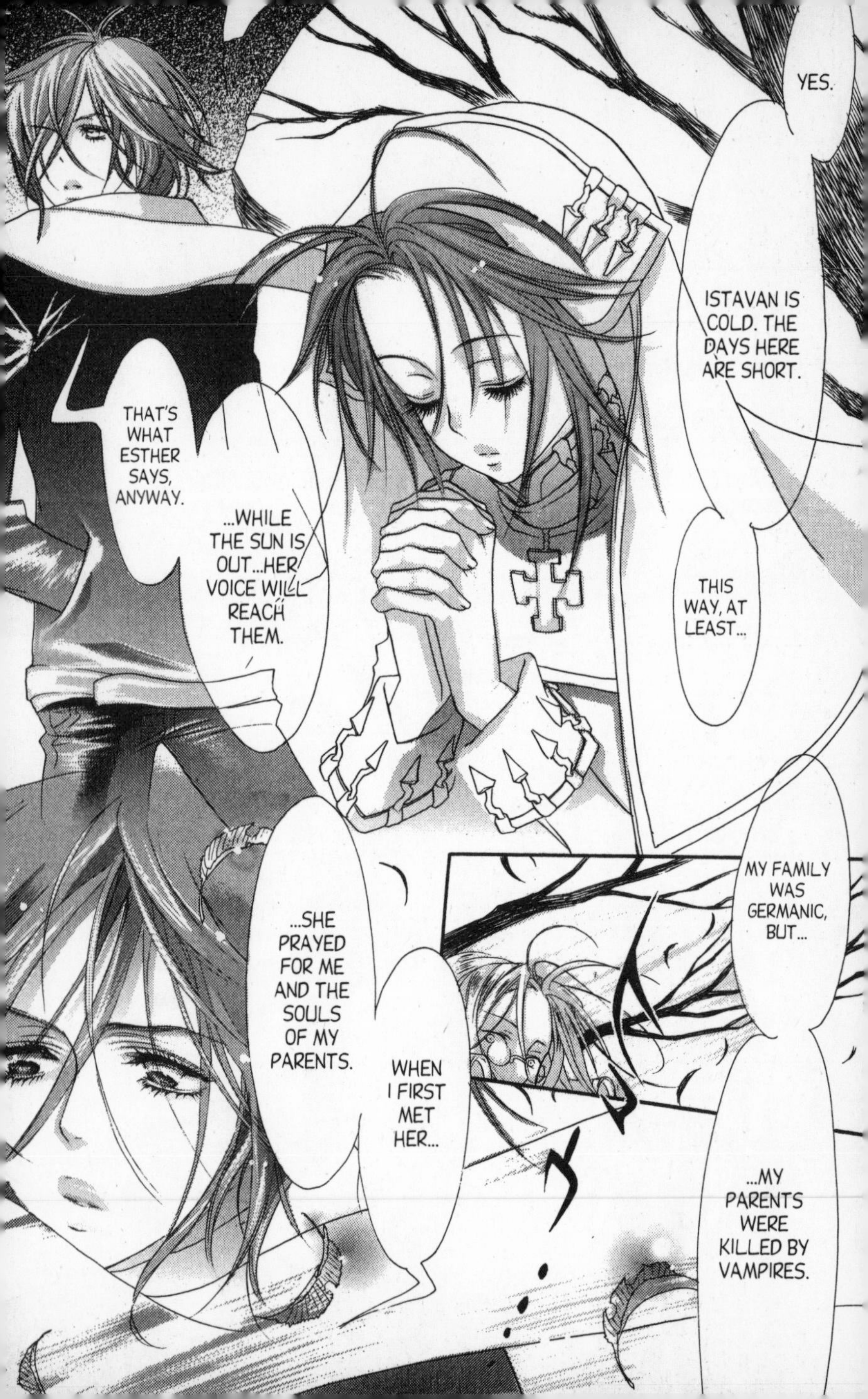
YES.
ISTAVAN IS COLD. THE DAYS HERE ARE SHORT.
THIS WAY, AT LEAST...
...WHILE THE SUN IS OUT...HER VOICE WILL REACH THEM.
THAT'S WHAT ESTHER SAYS, ANYWAY.
MY FAMILY WAS GERMANIC, BUT...
...MY PARENTS WERE KILLED BY VAMPIRES.
WHEN I FIRST MET HER...
...SHE PRAYED FOR ME AND THE SOULS OF MY PARENTS.

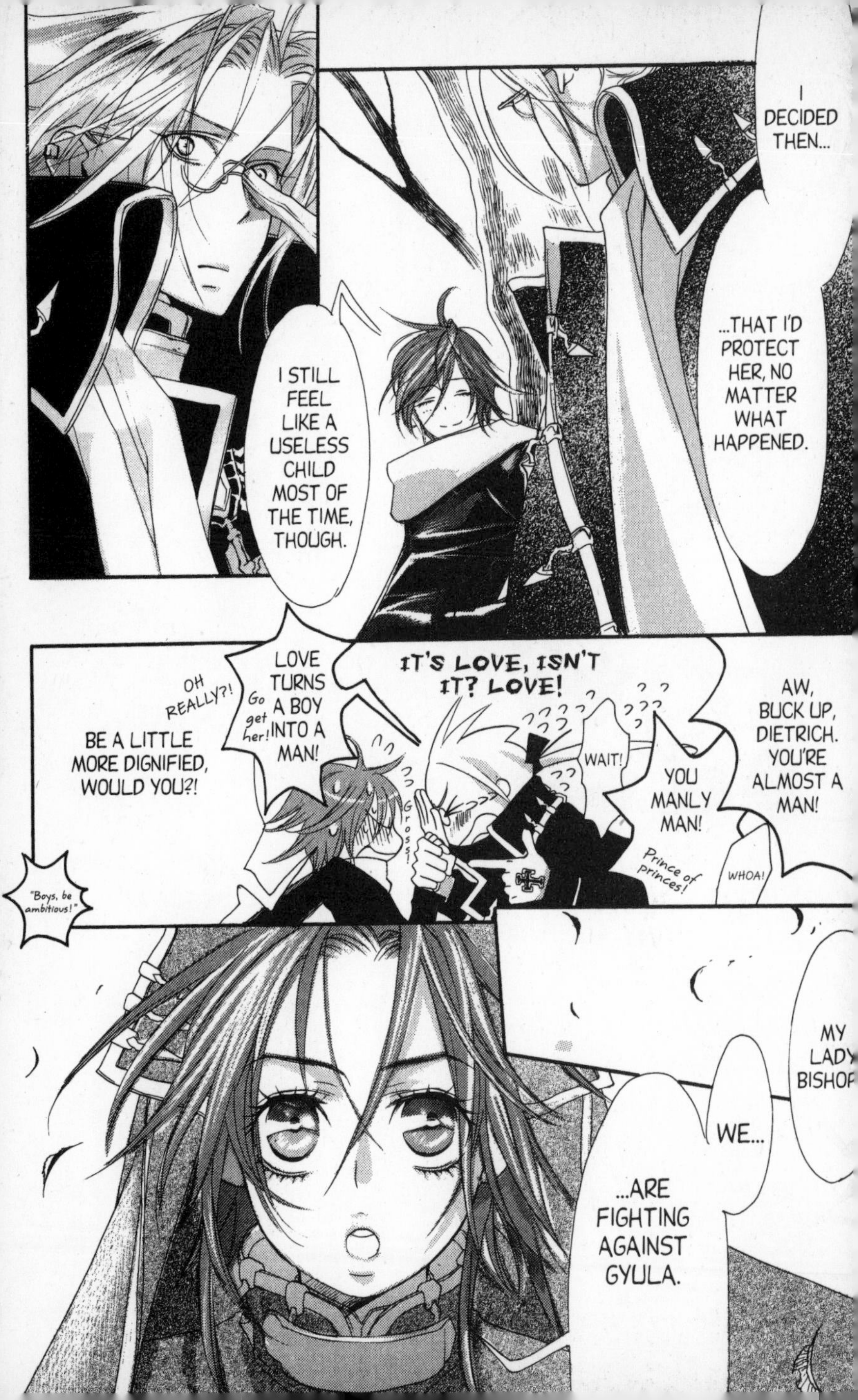
I DECIDED THEN...
...THAT I'D PROTECT HER, NO MATTER WHAT HAPPENED.
I STILL FEEL LIKE A USELESS CHILD MOST OF THE TIME, THOUGH.
AW, BUCK UP, DIETRICH. YOU'RE ALMOST A MAN!
WHOA!
YOU MANLY MAN!
Prince of princes!
WAIT!
IT'S LOVE, ISN'T IT? LOVE!
LOVE TURNS A BOY INTO A MAN!
Go get her!
Gross!
OH REALLY?!
BE A LITTLE MORE DIGNIFIED, WOULD YOU?!
"Boys, be ambitious!"
MY LADY BISHOP
WE...
...ARE FIGHTING AGAINST GYULA.

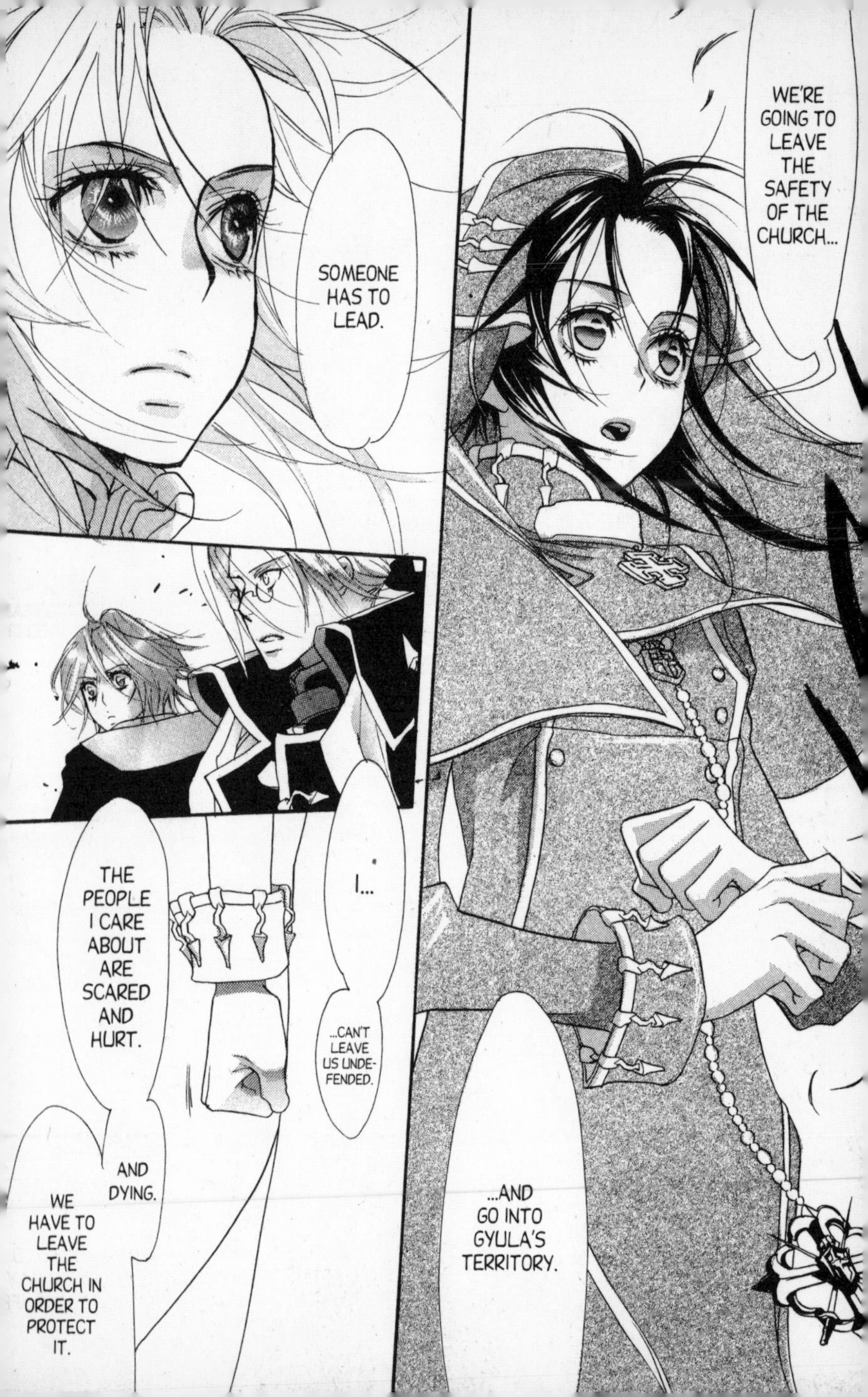
WE'RE GOING TO LEAVE THE SAFETY OF THE CHURCH...
...AND GO INTO GYULA'S TERRITORY.
SOMEONE HAS TO LEAD.
I...
...CAN'T LEAVE US UNDE-FENDED.
THE PEOPLE I CARE ABOUT ARE SCARED AND HURT.
AND DYING.
WE HAVE TO LEAVE THE CHURCH IN ORDER TO PROTECT IT.

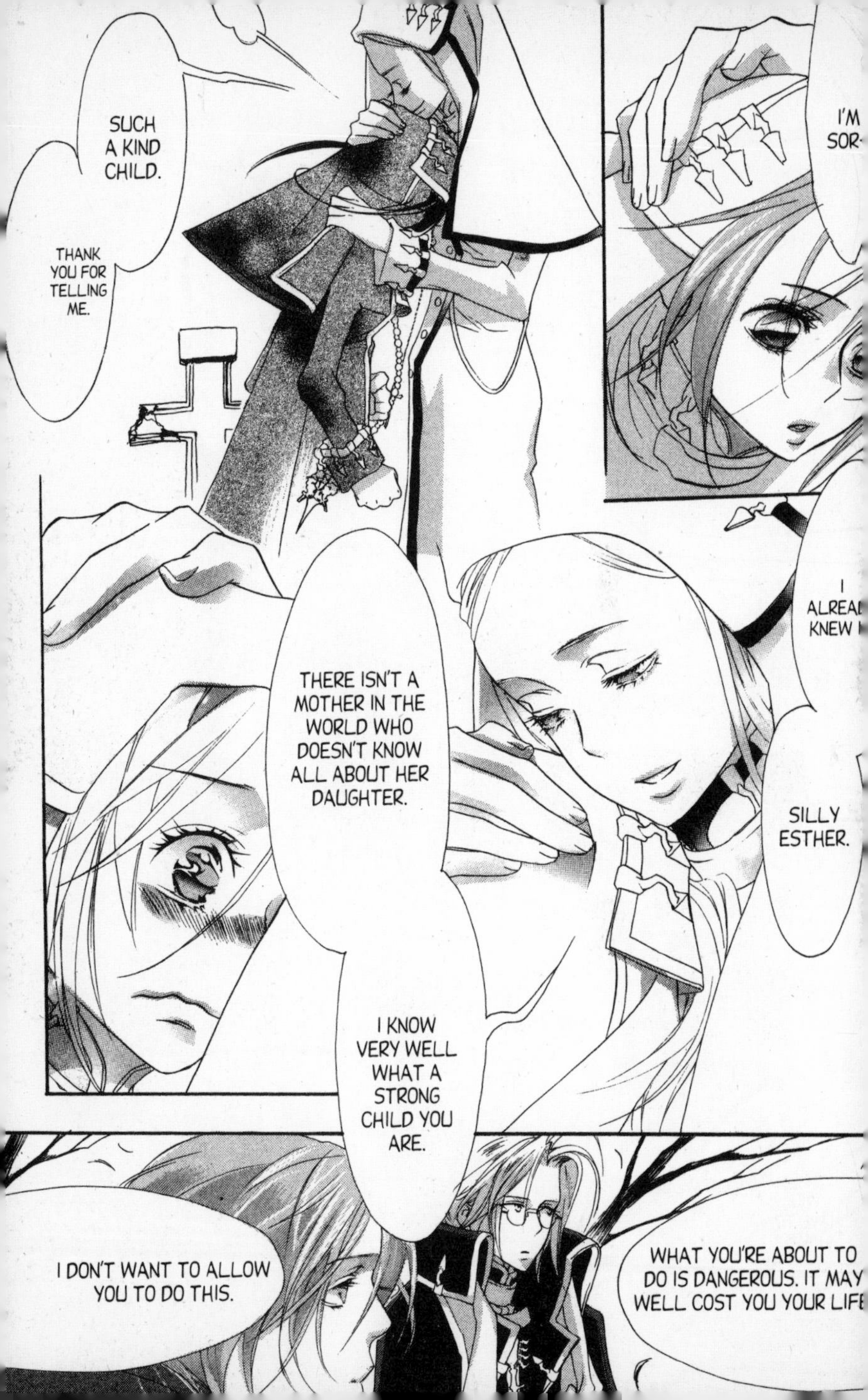
I'M SOR-
SUCH A KIND CHILD.
THANK YOU FOR TELLING ME.
I ALREAD KNEW
SILLY ESTHER.
THERE ISN'T A MOTHER IN THE WORLD WHO DOESN'T KNOW ALL ABOUT HER DAUGHTER.
I KNOW VERY WELL WHAT A STRONG CHILD YOU ARE.
WHAT YOU'RE ABOUT TO DO IS DANGEROUS. IT MAY WELL COST YOU YOUR LIF
I DON'T WANT TO ALLOW YOU TO DO THIS.

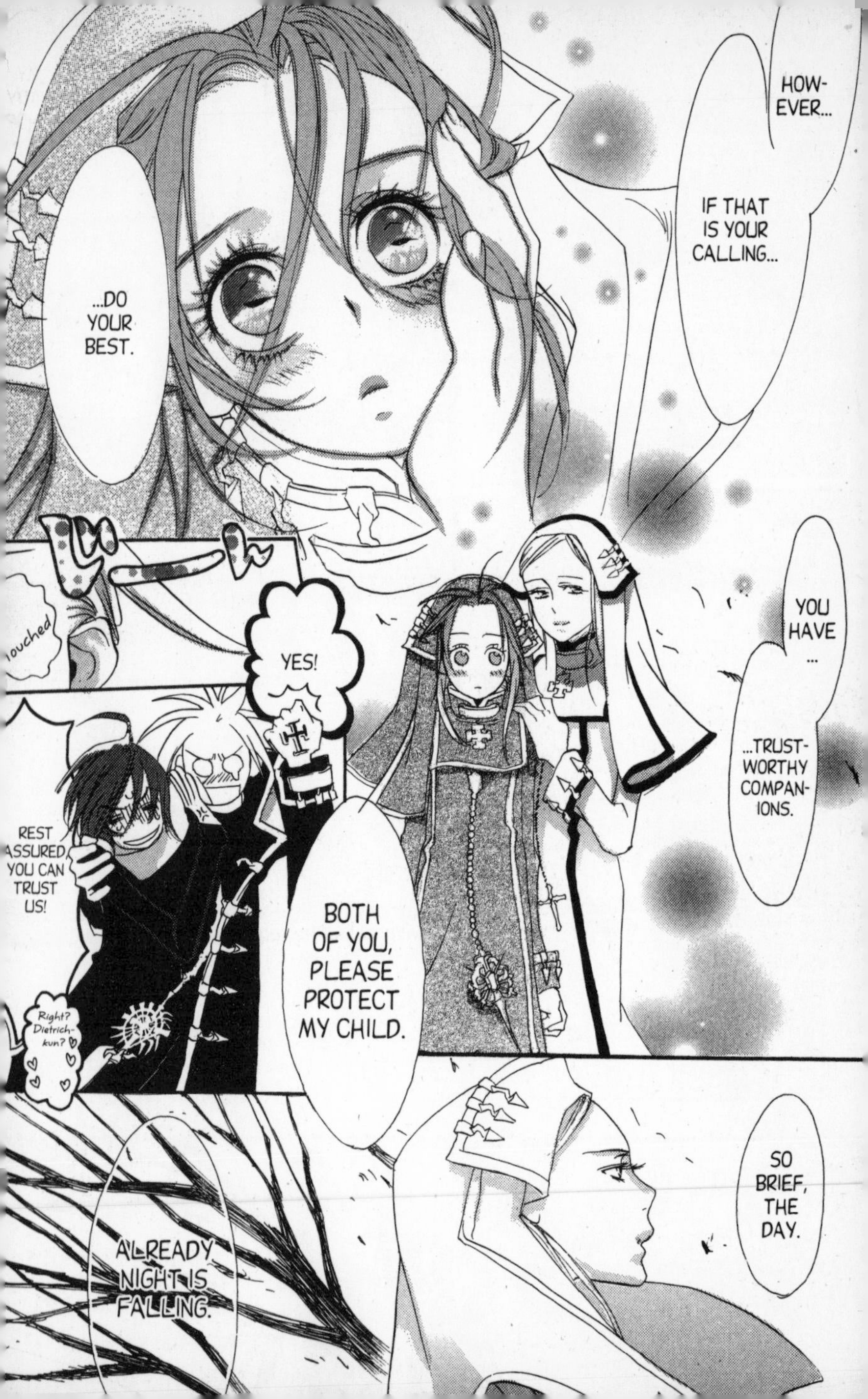
HOW-EVER...
IF THAT IS YOUR CALLING...
...DO YOUR BEST.
YOU HAVE ...
...TRUST-WORTHY COMPANIONS.
じーん
ouched
YES!
BOTH OF YOU, PLEASE PROTECT MY CHILD.
REST ASSURED YOU CAN TRUST US!
Right? Dietrich-kun?
SO BRIEF, THE DAY.
ALREADY NIGHT IS FALLING.

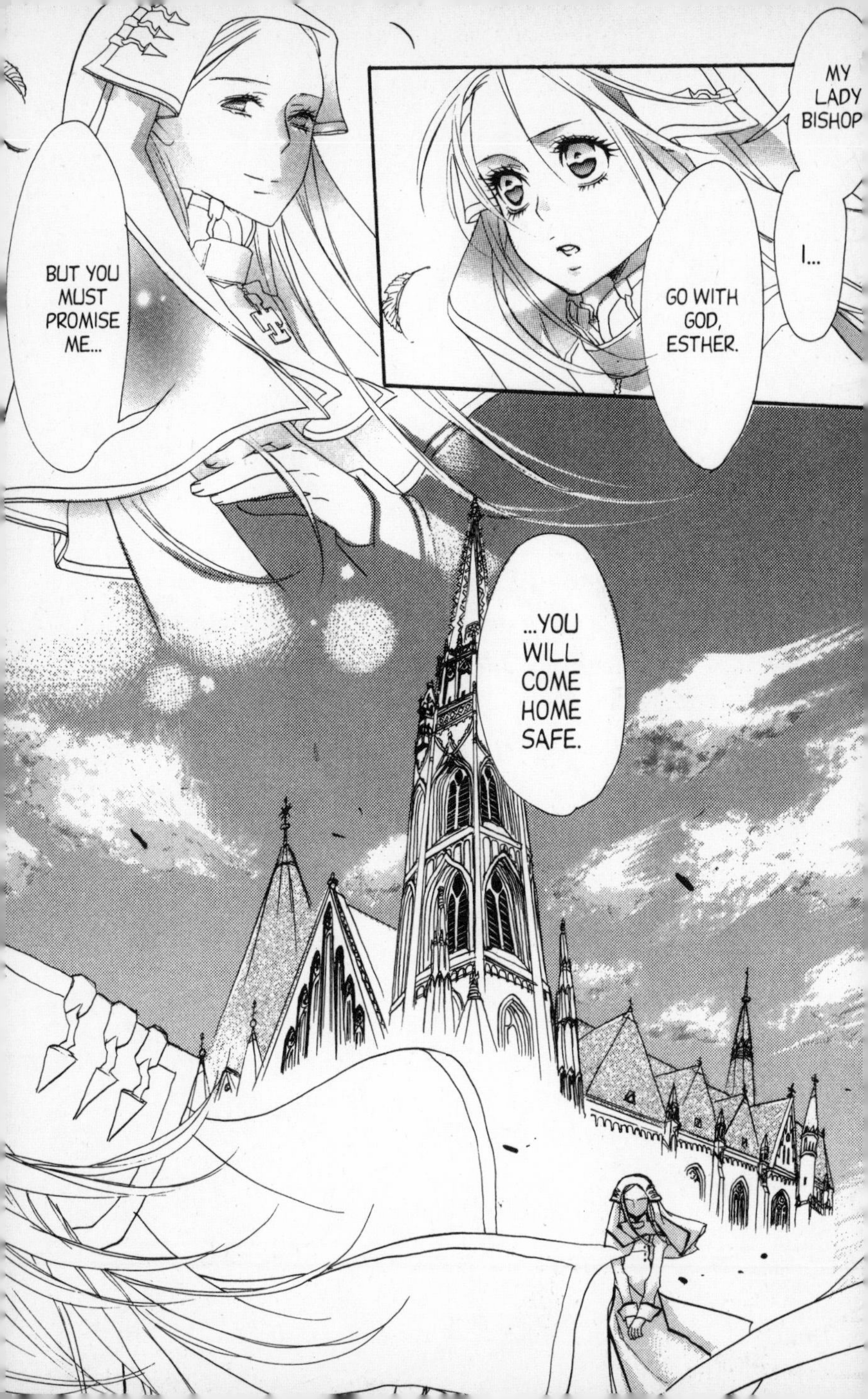
MY LADY BISHOP
I...
GO WITH GOD, ESTHER.
BUT YOU MUST PROMISE ME...
...YOU WILL COME HOME SAFE.

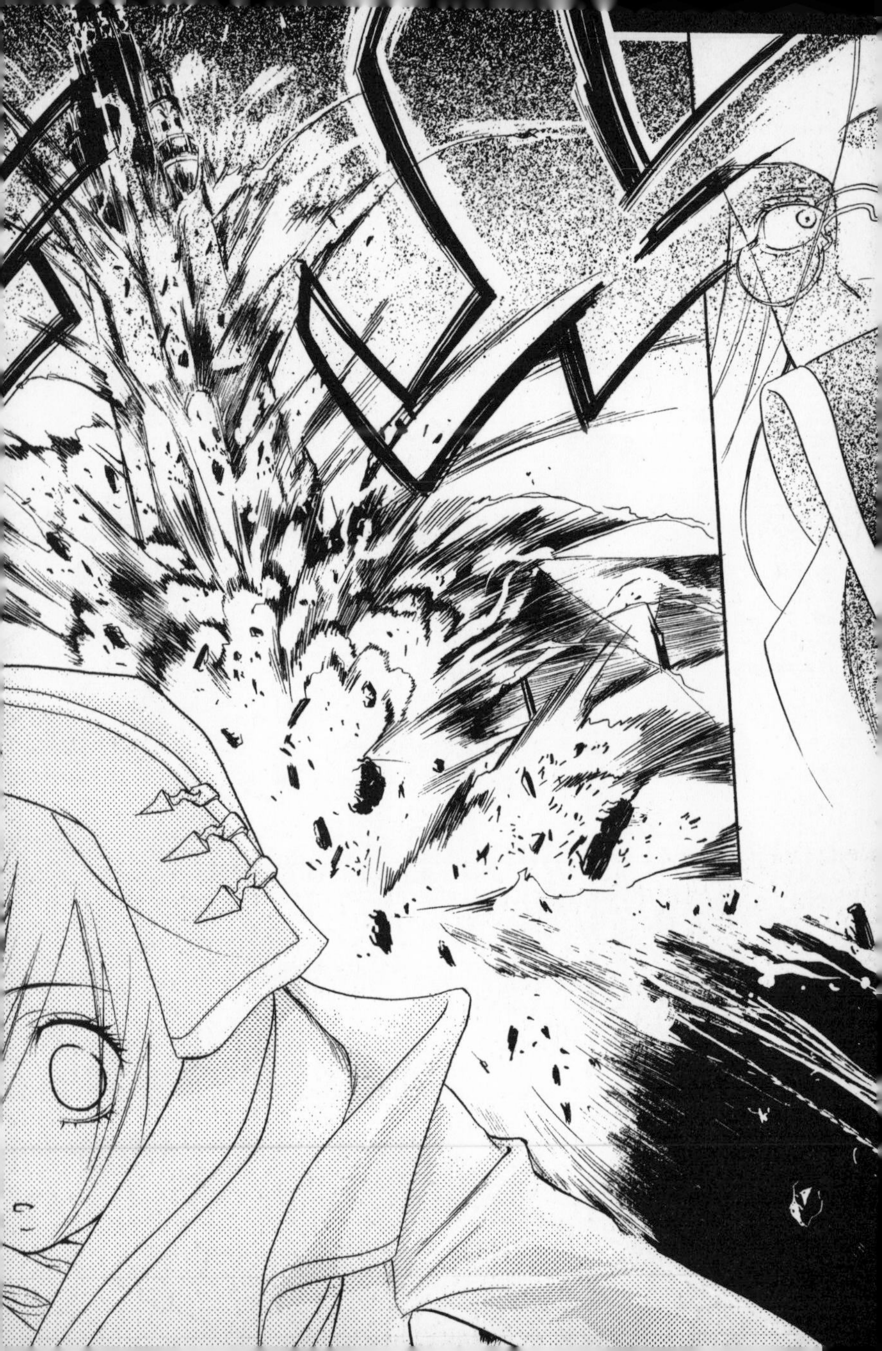

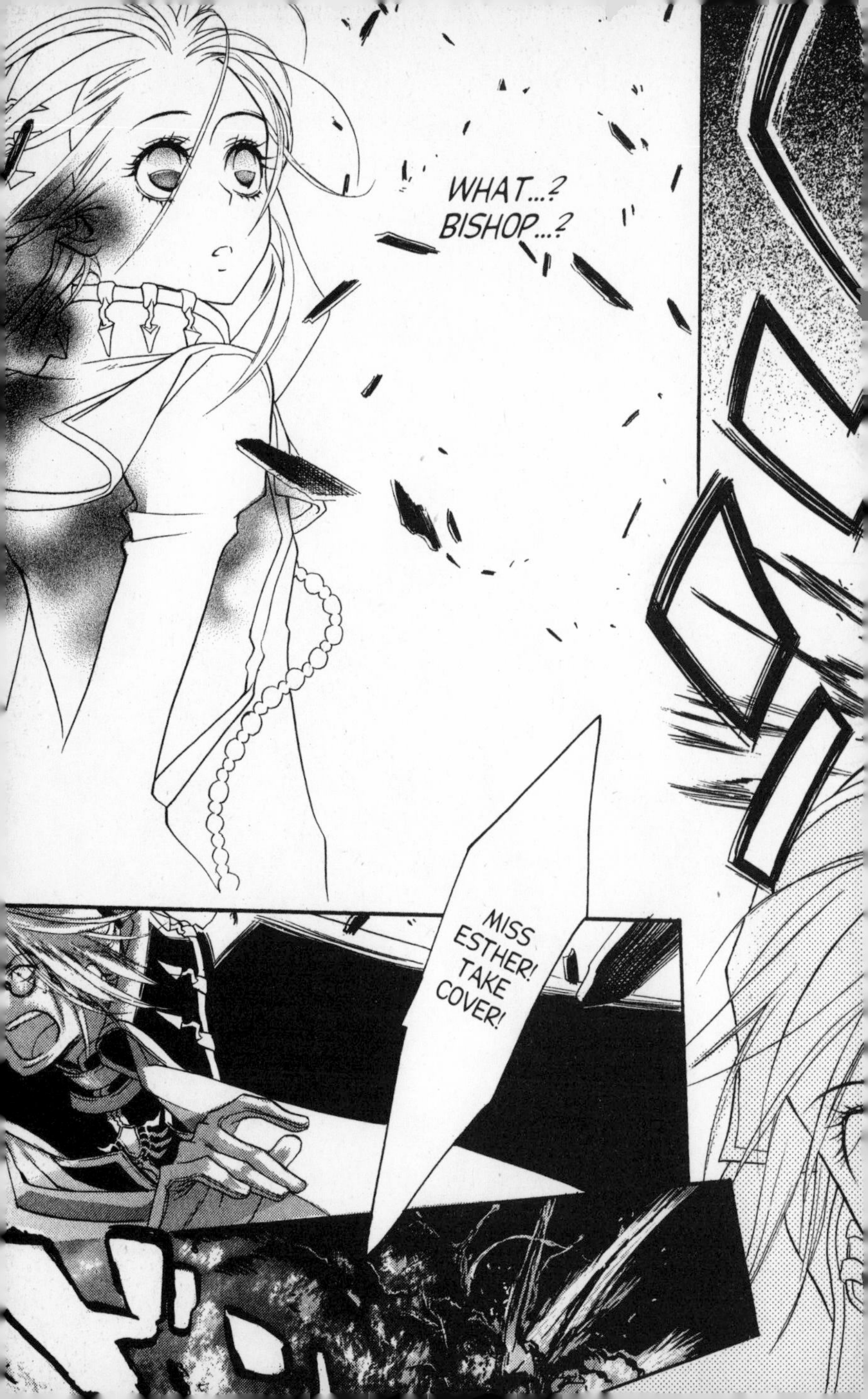
WHAT...?
BISHOP...?
MISS ESTHER! TAKE COVER!

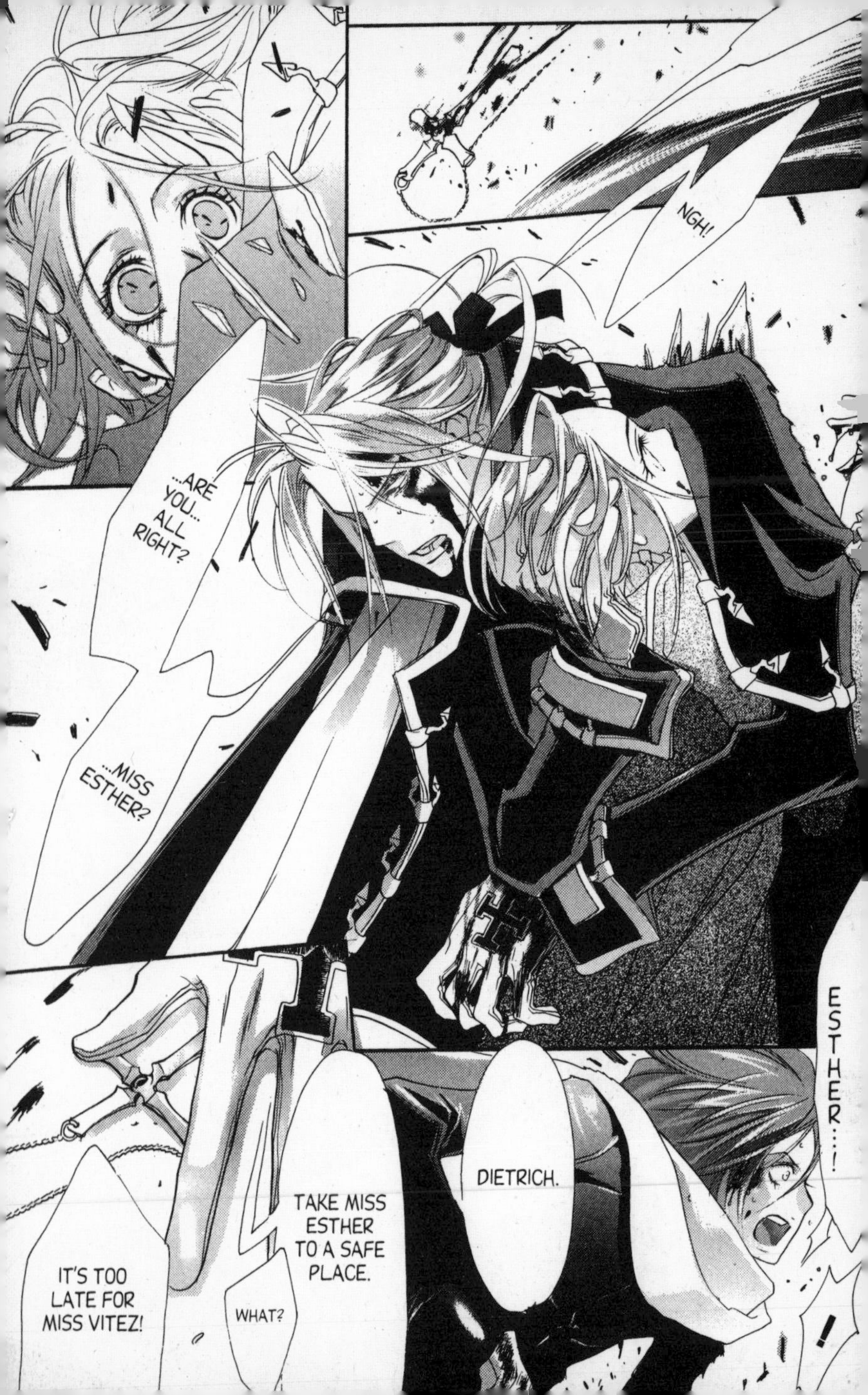
NGH!
...ARE YOU... ALL RIGHT?
...MISS ESTHER?
ESTHER...!
DIETRICH.
TAKE MISS ESTHER TO A SAFE PLACE.
WHAT?
IT'S TOO LATE FOR MISS VITEZ!

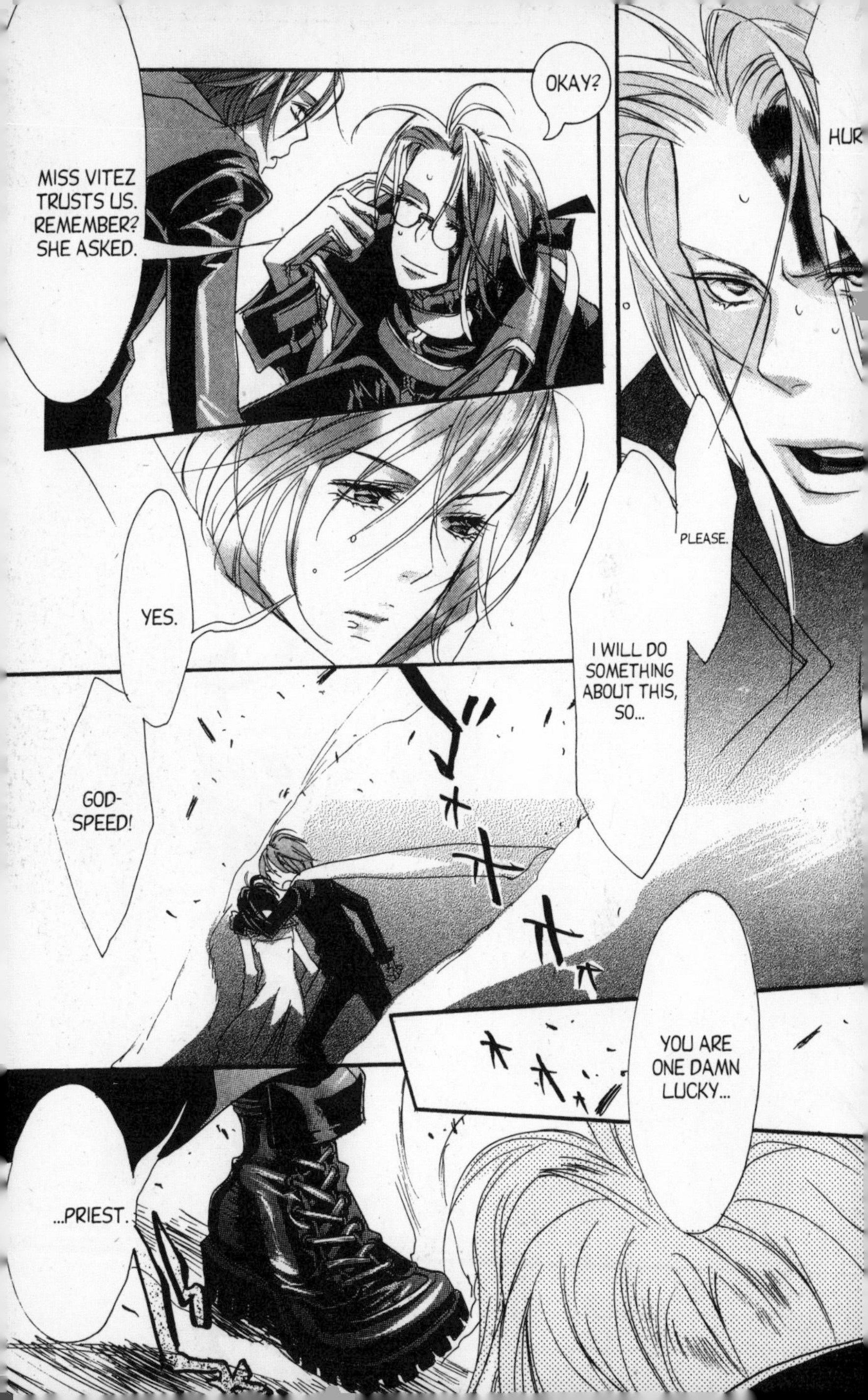

HUR
PLEASE.
I WILL DO SOMETHING ABOUT THIS, SO...
OKAY?
MISS VITEZ TRUSTS US. REMEMBER? SHE ASKED.
YES.
GOD-SPEED!
YOU ARE ONE DAMN LUCKY...
...PRIEST.

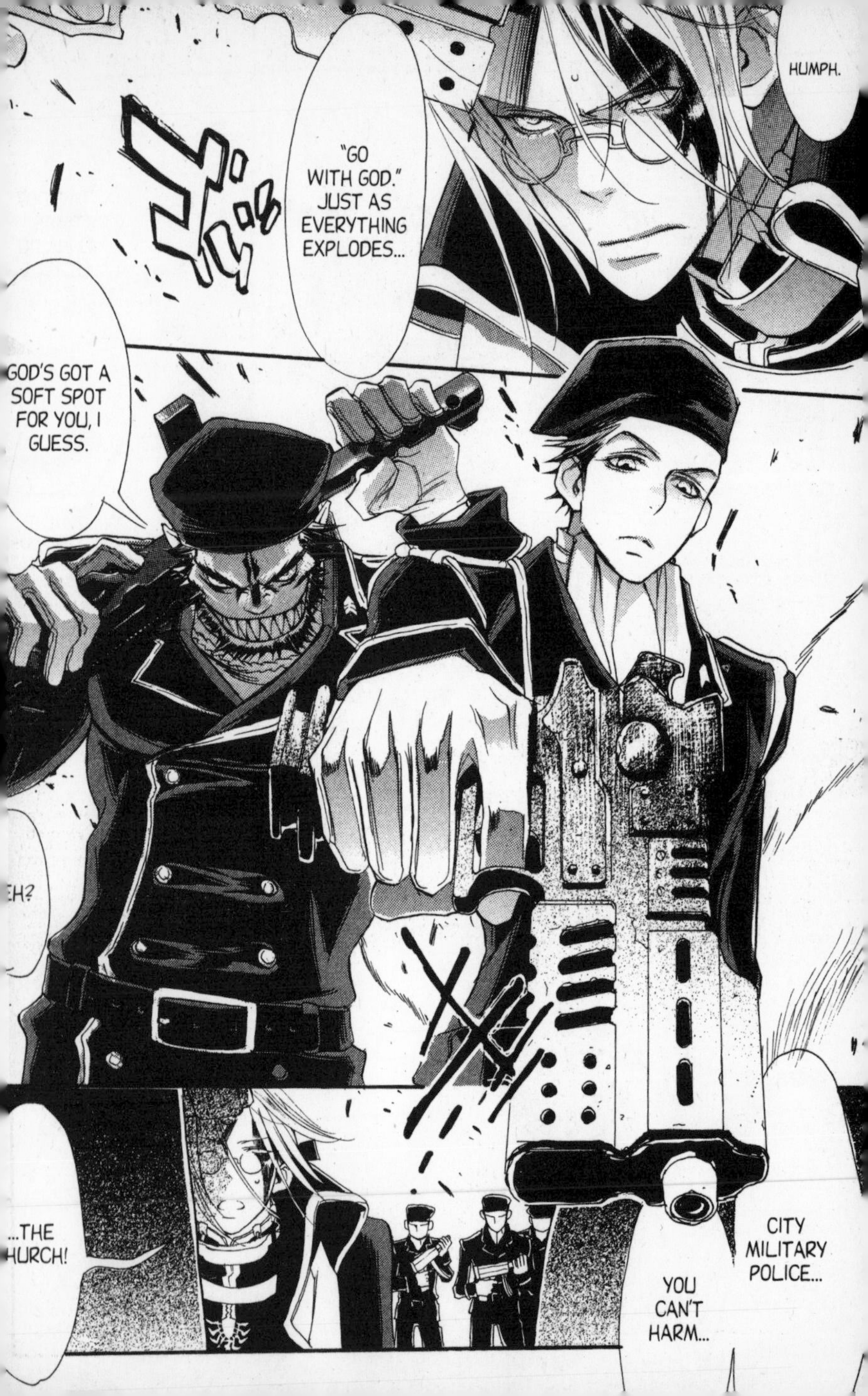
HUMPH.
"GO WITH GOD." JUST AS EVERYTHING EXPLODES...
GOD'S GOT A SOFT SPOT FOR YOU, I GUESS.
EH?
CITY MILITARY POLICE...
YOU CAN'T HARM...
...THE HURCH!

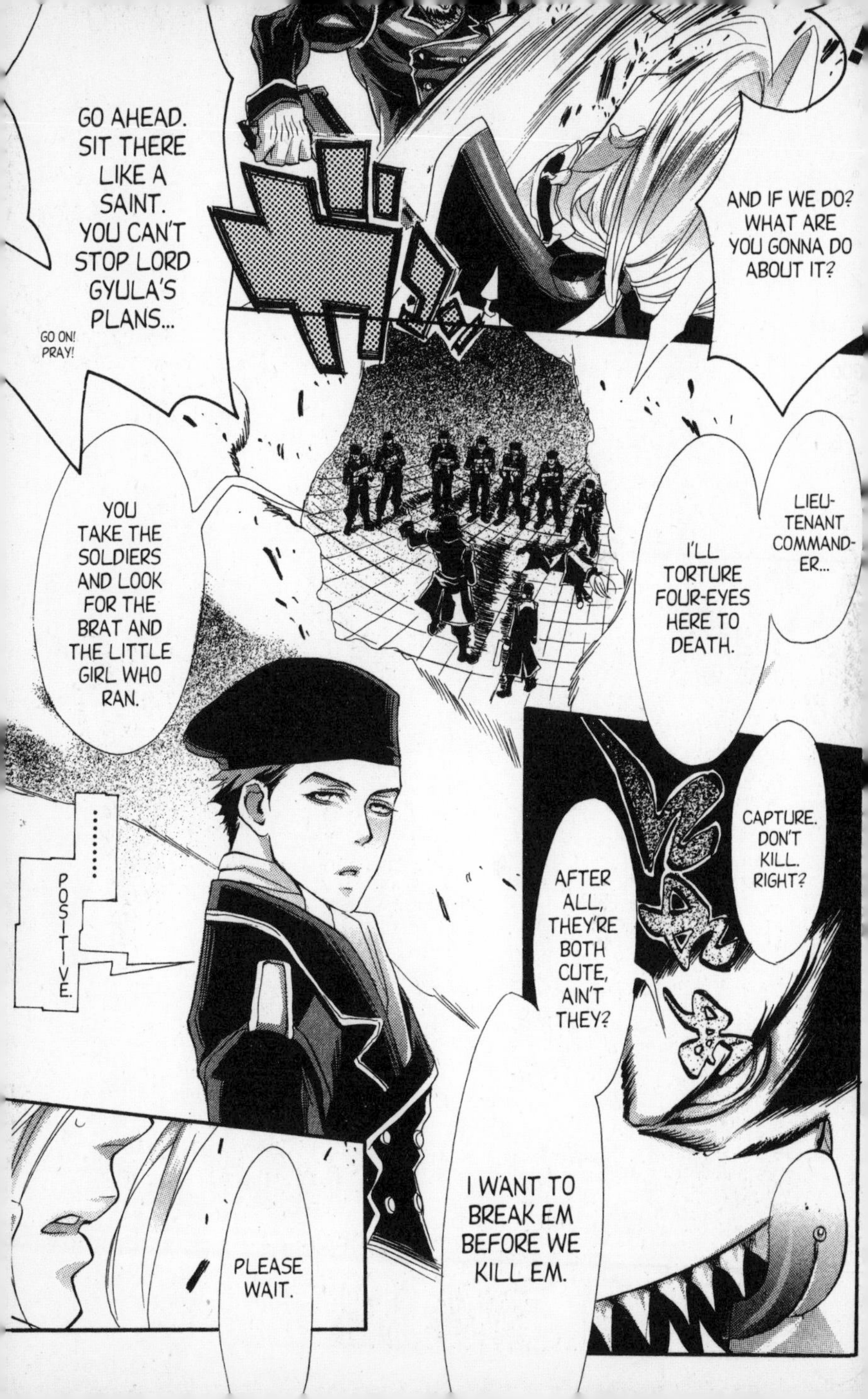

AND IF WE DO? WHAT ARE YOU GONNA DO ABOUT IT?
GO AHEAD. SIT THERE LIKE A SAINT. YOU CAN'T STOP LORD GYULA'S PLANS...
GO ON! PRAY!
LIEU-TENANT COMMAND-ER...
I'LL TORTURE FOUR-EYES HERE TO DEATH.
YOU TAKE THE SOLDIERS AND LOOK FOR THE BRAT AND THE LITTLE GIRL WHO RAN.
......
POSITIVE.
CAPTURE. DON'T KILL. RIGHT?
AFTER ALL, THEY'RE BOTH CUTE, AIN'T THEY?
I WANT TO BREAK EM BEFORE WE KILL EM.
PLEASE WAIT.

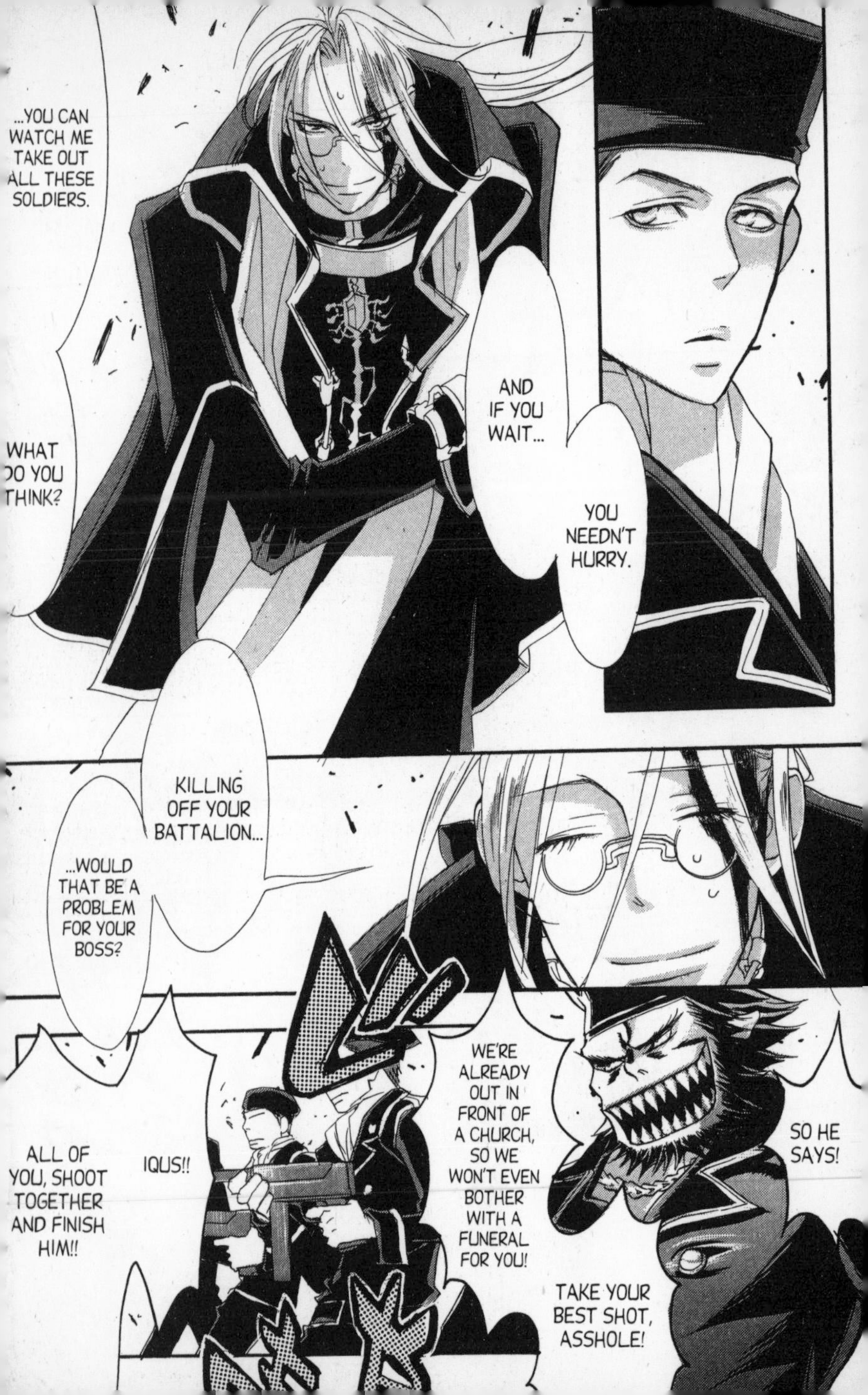
YOU NEEDN'T HURRY.
AND IF YOU WAIT...
...YOU CAN WATCH ME TAKE OUT ALL THESE SOLDIERS.
WHAT DO YOU THINK?
KILLING OFF YOUR BATTALION...
...WOULD THAT BE A PROBLEM FOR YOUR BOSS?
SO HE SAYS!
WE'RE ALREADY OUT IN FRONT OF A CHURCH, SO WE WON'T EVEN BOTHER WITH A FUNERAL FOR YOU!
TAKE YOUR BEST SHOT, ASSHOLE!
IQUS!!
ALL OF YOU, SHOOT TOGETHER AND FINISH HIM!!

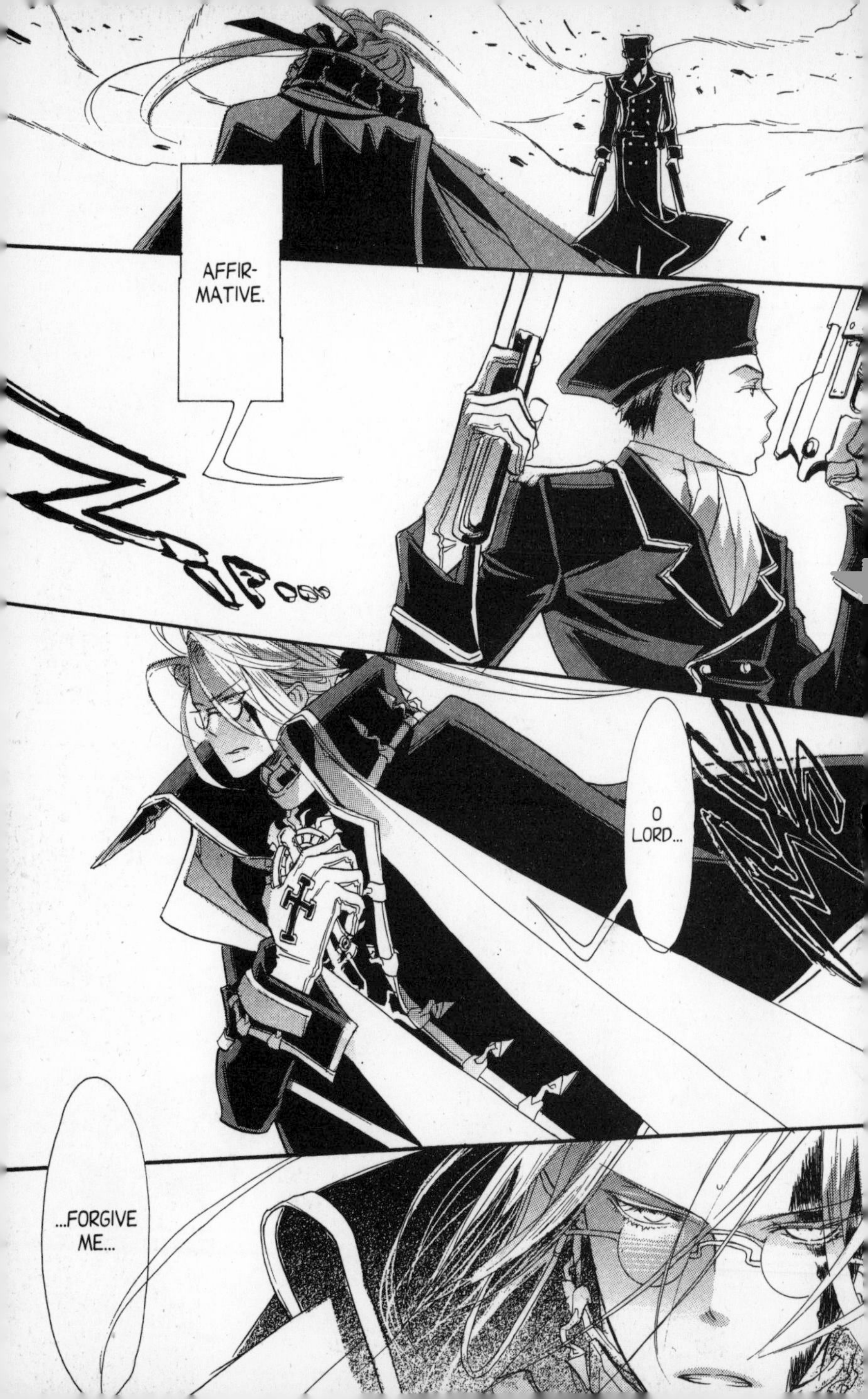
AFFIR-MATIVE.
O LORD...
...FORGIVE ME...

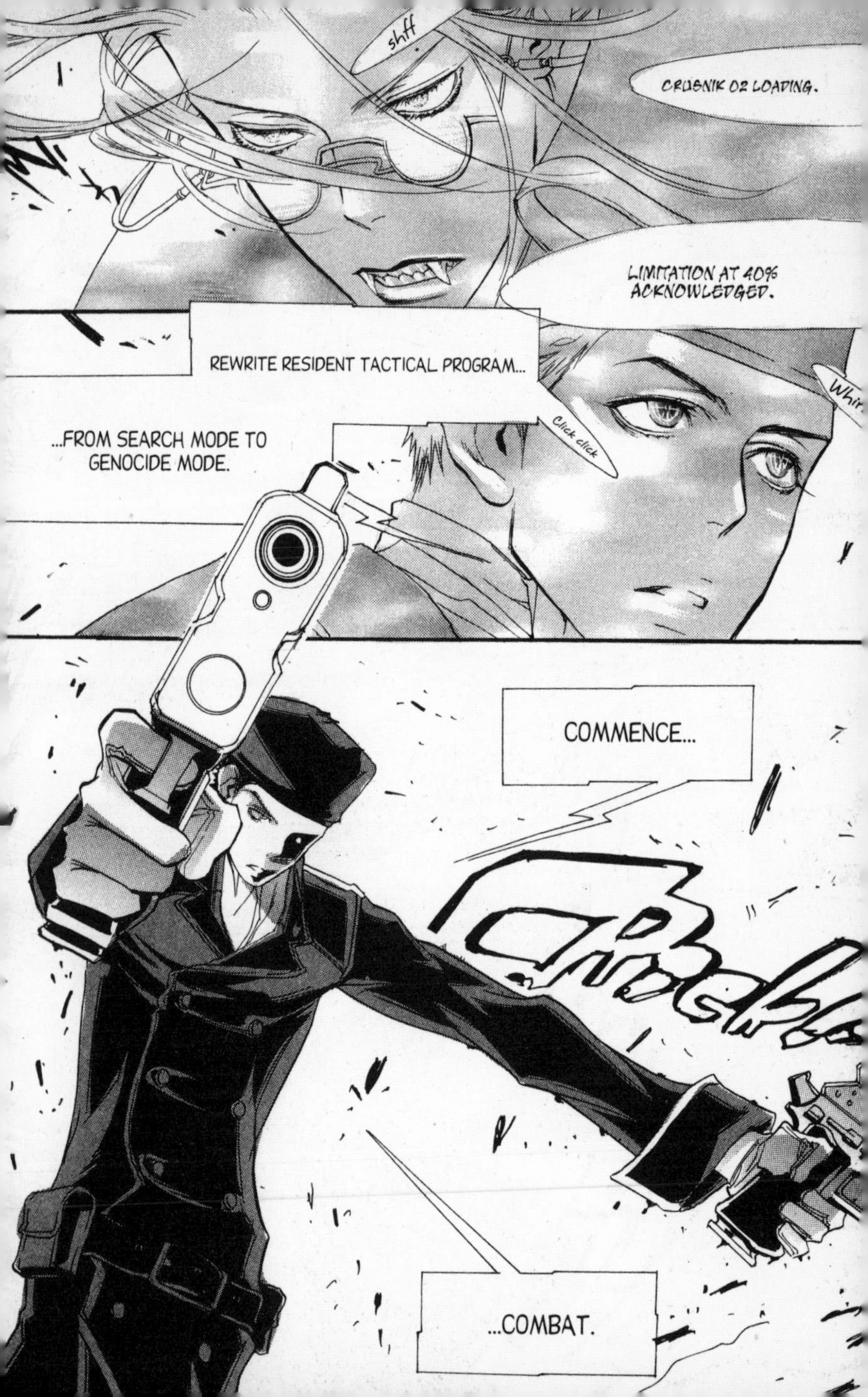

shff
CRUSNIK 02 LOADING.
LIMITATION AT 40% ACKNOWLEDGED.
Whir
REWRITE RESIDENT TACTICAL PROGRAM...
Click click
...FROM SEARCH MODE TO GENOCIDE MODE.
COMMENCE...
...COMBAT.

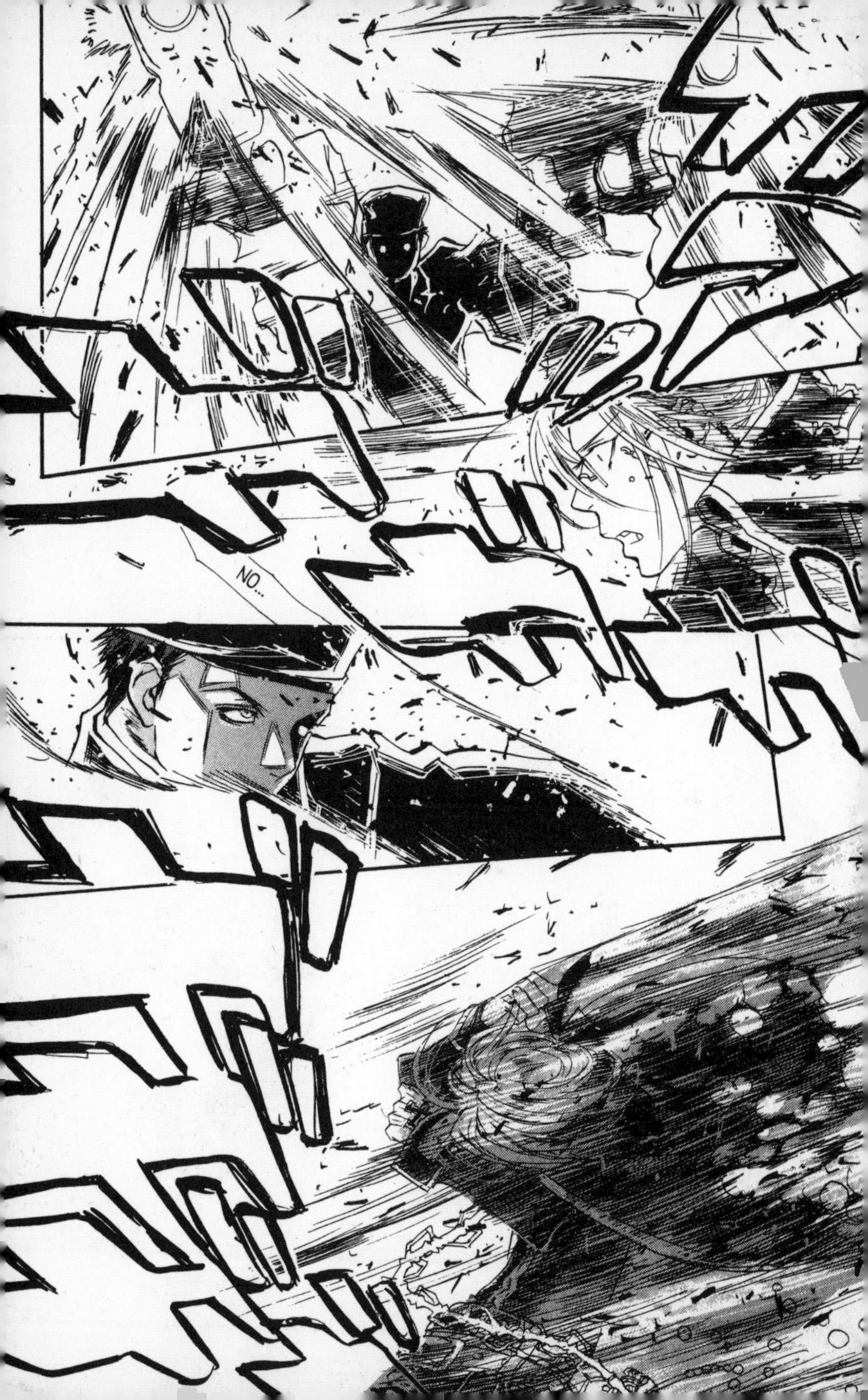
NO...

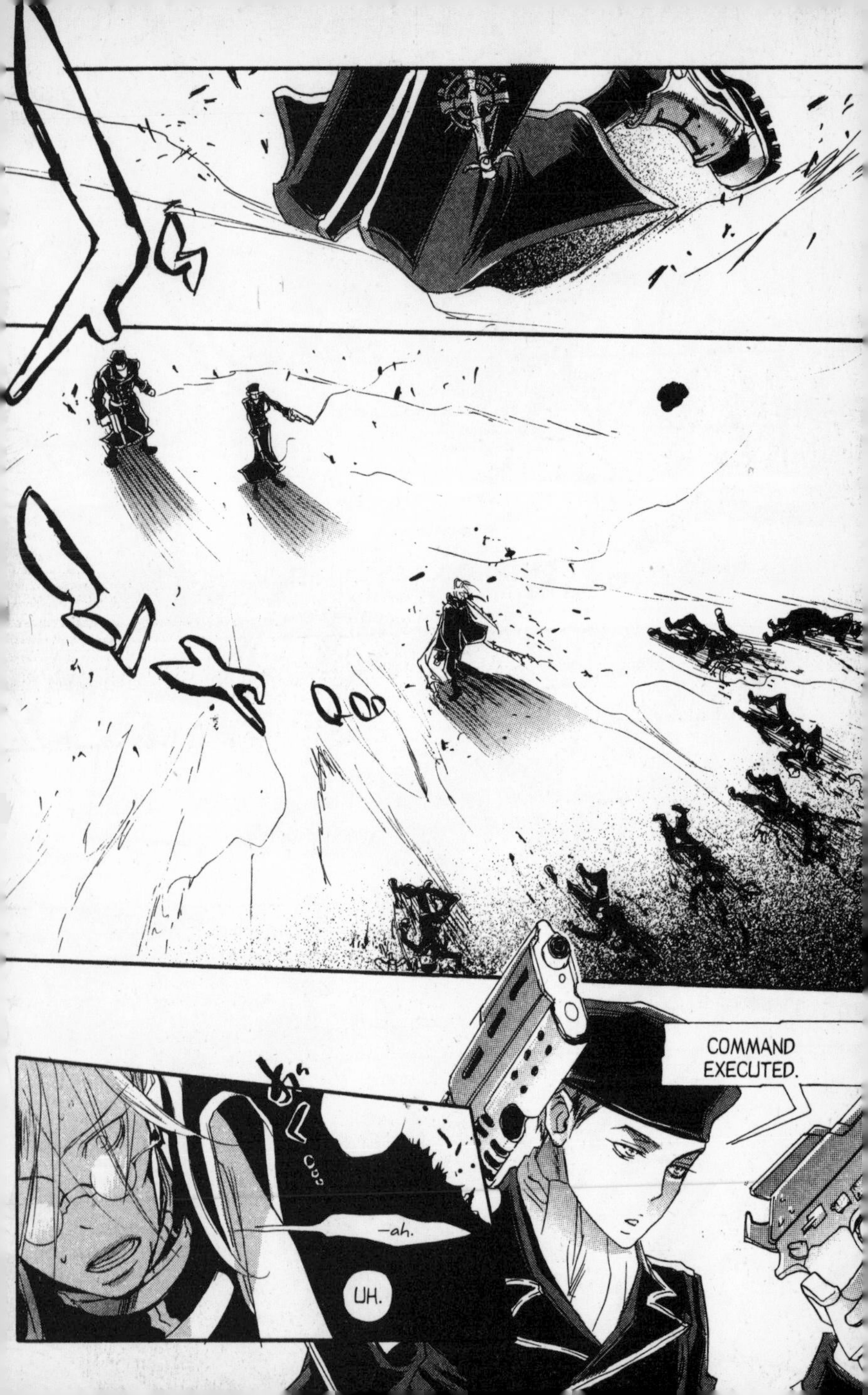
COMMAND EXECUTED.
—ah.
UH.

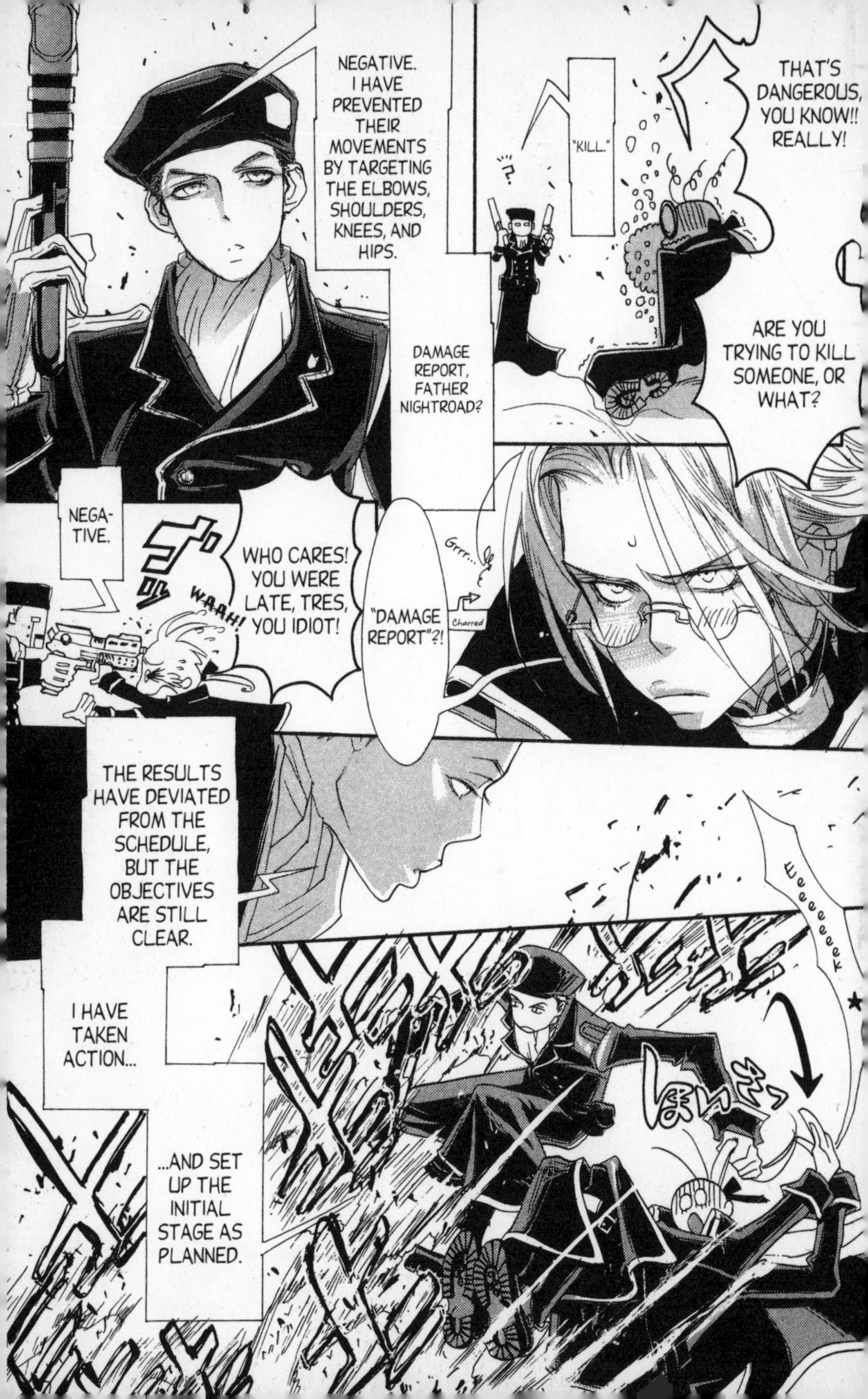

THAT'S DANGEROUS, YOU KNOW!! REALLY!
ARE YOU TRYING TO KILL SOMEONE, OR WHAT?
"KILL."
?
DAMAGE REPORT, FATHER NIGHTROAD?
NEGATIVE. I HAVE PREVENTED THEIR MOVEMENTS BY TARGETING THE ELBOWS, SHOULDERS, KNEES, AND HIPS.
Grrr...
Charred
"DAMAGE REPORT"?!
WHO CARES! YOU WERE LATE, TRES, YOU IDIOT!
WAAH!
NEGA-TIVE.
THE RESULTS HAVE DEVIATED FROM THE SCHEDULE, BUT THE OBJECTIVES ARE STILL CLEAR.
Eeeeeeeeek
I HAVE TAKEN ACTION...
...AND SET UP THE INITIAL STAGE AS PLANNED.

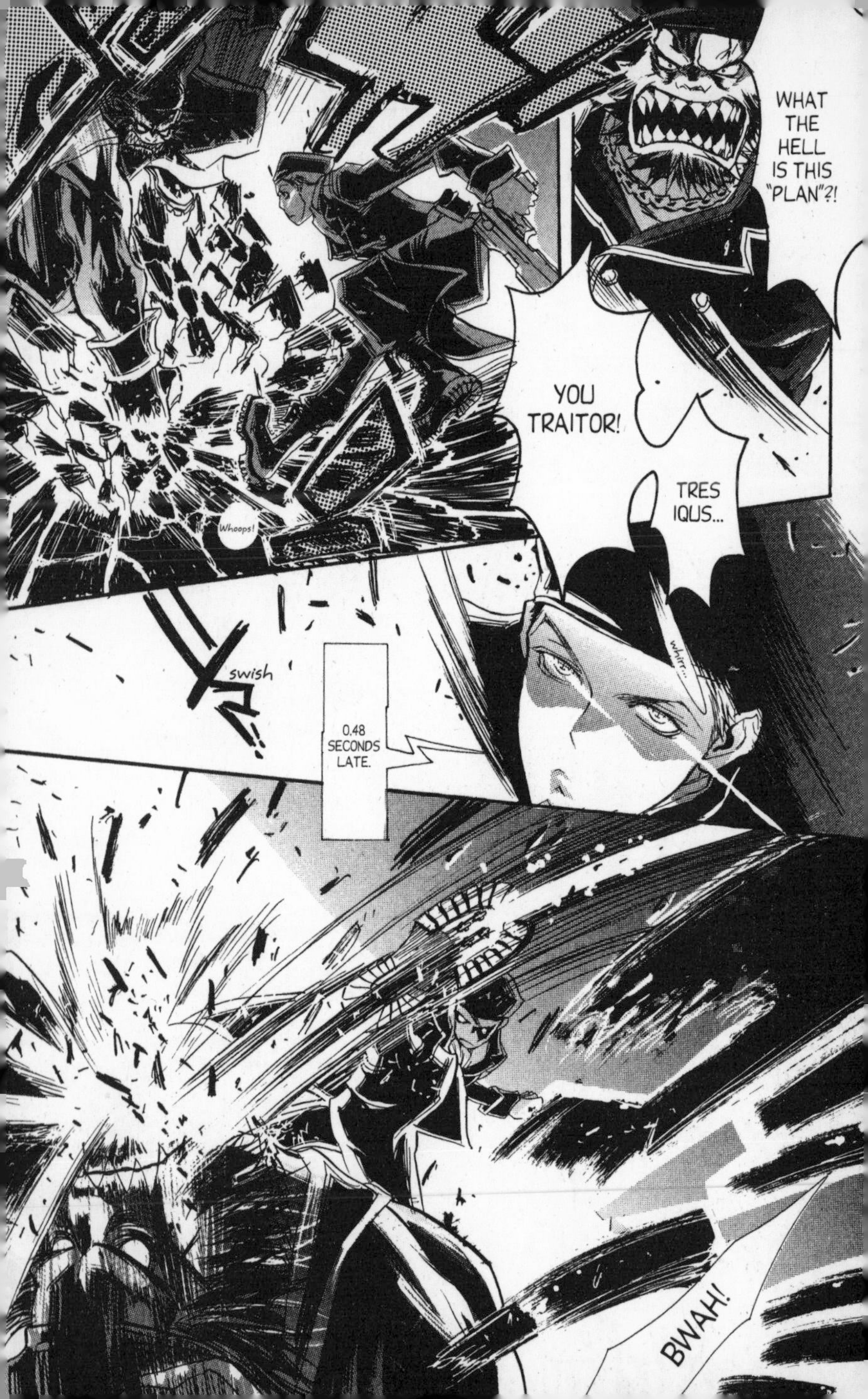
WHAT THE HELL IS THIS "PLAN"?!
YOU TRAITOR!
Whoops!
TRES IQUS...
whirr...
swish
0.48 SECONDS LATE.
BWAH!

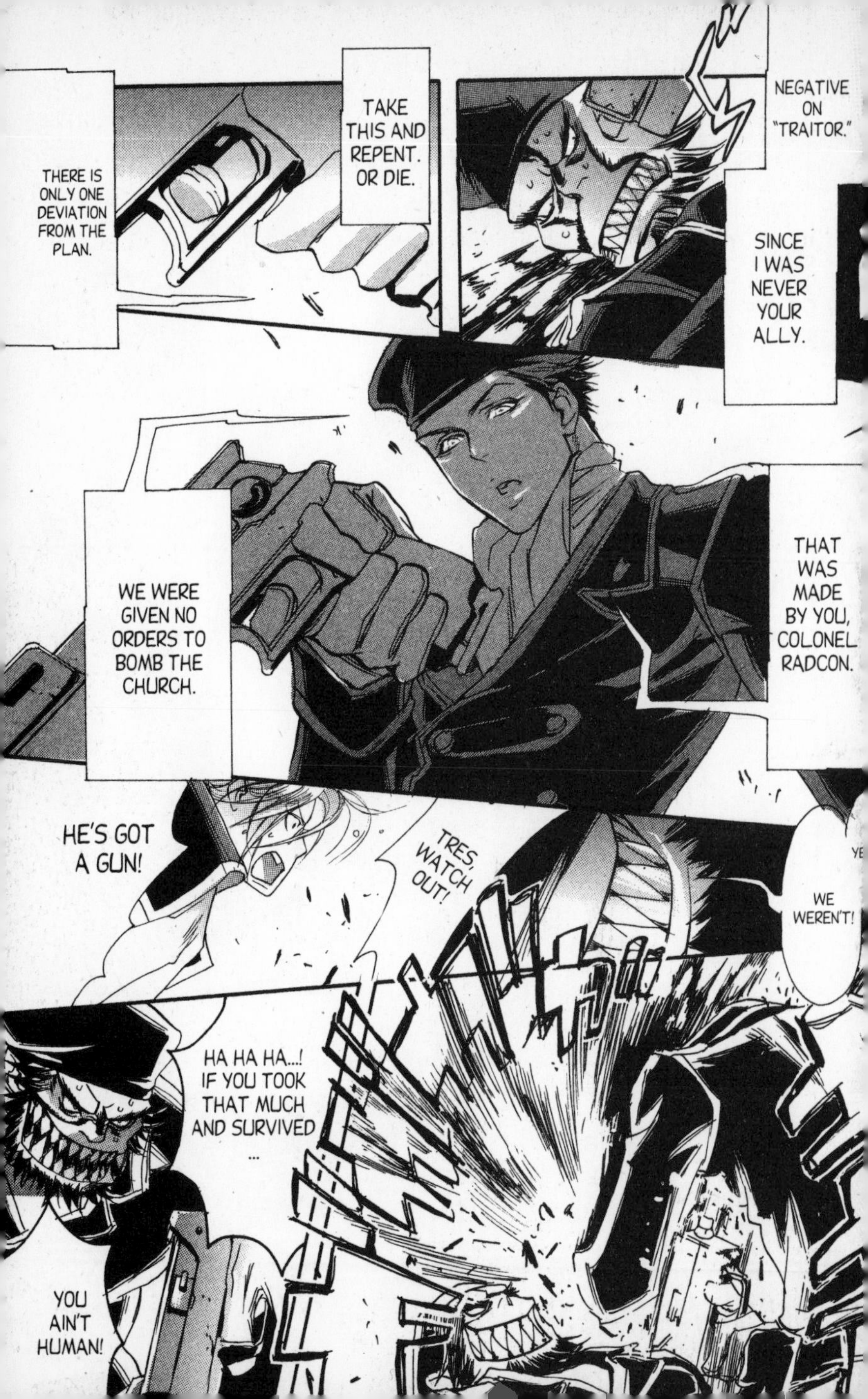
NEGATIVE ON "TRAITOR."
SINCE I WAS NEVER YOUR ALLY.
TAKE THIS AND REPENT. OR DIE.
THERE IS ONLY ONE DEVIATION FROM THE PLAN.
THAT WAS MADE BY YOU, COLONEL RADCON.
WE WERE GIVEN NO ORDERS TO BOMB THE CHURCH.
YE
WE WEREN'T!
TRES, WATCH OUT!
HE'S GOT A GUN!
HA HA HA...! IF YOU TOOK THAT MUCH AND SURVIVED
...
YOU AIN'T HUMAN!

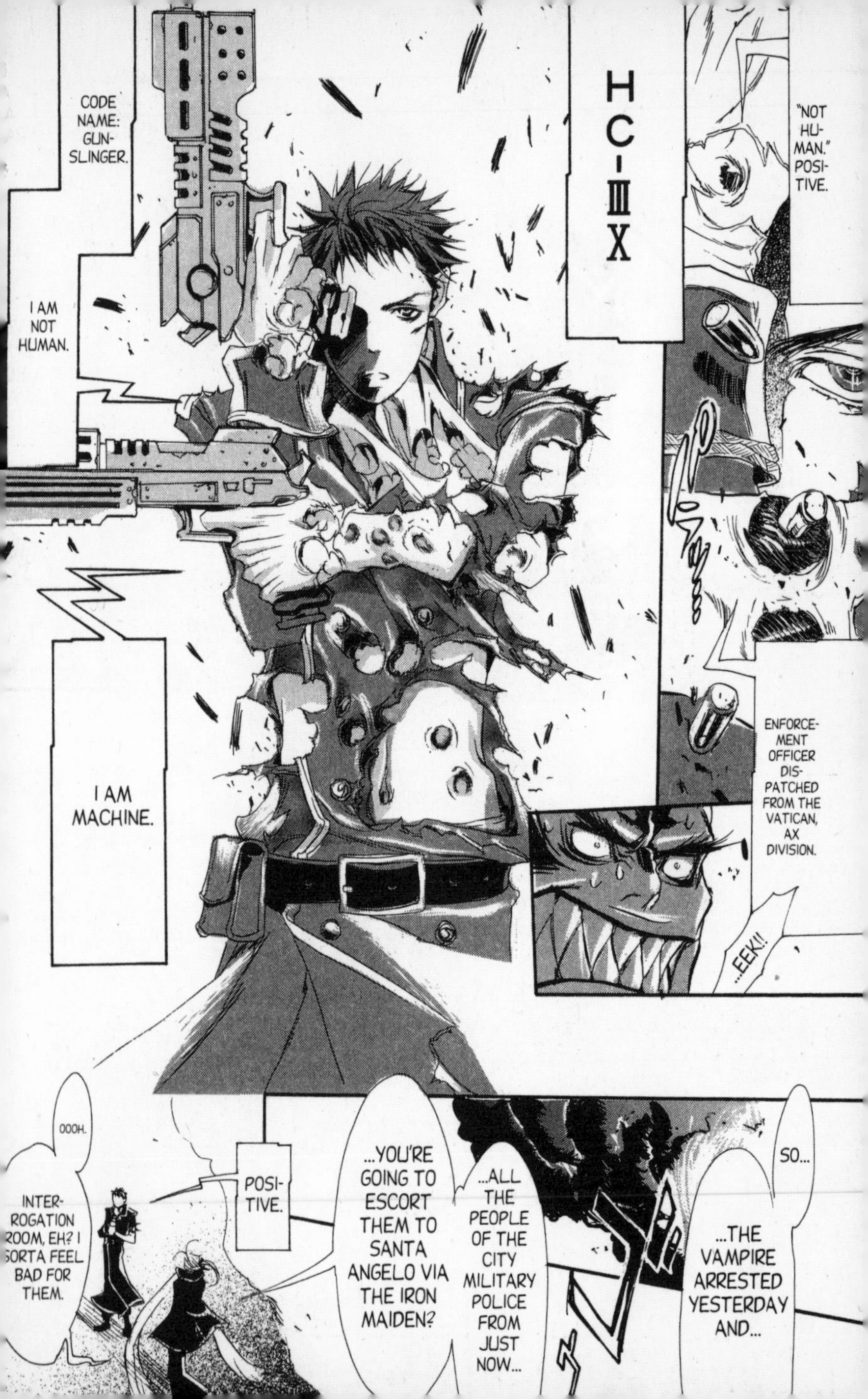
"NOT HUMAN." POSITIVE.
ENFORCEMENT OFFICER DISPATCHED FROM THE VATICAN, AX DIVISION.
...EEK!!
HC-IIIX
CODE NAME: GUNSLINGER.
I AM NOT HUMAN.
I AM MACHINE.
SO...
...THE VAMPIRE ARRESTED YESTERDAY AND...
...ALL THE PEOPLE OF THE CITY MILITARY POLICE FROM JUST NOW...
...YOU'RE GOING TO ESCORT THEM TO SANTA ANGELO VIA THE IRON MAIDEN?
POSITIVE.
OOOH.
INTERROGATION ROOM, EH? I SORTA FEEL BAD FOR THEM.

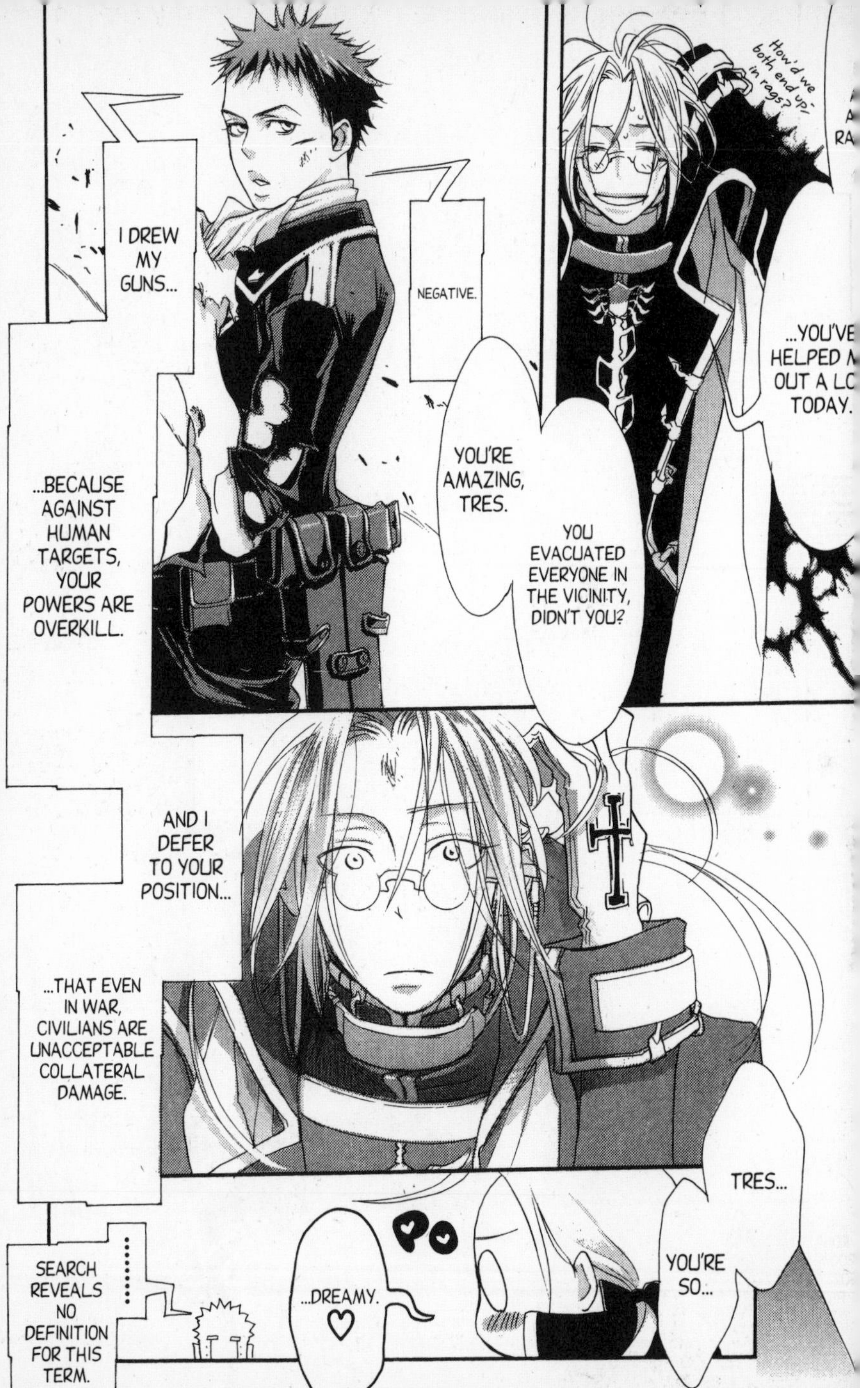

How'd we both end up in rags?
...YOU'VE HELPED M OUT A LO TODAY.
YOU'RE AMAZING, TRES.
YOU EVACUATED EVERYONE IN THE VICINITY, DIDN'T YOU?
NEGATIVE.
I DREW MY GUNS...
...BECAUSE AGAINST HUMAN TARGETS, YOUR POWERS ARE OVERKILL.
AND I DEFER TO YOUR POSITION...
...THAT EVEN IN WAR, CIVILIANS ARE UNACCEPTABLE COLLATERAL DAMAGE.
TRES...
YOU'RE SO...
PO
...DREAMY.
......
SEARCH REVEALS NO DEFINITION FOR THIS TERM.

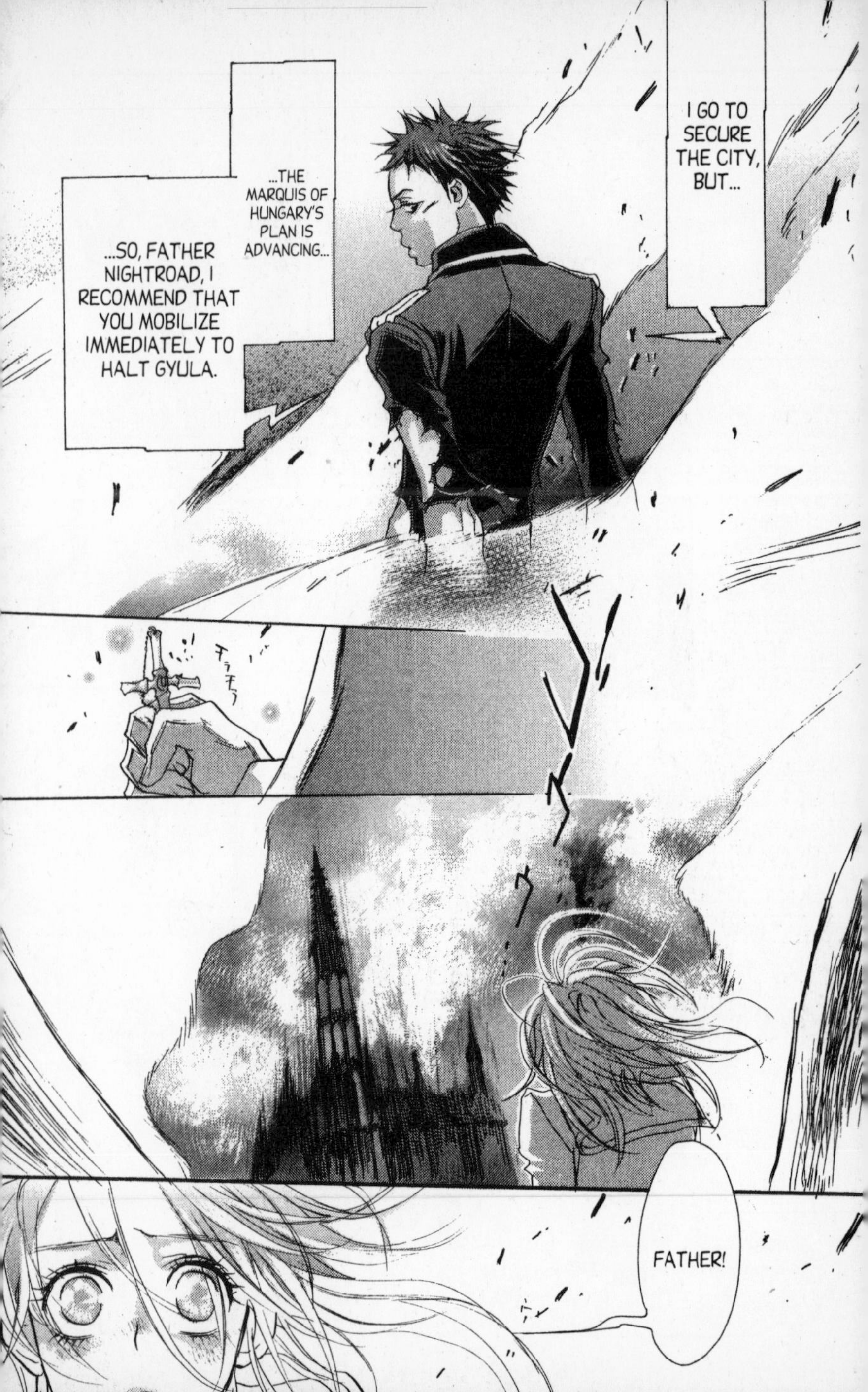
I GO TO SECURE THE CITY, BUT...
...THE MARQUIS OF HUNGARY'S PLAN IS ADVANCING...
...SO, FATHER NIGHTROAD, I RECOMMEND THAT YOU MOBILIZE IMMEDIATELY TO HALT GYULA.
FATHER!

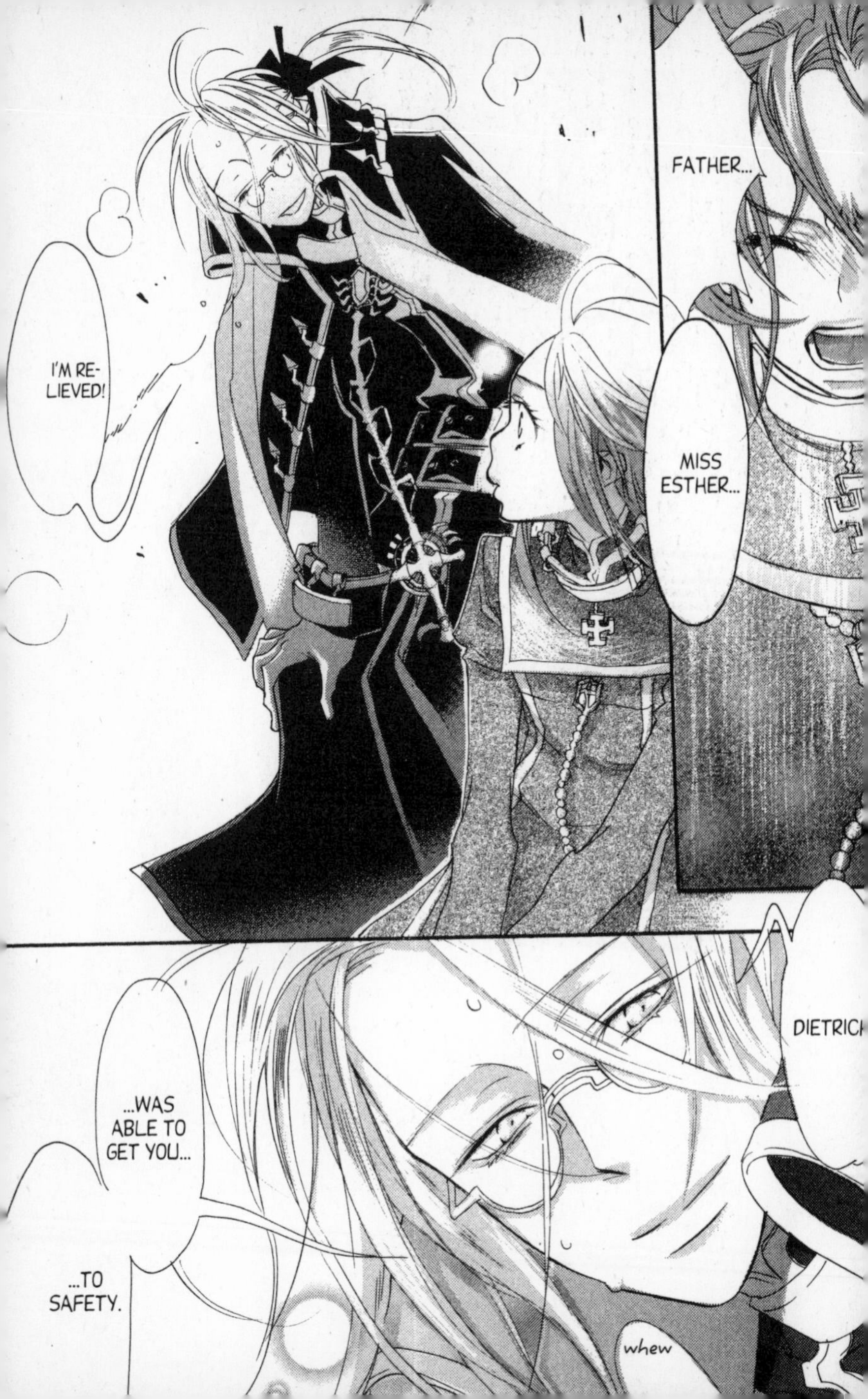
FATHER...
MISS ESTHER...
I'M RE-LIEVED!
DIETRICH
...WAS ABLE TO GET YOU...
...TO SAFETY.
whew

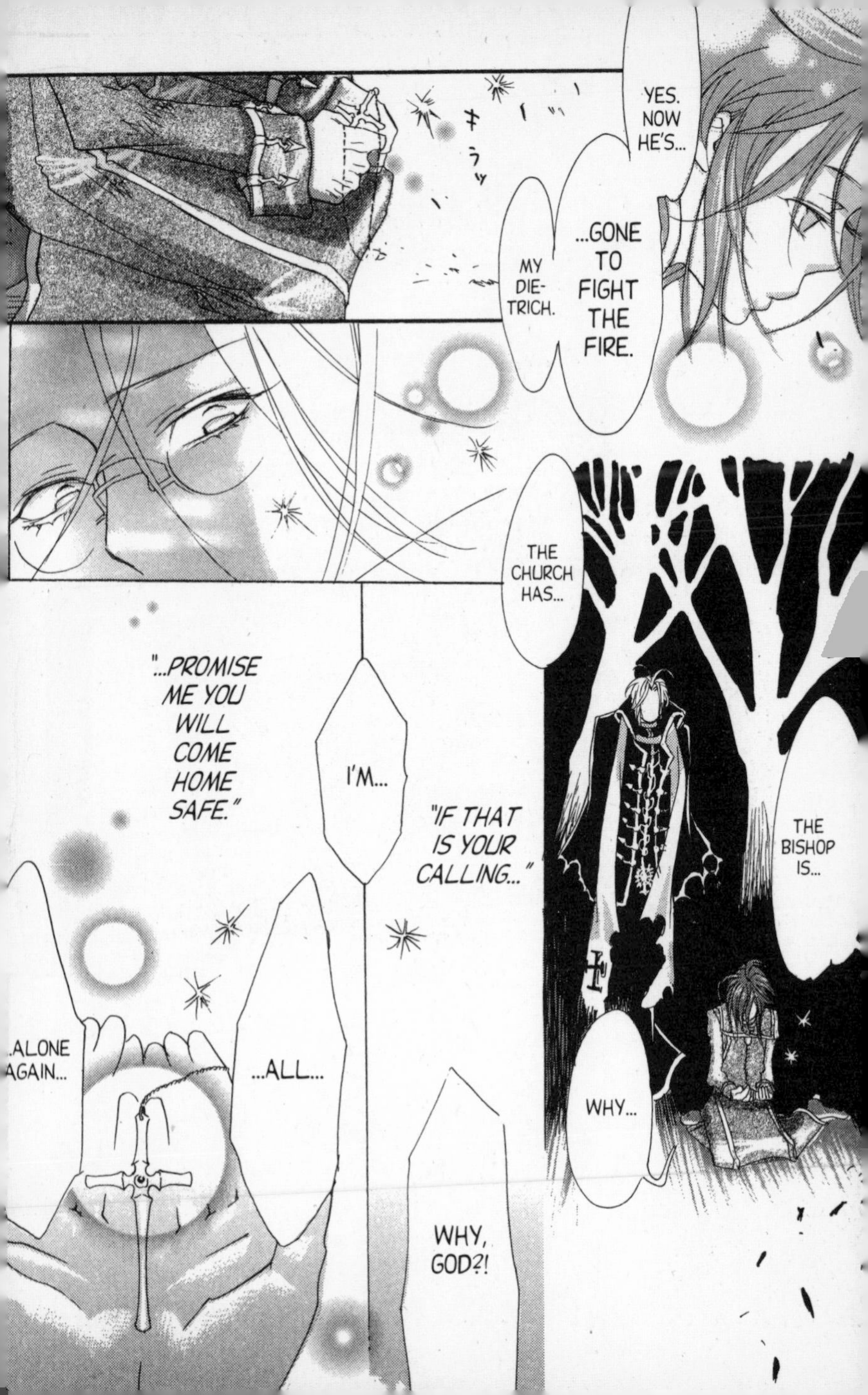
YES. NOW HE'S...
...GONE TO FIGHT THE FIRE.
MY DIE-TRICH.
キラッ
THE CHURCH HAS...
THE BISHOP IS...
WHY...
"IF THAT IS YOUR CALLING..."
"...PROMISE ME YOU WILL COME HOME SAFE."
I'M...
...ALL...
.ALONE AGAIN...
WHY, GOD?!

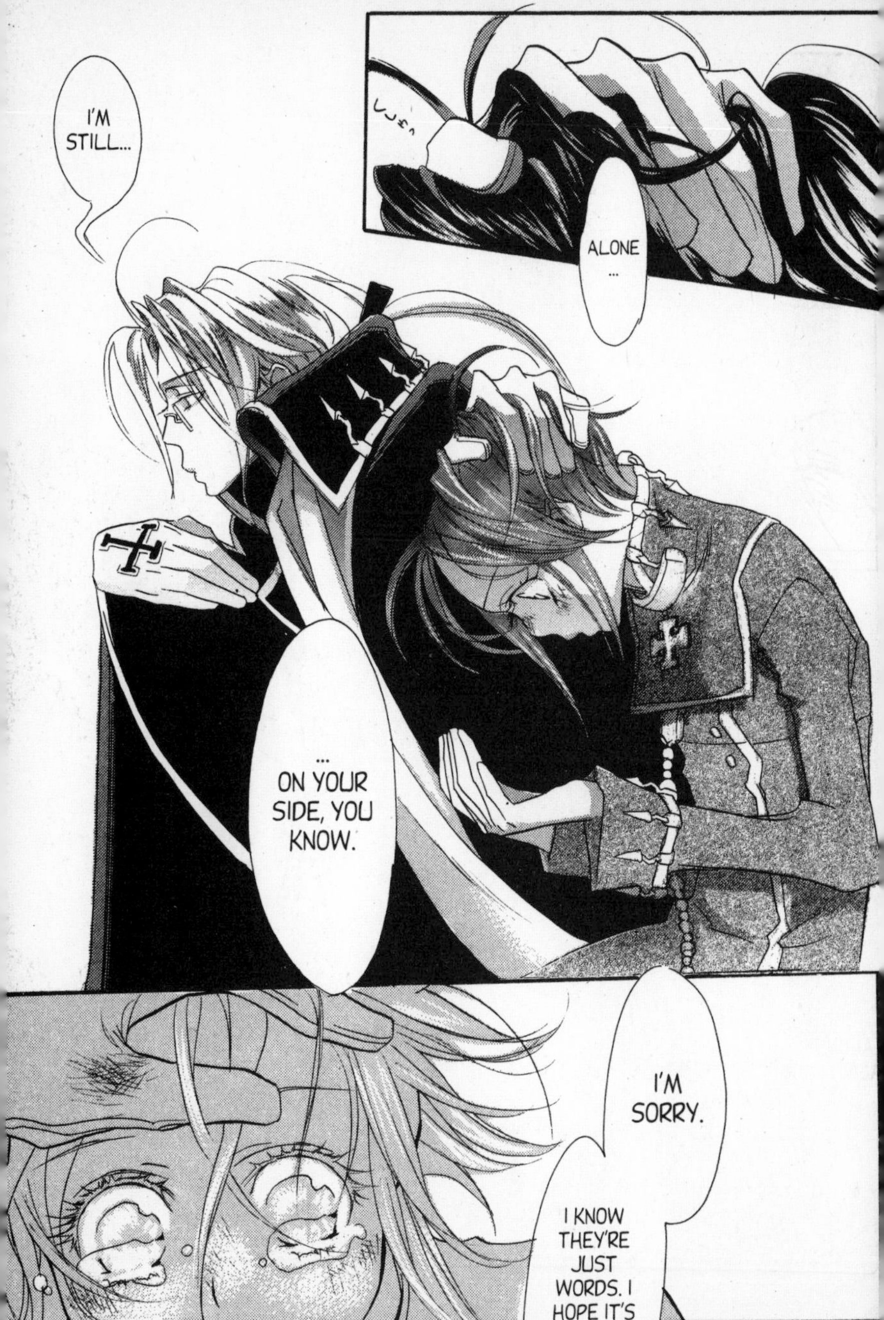
ALONE ...
I'M STILL...
... ON YOUR SIDE, YOU KNOW.
I'M SORRY.
I KNOW THEY'RE JUST WORDS. I HOPE IT'S ENOUGH.

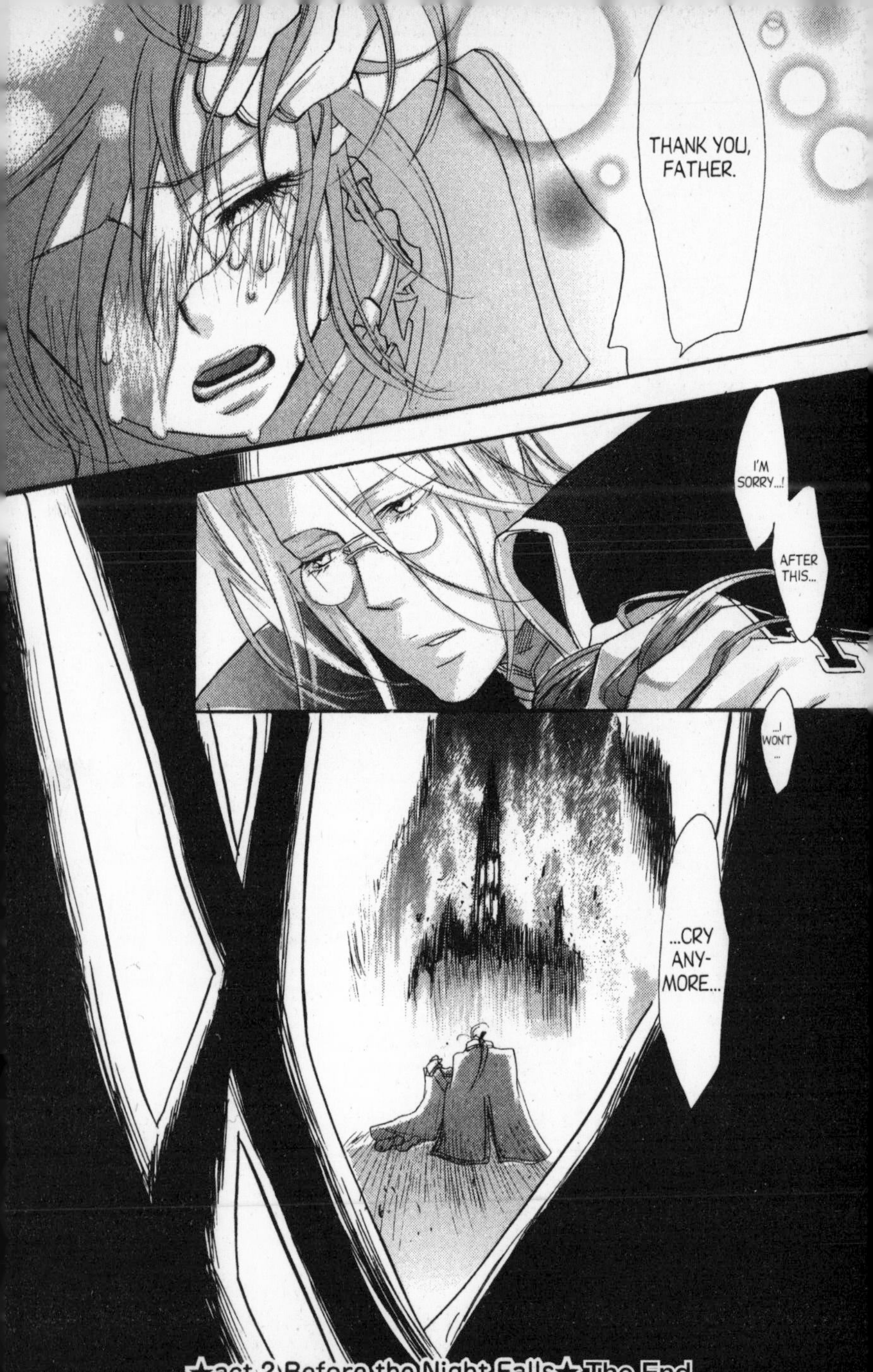
THANK YOU, FATHER.
I'M SORRY...!
AFTER THIS...
...I WON'T ...
...CRY ANY-MORE...

★act.2 Before the Night Falls★ The End

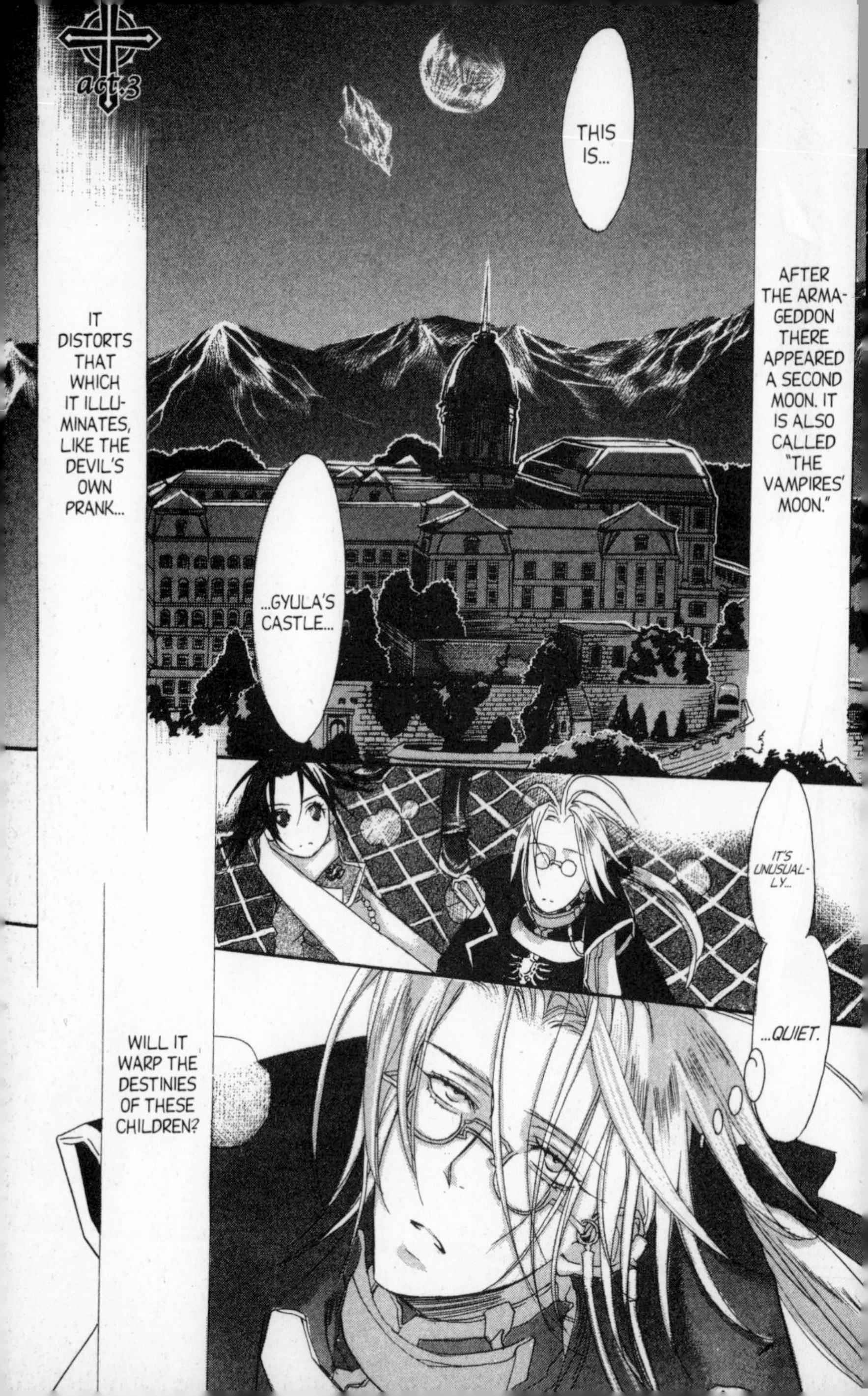
act.3
THIS IS...
AFTER THE ARMAGEDDON THERE APPEARED A SECOND MOON. IT IS ALSO CALLED "THE VAMPIRES' MOON."
...GYULA'S CASTLE...
IT DISTORTS THAT WHICH IT ILLUMINATES, LIKE THE DEVIL'S OWN PRANK...
IT'S UNUSUALLY...
...QUIET.
WILL IT WARP THE DESTINIES OF THESE CHILDREN?

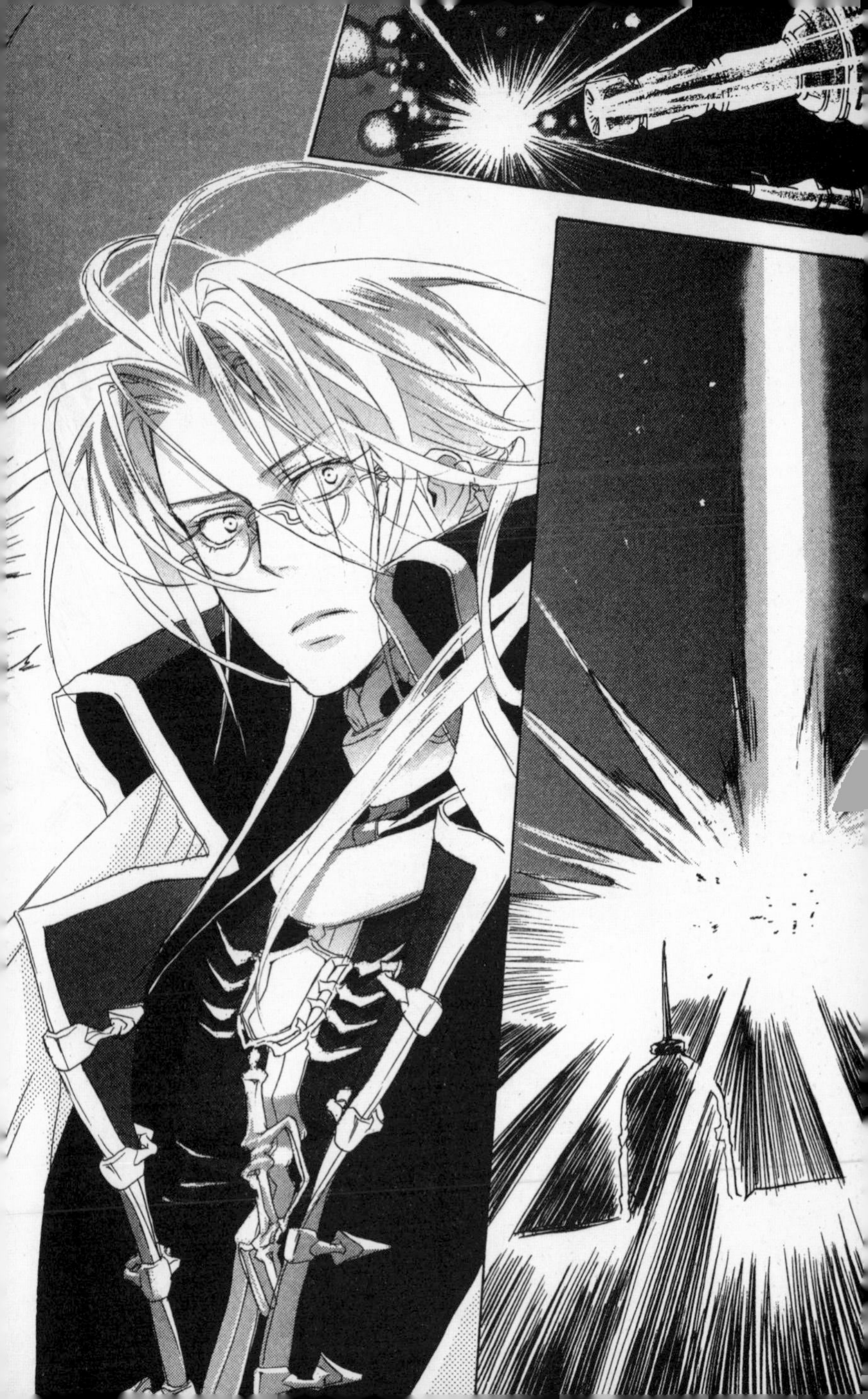

act.3 Beyond the Limit

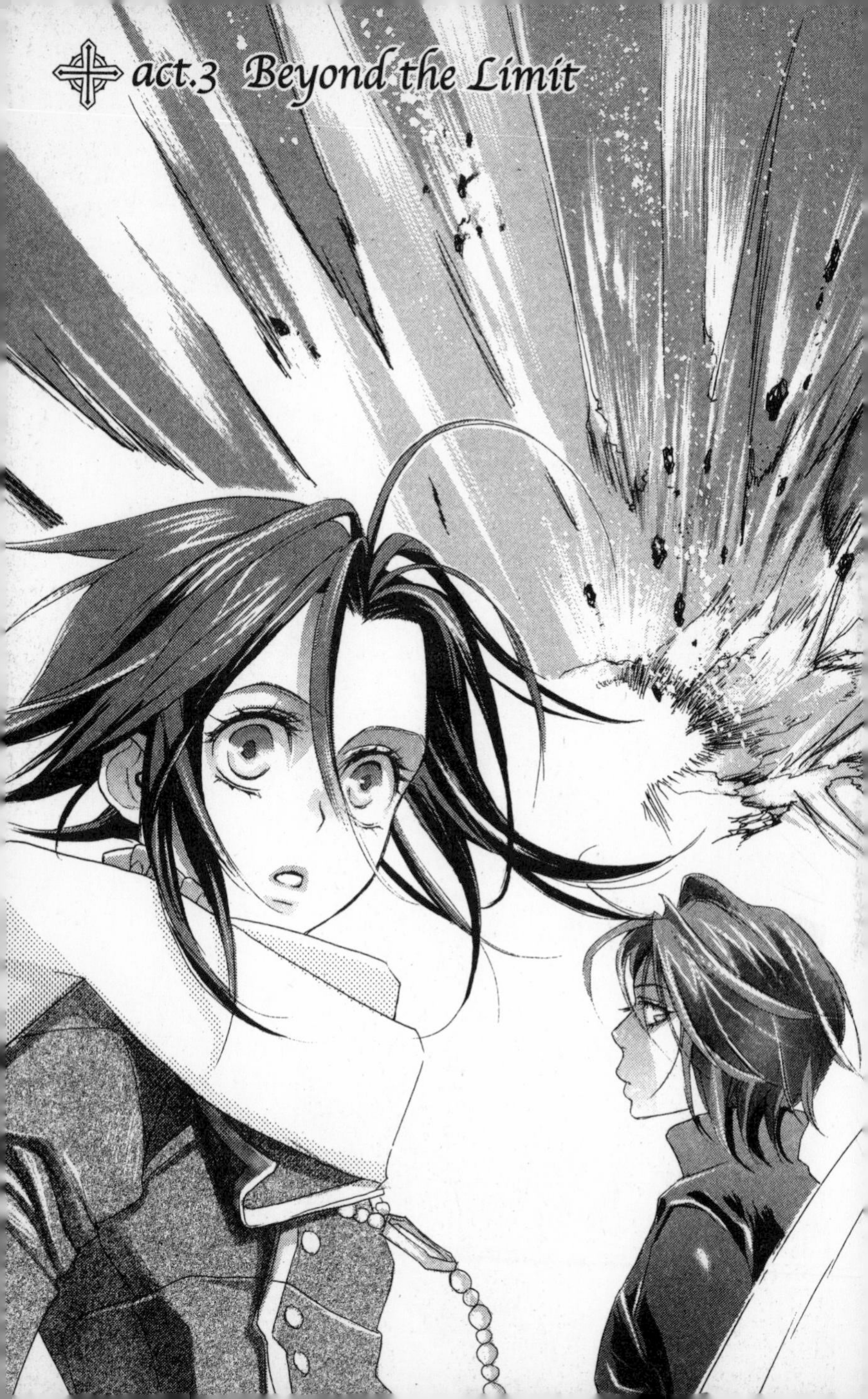

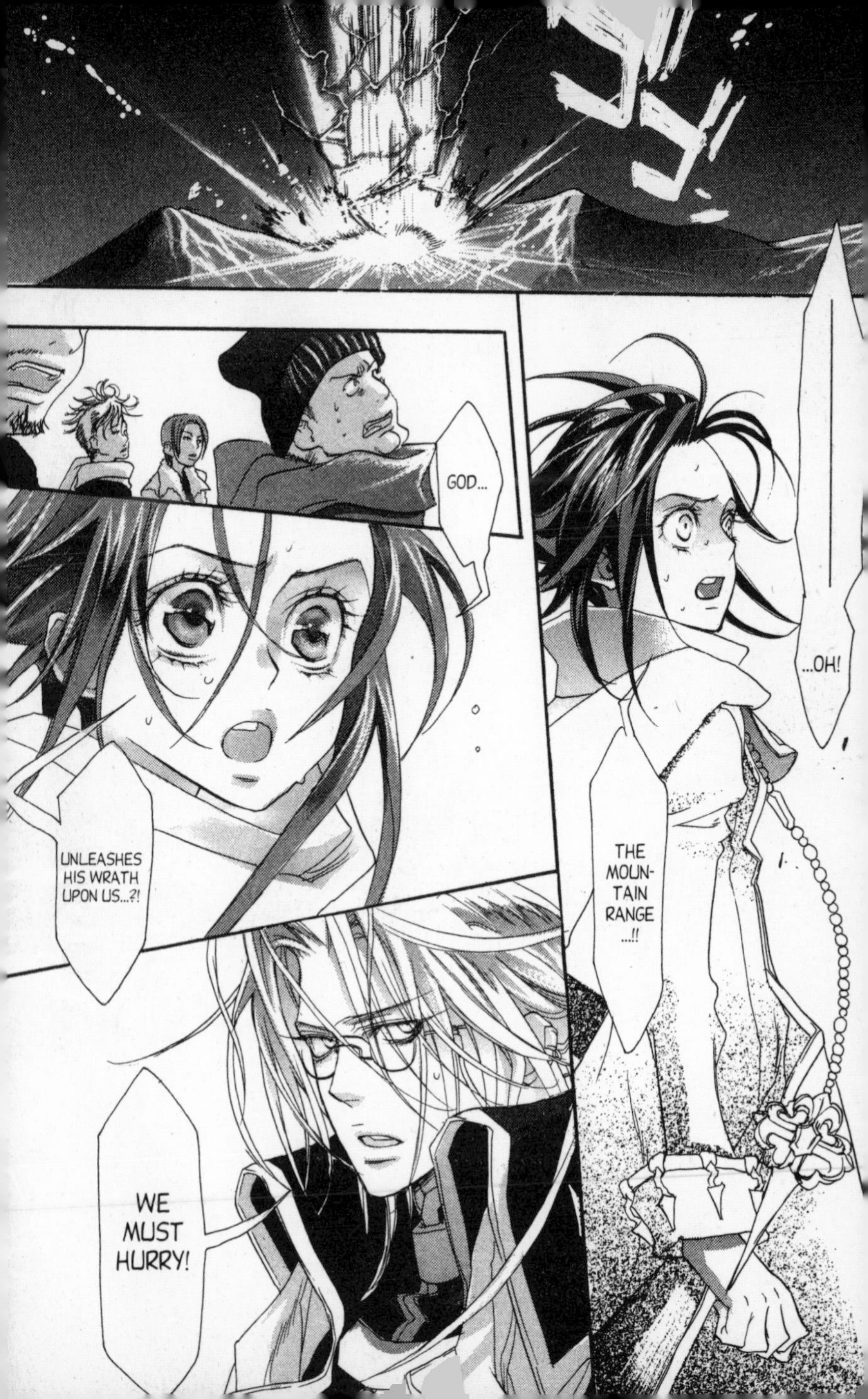
...OH!
THE MOUN-TAIN RANGE ...!!
GOD...
UNLEASHES HIS WRATH UPON US...?!
WE MUST HURRY!

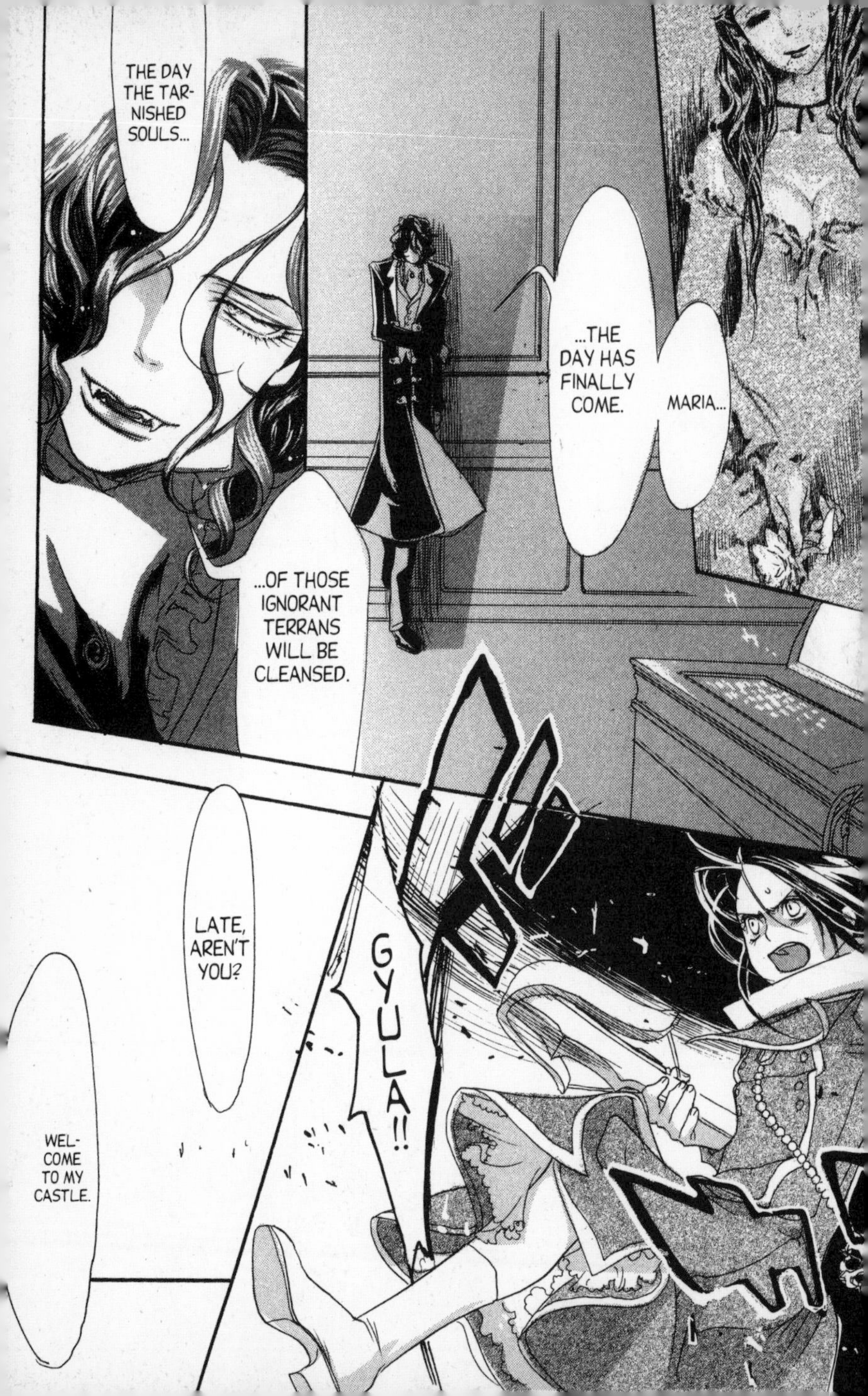
MARIA...
...THE DAY HAS FINALLY COME.
THE DAY THE TAR-NISHED SOULS...
...OF THOSE IGNORANT TERRANS WILL BE CLEANSED.
GYULA!!
LATE, AREN'T YOU?
WEL-COME TO MY CASTLE.

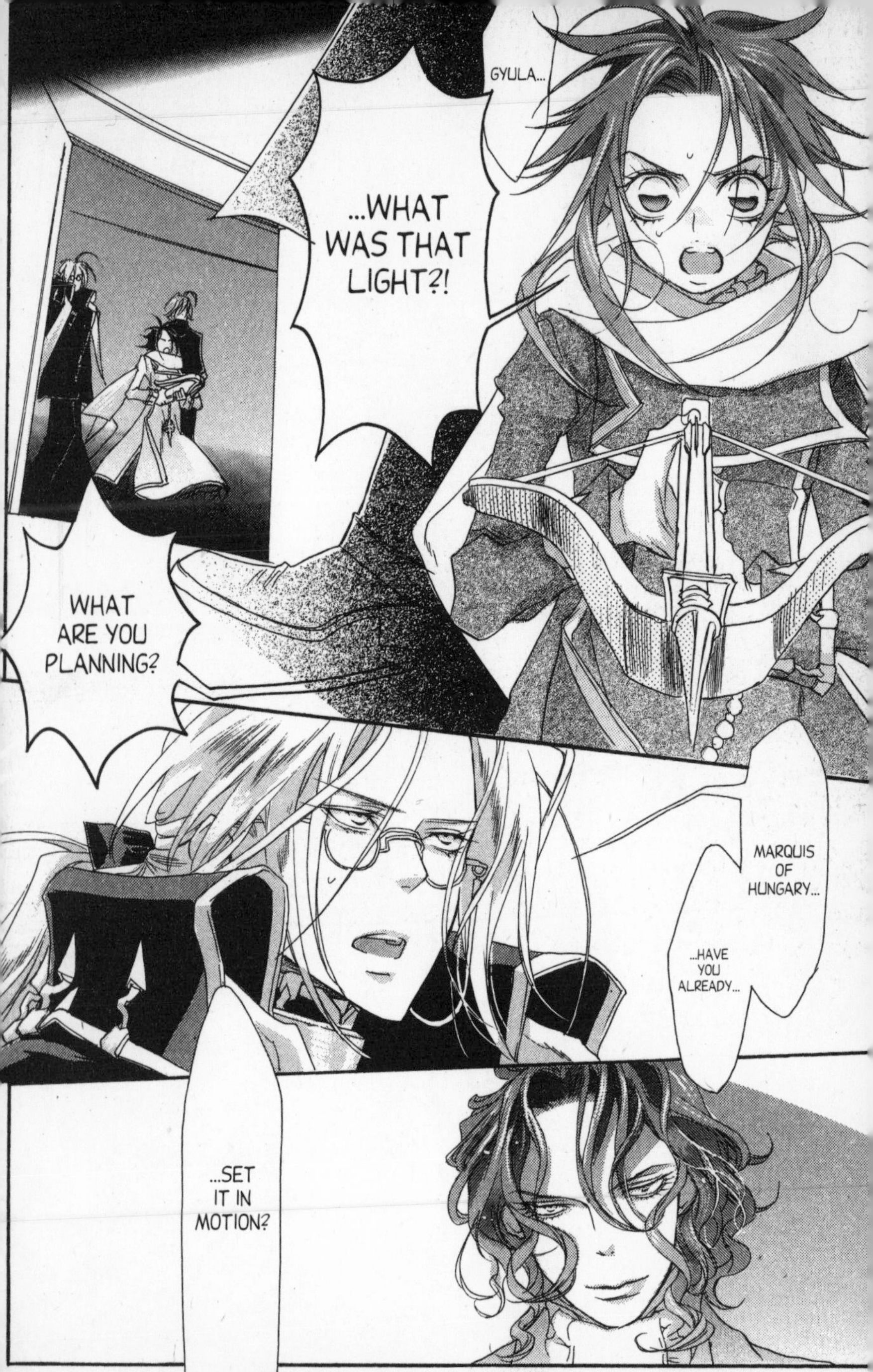
GYULA...
...WHAT WAS THAT LIGHT?!
WHAT ARE YOU PLANNING?
MARQUIS OF HUNGARY...
...HAVE YOU ALREADY...
...SET IT IN MOTION?

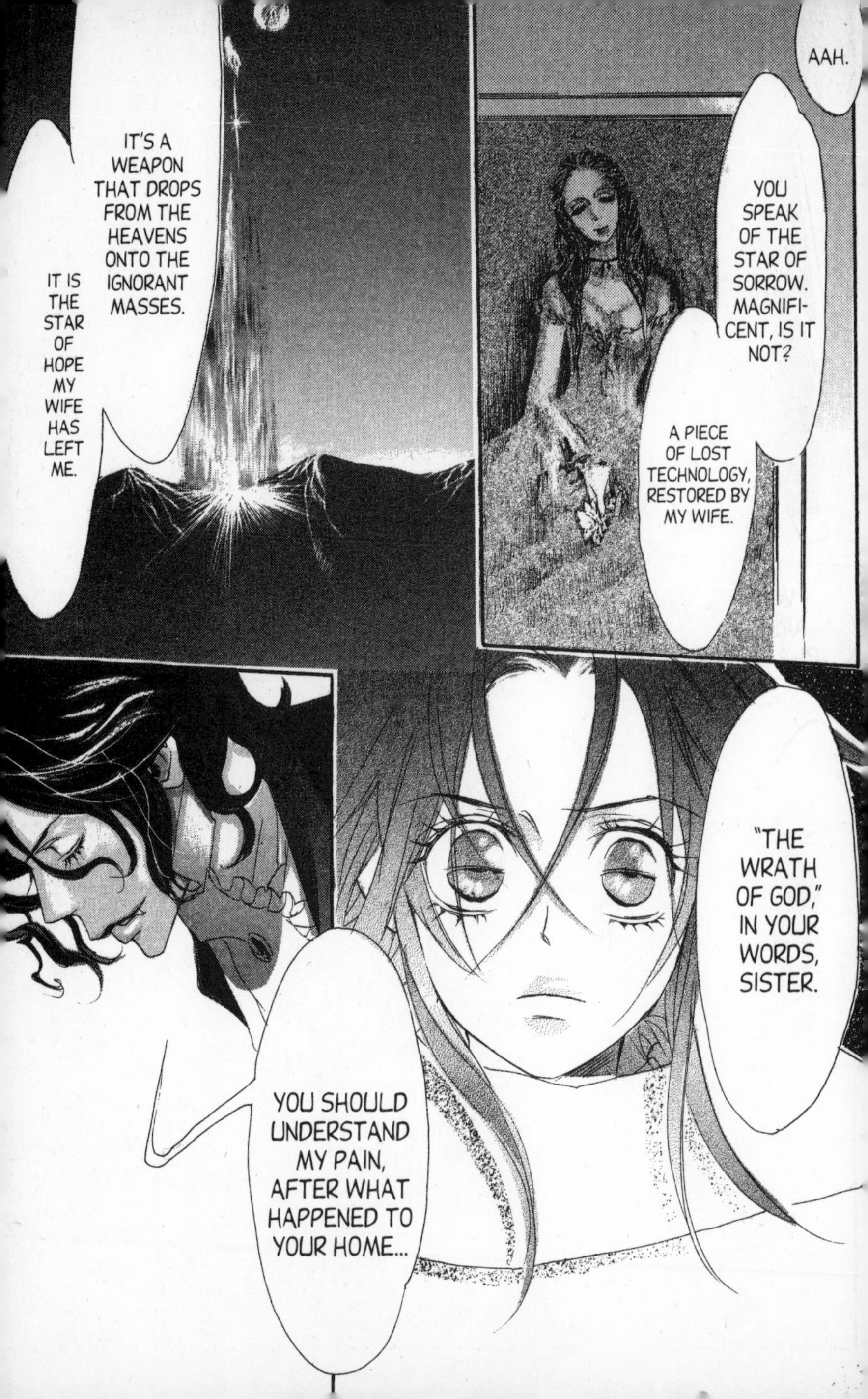
AAH.
YOU SPEAK OF THE STAR OF SORROW. MAGNIFI-CENT, IS IT NOT?
A PIECE OF LOST TECHNOLOGY, RESTORED BY MY WIFE.
IT'S A WEAPON THAT DROPS FROM THE HEAVENS ONTO THE IGNORANT MASSES.
IT IS THE STAR OF HOPE MY WIFE HAS LEFT ME.
"THE WRATH OF GOD," IN YOUR WORDS, SISTER.
YOU SHOULD UNDERSTAND MY PAIN, AFTER WHAT HAPPENED TO YOUR HOME...

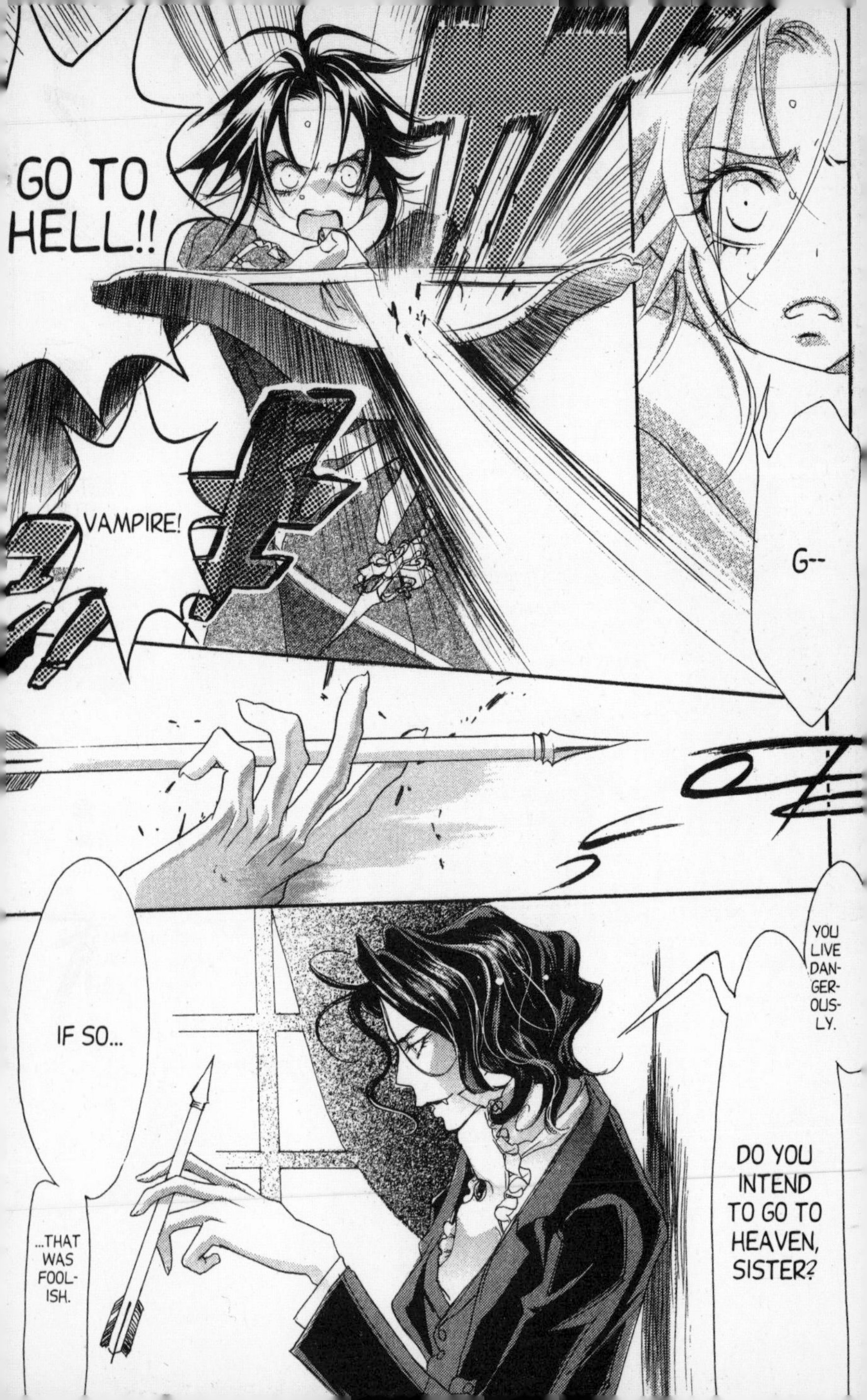
G--
GO TO HELL!!
VAMPIRE!
YOU LIVE DANGEROUSLY.
DO YOU INTEND TO GO TO HEAVEN, SISTER?
IF SO...
...THAT WAS FOOLISH.

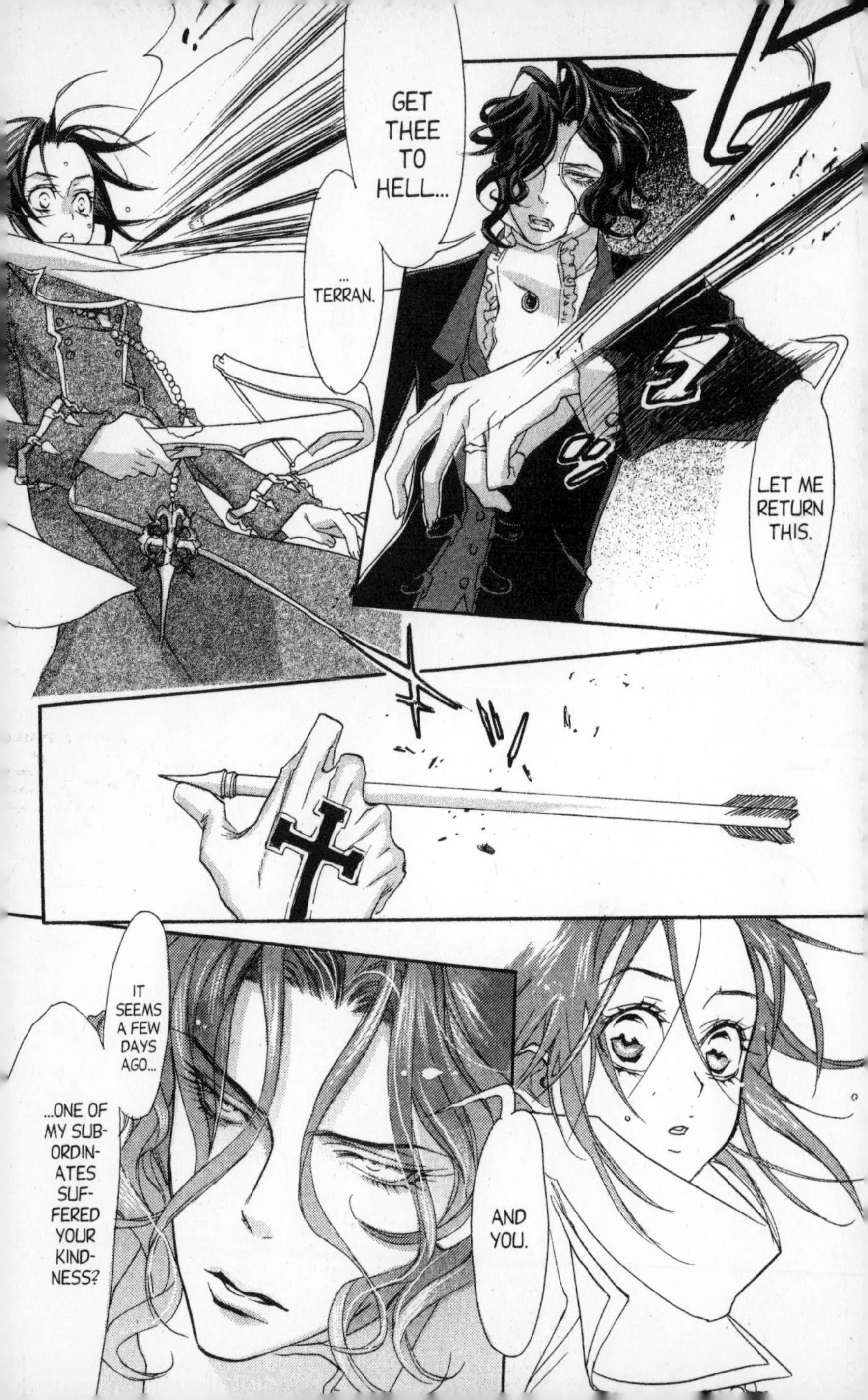

LET ME RETURN THIS.
GET THEE TO HELL...
... TERRAN.
!!
AND YOU.
IT SEEMS A FEW DAYS AGO...
...ONE OF MY SUB-ORDIN-ATES SUF-FERED YOUR KIND-NESS?

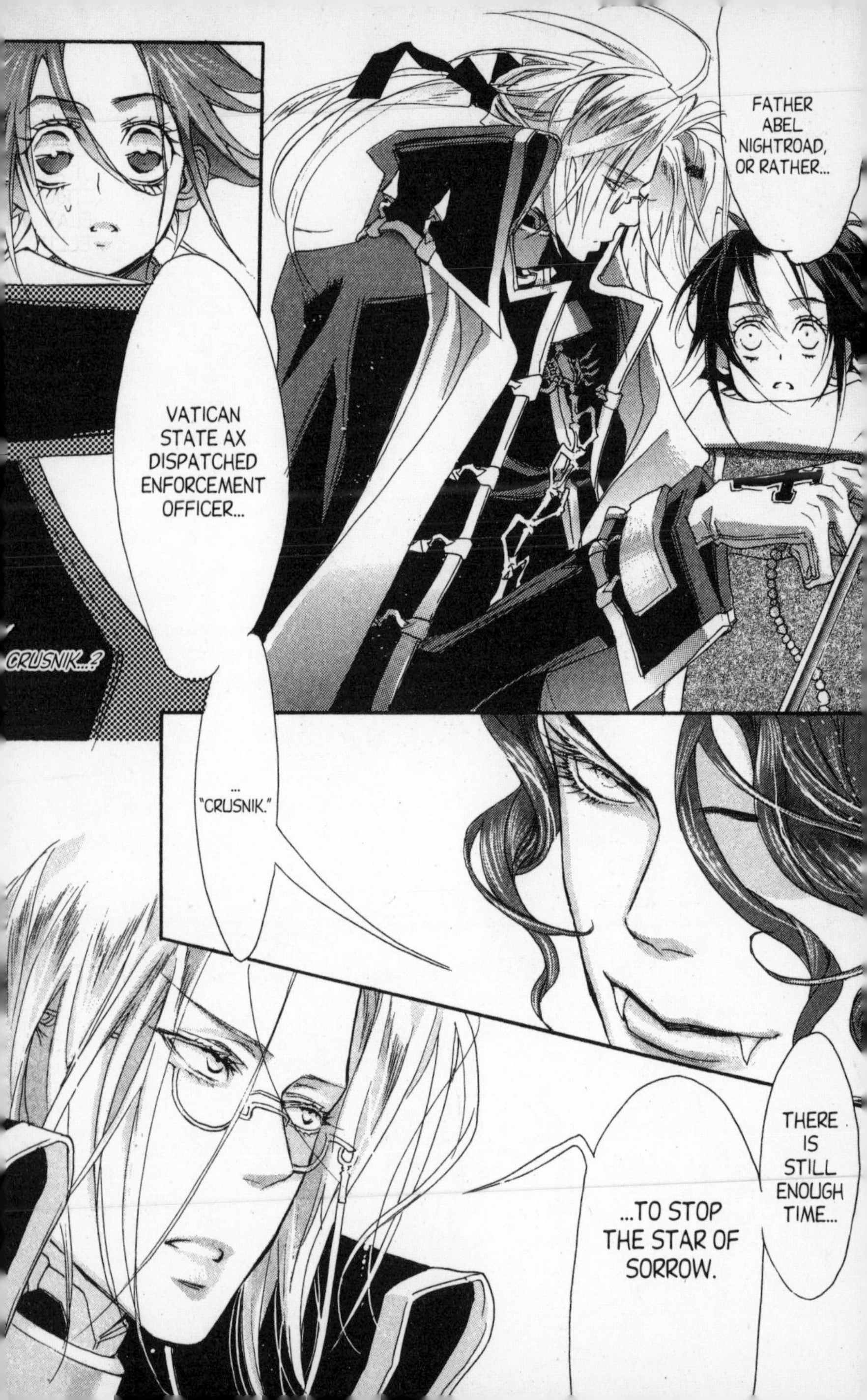
FATHER ABEL NIGHTROAD, OR RATHER...
VATICAN STATE AX DISPATCHED ENFORCEMENT OFFICER...
CRUSNIK...?
... "CRUSNIK."
THERE IS STILL ENOUGH TIME...
...TO STOP THE STAR OF SORROW.

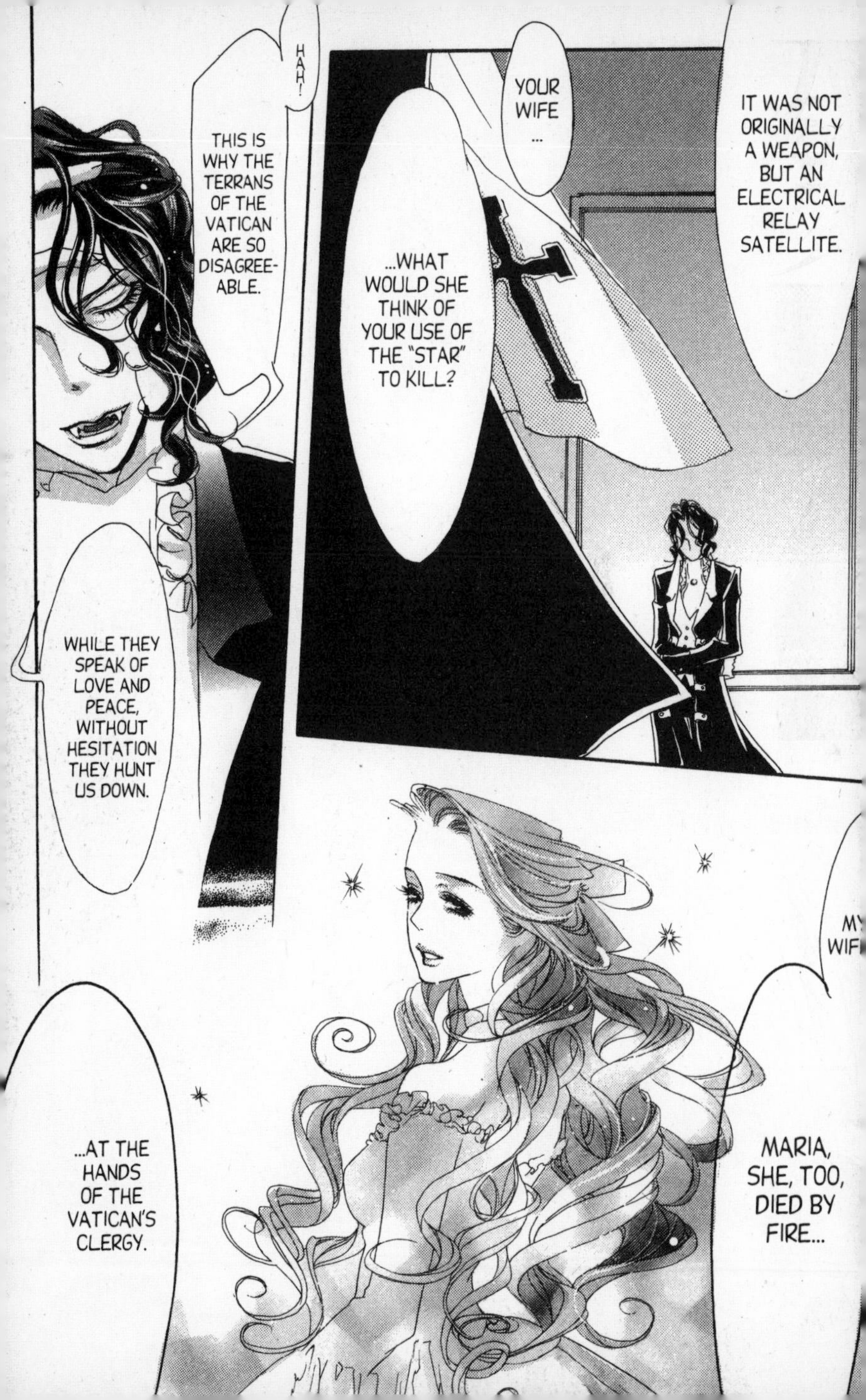
IT WAS NOT ORIGINALLY A WEAPON, BUT AN ELECTRICAL RELAY SATELLITE.
YOUR WIFE ...
...WHAT WOULD SHE THINK OF YOUR USE OF THE "STAR" TO KILL?
HAH!
THIS IS WHY THE TERRANS OF THE VATICAN ARE SO DISAGREE-ABLE.
WHILE THEY SPEAK OF LOVE AND PEACE, WITHOUT HESITATION THEY HUNT US DOWN.
MY WIF
MARIA, SHE, TOO, DIED BY FIRE...
...AT THE HANDS OF THE VATICAN'S CLERGY.

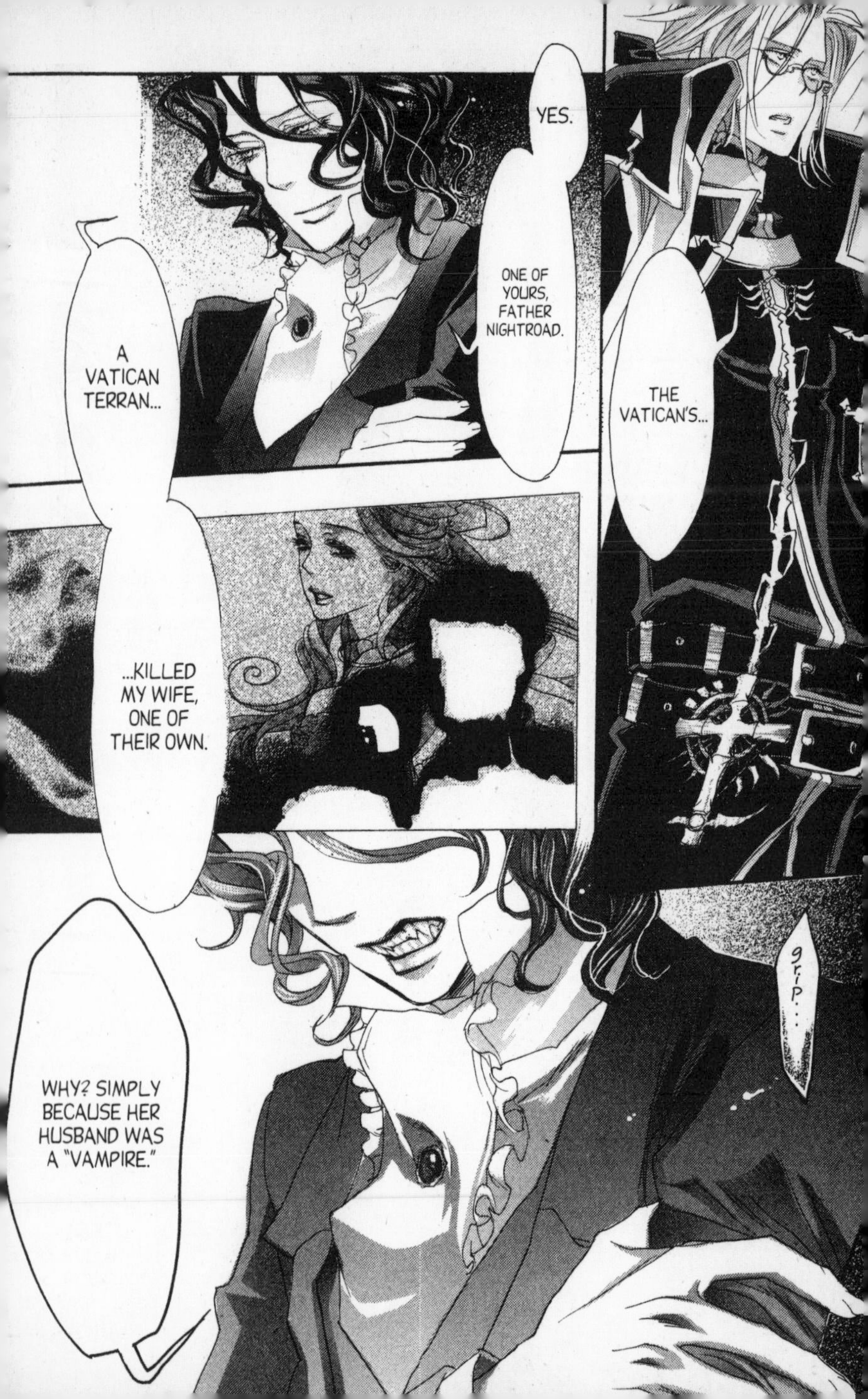
THE VATICAN'S...
YES.
ONE OF YOURS, FATHER NIGHTROAD.
A VATICAN TERRAN...
...KILLED MY WIFE, ONE OF THEIR OWN.
grip...
WHY? SIMPLY BECAUSE HER HUSBAND WAS A "VAMPIRE."

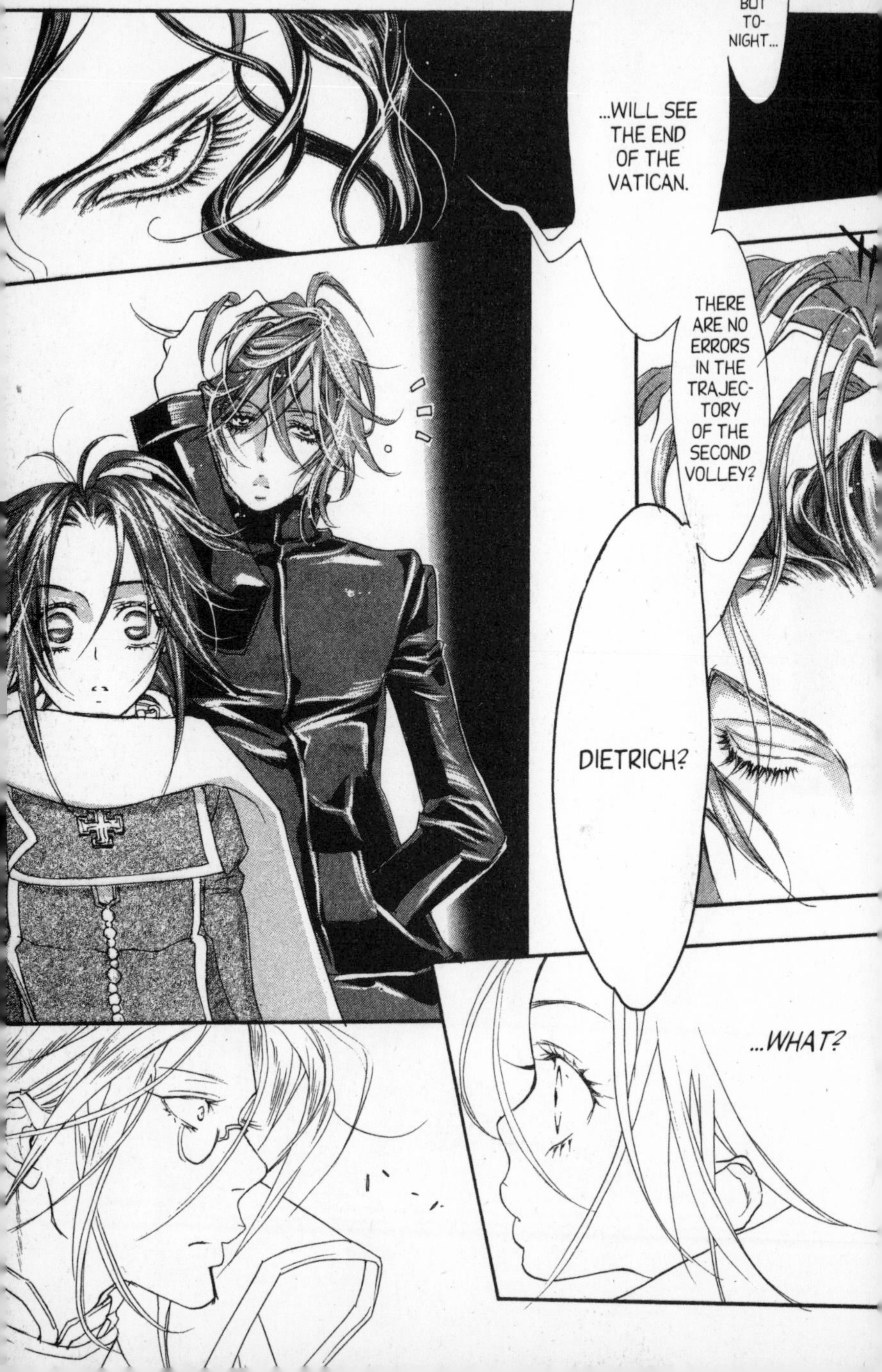
BUT TO-NIGHT...
...WILL SEE THE END OF THE VATICAN.
THERE ARE NO ERRORS IN THE TRAJEC-TORY OF THE SECOND VOLLEY?
DIETRICH?
...WHAT?

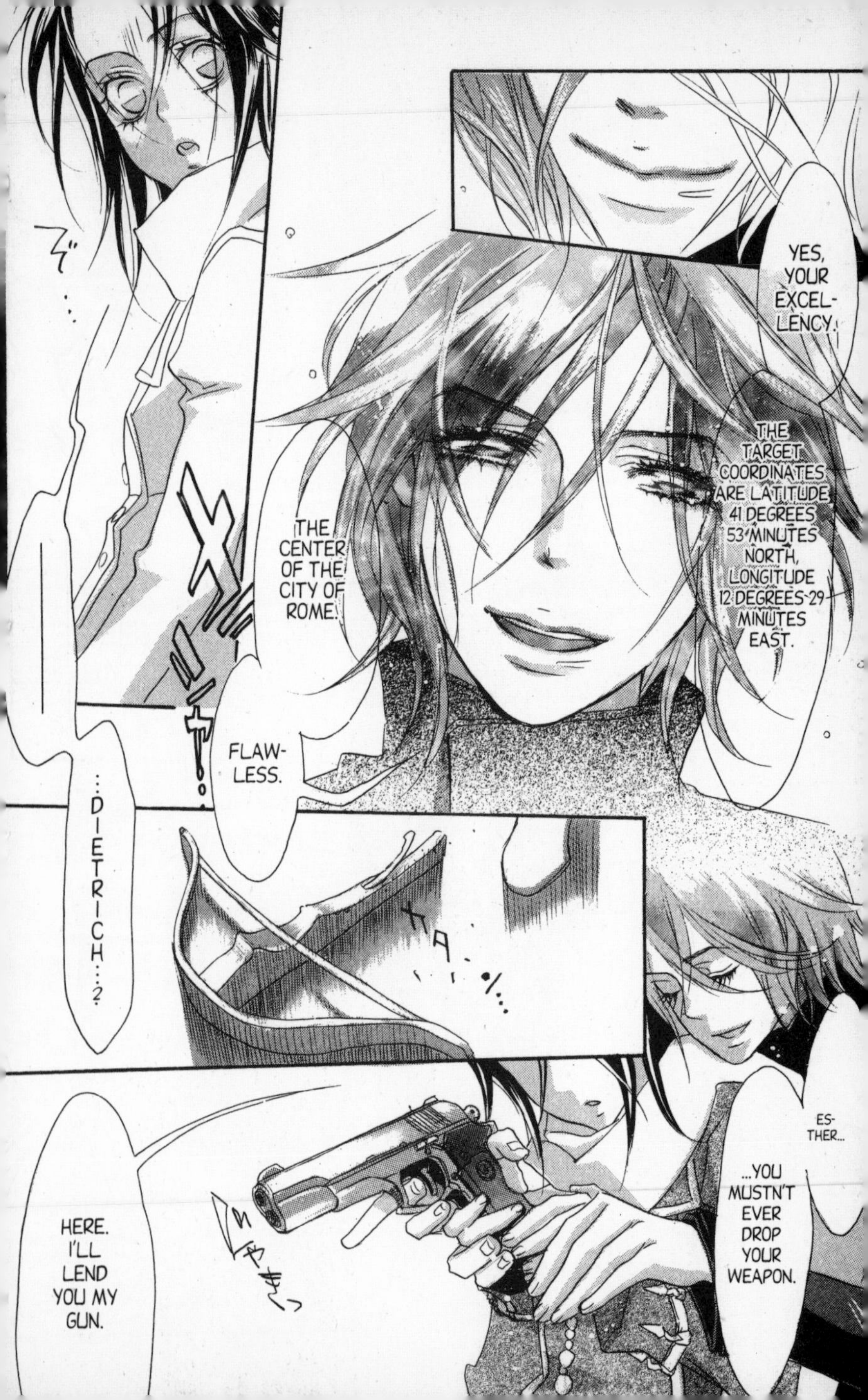
YES, YOUR EXCEL-LENCY.
THE TARGET COORDINATES ARE LATITUDE 41 DEGREES 53 MINUTES NORTH, LONGITUDE 12 DEGREES 29 MINUTES EAST.
THE CENTER OF THE CITY OF ROME.
FLAW-LESS.
...DIETRICH...?
ES-THER...
...YOU MUSTN'T EVER DROP YOUR WEAPON.
HERE. I'LL LEND YOU MY GUN.

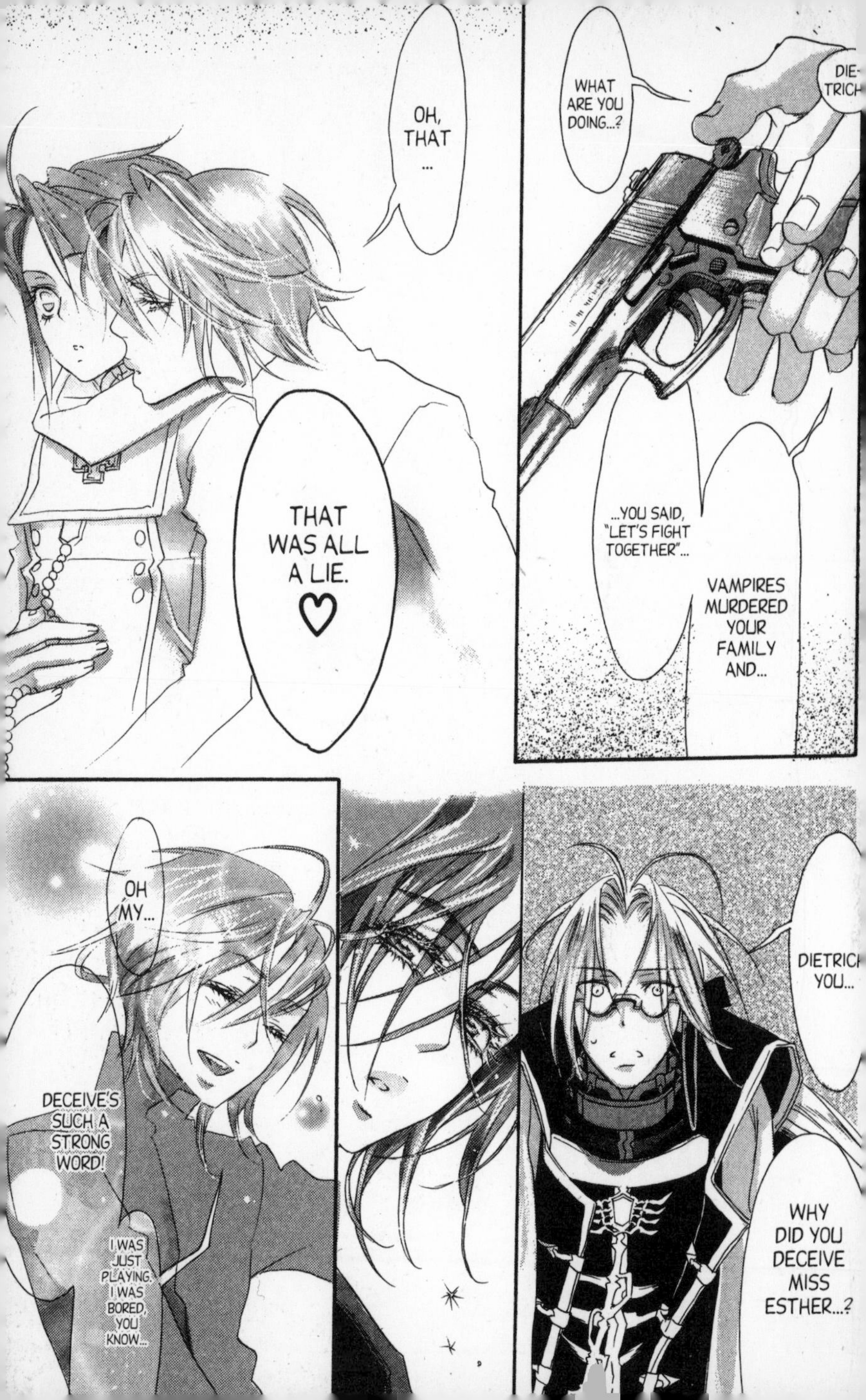
DIE-TRICH
WHAT ARE YOU DOING...?
...YOU SAID, "LET'S FIGHT TOGETHER"...
VAMPIRES MURDERED YOUR FAMILY AND...
OH, THAT ...
THAT WAS ALL A LIE. ♡
DIETRICH YOU...
WHY DID YOU DECEIVE MISS ESTHER...?
OH MY...
DECEIVE'S SUCH A STRONG WORD!
I WAS JUST PLAYING. I WAS BORED, YOU KNOW...

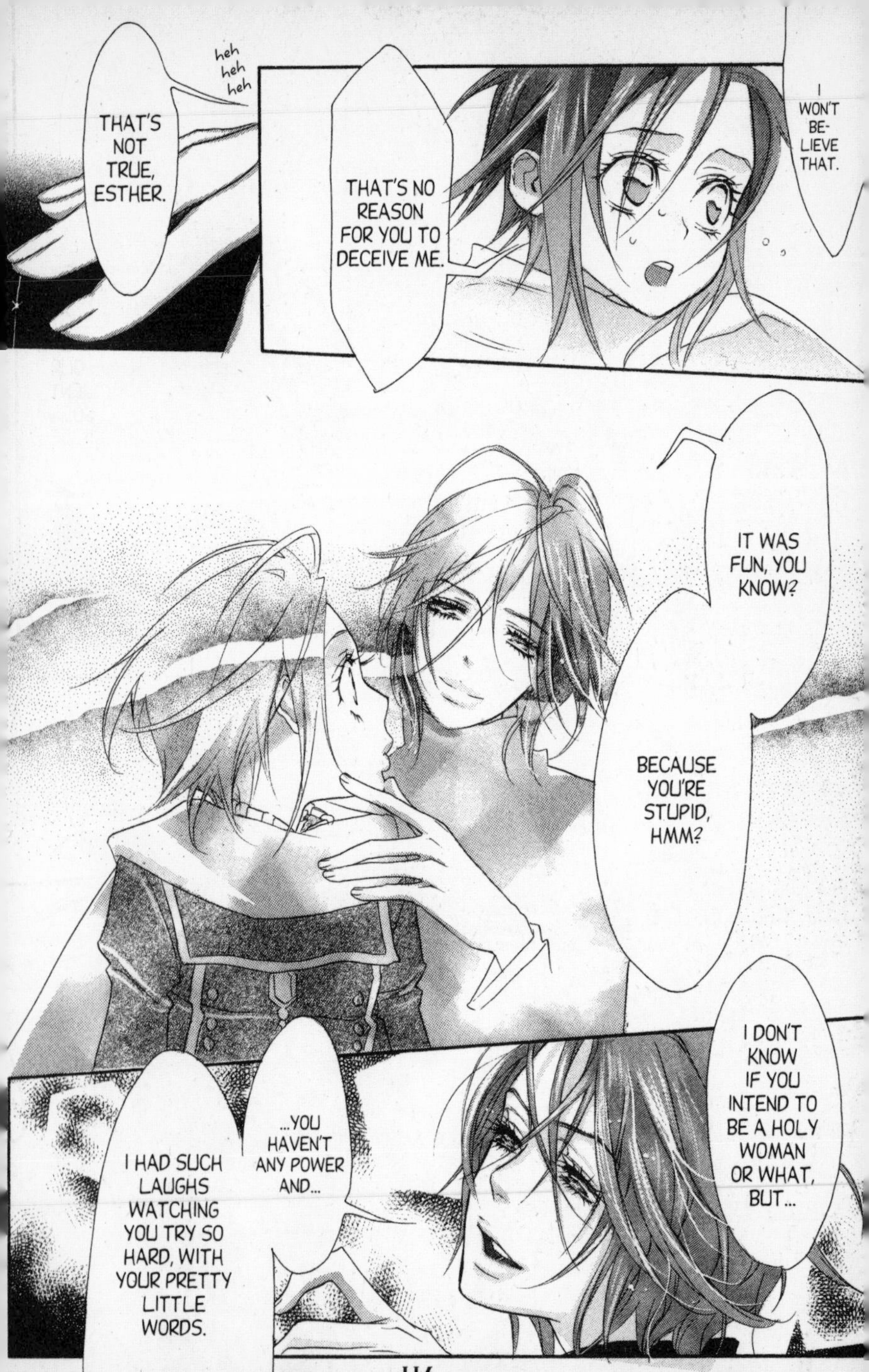
I WON'T BE-LIEVE THAT.
THAT'S NO REASON FOR YOU TO DECEIVE ME.
heh heh heh
THAT'S NOT TRUE, ESTHER.
IT WAS FUN, YOU KNOW?
BECAUSE YOU'RE STUPID, HMM?
I DON'T KNOW IF YOU INTEND TO BE A HOLY WOMAN OR WHAT, BUT...
...YOU HAVEN'T ANY POWER AND...
I HAD SUCH LAUGHS WATCHING YOU TRY SO HARD, WITH YOUR PRETTY LITTLE WORDS.

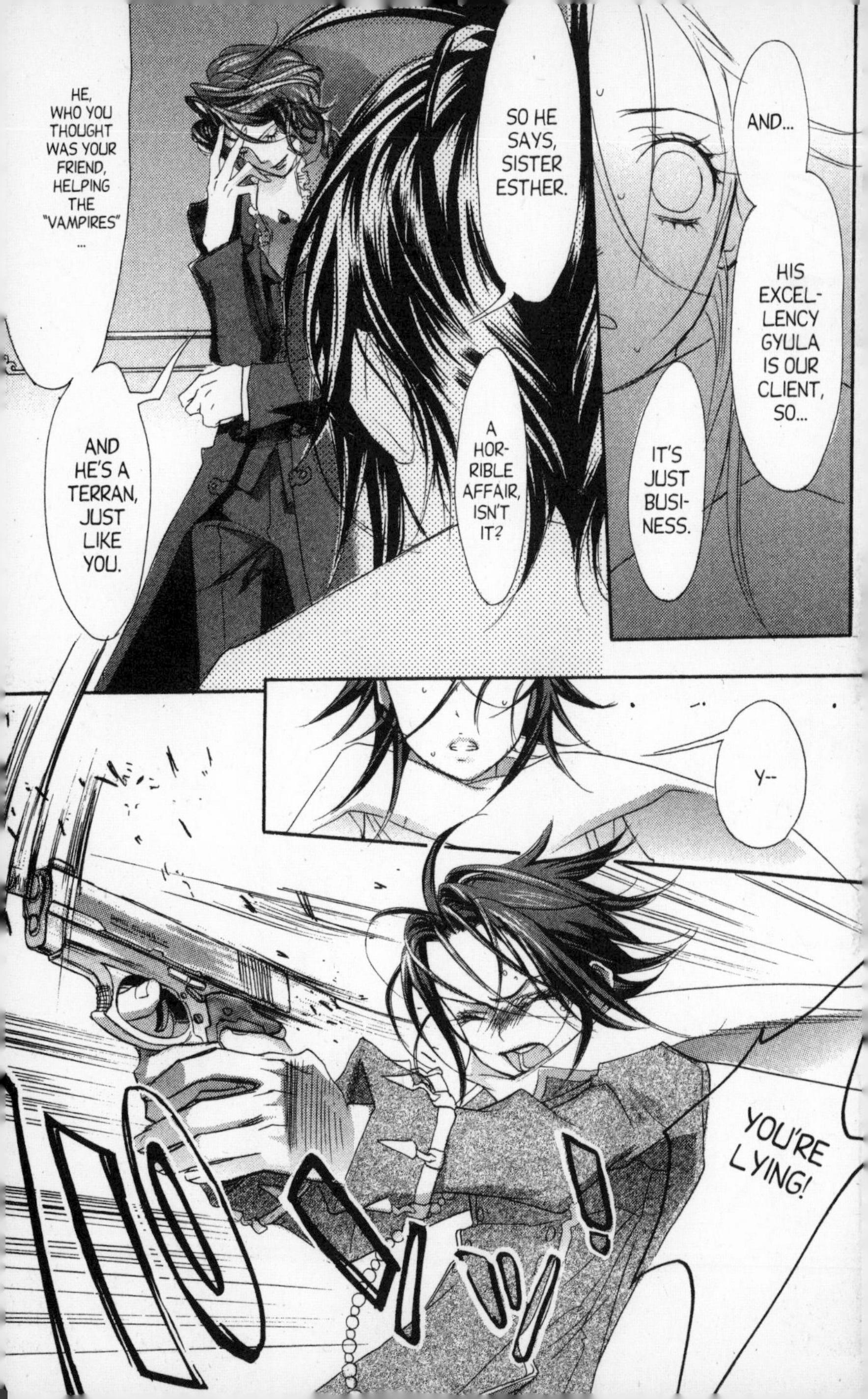
AND...
HIS EXCEL-LENCY GYULA IS OUR CLIENT, SO...
IT'S JUST BUSI-NESS.
SO HE SAYS, SISTER ESTHER.
A HOR-RIBLE AFFAIR, ISN'T IT?
HE, WHO YOU THOUGHT WAS YOUR FRIEND, HELPING THE "VAMPIRES" ...
AND HE'S A TERRAN, JUST LIKE YOU.
Y--
YOU'RE LYING!

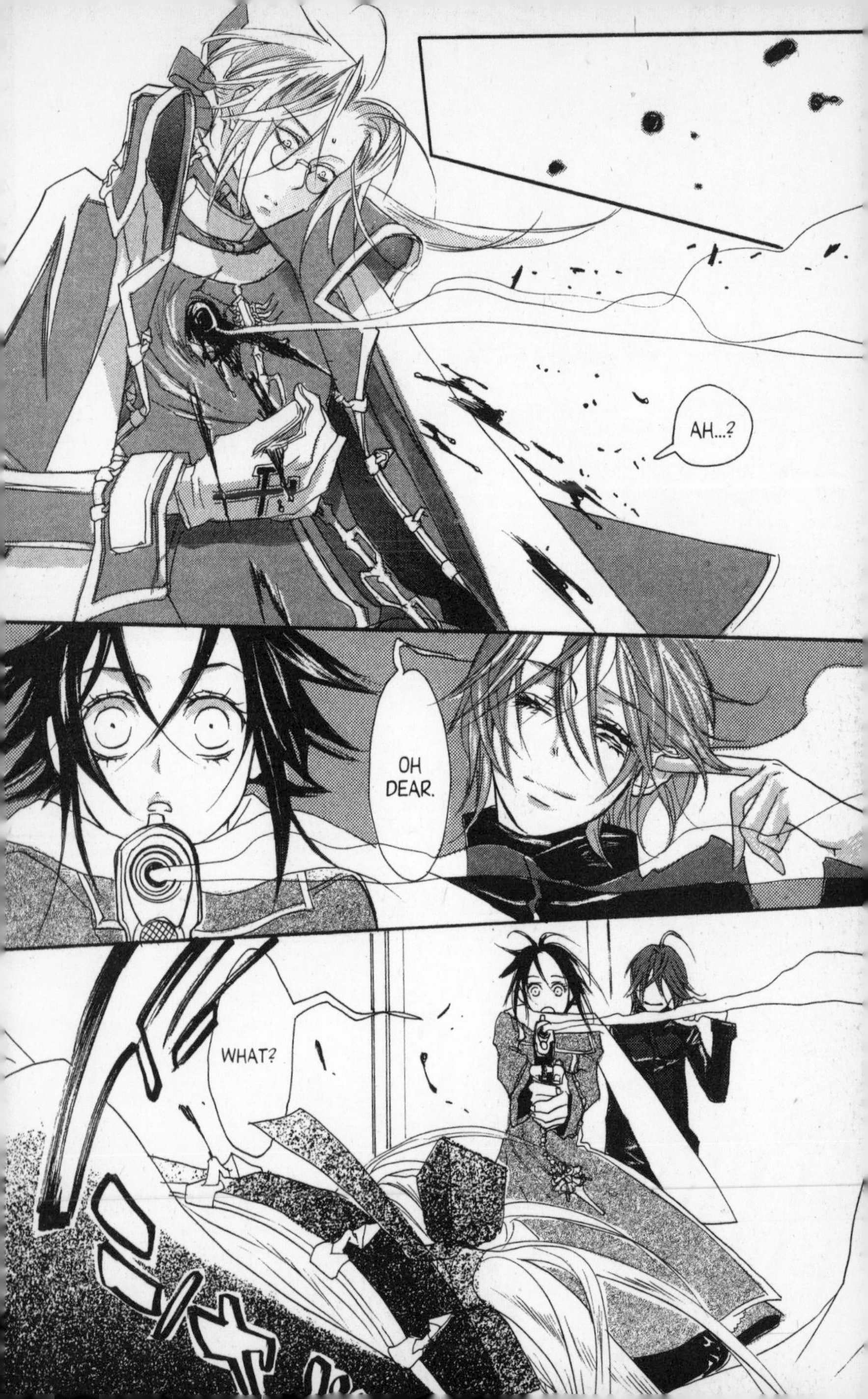
AH...?
OH DEAR.
WHAT?

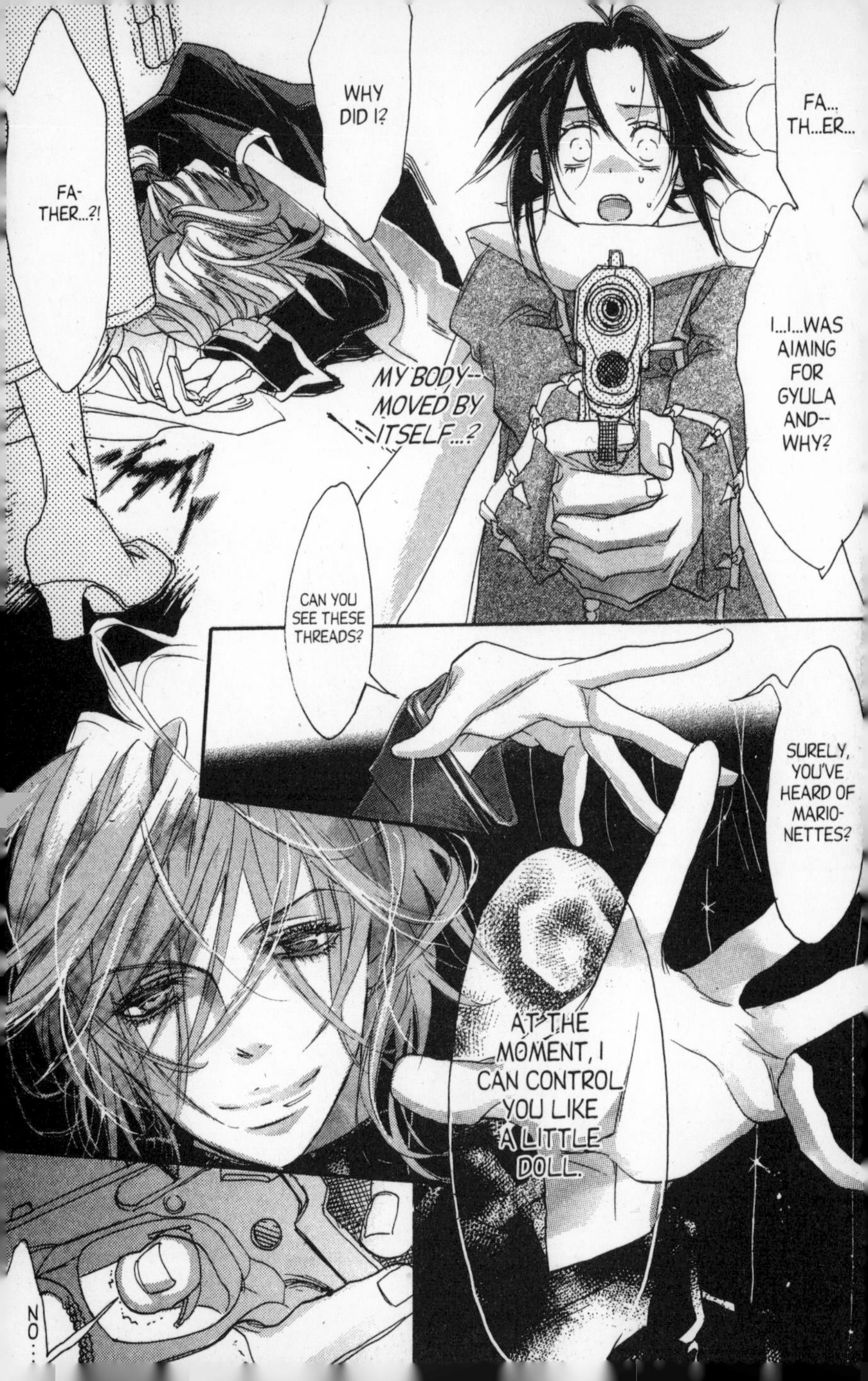
FA... TH...ER...
I...I...WAS AIMING FOR GYULA AND-- WHY?
WHY DID I?
FA-THER...?!
MY BODY-- MOVED BY ITSELF...?
CAN YOU SEE THESE THREADS?
SURELY, YOU'VE HEARD OF MARIO-NETTES?
AT THE MOMENT, I CAN CONTROL YOU LIKE A LITTLE DOLL.
NO...

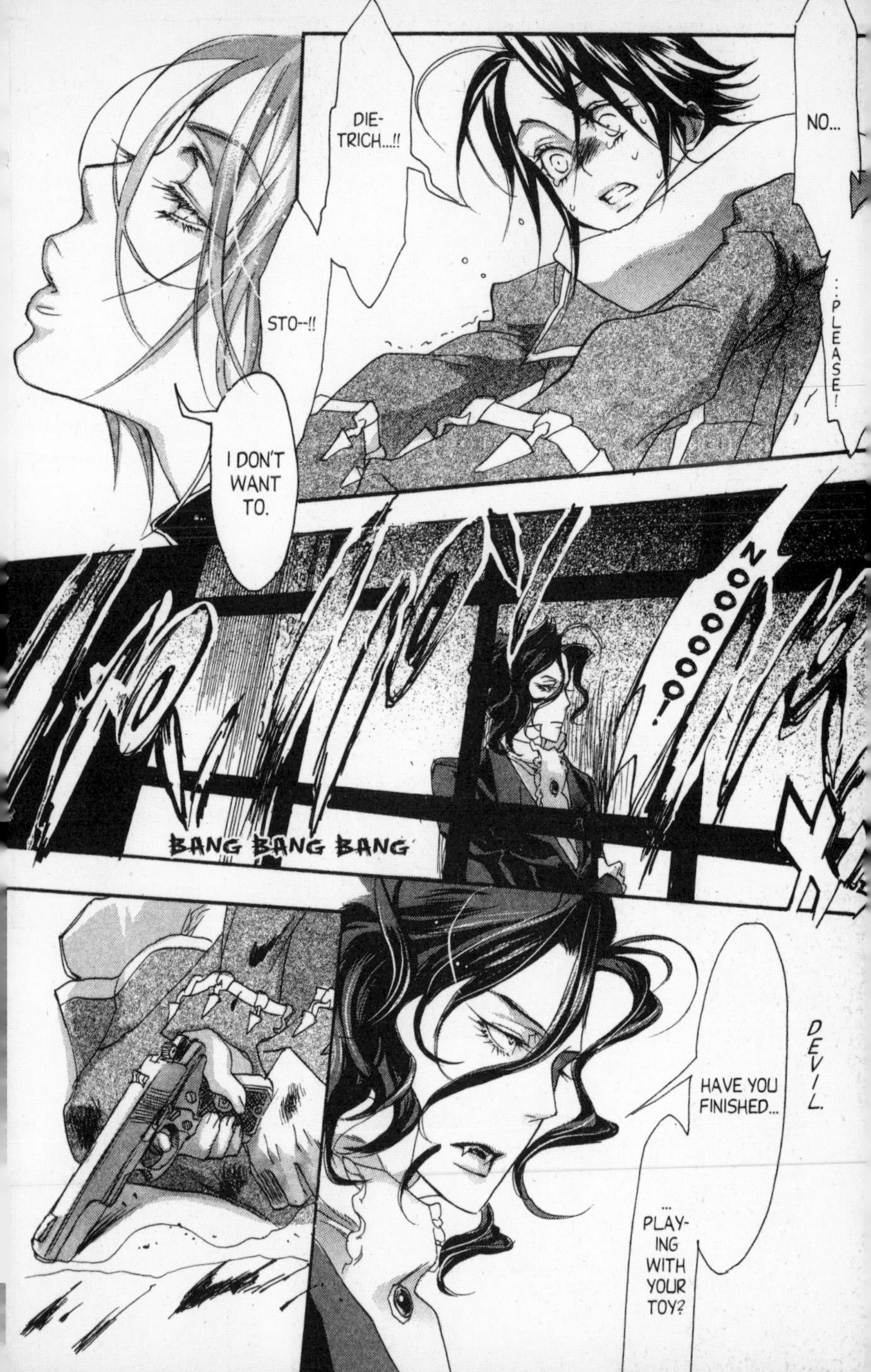
NO...
...PLEASE!
DIE-TRICH...!!
STO--!!
I DON'T WANT TO.
NOOOOOOO!
BANG BANG BANG
DEVIL.
HAVE YOU FINISHED...
...PLAYING WITH YOUR TOY?

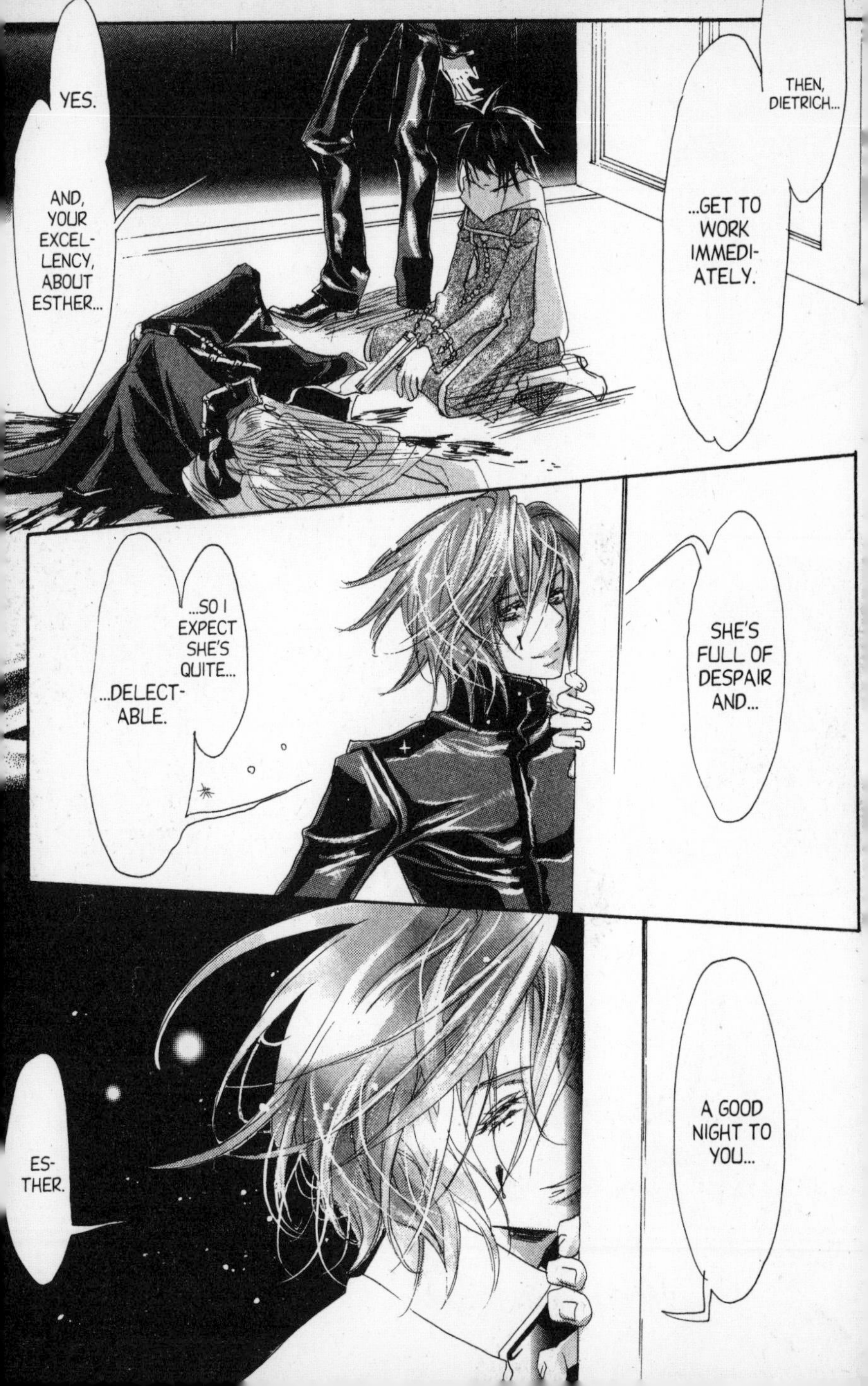
THEN, DIETRICH...
...GET TO WORK IMMEDIATELY.
YES.
AND, YOUR EXCELLENCY, ABOUT ESTHER...
SHE'S FULL OF DESPAIR AND...
...SO I EXPECT SHE'S QUITE... ...DELECTABLE.
A GOOD NIGHT TO YOU...
ESTHER.

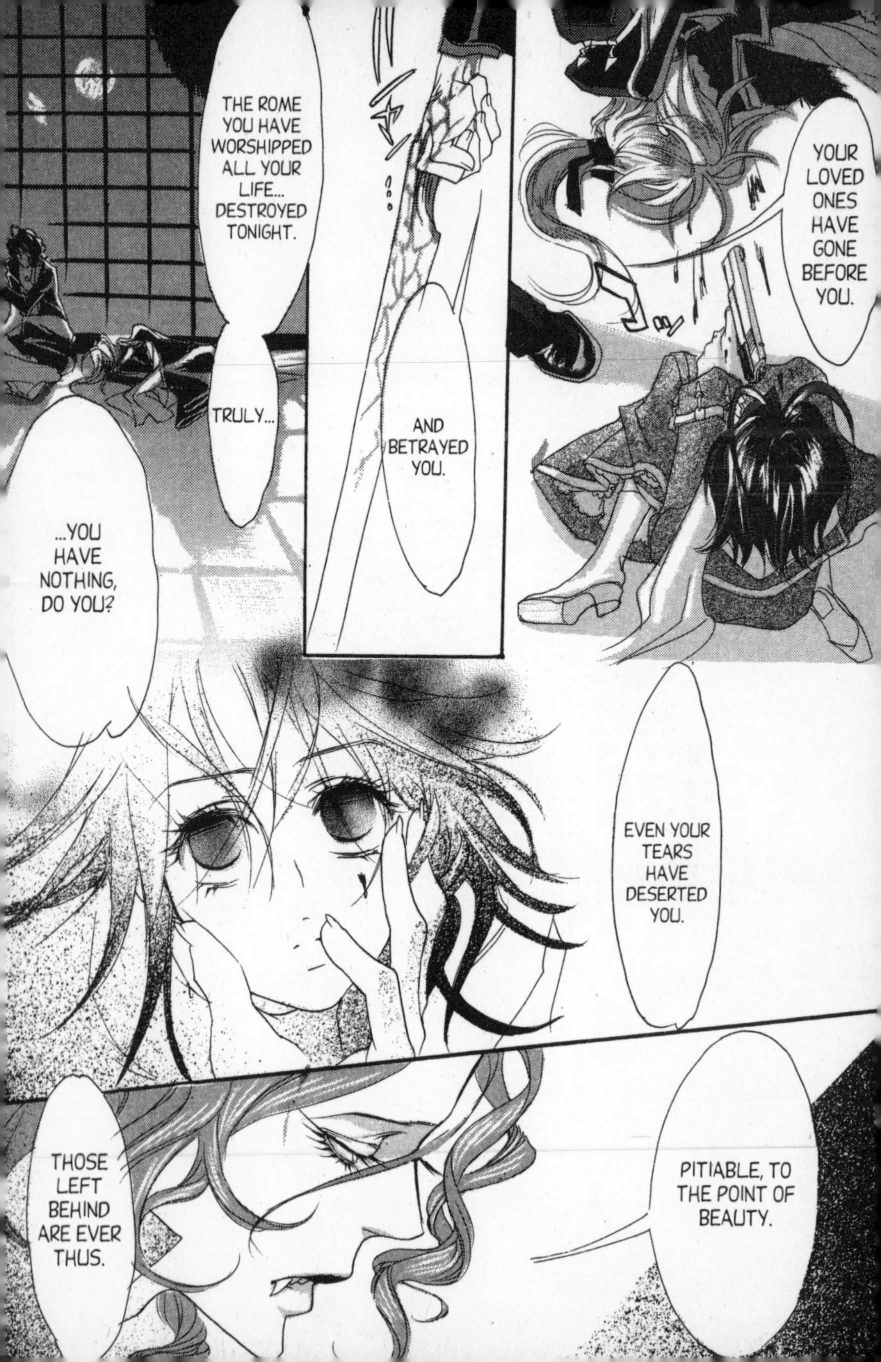
YOUR LOVED ONES HAVE GONE BEFORE YOU.
AND BETRAYED YOU.
THE ROME YOU HAVE WORSHIPPED ALL YOUR LIFE... DESTROYED TONIGHT.
TRULY...
...YOU HAVE NOTHING, DO YOU?
EVEN YOUR TEARS HAVE DESERTED YOU.
PITIABLE, TO THE POINT OF BEAUTY.
THOSE LEFT BEHIND ARE EVER THUS.

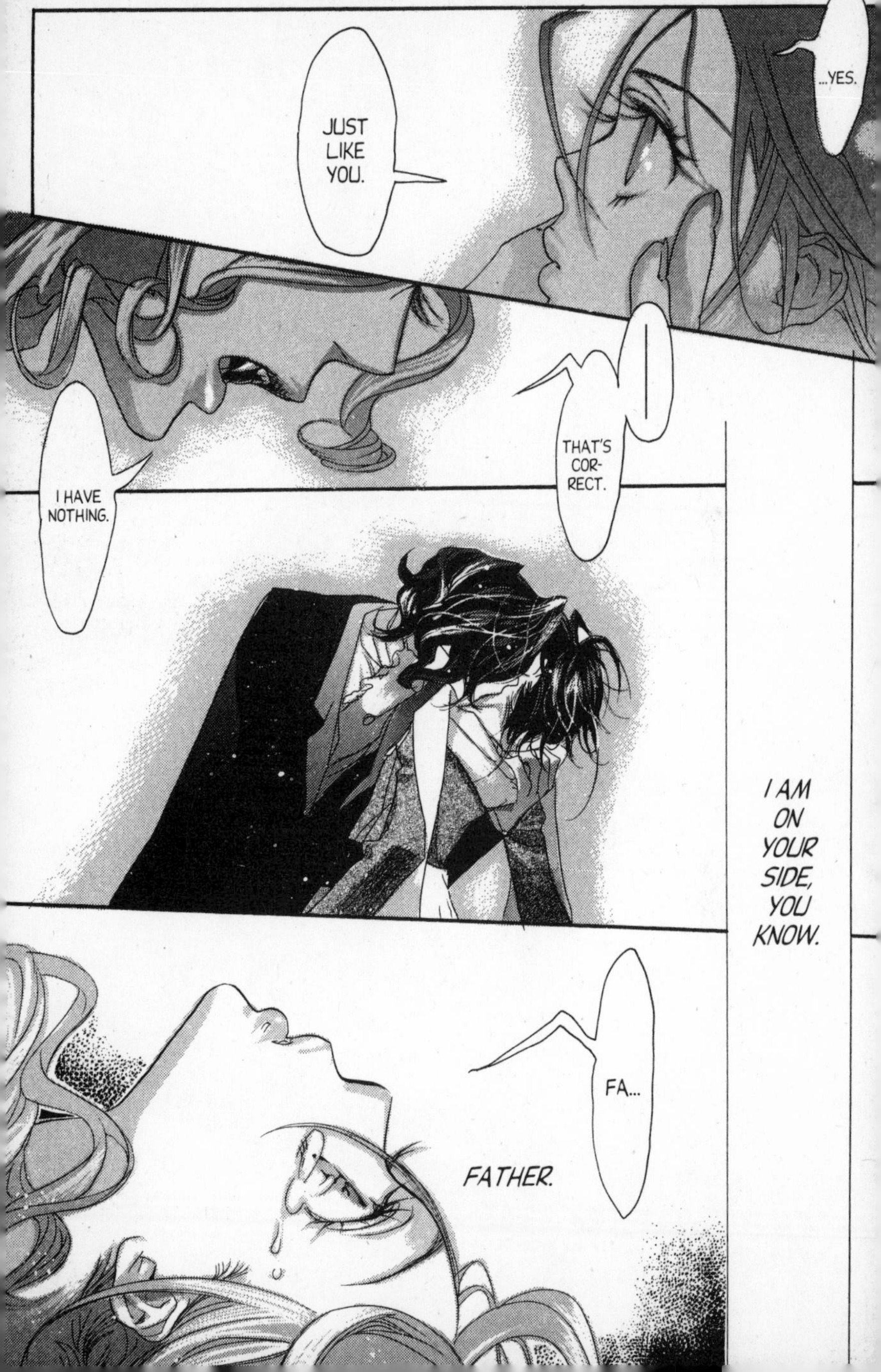
...YES.
JUST LIKE YOU.
THAT'S COR-RECT.
I HAVE NOTHING.
I AM ON YOUR SIDE, YOU KNOW.
FA...
FATHER.

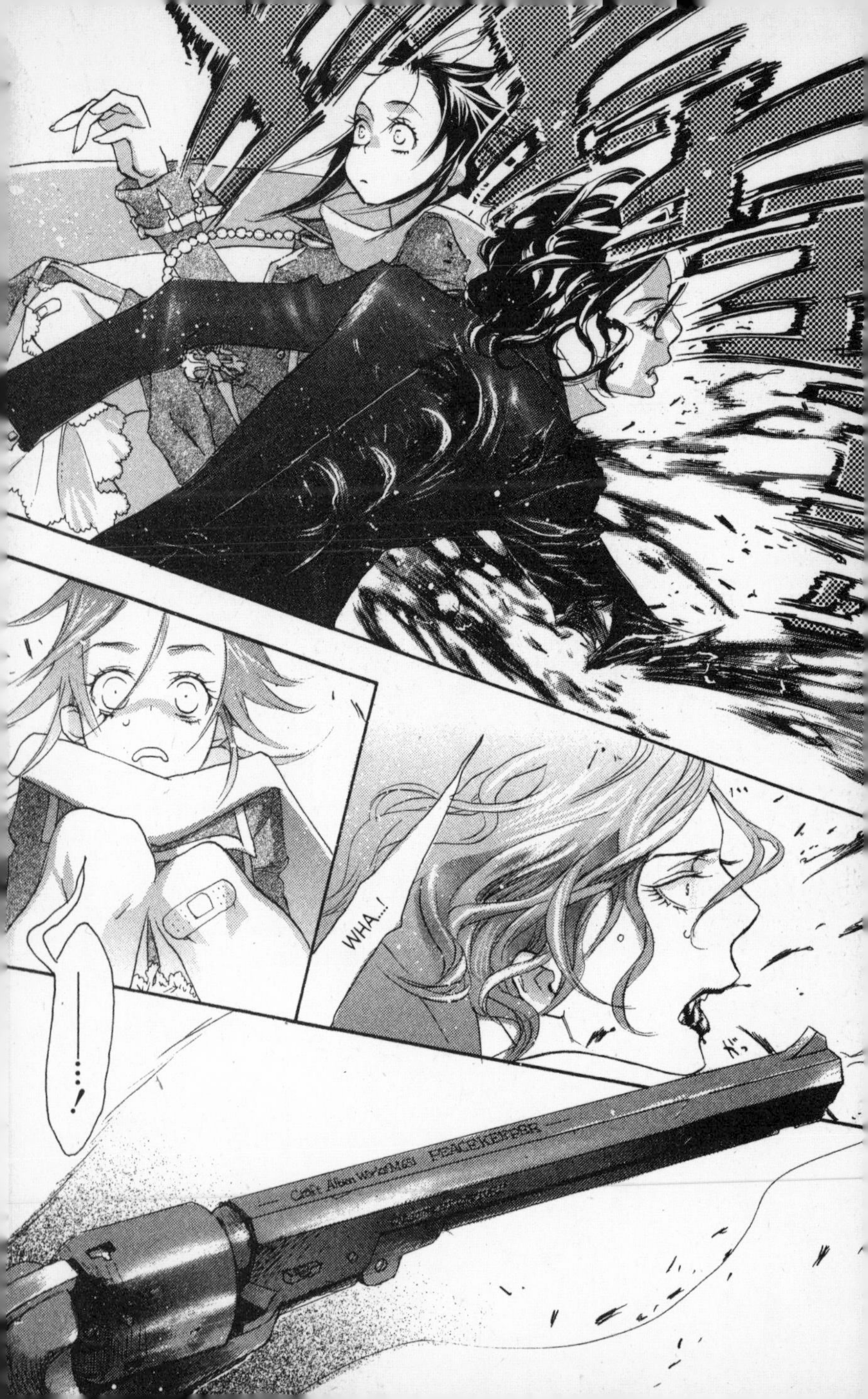
WHA...!
PEACEKEEPER
......!

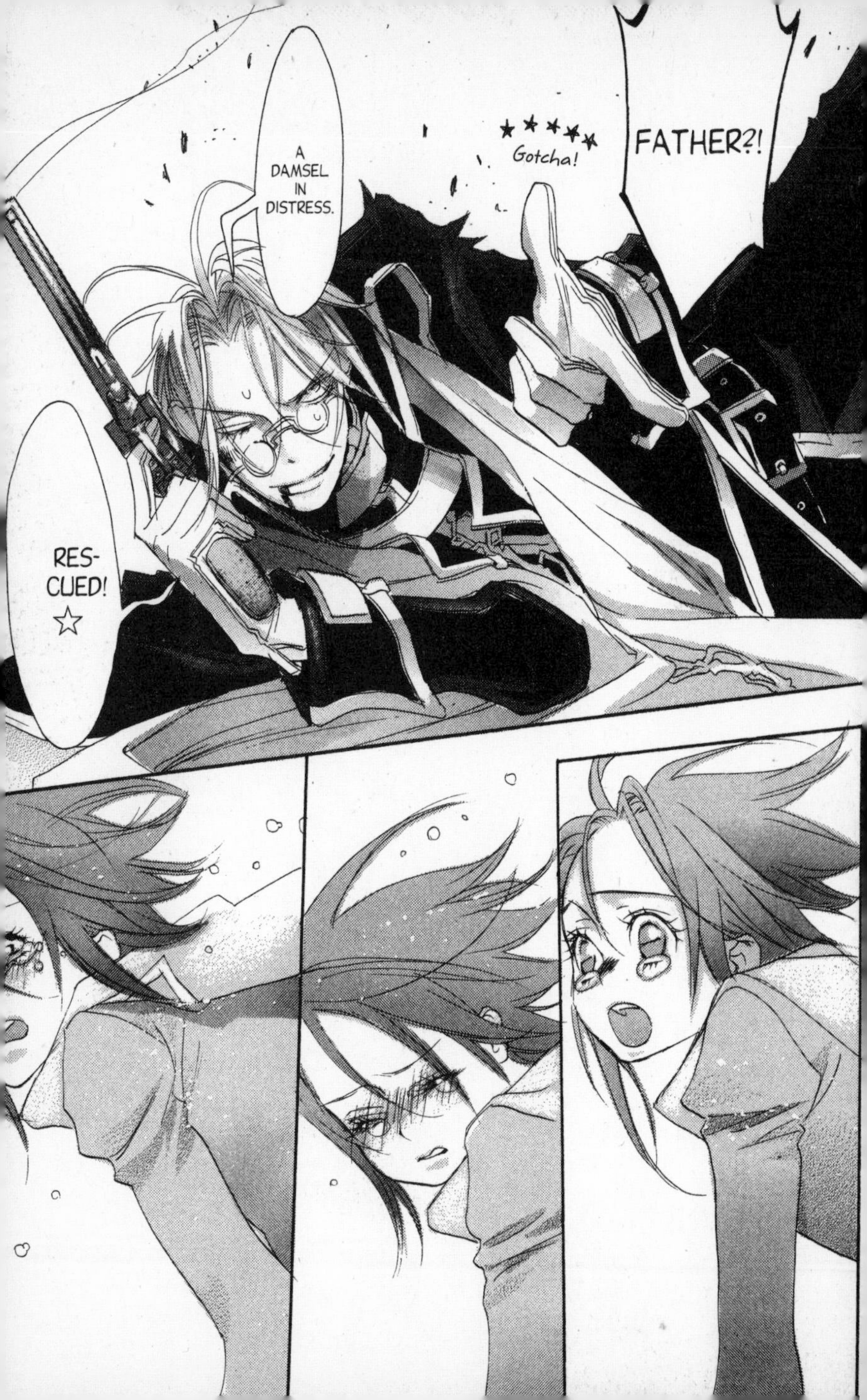
FATHER?!
★★★★★ Gotcha!
A DAMSEL IN DISTRESS.
RES-CUED! ☆

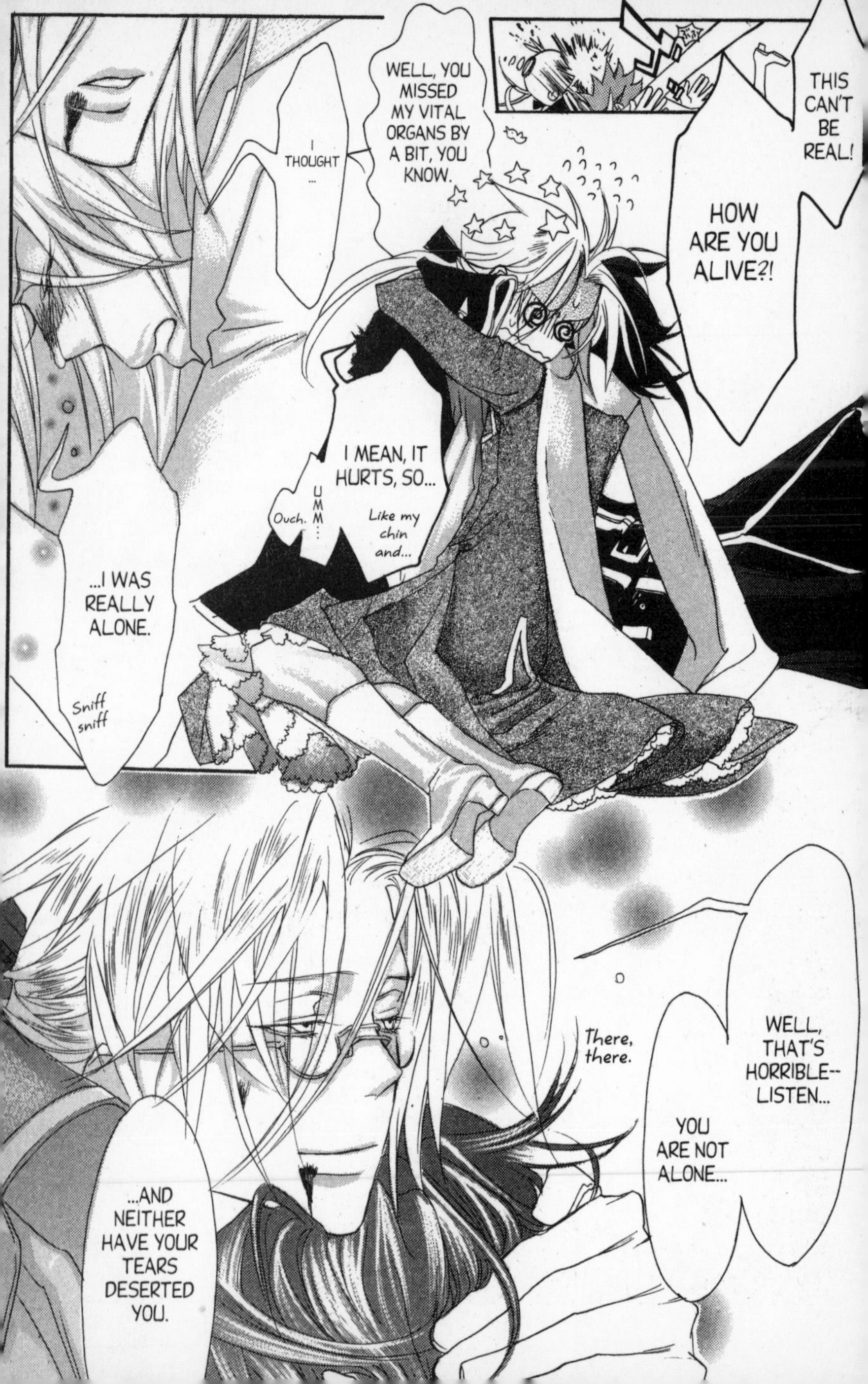
THIS CAN'T BE REAL!
HOW ARE YOU ALIVE?!
WELL, YOU MISSED MY VITAL ORGANS BY A BIT, YOU KNOW.
I MEAN, IT HURTS, SO...
Like my chin and...
UMM...
Ouch.
I THOUGHT...
...I WAS REALLY ALONE.
Sniff sniff
WELL, THAT'S HORRIBLE-- LISTEN...
YOU ARE NOT ALONE...
There, there.
...AND NEITHER HAVE YOUR TEARS DESERTED YOU.

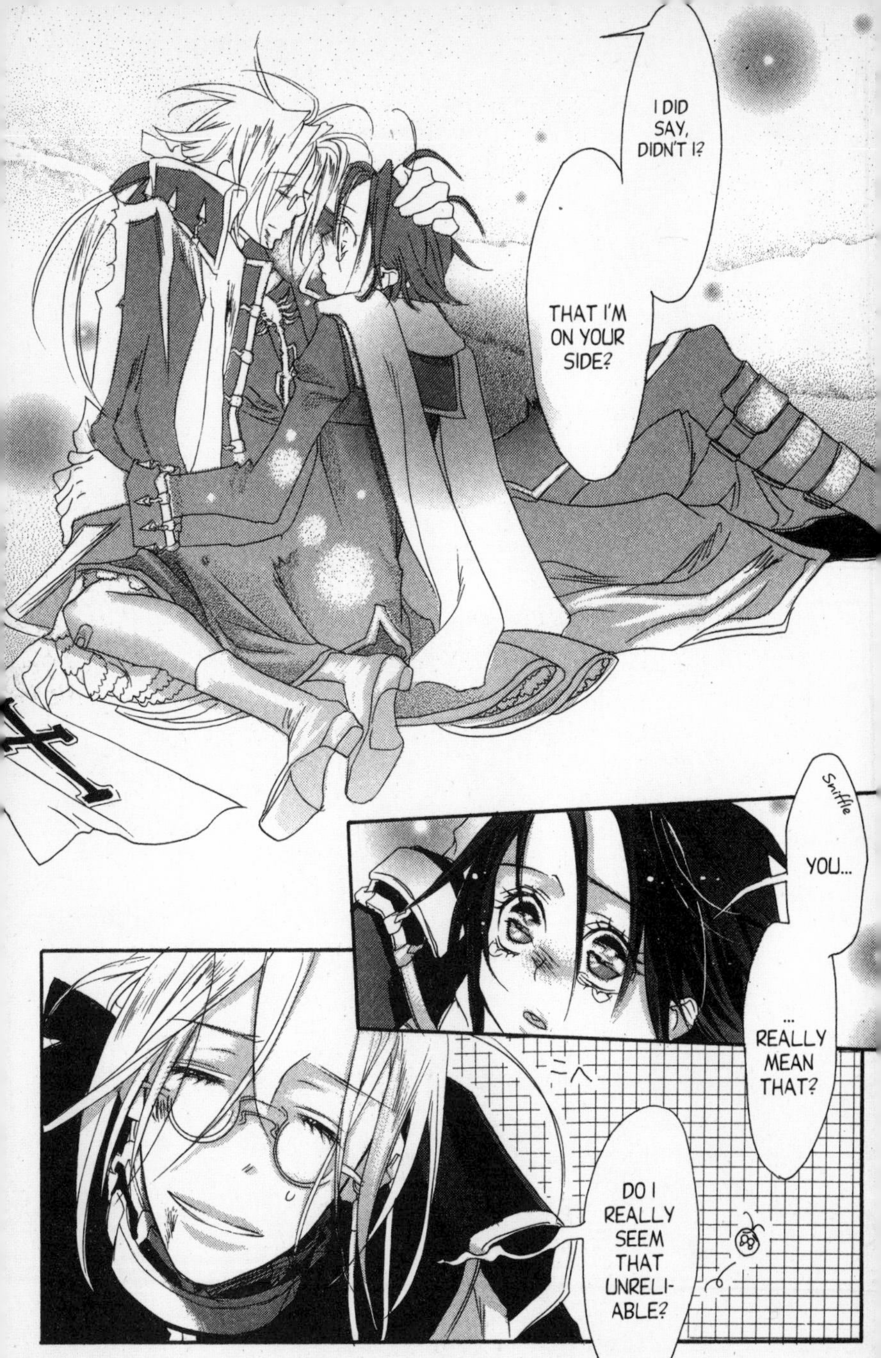
I DID SAY, DIDN'T I?
THAT I'M ON YOUR SIDE?
Sniffle
YOU...
... REALLY MEAN THAT?
ニヘ
DO I REALLY SEEM THAT UNRELI-ABLE?

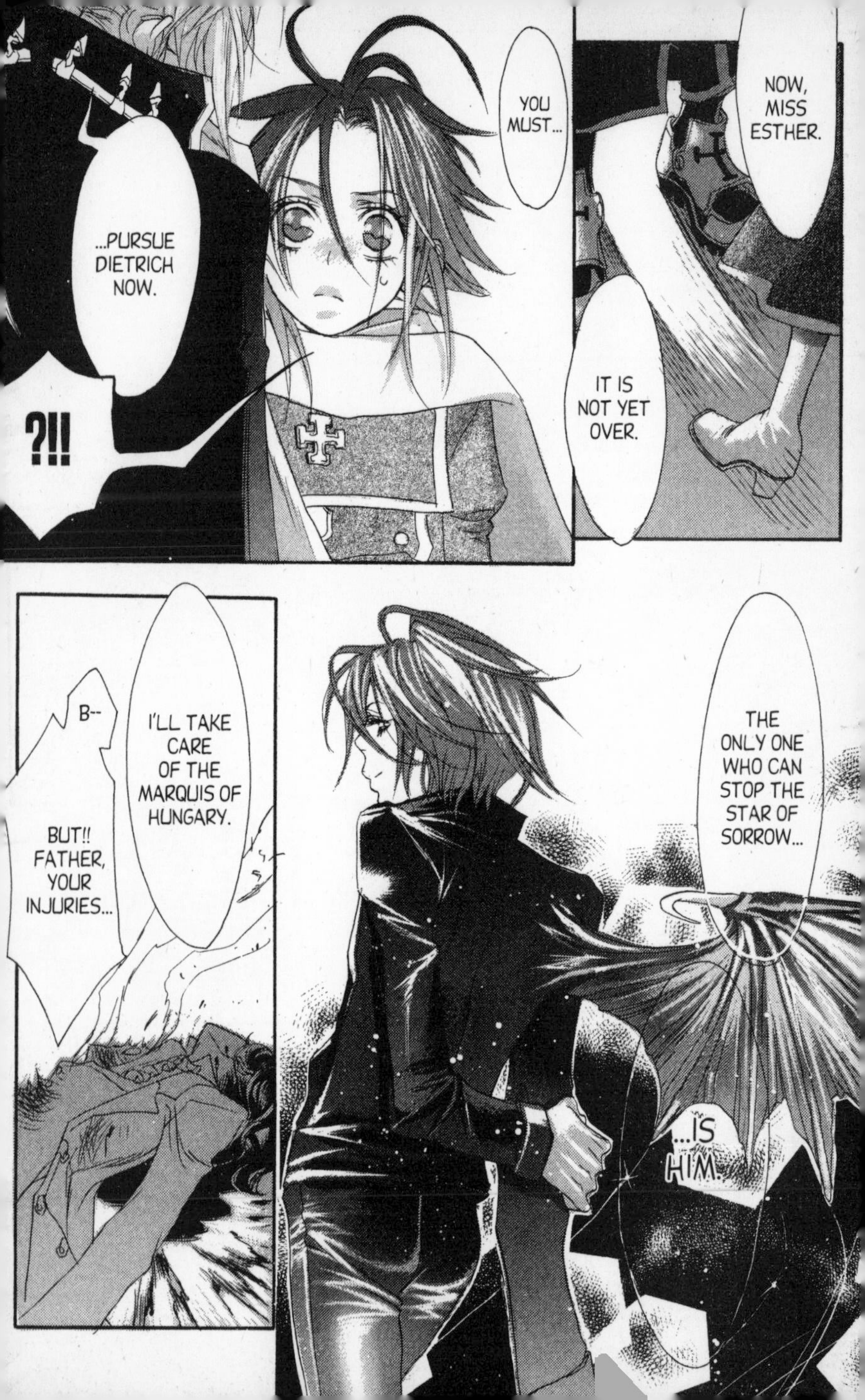
NOW, MISS ESTHER.
IT IS NOT YET OVER.
YOU MUST...
...PURSUE DIETRICH NOW.
?!!
THE ONLY ONE WHO CAN STOP THE STAR OF SORROW...
...IS HIM.
I'LL TAKE CARE OF THE MARQUIS OF HUNGARY.
B--
BUT!! FATHER, YOUR INJURIES...

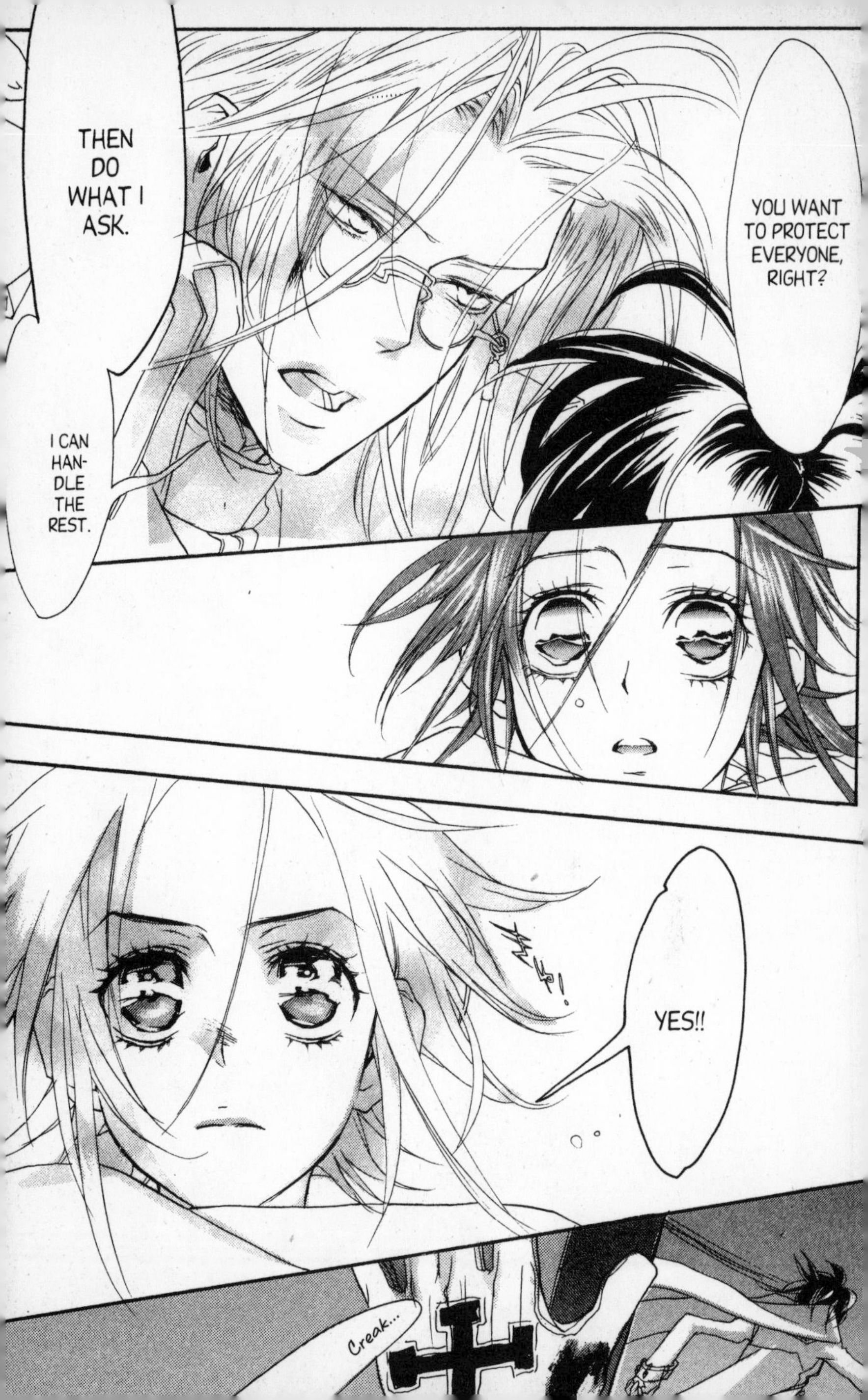
YOU WANT TO PROTECT EVERYONE, RIGHT?
THEN DO WHAT I ASK.
I CAN HAN-DLE THE REST.
YES!!
Creak...

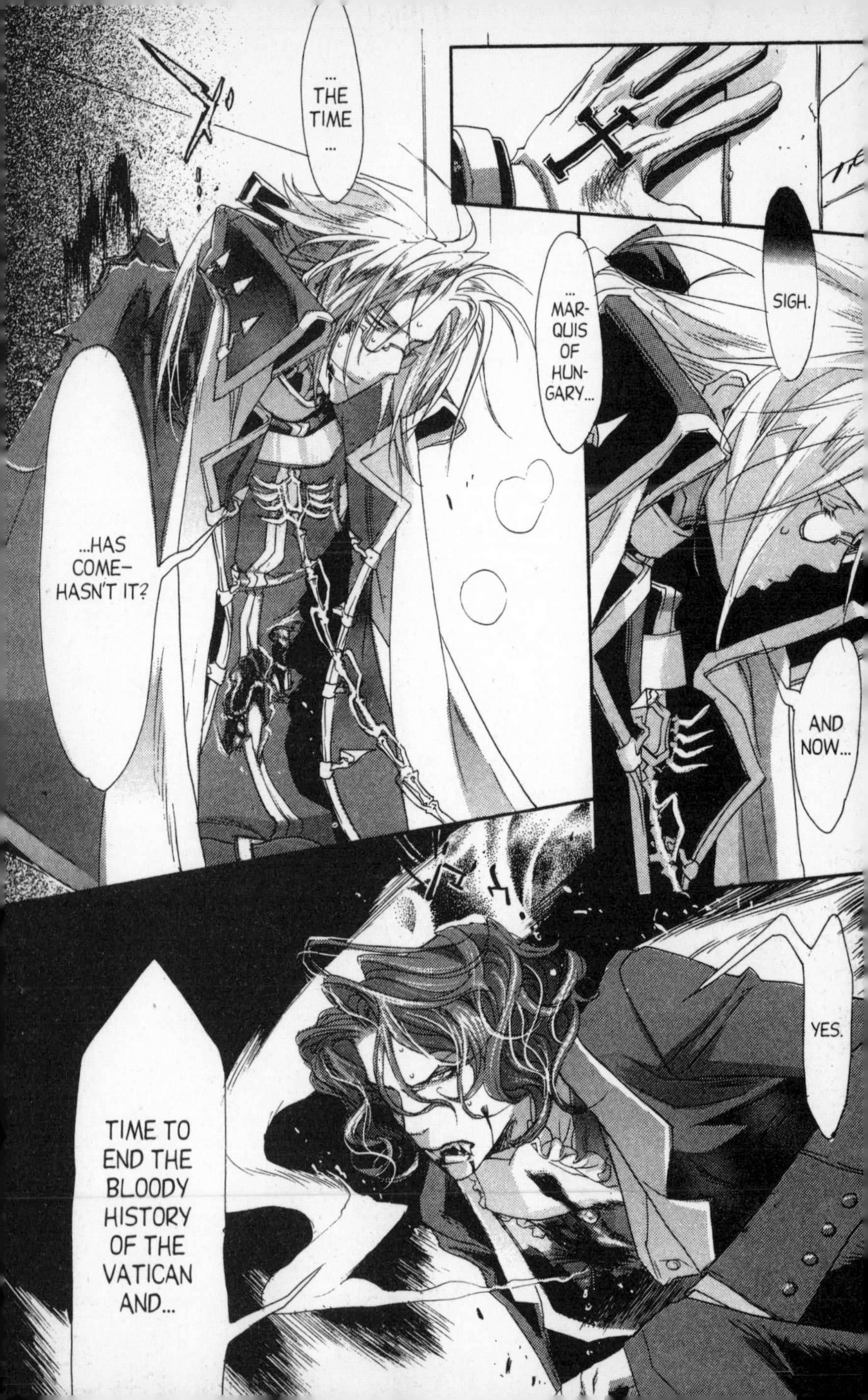
SIGH.
... MARQUIS OF HUNGARY...
AND NOW...
... THE TIME ...
...HAS COME—HASN'T IT?
YES.
TIME TO END THE BLOODY HISTORY OF THE VATICAN AND...

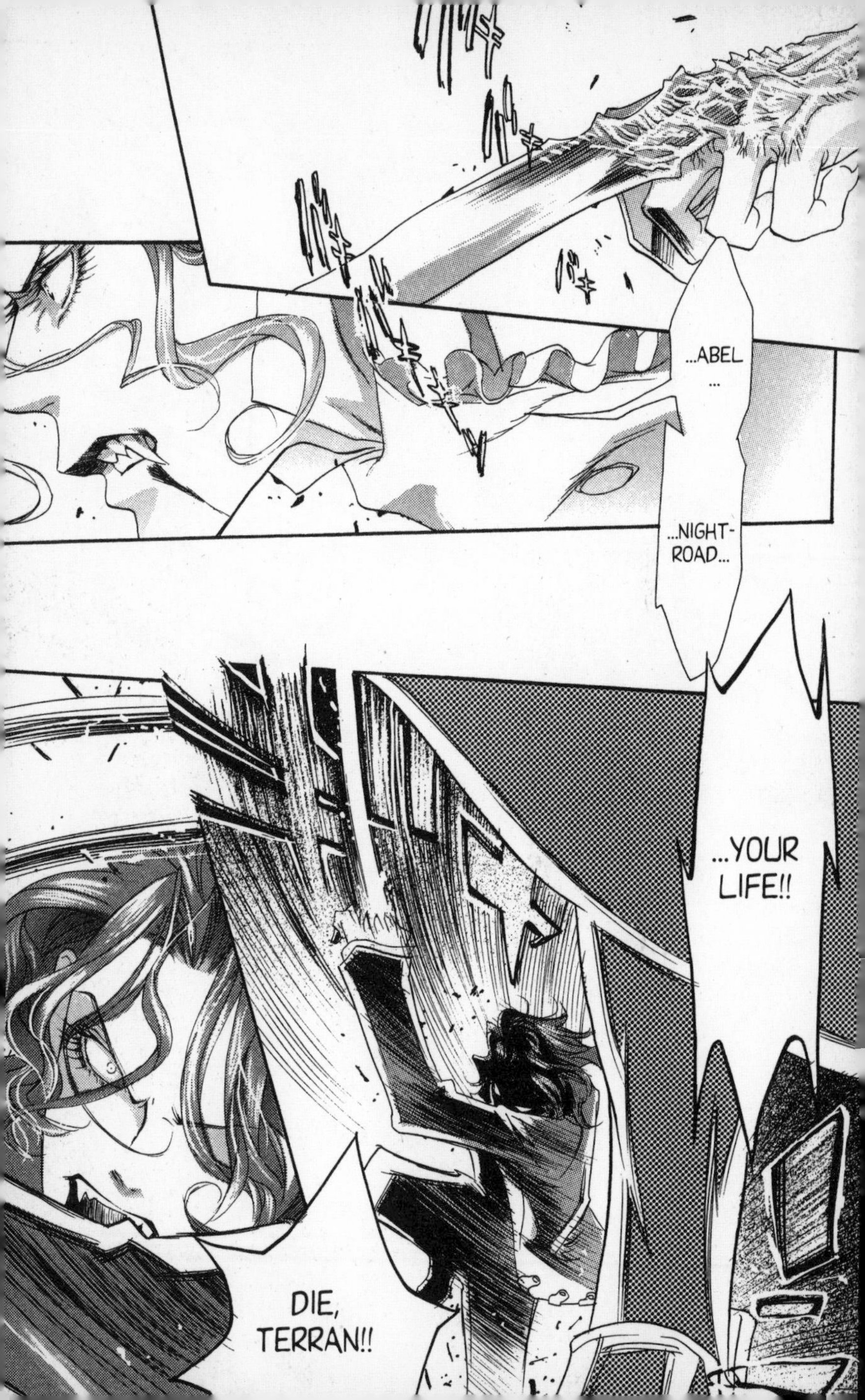
...ABEL ...
...NIGHT-ROAD...
...YOUR LIFE!!
DIE, TERRAN!!

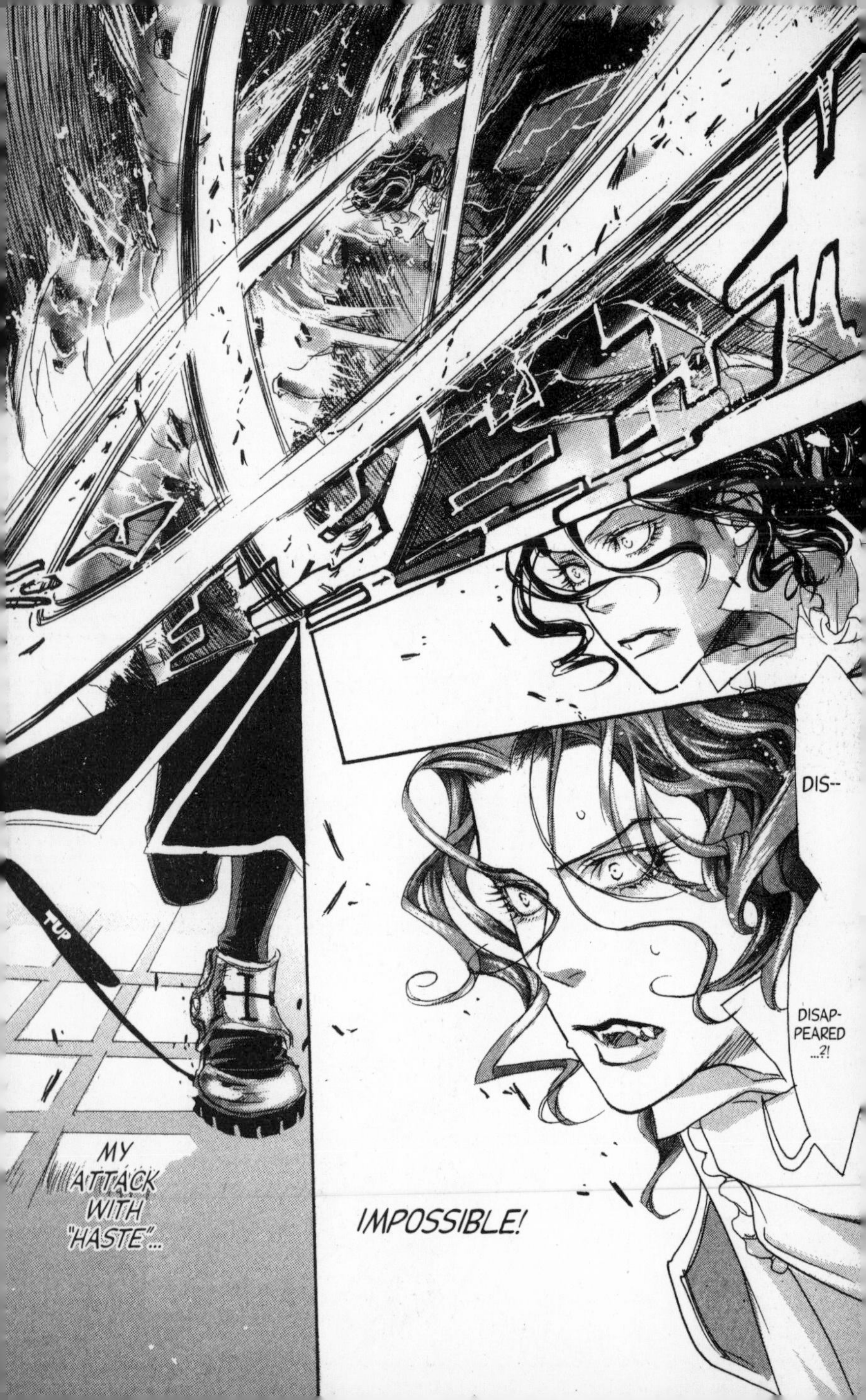
DIS--
DISAP-PEARED ...?!
IMPOSSIBLE!
TUP
MY ATTACK WITH "HASTE"...

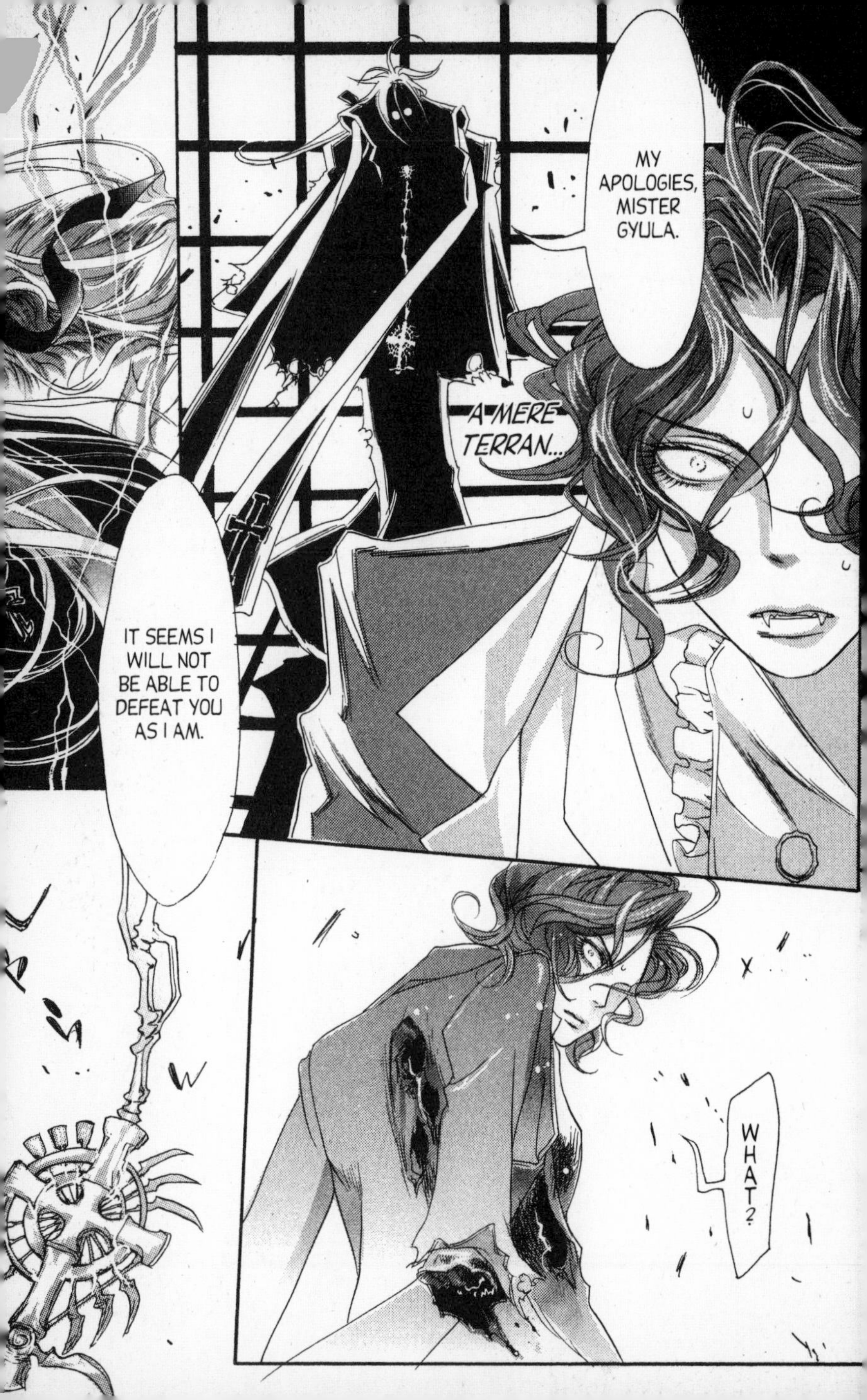
MY APOLOGIES, MISTER GYULA.
A MERE TERRAN...
IT SEEMS I WILL NOT BE ABLE TO DEFEAT YOU AS I AM.
WHAT?

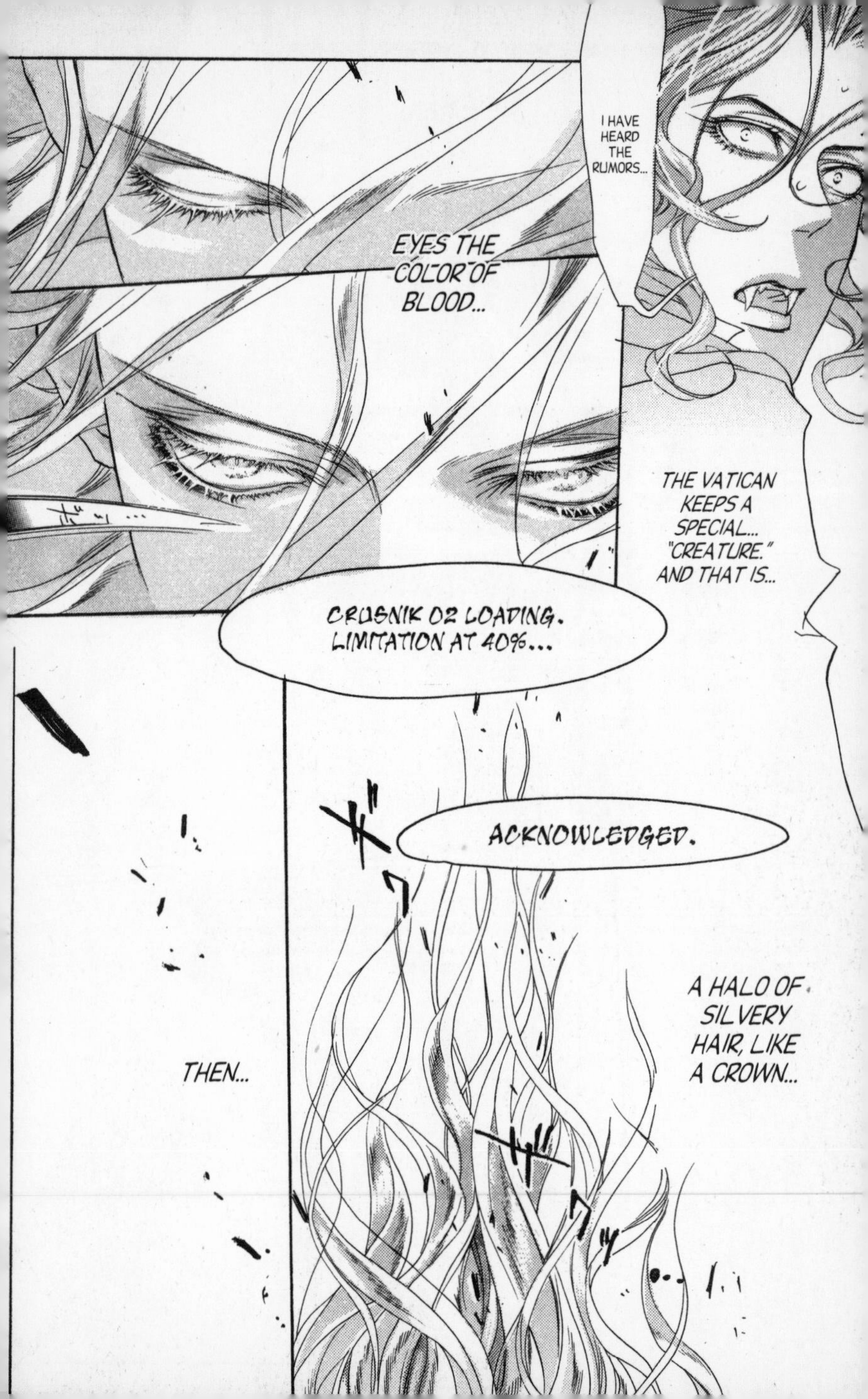
I HAVE HEARD THE RUMORS...
EYES THE COLOR OF BLOOD...
THE VATICAN KEEPS A SPECIAL... "CREATURE." AND THAT IS...
CRUSNIK 02 LOADING. LIMITATION AT 40%...
ACKNOWLEDGED.
A HALO OF SILVERY HAIR, LIKE A CROWN...
THEN...

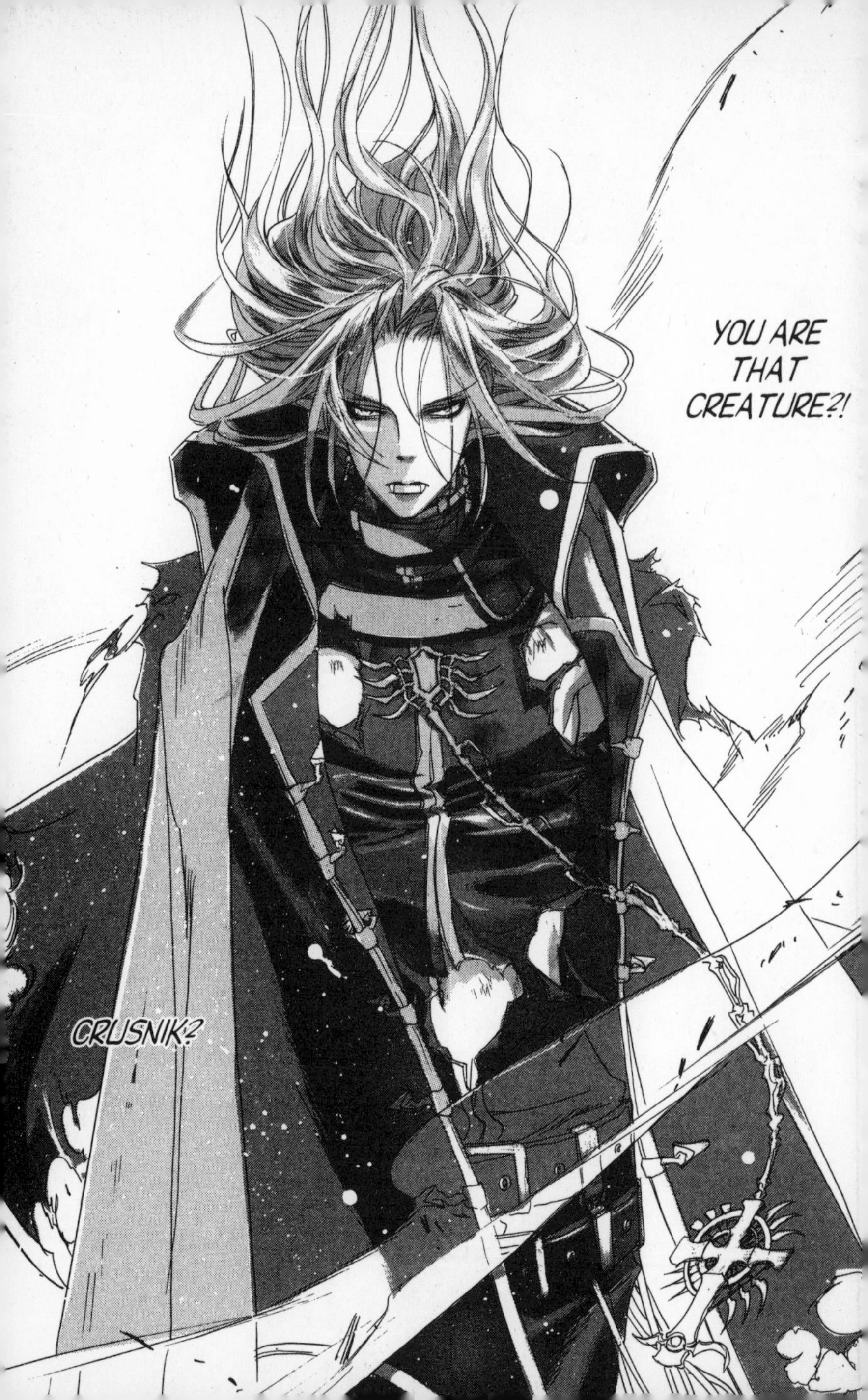
YOU ARE THAT CREATURE?!
CRUSNIK?

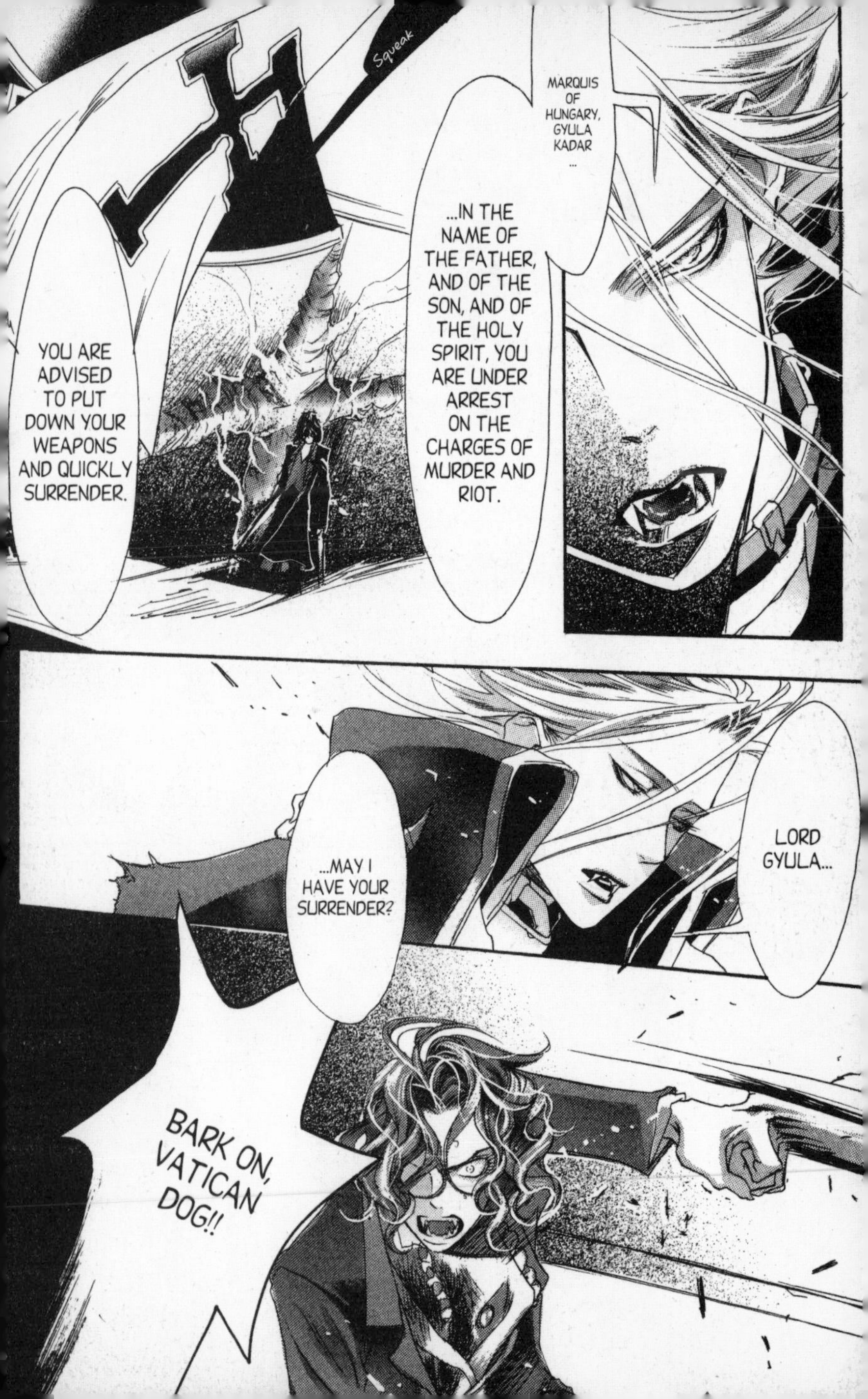
MARQUIS OF HUNGARY, GYULA KADAR ...
...IN THE NAME OF THE FATHER, AND OF THE SON, AND OF THE HOLY SPIRIT, YOU ARE UNDER ARREST ON THE CHARGES OF MURDER AND RIOT.
Squeak
YOU ARE ADVISED TO PUT DOWN YOUR WEAPONS AND QUICKLY SURRENDER.
LORD GYULA...
...MAY I HAVE YOUR SURRENDER?
BARK ON, VATICAN DOG!!

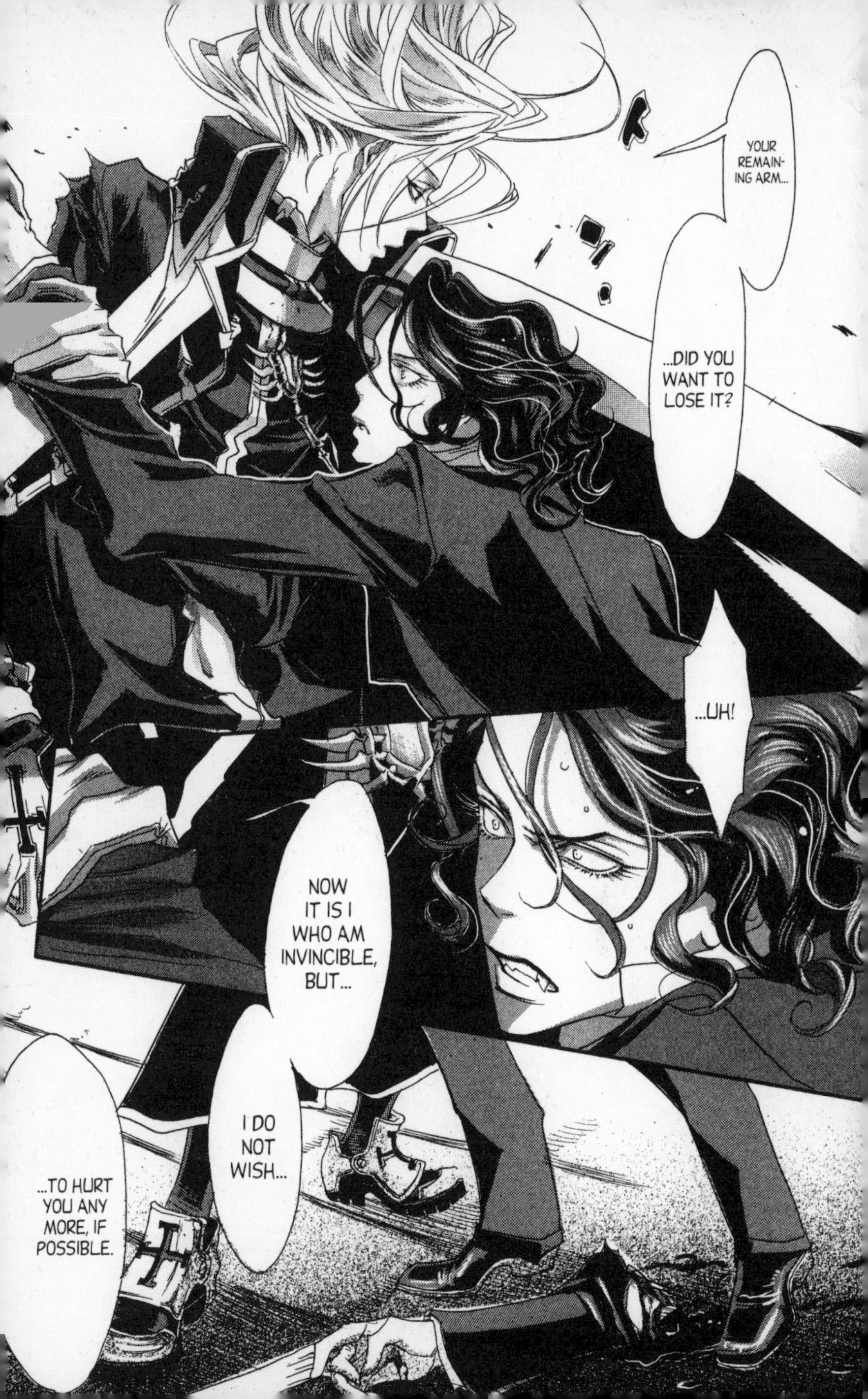
YOUR REMAINING ARM...
...DID YOU WANT TO LOSE IT?
...UH!
NOW IT IS I WHO AM INVINCIBLE, BUT...
I DO NOT WISH...
...TO HURT YOU ANY MORE, IF POSSIBLE.

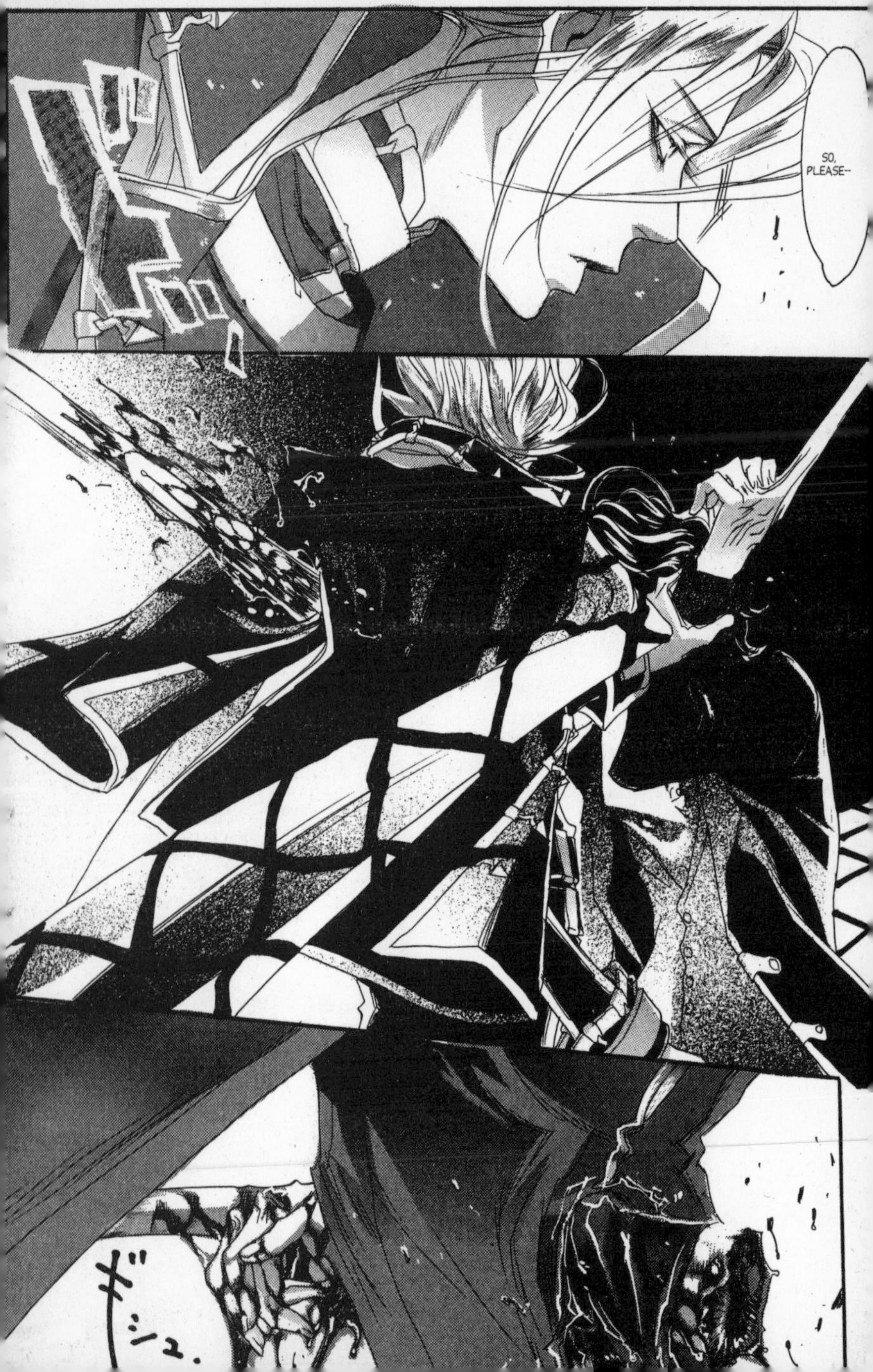
SO, PLEASE--
ザシュ.

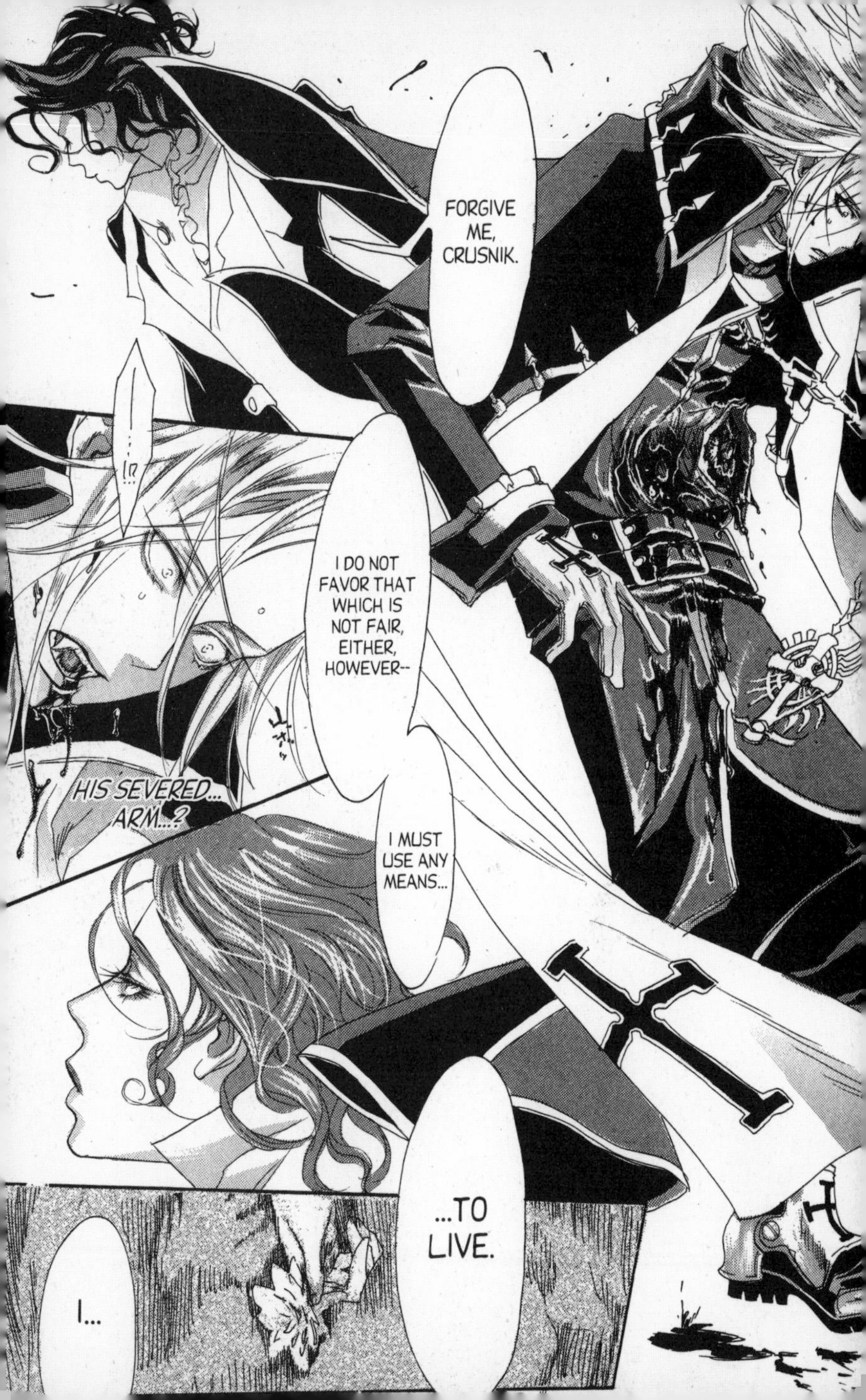

FORGIVE ME, CRUSNIK.
I DO NOT FAVOR THAT WHICH IS NOT FAIR, EITHER, HOWEVER--
...!?
HIS SEVERED... ARM...?
I MUST USE ANY MEANS...
...TO LIVE.
I...

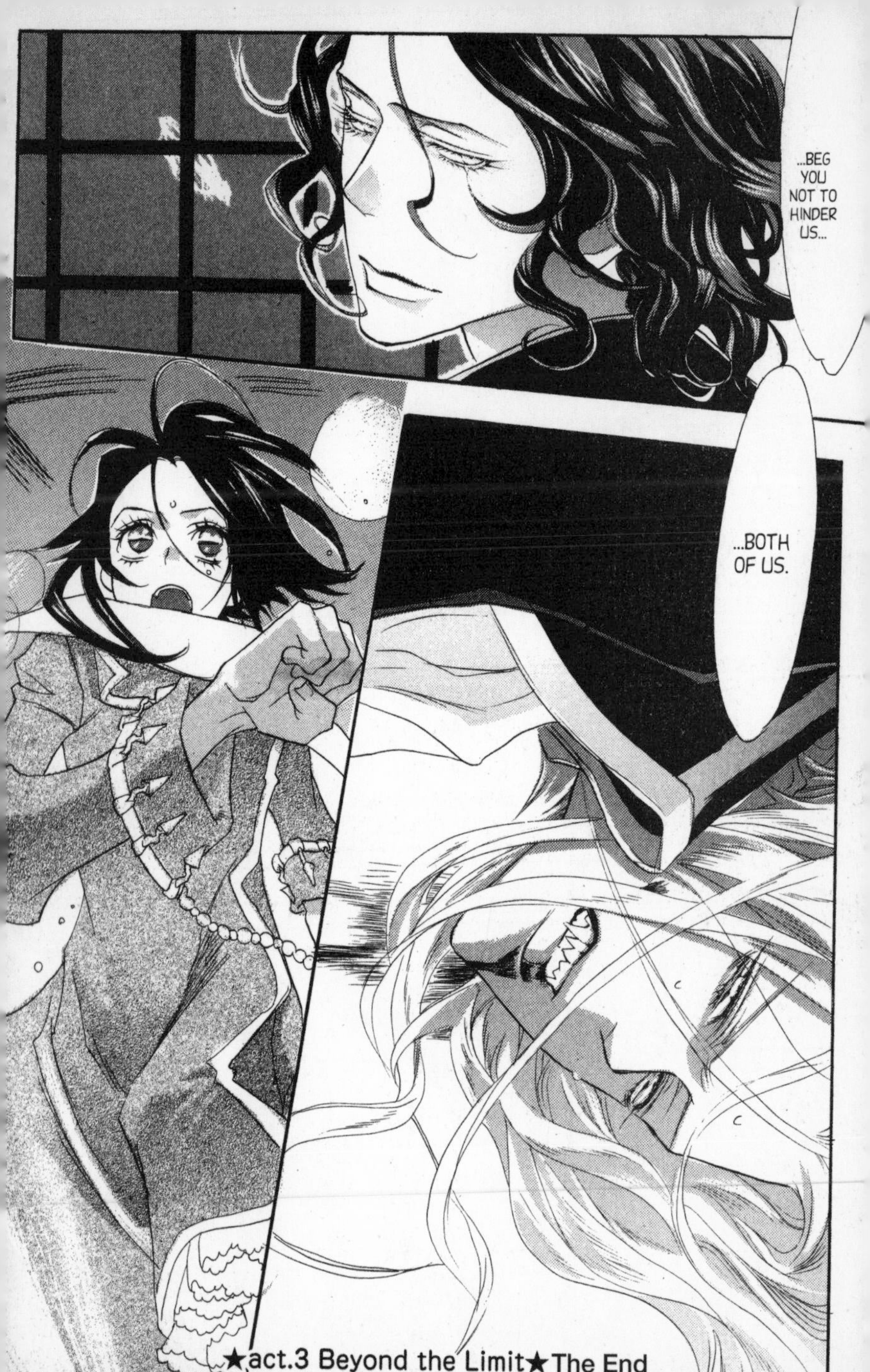
...BEG YOU NOT TO HINDER US...
...BOTH OF US.

★act.3 Beyond the Limit★The End

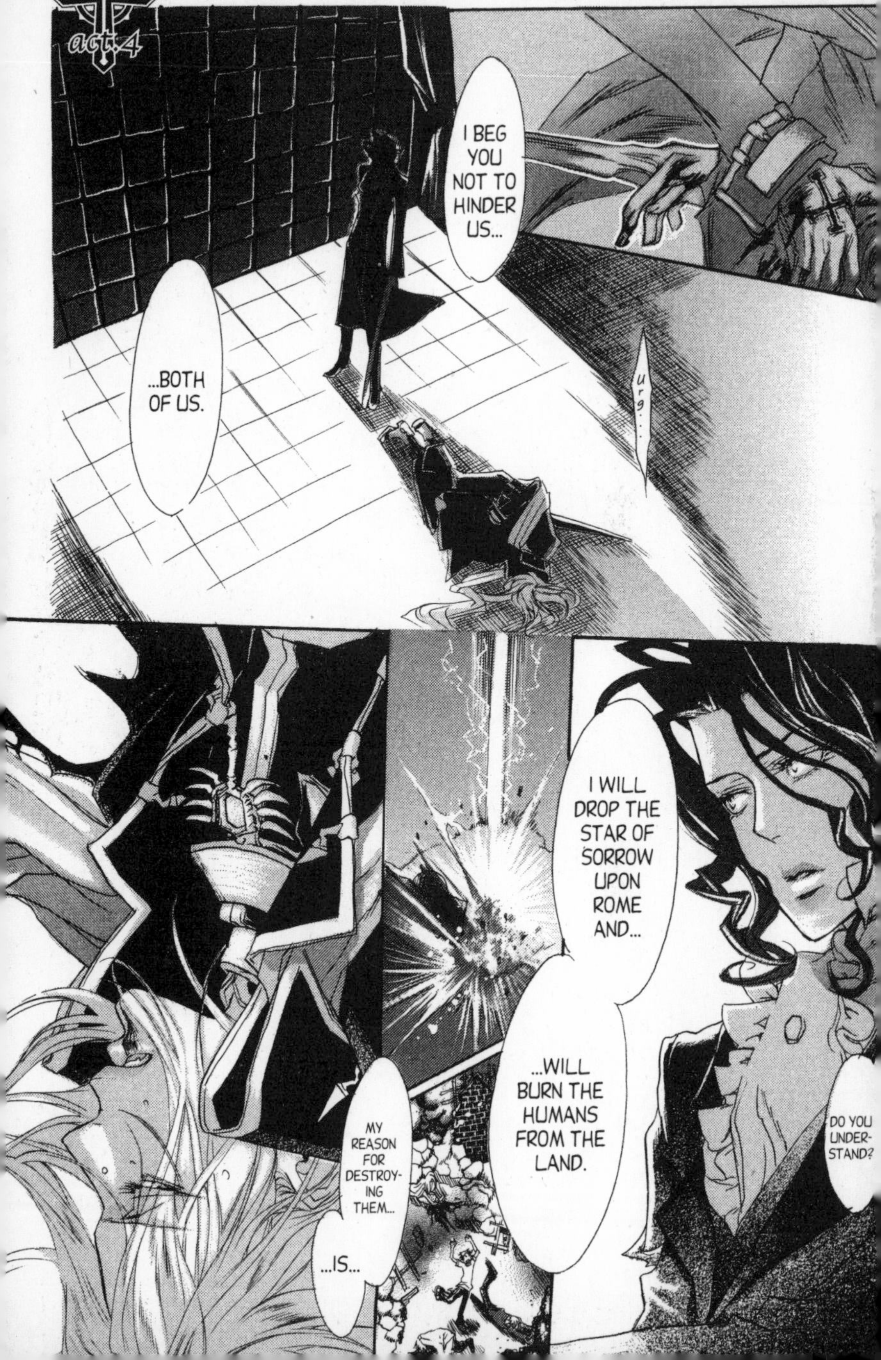
I BEG YOU NOT TO HINDER US...
urg...
...BOTH OF US.
I WILL DROP THE STAR OF SORROW UPON ROME AND...
...WILL BURN THE HUMANS FROM THE LAND.
DO YOU UNDERSTAND?
MY REASON FOR DESTROYING THEM...
...IS...

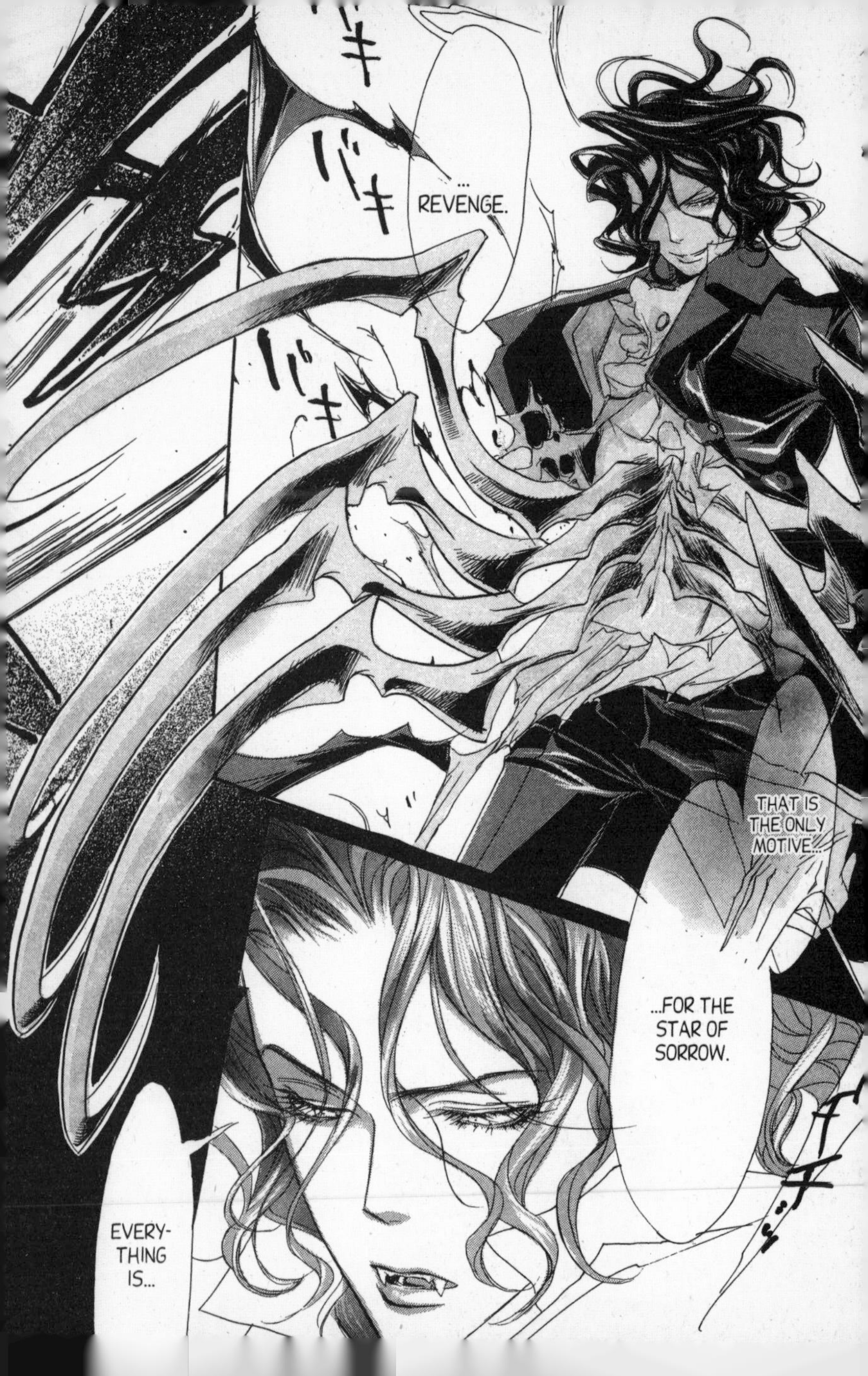

...REVENGE.
バキ
バキ
THAT IS THE ONLY MOTIVE...
...FOR THE STAR OF SORROW.
EVERY-THING IS...

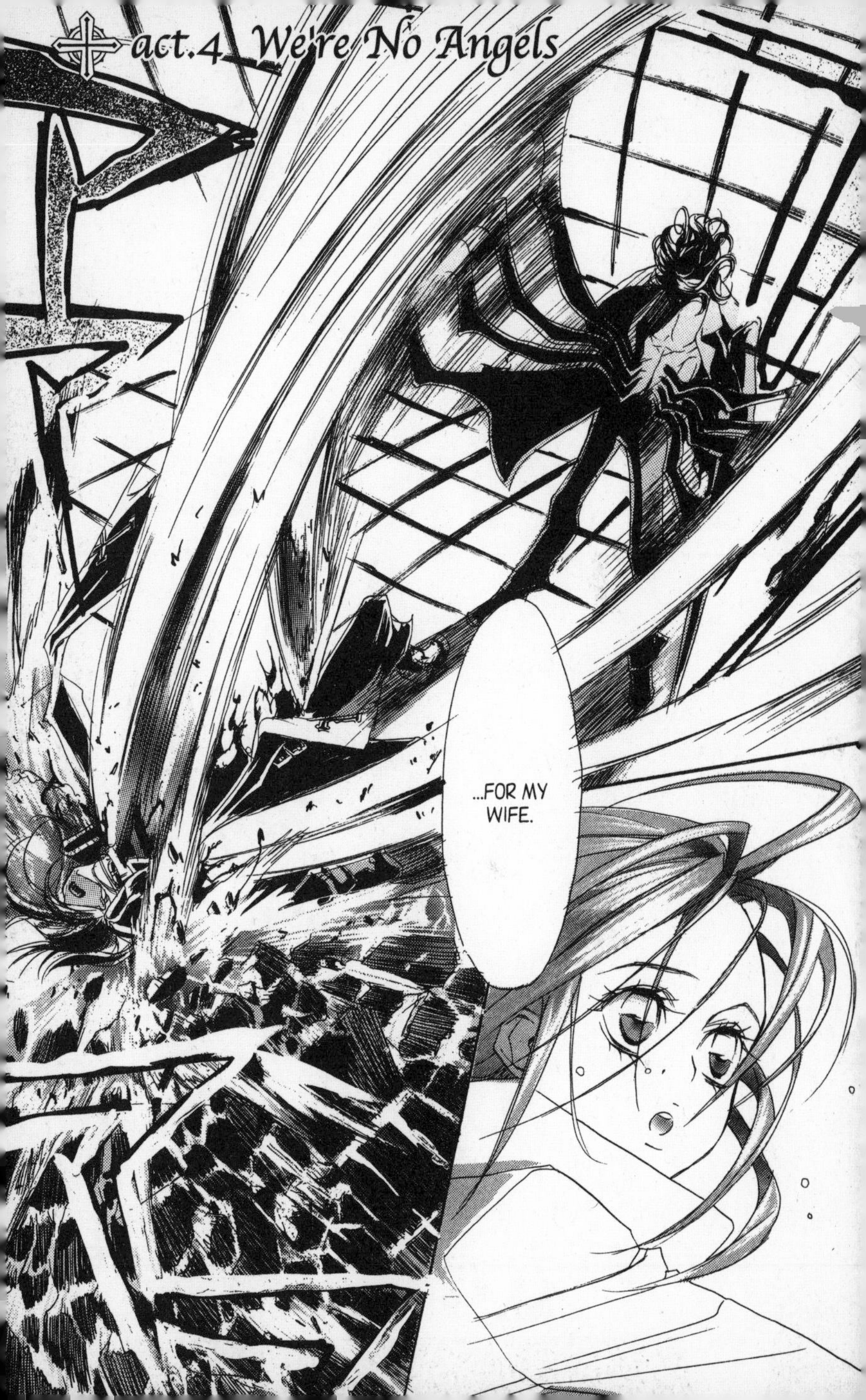
act.4 We're No Angels
...FOR MY WIFE.

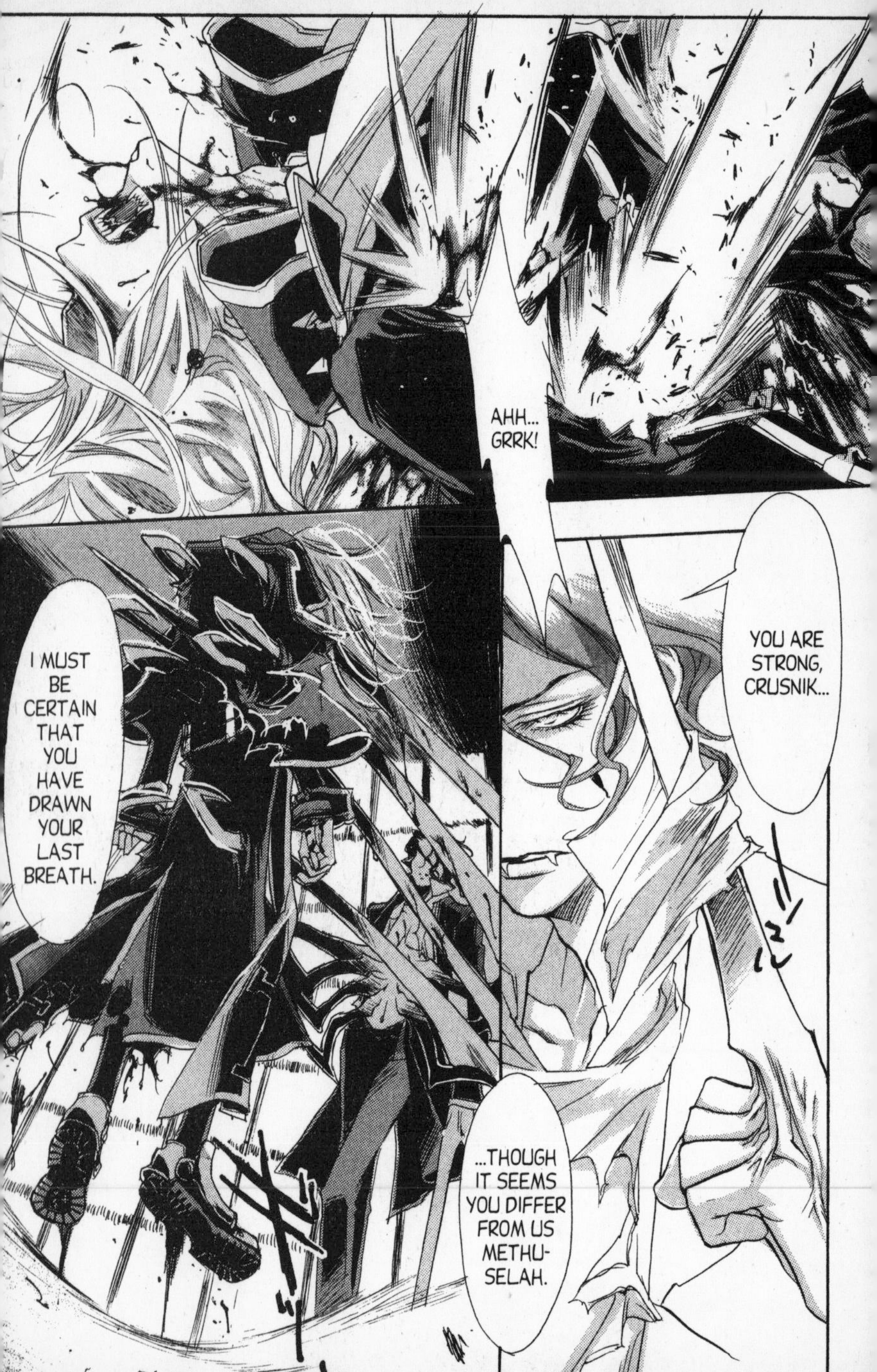
AHH... GRRK!
YOU ARE STRONG, CRUSNIK...
...THOUGH IT SEEMS YOU DIFFER FROM US METHU-SELAH.
I MUST BE CERTAIN THAT YOU HAVE DRAWN YOUR LAST BREATH.

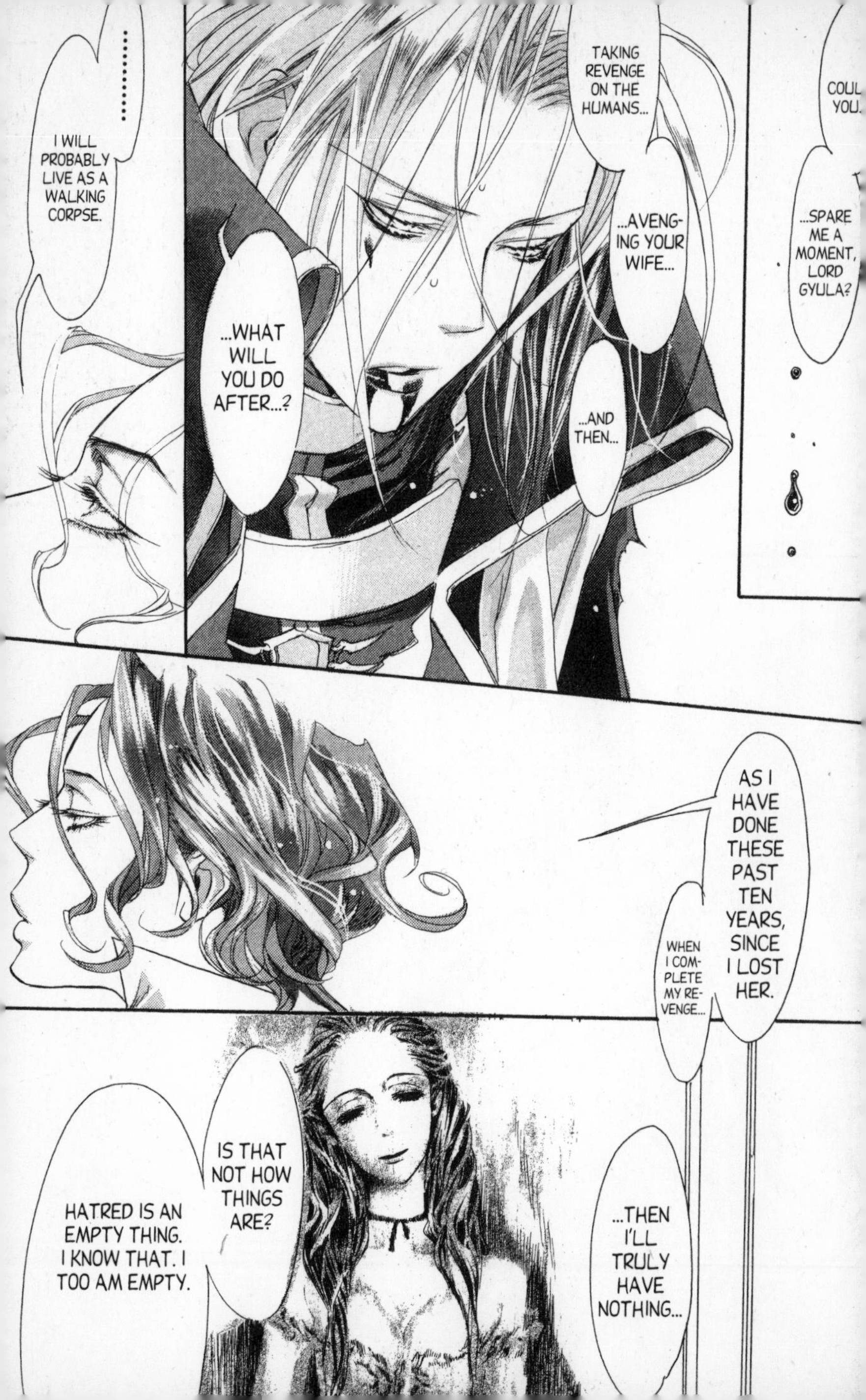
COUL YOU.
...SPARE ME A MOMENT, LORD GYULA?
TAKING REVENGE ON THE HUMANS...
...AVENGING YOUR WIFE...
...AND THEN...
...WHAT WILL YOU DO AFTER...?
......
I WILL PROBABLY LIVE AS A WALKING CORPSE.
AS I HAVE DONE THESE PAST TEN YEARS, SINCE I LOST HER.
WHEN I COMPLETE MY REVENGE...
...THEN I'LL TRULY HAVE NOTHING...
IS THAT NOT HOW THINGS ARE?
HATRED IS AN EMPTY THING. I KNOW THAT. I TOO AM EMPTY.

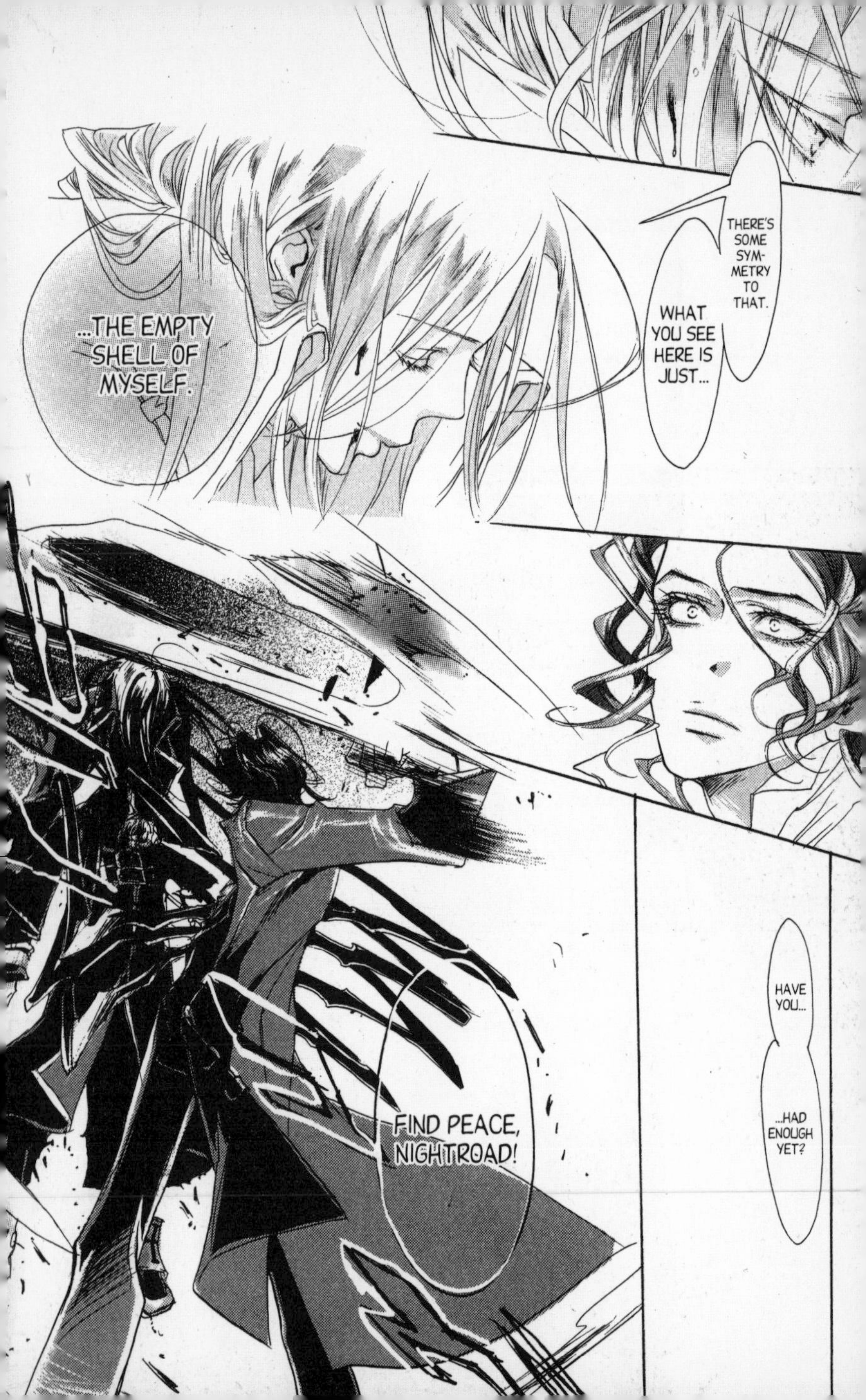
THERE'S SOME SYMMETRY TO THAT.
WHAT YOU SEE HERE IS JUST...
...THE EMPTY SHELL OF MYSELF.
HAVE YOU...
...HAD ENOUGH YET?
FIND PEACE, NIGHTROAD!

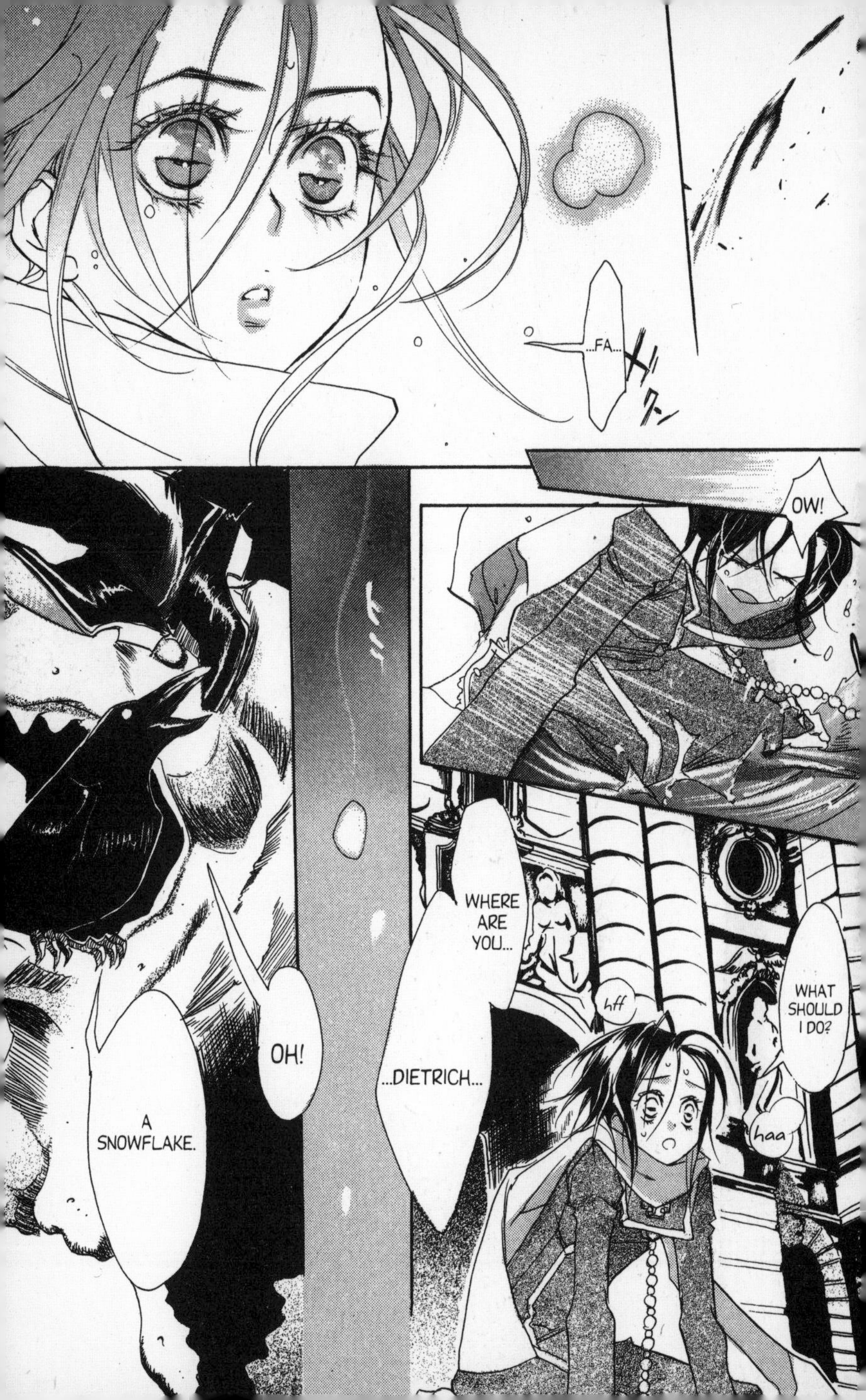
...FA...
OW!
WHERE ARE YOU...
hff
WHAT SHOULD I DO?
haa
...DIETRICH...
OH!
A SNOWFLAKE.

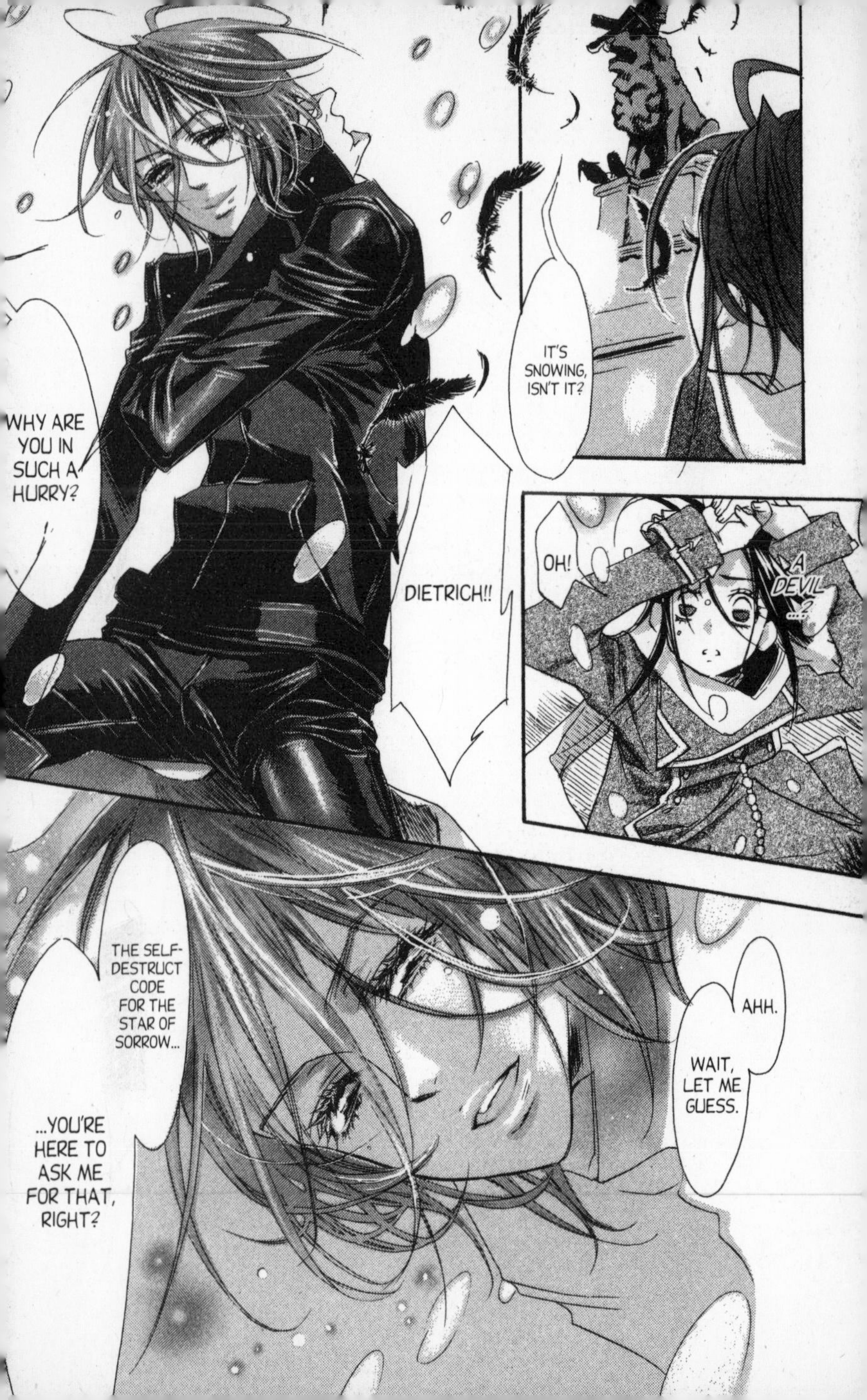
IT'S SNOWING, ISN'T IT?
OH!
A DEVIL ...?
DIETRICH!!
WHY ARE YOU IN SUCH A HURRY?
AHH.
WAIT, LET ME GUESS.
THE SELF-DESTRUCT CODE FOR THE STAR OF SORROW...
...YOU'RE HERE TO ASK ME FOR THAT, RIGHT?

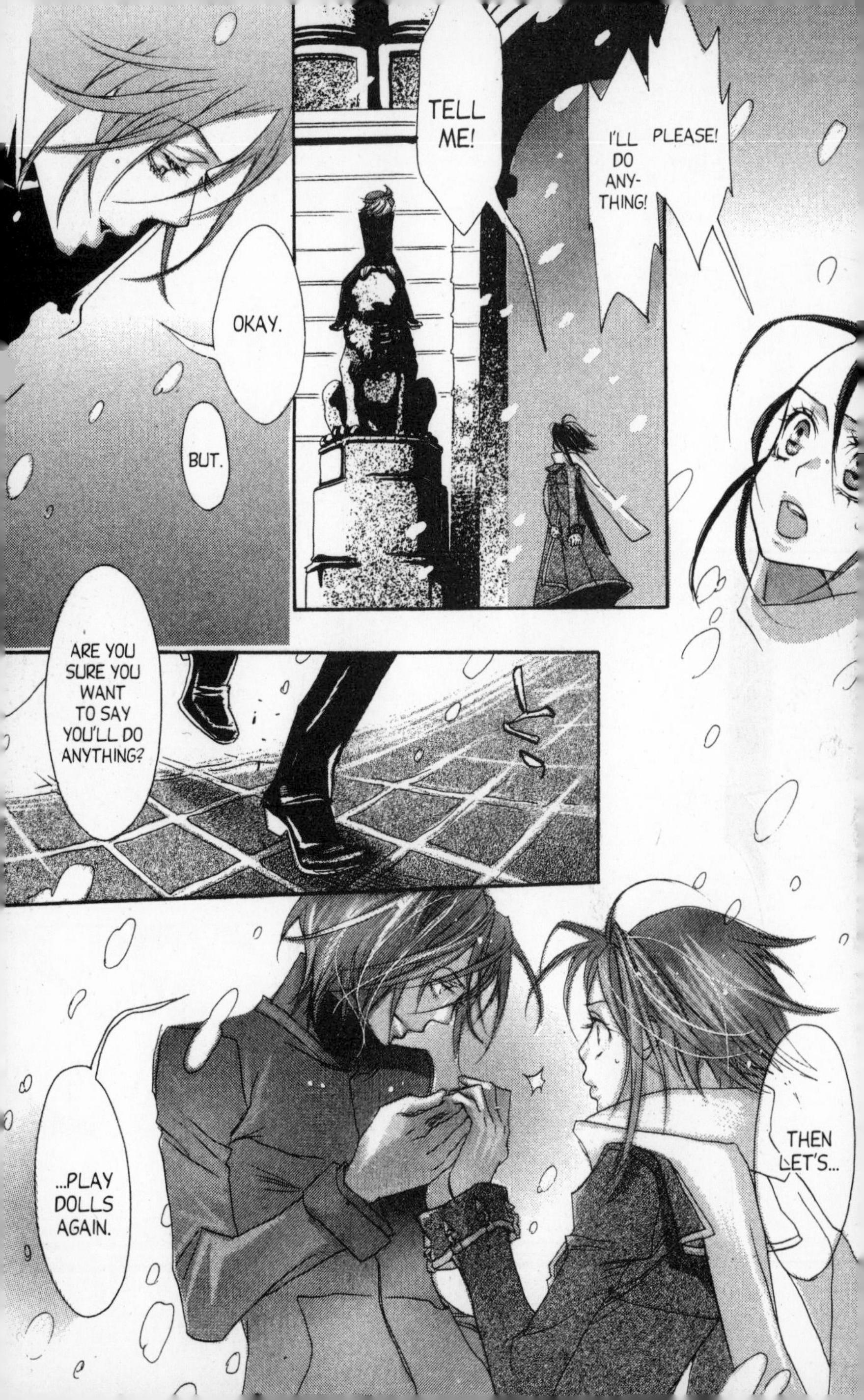
TELL ME!
PLEASE!
I'LL DO ANYTHING!
OKAY.
BUT.
ARE YOU SURE YOU WANT TO SAY YOU'LL DO ANYTHING?
THEN LET'S...
...PLAY DOLLS AGAIN.

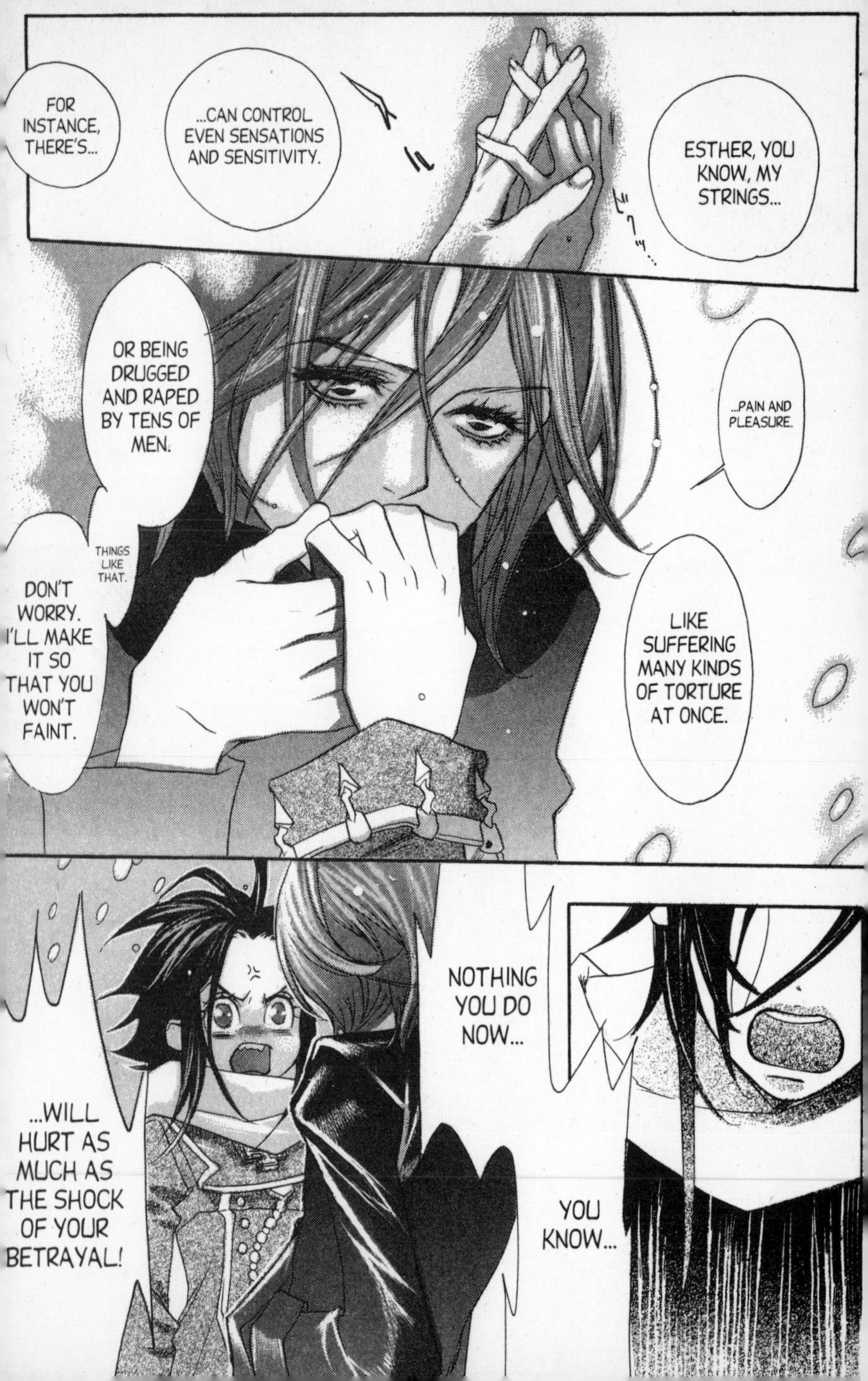
ESTHER, YOU KNOW, MY STRINGS...
...CAN CONTROL EVEN SENSATIONS AND SENSITIVITY.
FOR INSTANCE, THERE'S...
...PAIN AND PLEASURE.
LIKE SUFFERING MANY KINDS OF TORTURE AT ONCE.
OR BEING DRUGGED AND RAPED BY TENS OF MEN.
THINGS LIKE THAT.
DON'T WORRY. I'LL MAKE IT SO THAT YOU WON'T FAINT.
YOU KNOW...
NOTHING YOU DO NOW...
...WILL HURT AS MUCH AS THE SHOCK OF YOUR BETRAYAL!

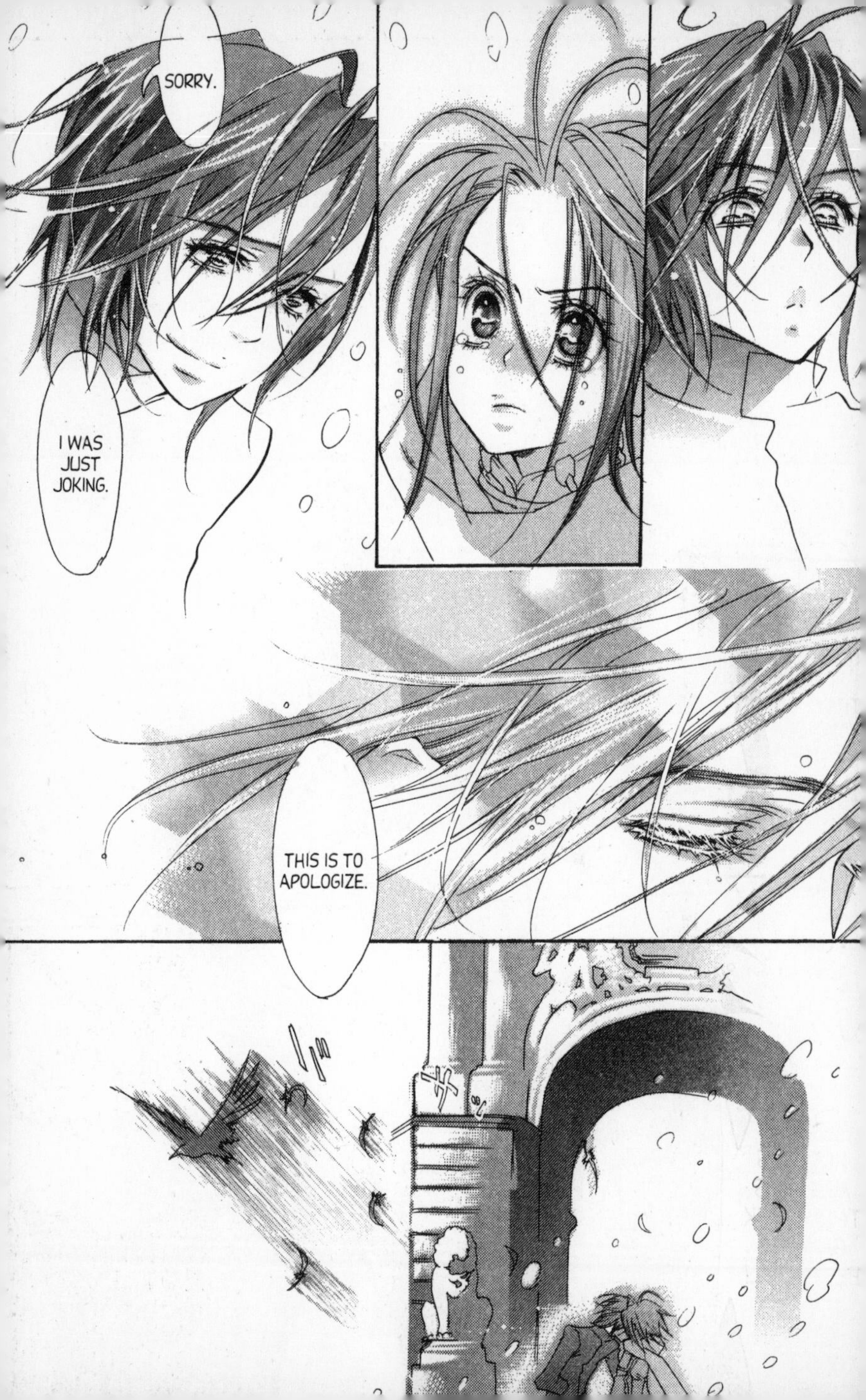
SORRY.
I WAS JUST JOKING.
THIS IS TO APOLOGIZE.

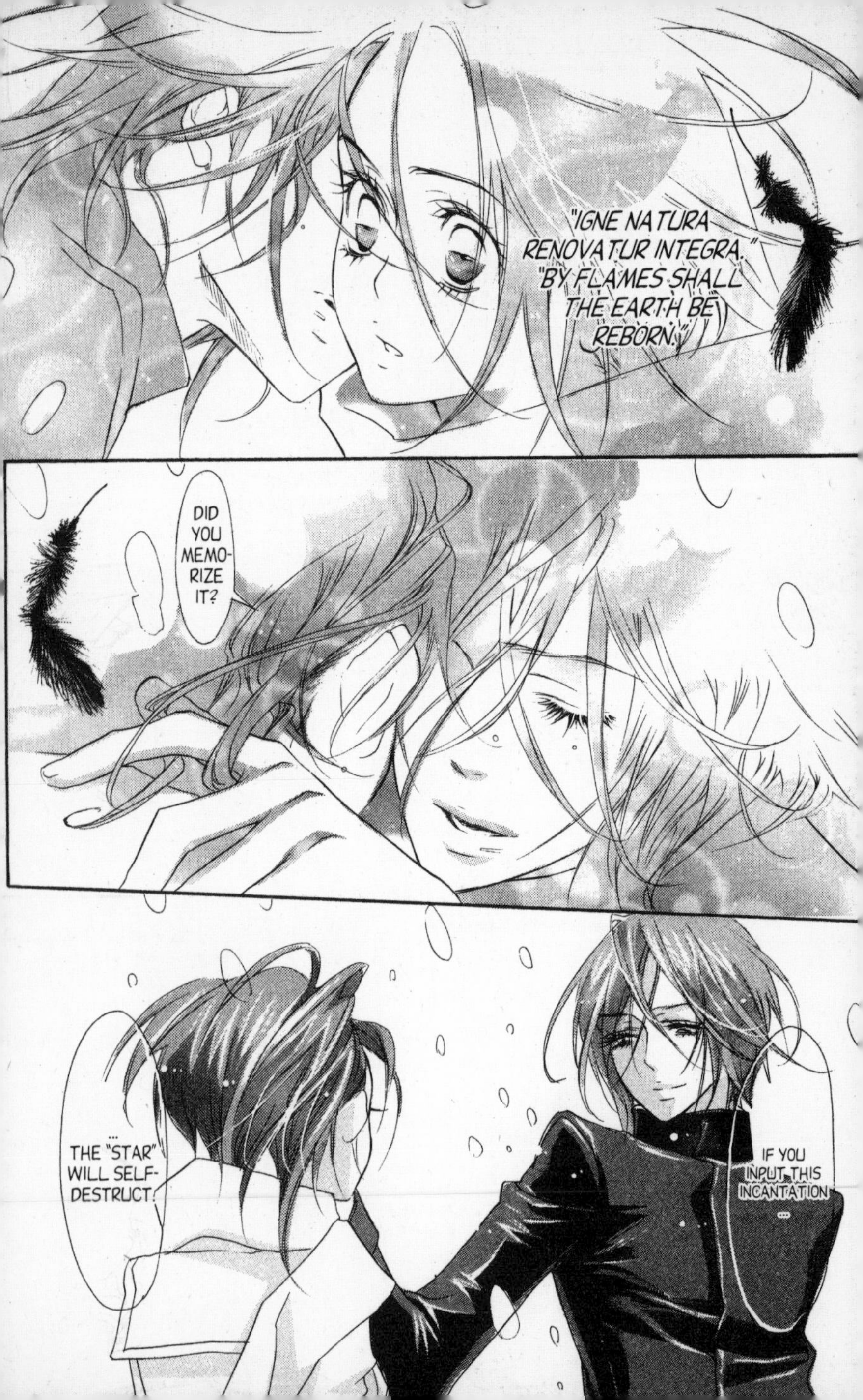
"IGNE NATURA RENOVATUR INTEGRA." "BY FLAMES SHALL THE EARTH BE REBORN."
DID YOU MEMORIZE IT?
IF YOU INPUT THIS INCANTATION ...
... THE "STAR" WILL SELF-DESTRUCT!

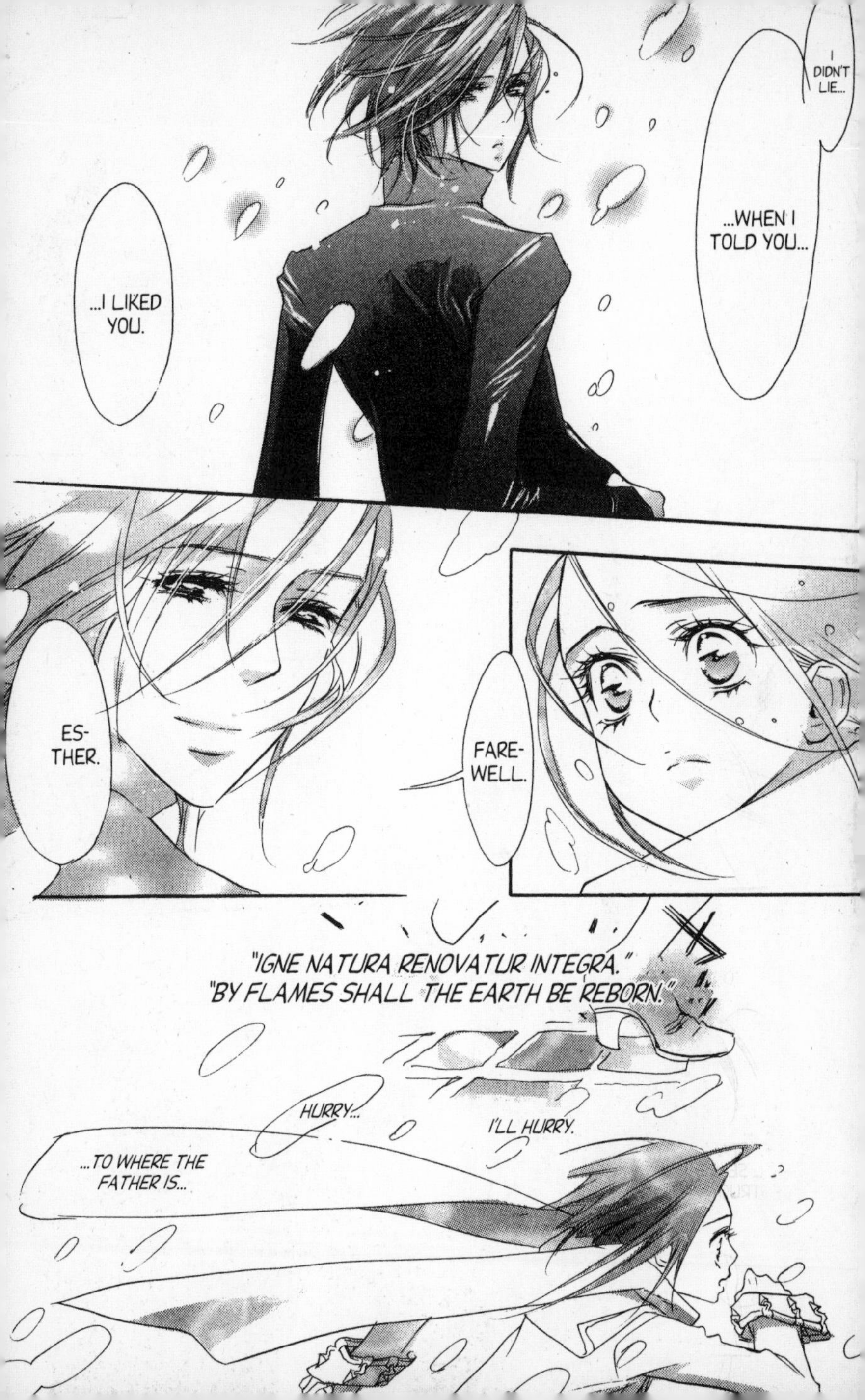
I DIDN'T LIE...
...WHEN I TOLD YOU...
...I LIKED YOU.
FARE-WELL.
ES-THER.
"IGNE NATURA RENOVATUR INTEGRA."
"BY FLAMES SHALL THE EARTH BE REBORN."
I'LL HURRY.
HURRY...
...TO WHERE THE FATHER IS...

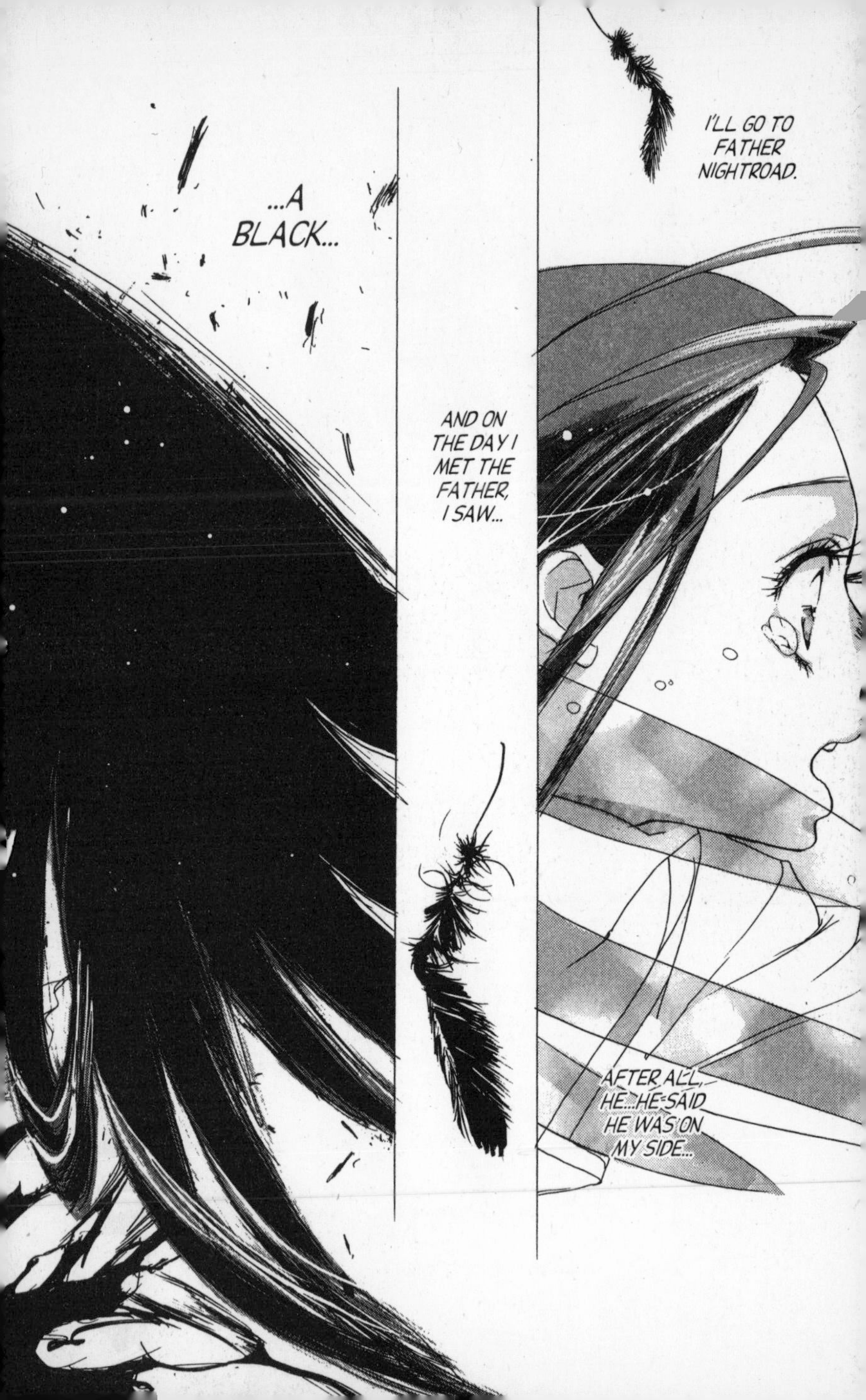
I'LL GO TO FATHER NIGHTROAD.
AFTER ALL, HE...HE SAID HE WAS ON MY SIDE...
AND ON THE DAY I MET THE FATHER, I SAW...
...A BLACK...

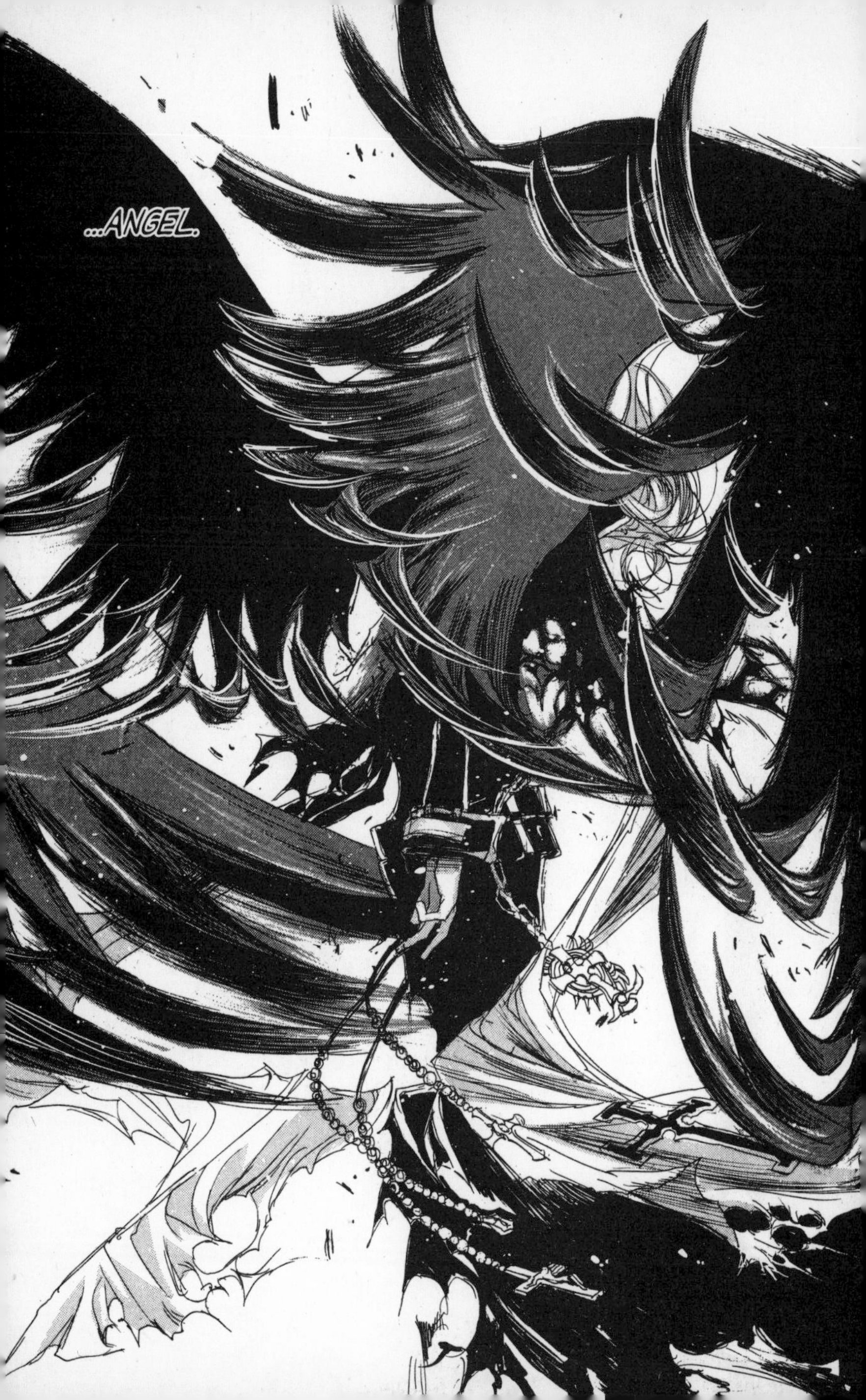
...ANGEL...

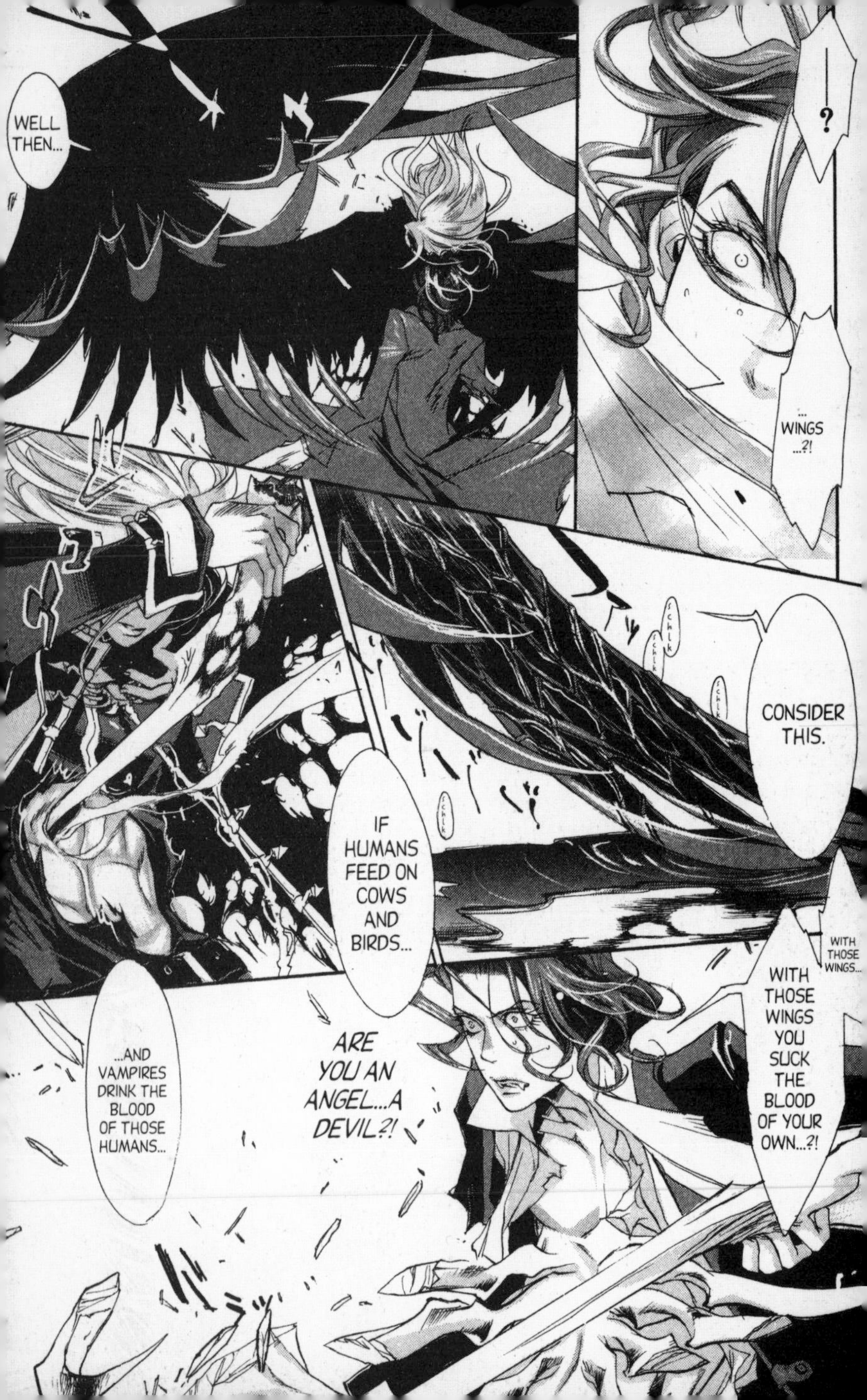
?
...WINGS...?!
WELL THEN...
schlk schlk schlk
CONSIDER THIS.
schlk
IF HUMANS FEED ON COWS AND BIRDS...
WITH THOSE WINGS...
WITH THOSE WINGS YOU SUCK THE BLOOD OF YOUR OWN...?!
ARE YOU AN ANGEL...A DEVIL?!
...AND VAMPIRES DRINK THE BLOOD OF THOSE HUMANS...

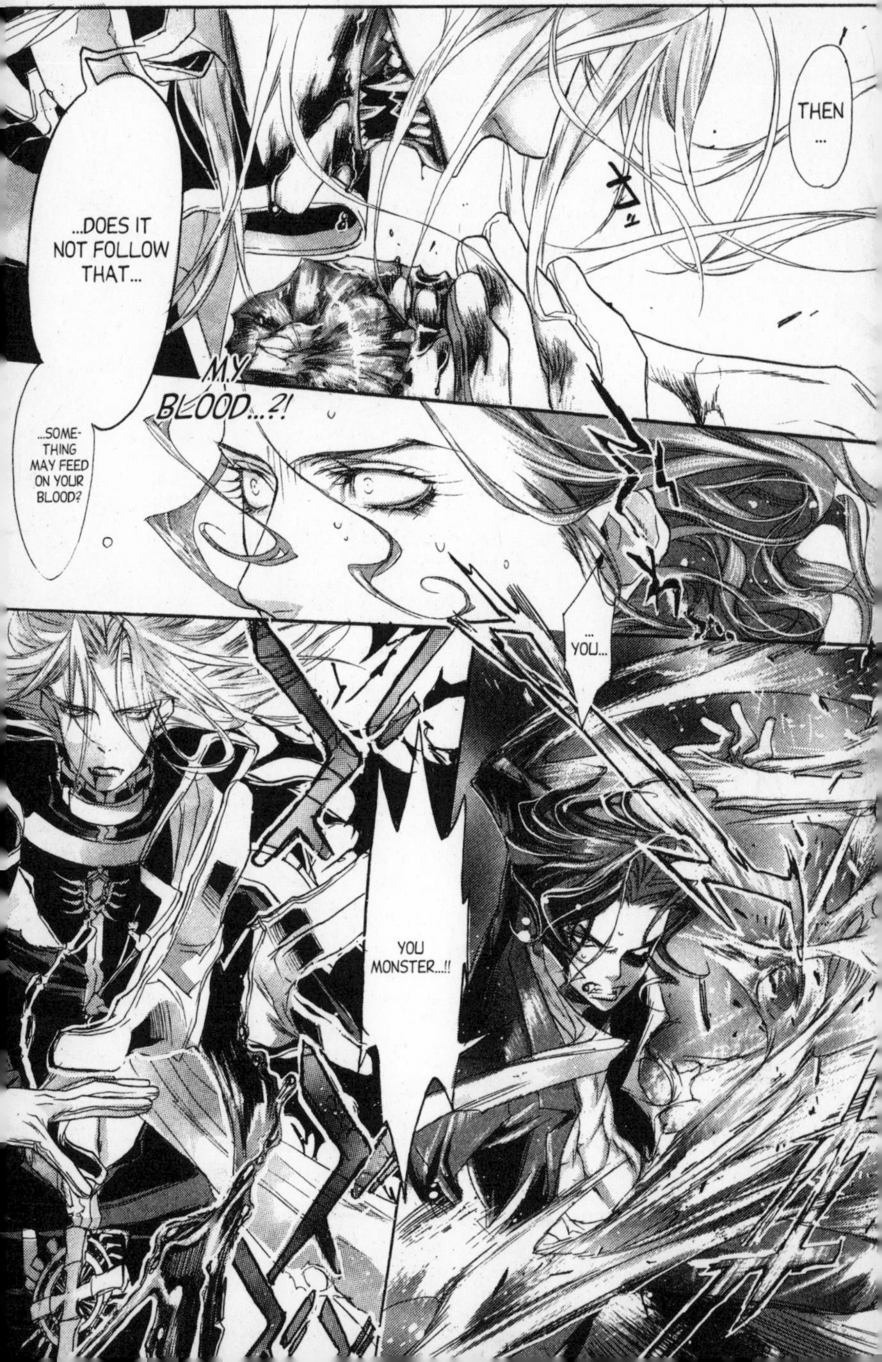
THEN ...
...DOES IT NOT FOLLOW THAT...
...SOME-THING MAY FEED ON YOUR BLOOD?
MY BLOOD...?!
... YOU...
YOU MONSTER...!!

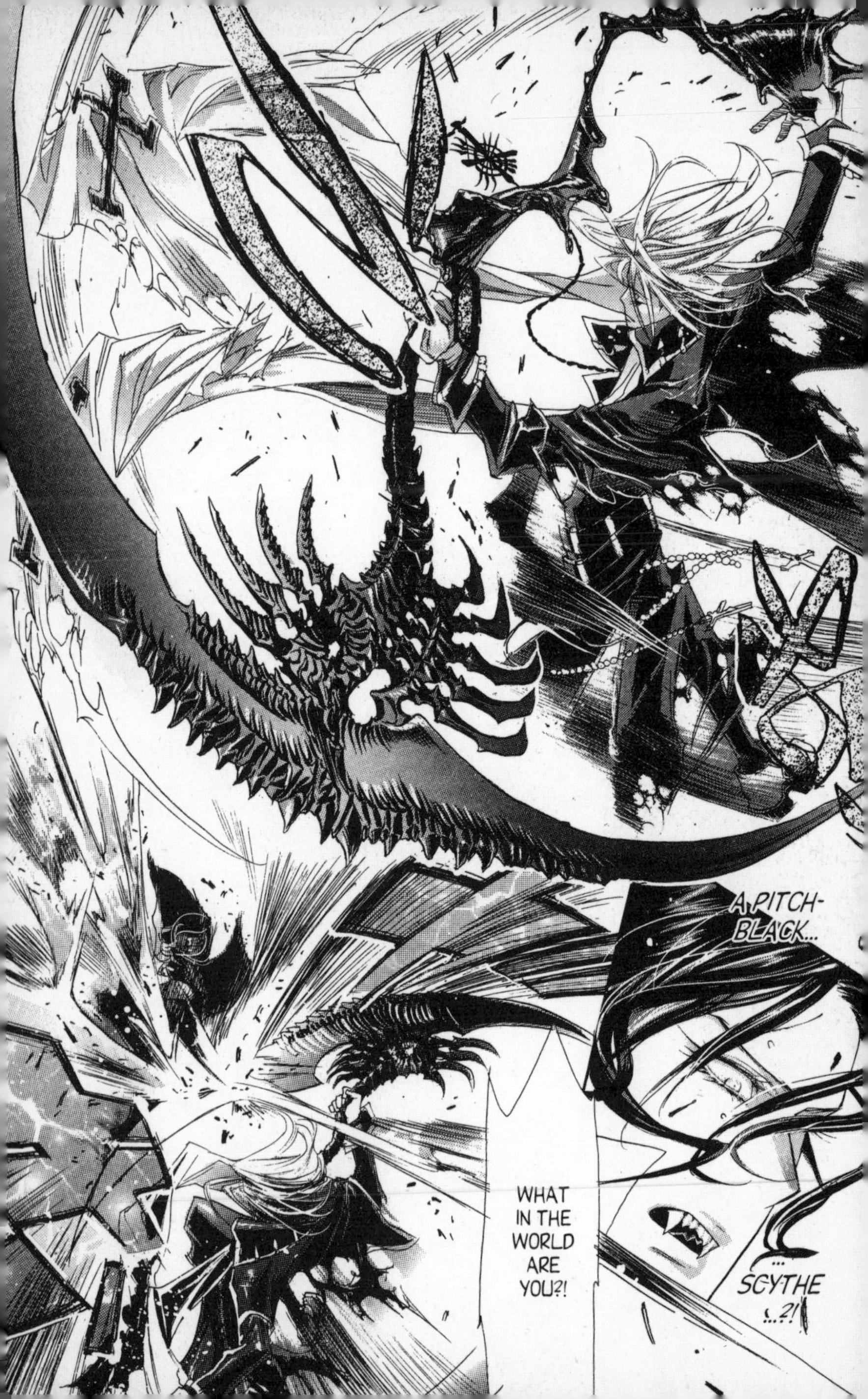
A PITCH-BLACK...
...SCYTHE ...?!
WHAT IN THE WORLD ARE YOU?!

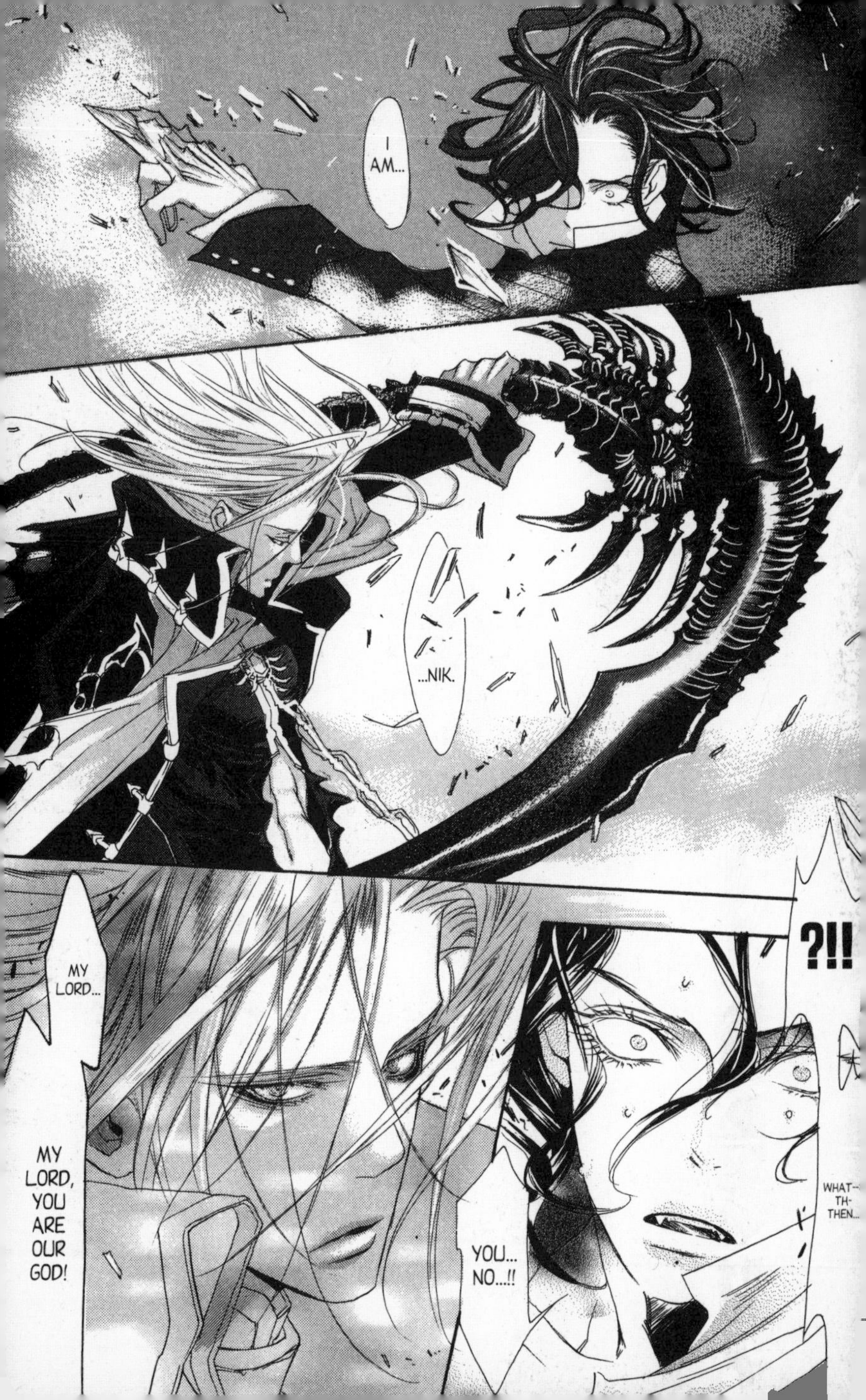
I AM...
...NIK.
?!!
WHAT-- TH- THEN...
YOU... NO...!!
MY LORD...
MY LORD, YOU ARE OUR GOD!

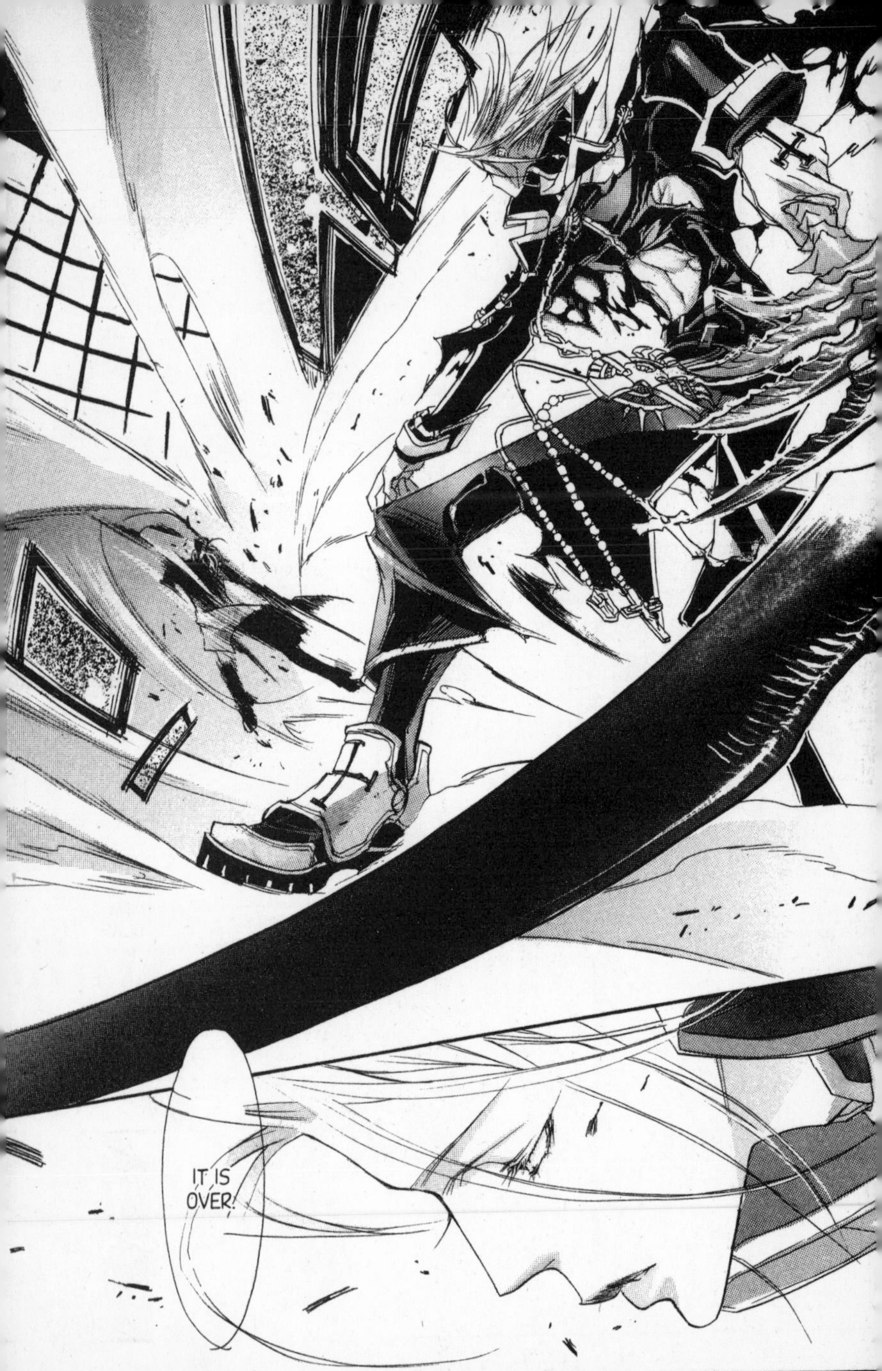
IT IS OVER!

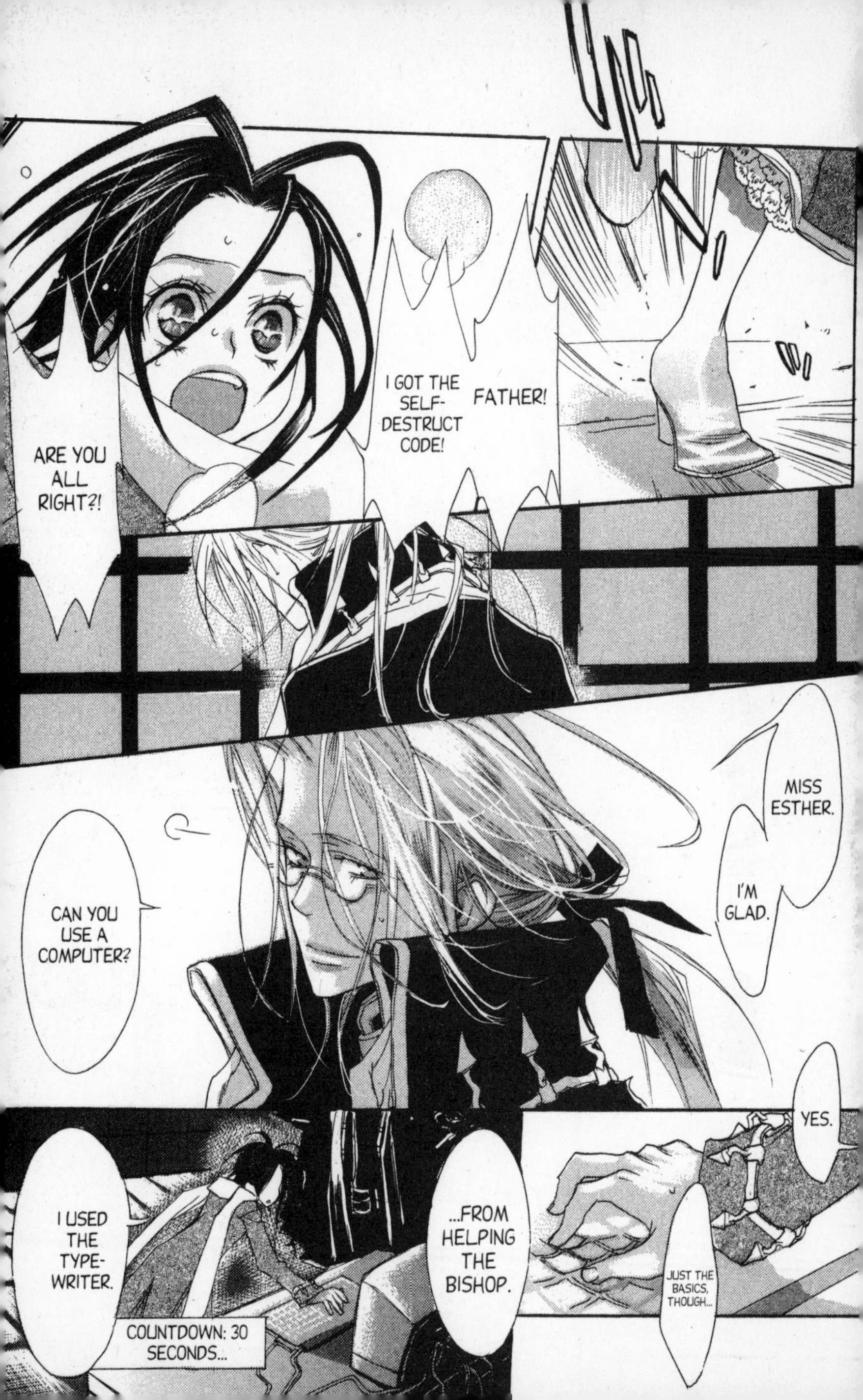
FATHER!
I GOT THE SELF-DESTRUCT CODE!
ARE YOU ALL RIGHT?!
MISS ESTHER.
I'M GLAD.
CAN YOU USE A COMPUTER?
YES.
JUST THE BASICS, THOUGH...
...FROM HELPING THE BISHOP.
I USED THE TYPE-WRITER.
COUNTDOWN: 30 SECONDS...

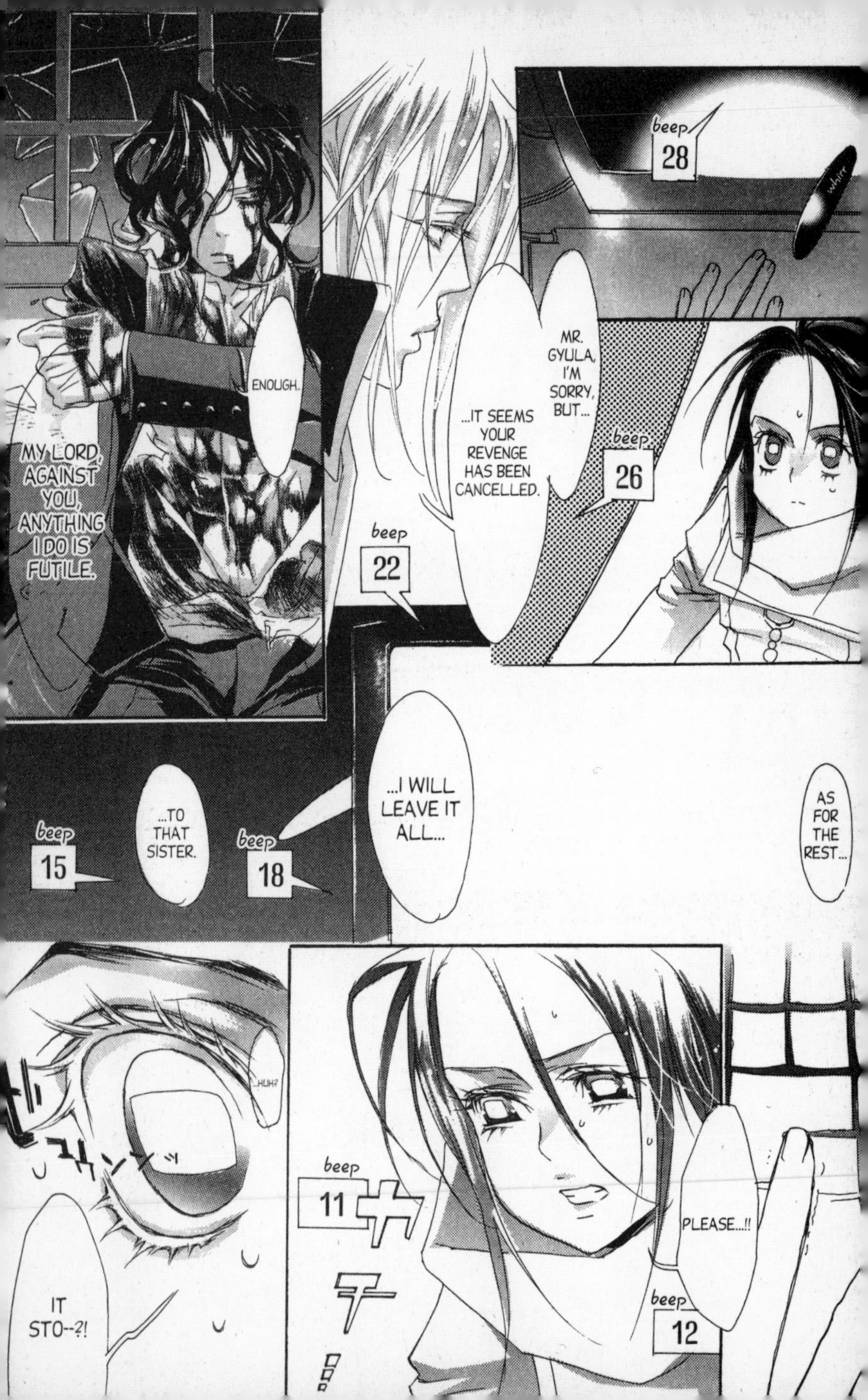

beep
28
whirr
MR. GYULA, I'M SORRY, BUT...
beep
26
...IT SEEMS YOUR REVENGE HAS BEEN CANCELLED.
beep
22
ENOUGH.
MY LORD, AGAINST YOU, ANYTHING I DO IS FUTILE.
AS FOR THE REST...
...I WILL LEAVE IT ALL...
beep
18
...TO THAT SISTER.
beep
15
beep
12
PLEASE...!!
beep
11
...HUH?
IT STO--?!

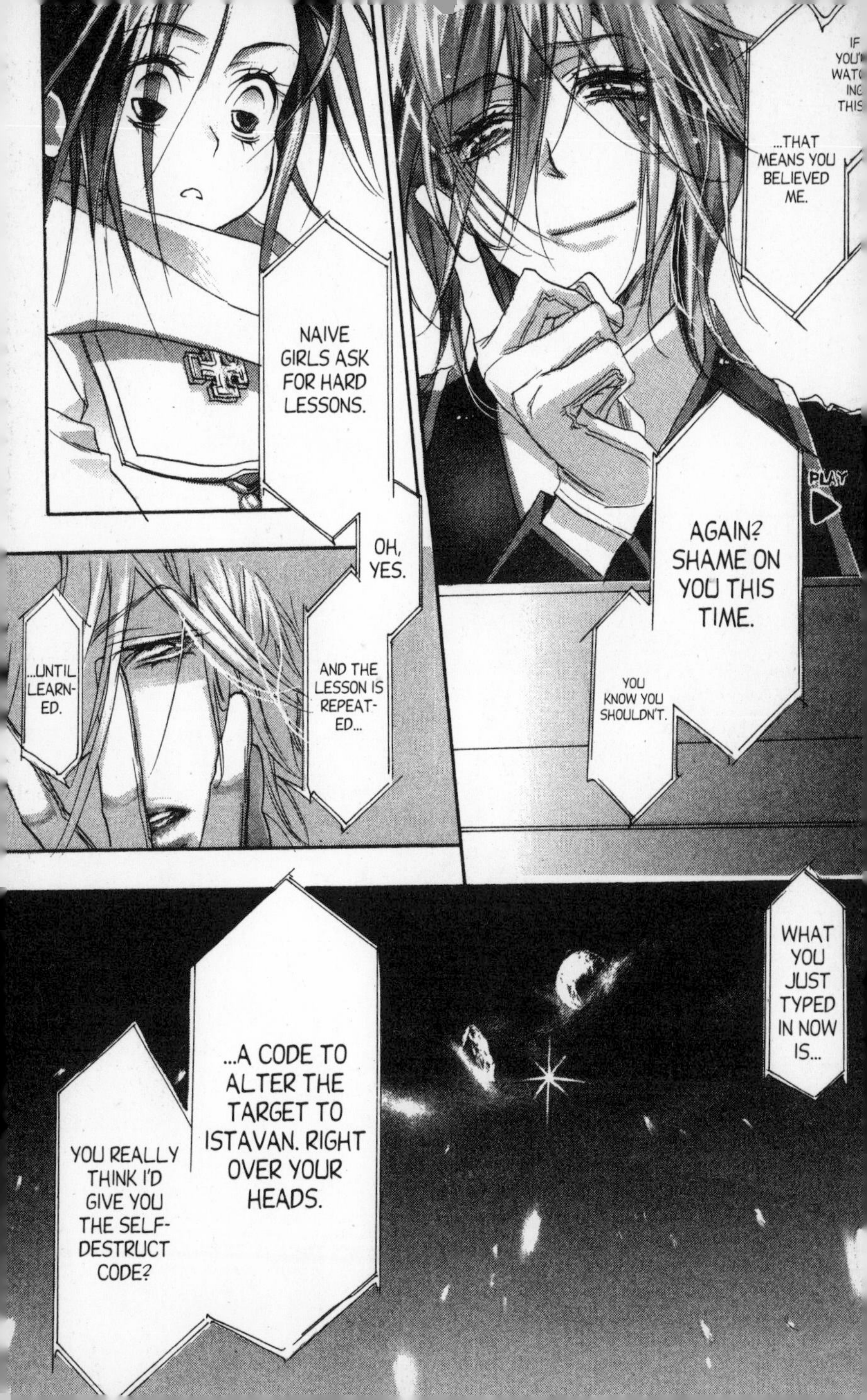
IF YOU' WATC ING THIS
...THAT MEANS YOU BELIEVED ME.
PLAY
AGAIN? SHAME ON YOU THIS TIME.
NAIVE GIRLS ASK FOR HARD LESSONS.
OH, YES.
YOU KNOW YOU SHOULDN'T.
AND THE LESSON IS REPEAT-ED...
...UNTIL LEARN-ED.
WHAT YOU JUST TYPED IN NOW IS...
...A CODE TO ALTER THE TARGET TO ISTAVAN. RIGHT OVER YOUR HEADS.
YOU REALLY THINK I'D GIVE YOU THE SELF-DESTRUCT CODE?

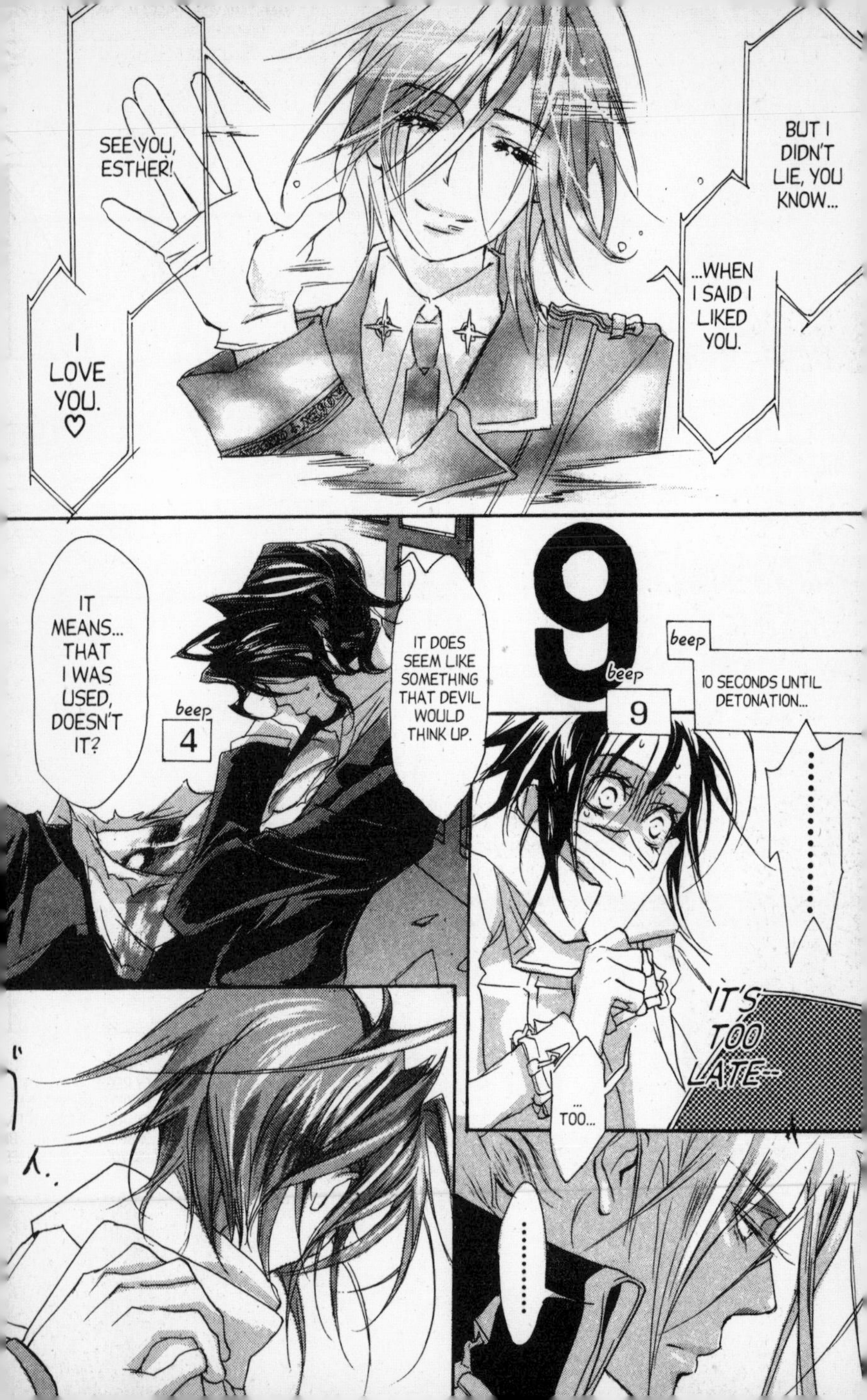
BUT I DIDN'T LIE, YOU KNOW...
...WHEN I SAID I LIKED YOU.
SEE YOU, ESTHER!
I LOVE YOU. ♡
9
beep
beep
10 SECONDS UNTIL DETONATION...
9
......
IT'S TOO LATE--
...TOO...
IT DOES SEEM LIKE SOMETHING THAT DEVIL WOULD THINK UP.
beep
4
IT MEANS... THAT I WAS USED, DOESN'T IT?
......

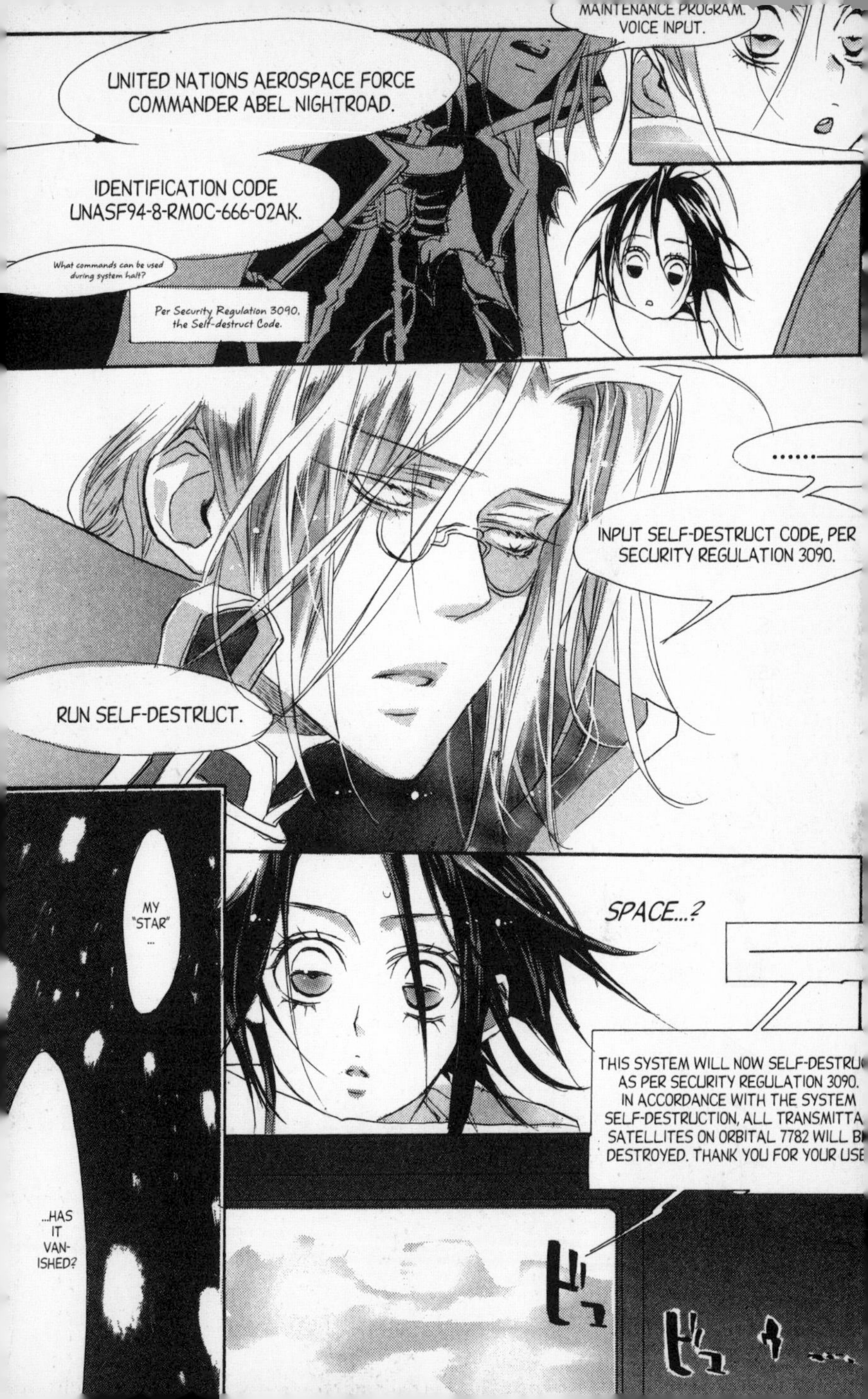

MAINTENANCE PROGRAM. VOICE INPUT.
UNITED NATIONS AEROSPACE FORCE COMMANDER ABEL NIGHTROAD.
IDENTIFICATION CODE UNASF94-8-RMOC-666-02AK.
What commands can be used during system halt?
Per Security Regulation 3090, the Self-destruct Code.
......
INPUT SELF-DESTRUCT CODE, PER SECURITY REGULATION 3090.
RUN SELF-DESTRUCT.
SPACE...?
THIS SYSTEM WILL NOW SELF-DESTRU AS PER SECURITY REGULATION 3090. IN ACCORDANCE WITH THE SYSTEM SELF-DESTRUCTION, ALL TRANSMITTA SATELLITES ON ORBITAL 7782 WILL B DESTROYED. THANK YOU FOR YOUR USE
MY "STAR" ...
...HAS IT VAN-ISHED?

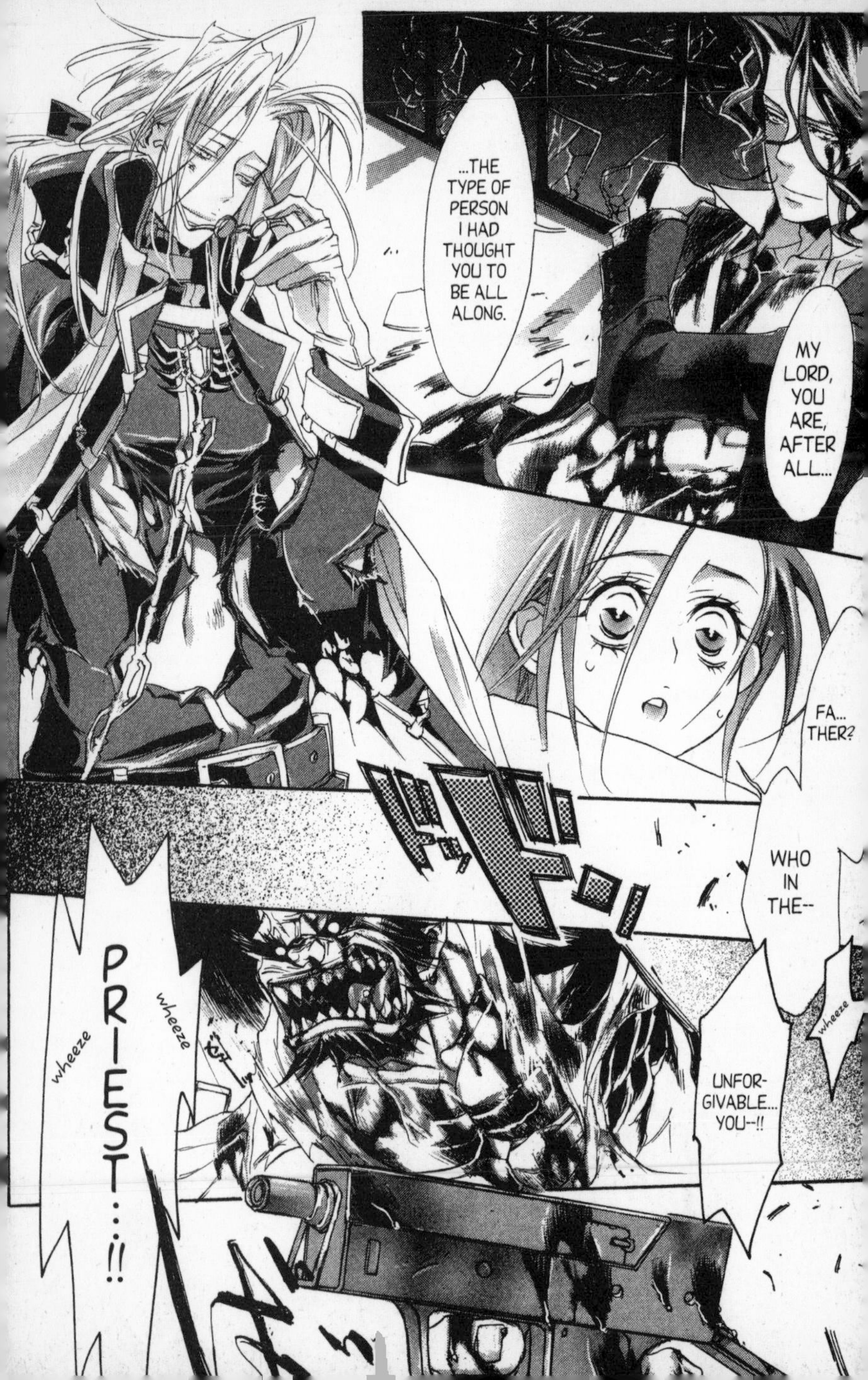
MY LORD, YOU ARE, AFTER ALL...
...THE TYPE OF PERSON I HAD THOUGHT YOU TO BE ALL ALONG.
FA... THER?
WHO IN THE--
wheeze
UNFORGIVABLE... YOU--!!
wheeze
PRIEST...!!
wheeze

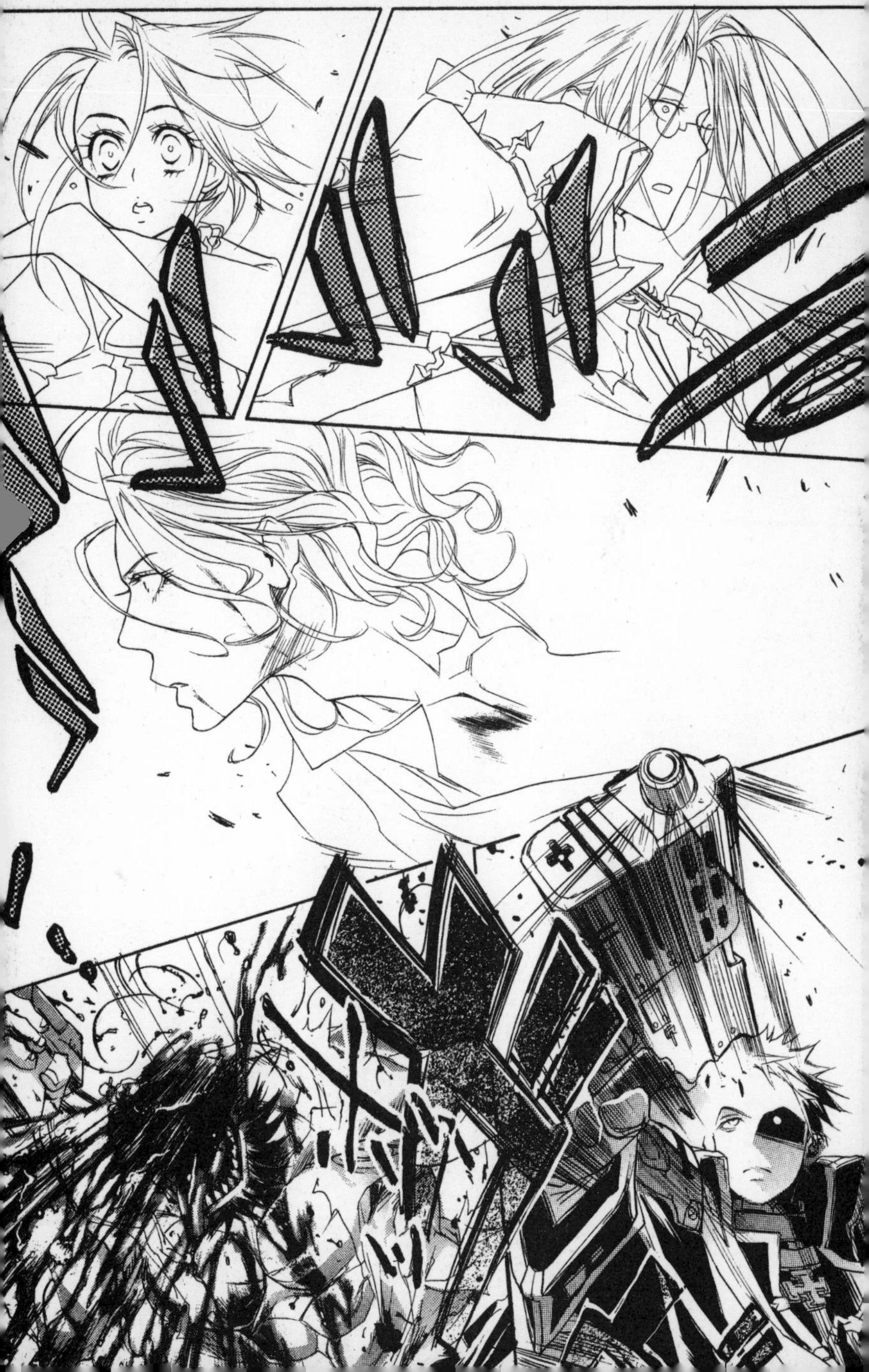

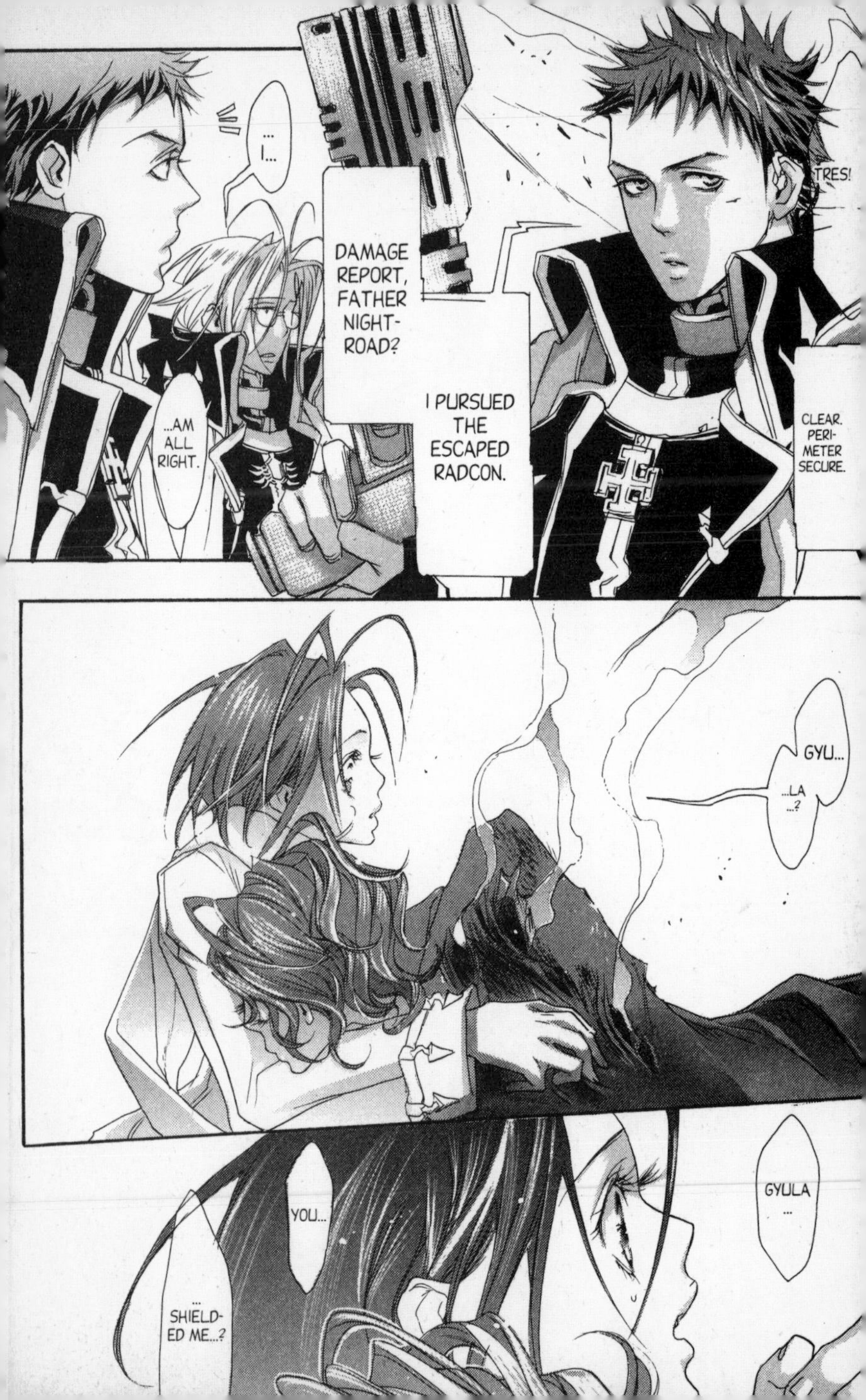
TRES!
CLEAR. PERIMETER SECURE.
DAMAGE REPORT, FATHER NIGHTROAD?
I PURSUED THE ESCAPED RADCON.
... I...
...AM ALL RIGHT.
GYU...
...LA ...?
GYULA ...
YOU...
... SHIELDED ME...?

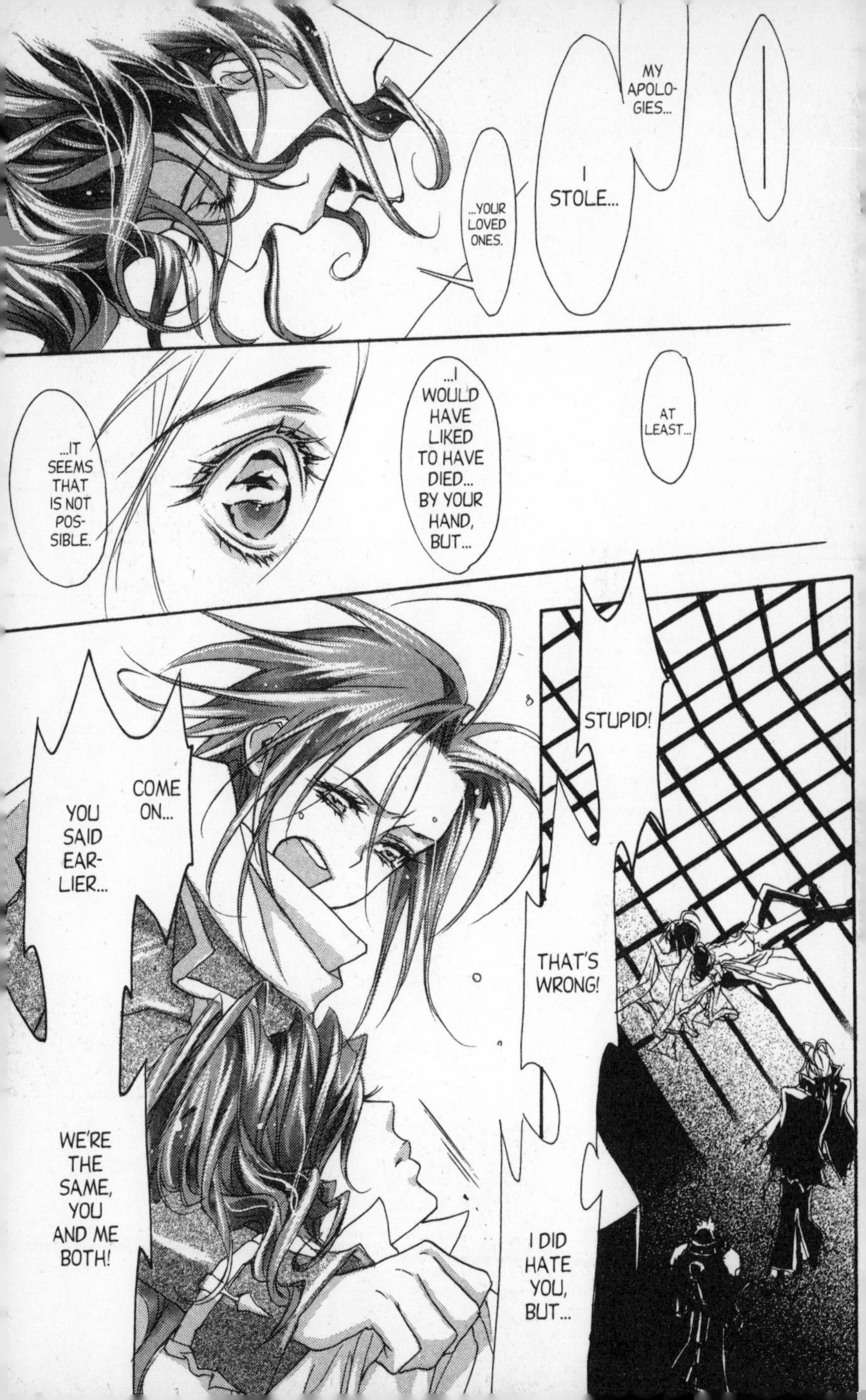
MY APOLOGIES...
I STOLE...
...YOUR LOVED ONES.
AT LEAST...
...I WOULD HAVE LIKED TO HAVE DIED... BY YOUR HAND, BUT...
...IT SEEMS THAT IS NOT POSSIBLE.
STUPID!
THAT'S WRONG!
I DID HATE YOU, BUT...
COME ON...
YOU SAID EARLIER...
WE'RE THE SAME, YOU AND ME BOTH!

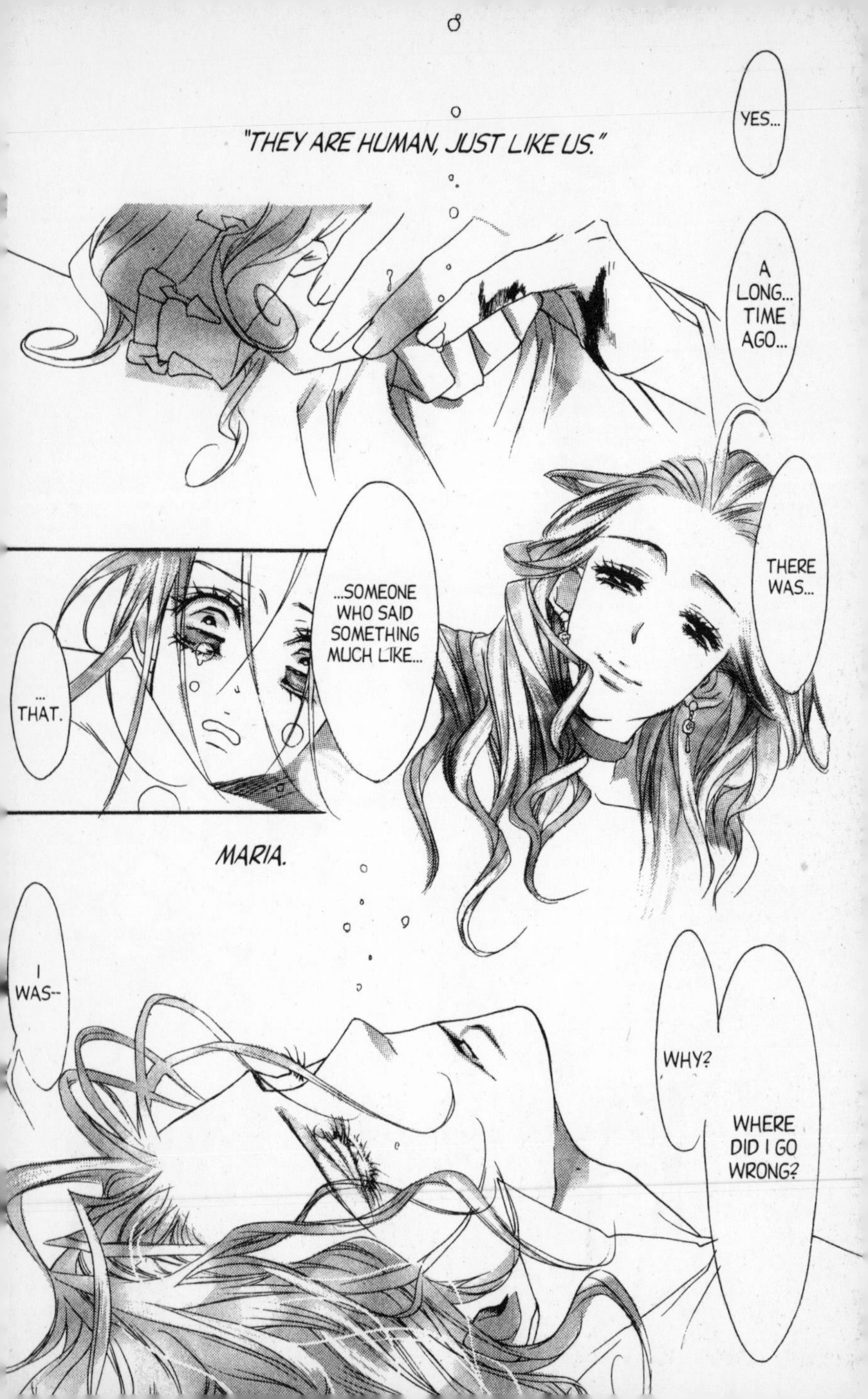

"THEY ARE HUMAN, JUST LIKE US."
YES...
A LONG... TIME AGO...
THERE WAS...
...SOMEONE WHO SAID SOMETHING MUCH LIKE...
... THAT.
MARIA.
WHY?
WHERE DID I GO WRONG?
I WAS--

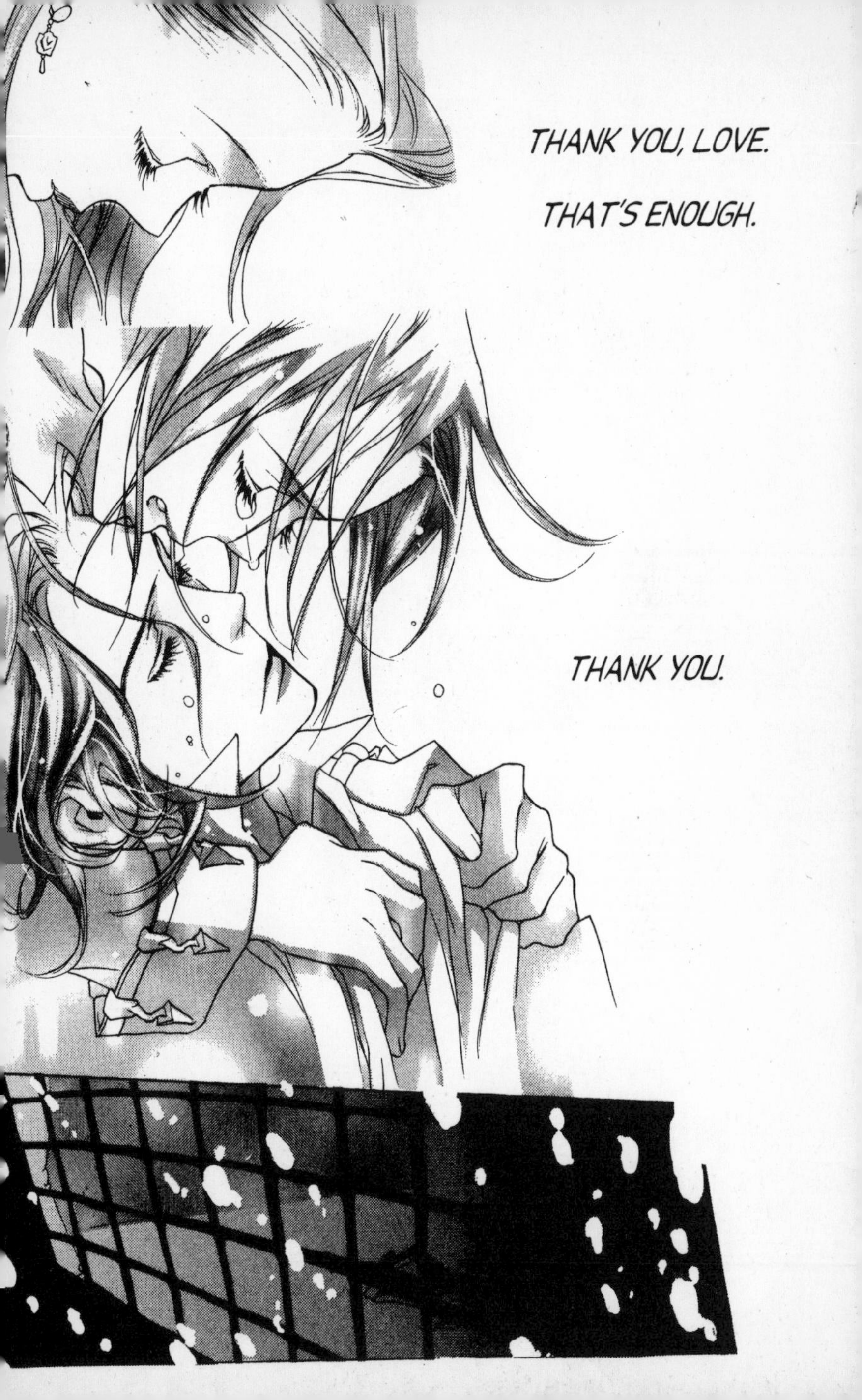
THANK YOU, LOVE.
THAT'S ENOUGH.
THANK YOU.

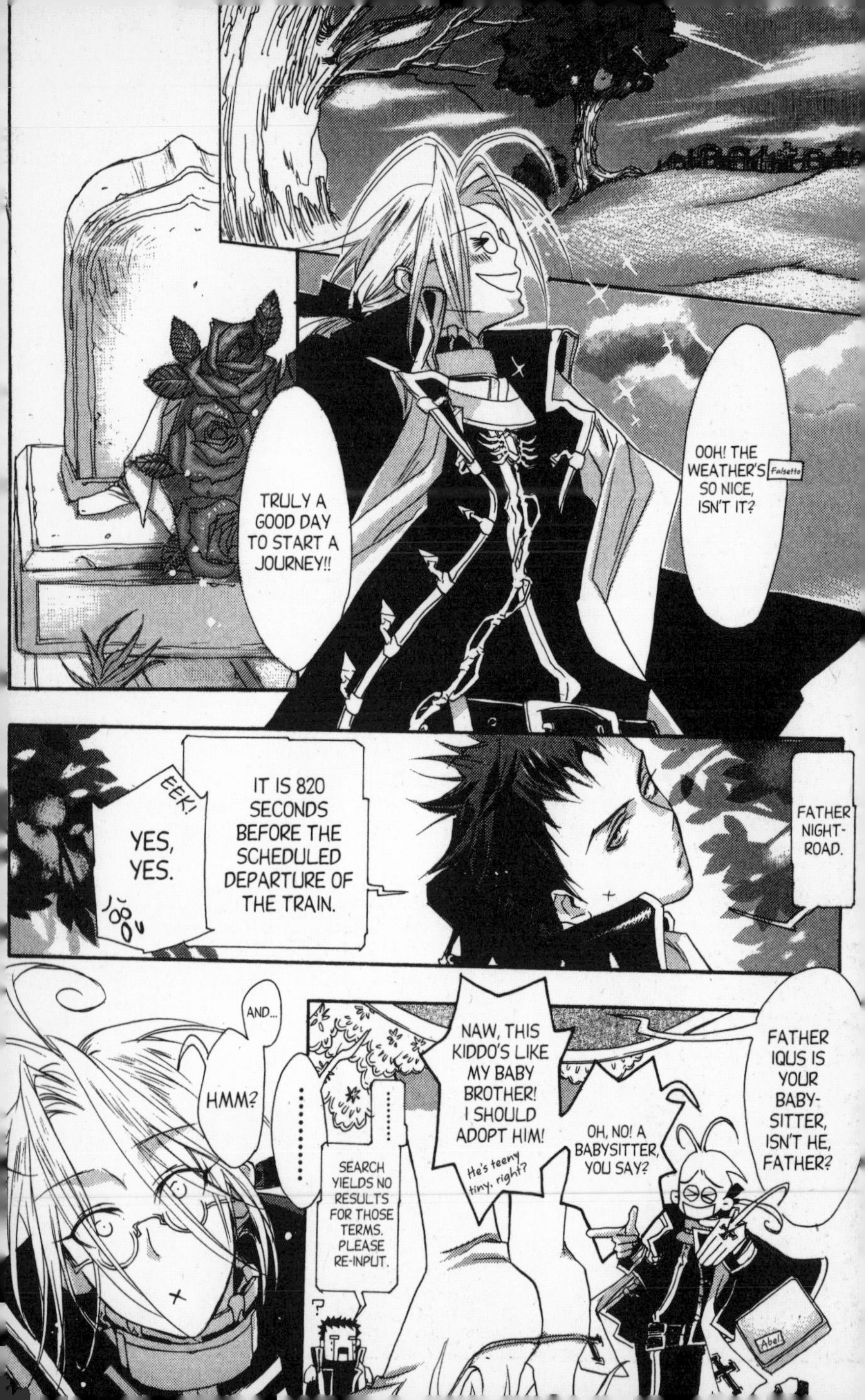
OOH! THE WEATHER'S SO NICE, ISN'T IT?
Falsetto
TRULY A GOOD DAY TO START A JOURNEY!!
FATHER NIGHT-ROAD.
IT IS 820 SECONDS BEFORE THE SCHEDULED DEPARTURE OF THE TRAIN.
EEK!
YES, YES.
FATHER IQUS IS YOUR BABY-SITTER, ISN'T HE, FATHER?
OH, NO! A BABYSITTER, YOU SAY?
Abel!
NAW, THIS KIDDO'S LIKE MY BABY BROTHER! I SHOULD ADOPT HIM!
He's teeny tiny, right?
......
SEARCH YIELDS NO RESULTS FOR THOSE TERMS. PLEASE RE-INPUT.
?
......
AND...
HMM?

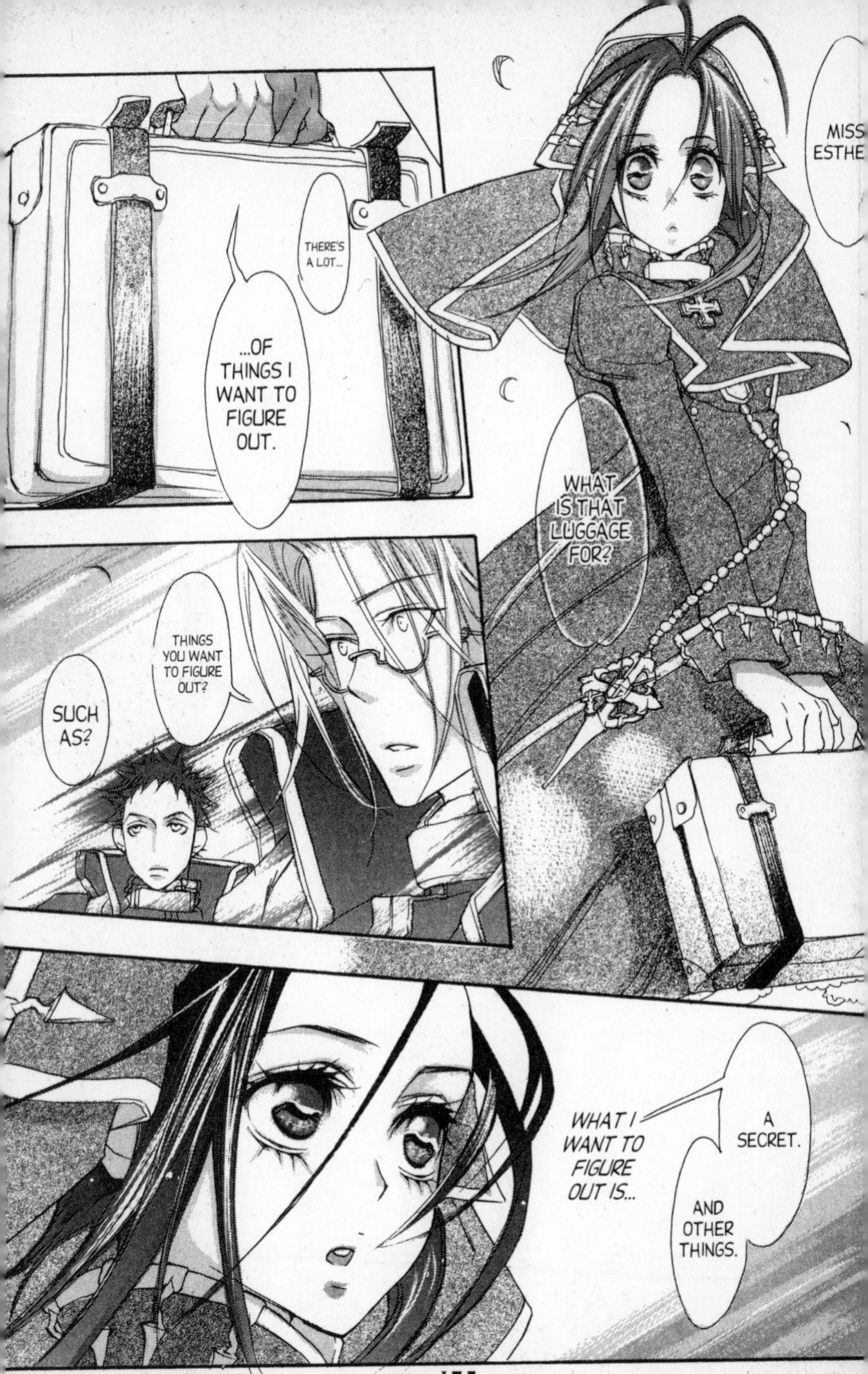
MISS ESTHE
WHAT IS THAT LUGGAGE FOR?
THERE'S A LOT...
...OF THINGS I WANT TO FIGURE OUT.
THINGS YOU WANT TO FIGURE OUT?
SUCH AS?
A SECRET.
AND OTHER THINGS.
WHAT I WANT TO FIGURE OUT IS...

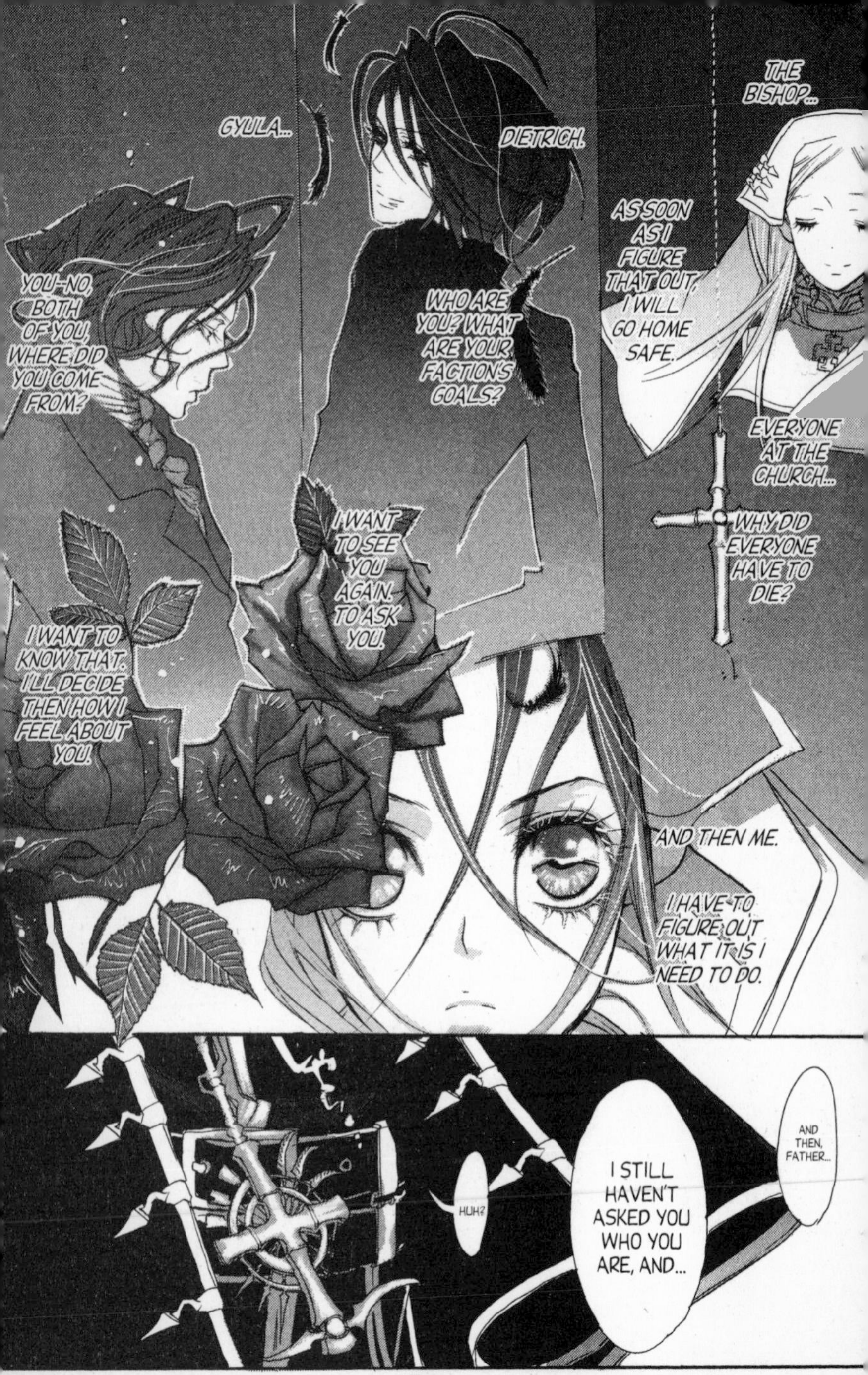
THE BISHOP...
AS SOON AS I FIGURE THAT OUT, I WILL GO HOME SAFE.
EVERYONE AT THE CHURCH...
WHY DID EVERYONE HAVE TO DIE?
DIETRICH.
WHO ARE YOU? WHAT ARE YOUR FACTION'S GOALS?
I WANT TO SEE YOU AGAIN. TO ASK YOU.
GYULA...
YOU--NO, BOTH OF YOU, WHERE DID YOU COME FROM?
I WANT TO KNOW THAT. I'LL DECIDE THEN HOW I FEEL ABOUT YOU.
AND THEN ME.
I HAVE TO FIGURE OUT WHAT IT IS I NEED TO DO.
AND THEN, FATHER...
I STILL HAVEN'T ASKED YOU WHO YOU ARE, AND...
HUH?

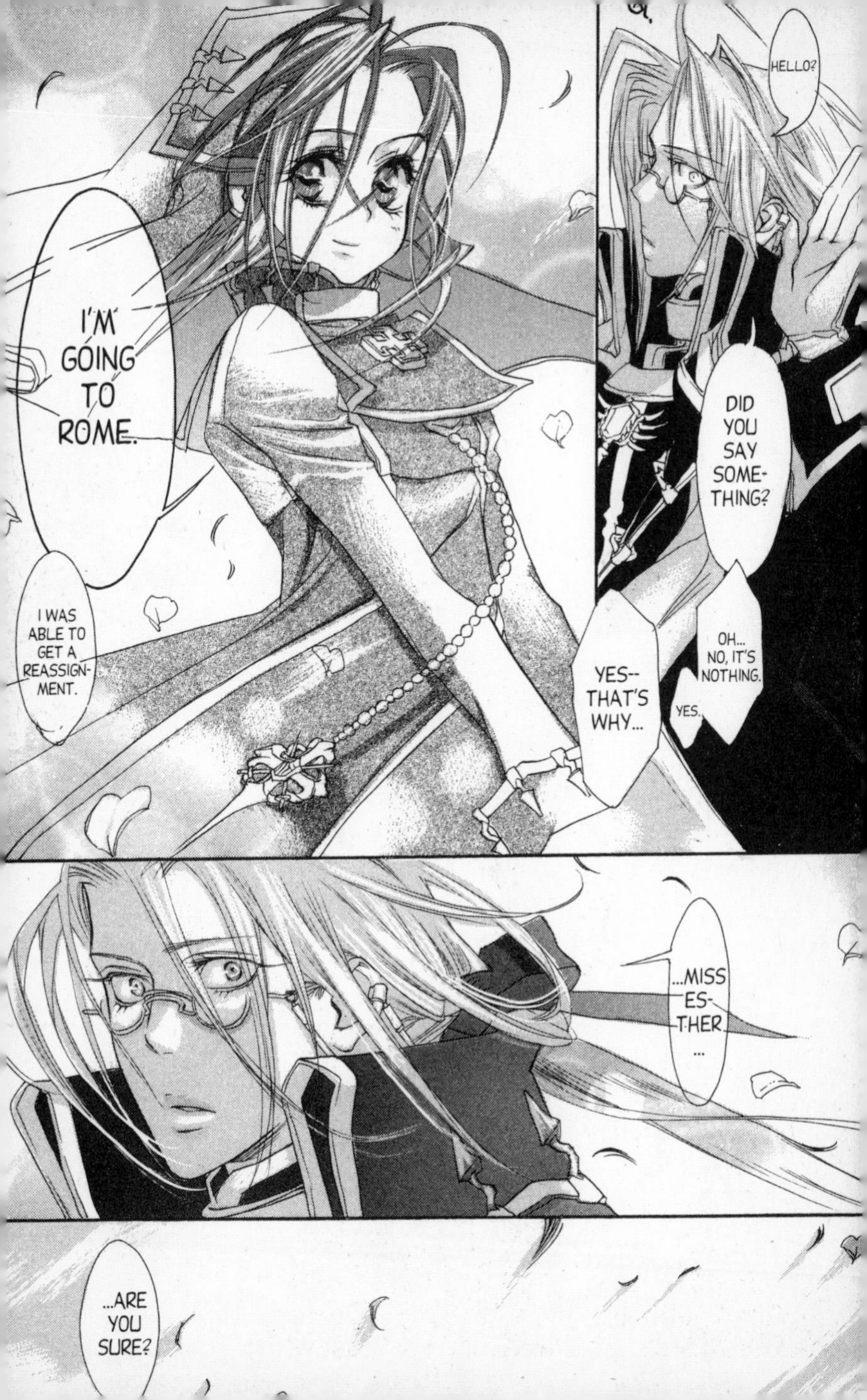
HELLO?
DID YOU SAY SOME-THING?
OH... NO, IT'S NOTHING.
YES.
I'M GOING TO ROME.
I WAS ABLE TO GET A REASSIGN-MENT.
YES-- THAT'S WHY...
...MISS ES-THER...
...ARE YOU SURE?

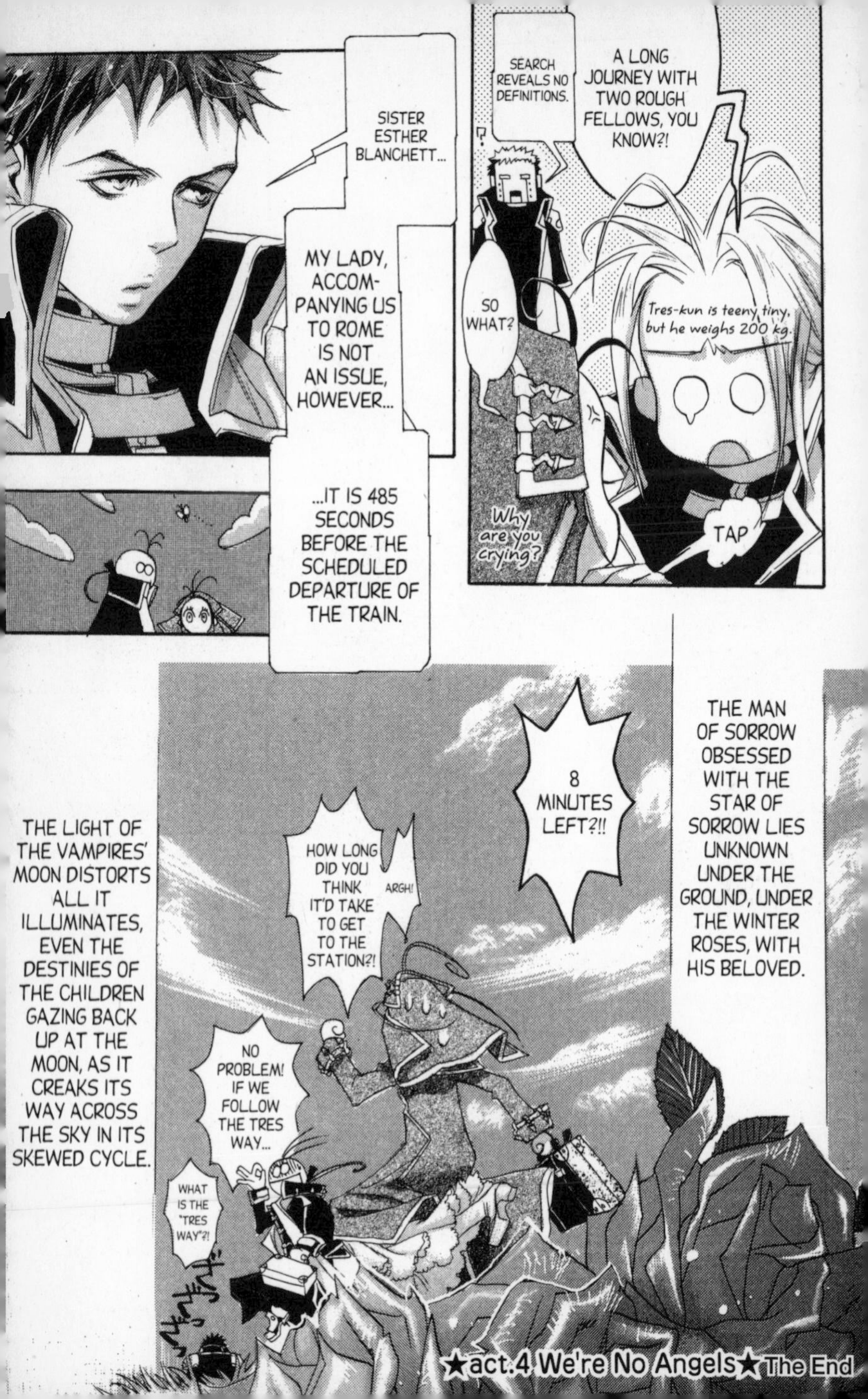
A LONG JOURNEY WITH TWO ROUGH FELLOWS, YOU KNOW?!
SEARCH REVEALS NO DEFINITIONS.
SO WHAT?
Tres-kun is teeny tiny, but he weighs 200 kg.
TAP
Why are you crying?
SISTER ESTHER BLANCHETT...
MY LADY, ACCOMPANYING US TO ROME IS NOT AN ISSUE, HOWEVER...
...IT IS 485 SECONDS BEFORE THE SCHEDULED DEPARTURE OF THE TRAIN.
THE MAN OF SORROW OBSESSED WITH THE STAR OF SORROW LIES UNKNOWN UNDER THE GROUND, UNDER THE WINTER ROSES, WITH HIS BELOVED.
8 MINUTES LEFT?!!
HOW LONG DID YOU THINK IT'D TAKE TO GET TO THE STATION?!
ARGH!
NO PROBLEM! IF WE FOLLOW THE TRES WAY...
WHAT IS THE "TRES WAY"?!
THE LIGHT OF THE VAMPIRES' MOON DISTORTS ALL IT ILLUMINATES, EVEN THE DESTINIES OF THE CHILDREN GAZING BACK UP AT THE MOON, AS IT CREAKS ITS WAY ACROSS THE SKY IN ITS SKEWED CYCLE.
★act.4 We're No Angels★ The End

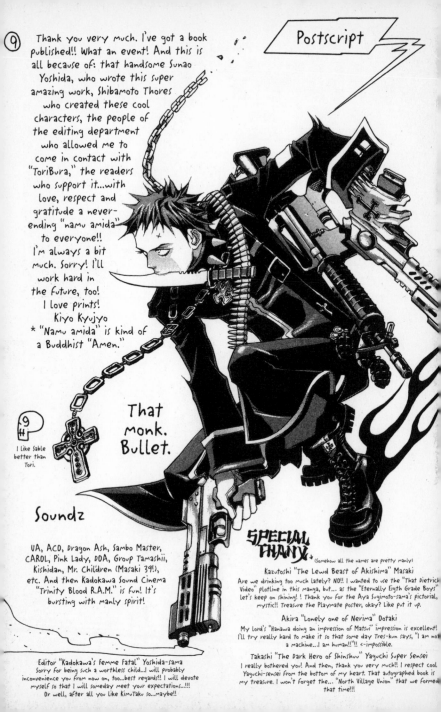

Postscript

9 Thank you very much. I've got a book published!! What an event! And this is all because of: that handsome Sunao Yoshida, who wrote this super amazing work, Shibamoto Thores who created these cool characters, the people of the editing department who allowed me to come in contact with "ToriBura," the readers who support it...with love, respect and gratitude a never-ending "namu amida" to everyone!!
I'm always a bit much. Sorry! I'll work hard in the future, too!
I love prints!
Kiyo Kyujyo
* "Namu amida" is kind of a Buddhist "Amen."

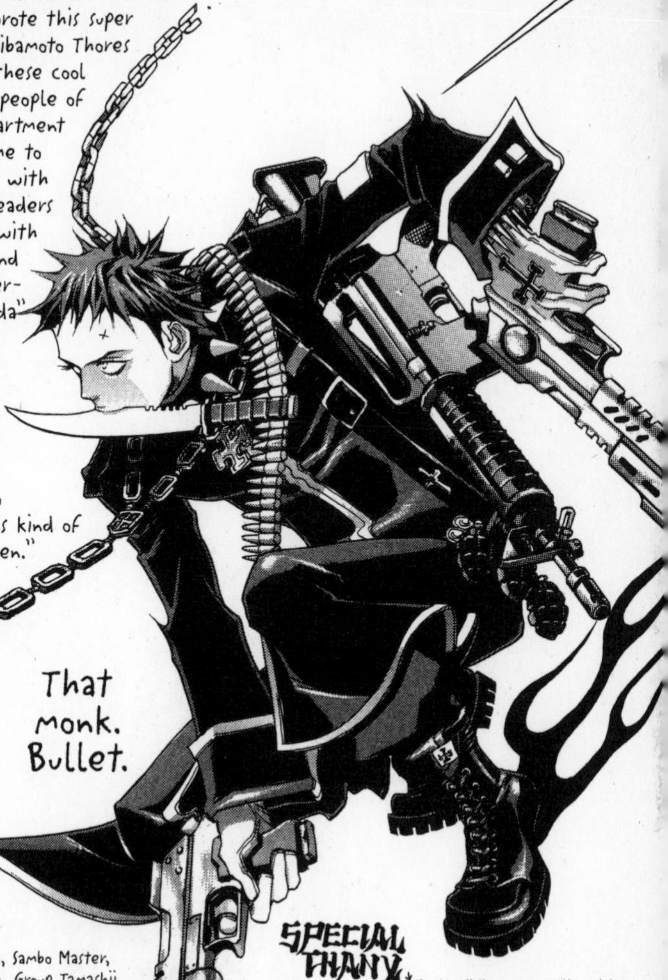

That monk. Bullet.

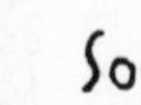

9
#

I like Sable better than Tori.

Soundz

UA, ACO, Dragon Ash, Sambo Master, CAROL, Pink Lady, DDA, Group Tamashii, Kishidan, Mr. Children (Masaki 39!), etc. And then Kadokawa Sound Cinema "Trinity Blood R.A.M." is fun! It's bursting with manly spirit!

Editor "Kadokawa's Femme Fatal" Yoshida-sama
Sorry for being such a worthless child...I will probably inconvenience you from now on, too...best regards!! I will devote myself so that I will someday meet your expectations...!!! Or well, after all you like KimuTaku so...maybe!!

SPECIAL THANX

(Somehow all the names are pretty manly)

Kazutoshi "The Lewd Beast of Akishima" Masaki
Are we drinking too much lately? NO!! I wanted to use the "That Dietrich Video" plotline in this manga, but... as the "Eternally Eigth Grade Boys" let's keep on shining! ! Thank you for the Aya Sugimoto-sama's pictorial, mystic!! Treasure the Playmate poster, okay? Like put it up.

Akira "Lonely one of Nerima" Dotaki
My lord's "Hanawa doing an impression of Matsui" impression is excellent! I'll try really hard to make it so that some day Tres-kun says, "I am not a machine...I am human!!"!! <-impossible.

Takashi "The Dark Hero of Shinshuu" Yaguchi Super Sensei
I really bothered you! And then, thank you very much!! I respect cool Yaguchi-sensei from the bottom of my heart. That autographed book is my treasure. I won't forget the... "North Village Union" that we formed that time!!!

IN THE NEXT VOLUME OF TRINITY BLOOD™

The road to Rome is paved with many obstacles...
Abel, Tres and Esther head off on their journey to the
holy city and the Vatican, but nothing goes quite as they
planned. Between a powerful vampire who assaults them
on the train, a bloodsucking tree, and a dangerously beautiful
mermaid, the trio will have to keep their wits sharp and
their weapons even sharper in order to survive the journey.
But while mysterious figures from their pasts continue to
haunt Abel and Esther, there are also allies waiting along
the journey to lend a hand when it is most needed.

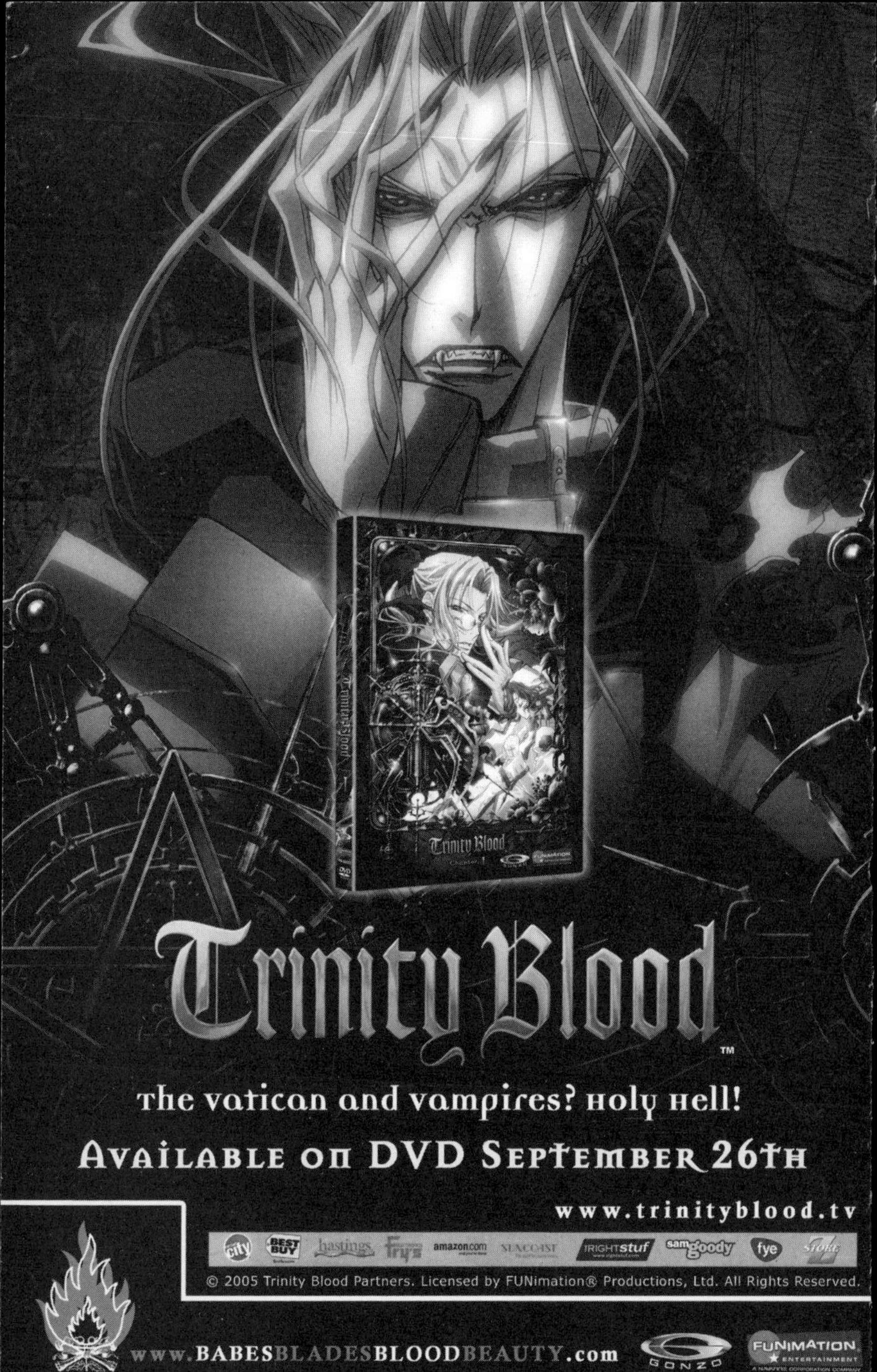
Trinity Blood™
the vatican and vampires? holy hell!
Available on DVD September 26th
www.trinityblood.tv
© 2005 Trinity Blood Partners. Licensed by FUNimation® Productions, Ltd. All Rights Reserved.
www.BABESBLADESBLOODBEAUTY.com
GONZO
FUNIMATION ENTERTAINMENT

The following is a preview of the novel series.
Please flip ahead six pages, and be sure to read
left-to-right.

TRINITY BLOOD™
RAGE AGAINST THE MOONS

FROM THE EMPIRE
SUNAO YOSHIDA

Coming to stores in April 2007

The priest smiled, one eye visible beneath dripping wet hair. He threw his head back and laughed. "Oh, it's okay. Only a cup of tea. No problem. I'm not worried about it. Not at all."

Jessica smiled until her eyes crinkled with pleasure. "Isn't he such a nice priest? Well, you need to get to bed. Make sure you go straight to your mother."

The little boy nodded and ran off. Jessica made sure he'd safely left the lounge before she looked at the priest.

He stared at the spilled tea. He just stared and stared, his expression so remorseful.

"Father, would you like a sandwich? You don't have to pay—it'll be on the house."

He brightened. "On the house? Really? Oh, Lord, thank you, stewardess. Are you an angel? Now that I think about it, there's a picture of you in our church."

She rolled her eyes. "I'm just a stewardess."

After a short sputtering noise, an automated voice piped in through the intercom on the lunch counter.

"This is the bridge—Jessica, can you bring us our meals?"

"Yes, Captain Connely . . . Um, Father, can you hold on a minute? I'll be right back," she said.

"I'll wait as long as you ask me to, Miss . . . ?"

"Lang. I'm Jessica Lang."

"Lang?" the priest repeated. He thought for a moment. "Any relation to the airship designer, Doctor Catherine Lang?"

"Yes. She's my mother."

The priest's eyebrows shot up. "Wow. Can you fly this ship?"

"No! I'm just a stewardess. I've studied flying a little, but I'm not certified yet, since I'm a woman, you know . . ."

"There's no law stopping you from flying, Jessica. I know a woman that flies an airship . . ." He trailed off, then shook his head. "Oh, I beg your pardon. I'm Abel." The priest bowed low as he introduced himself. "Abel Nightroad—wandering priest, at your service."

"My job always makes me cry," he joked. "The cafeteria here charges a hundred dinars for dinner. What a rip-off! I'm so poor, one meal will clean out my bank account."

"Don't tell me you haven't eaten?" she asked.

He shrugged. "Not for about twenty hours. I was trying not to exert myself by just sleeping in my room, but I was starting to feel lightheaded anyway. I thought that maybe if I raised my blood sugar a little, I could hold off until we reached Rome," he replied earnestly.

"Priests live such a hard life."

The priest took Jessica's sympathy as a compliment. He nodded as if he were praying to God. "Sometimes our jobs mean life and death for the faithful . . . So, can I have the tea and sugar now?"

She nodded. "Sure. Here you go."

"Mm. This tea tastes so smooth. It's authentic, isn't it? Not that brewed-in-a-bag stuff that leaves you—"

WHAPT!

Before the thick liquid could reach his lips for a second sip, a little child running through the lounge with a balloon bumped into the priest's elbow. The glass bonked the priest's chin. Sugary tea spilled everywhere—his long hair, his robes, his glasses . . . everywhere. Meanwhile, the child tripped, fell on the floor, and started crying.

"Are you okay, little boy? Are you hurt?" Jessica asked.

She completely ignored the silver-haired priest, who stood there with tea dripping down his face. Instead, she ran to the child. Luckily, the boy was more startled than hurt.

Jessica snatched up the balloon's string. She'd given a balloon to all the children as they boarded. Returning it now, she gently hugged the boy.

"Th-thank you, miss," the boy stammered.

"You're welcome. But you need to go back to your mother. It's close to your bedtime."

"Y-yes . . . I'm sorry, Father." The boy looked sheepish.

CHAPTER I

Stewardess? May I please have milk in my tea? And about twelve . . . no, thirteen sugars?" he asked.

Jessica peered back at the young man on the other side of the counter. He wore thick glasses and a plain, faded priest's robe. This poor traveler looked very out of place.

Though recent times had been hard, the observation lounge was elegant and lively. Well-dressed ladies and gentlemen chatted and chuckled, lively music played, glasses clinked, and cigar smoke hung in the air. The lounge was full of rich and gorgeous people. It was a perfect night for flying.

"Um, stewardess? Ma'am?" he asked again.

"Huh? Y-yes!" she replied.

Jessica ran a hand through her brown shoulder-length hair, forcing herself to wake from her daydream. She tied on her apron. Her smile made her youthful, freckled face light up. "Uh, did you ask for a scotch?"

"No, tea with milk. And thirteen sugars."

She blinked. "Well, if you want some sweets, we have cakes and pies, sir."

"I'm sure they're wonderful, but . . ." The priest looked into his wallet. His shoulders slumped. "I only have four dinars . . . so I'll just have some tea, please."

Even the rich children running amok in the lounge had more money than that. In fact, Jessica's pay the previous week was two thousand dinars. How did this poor priest even get on the *Tristan*—the most luxurious airship that flew between Londinium and Rome?

of believing in themselves. Your faith made me want to show you compassion, but . . ." the shadowed figure trailed off.

"H-how . . . ?" The elderly priest, who had traded sunlight and decency for the strength and power of immortal evil, now cowered, frozen in fear. "Are you a vampire too?"

"No. I am . . . what I am." Suddenly, the sound of metal bending and popping split through the air. The figure stepped forward, his own priest's robes slowly absorbing the knife, until it was engulfed deep into his chest.

The vampire growled. "I'd heard of your kind, when I was still human. In Rome, at the Vatican headquarters, there was a sect of priests that kept a monster. When the Vatican had problems beyond the scope of mortal men, they sent the monster to do their bidding. Is that you?" the vampire asked.

The stranger cocked his head. "AX. Spelled out, it is the Arcanum Cella ex Dono Dei. My boss doesn't like scandals, you see. She wouldn't want news spreading that a priest 'changed.' That's why I'm here."

From out of nowhere, the shadow-clad man raised a double-bladed scythe high into the air.

Father Scott glanced at the scythe and then shrieked in horror. "You're Caterina's hound! AX Agent Crusnik—!"

A whipping winter wind drowned out his scream.

The old man flashed a wicked smile; long white fangs poked past his lips. Unable to check his bloodlust, the old man pointed the knife at Angelina's white breast. But just as he was about to slice into her heart—

A whisper came from the shadows. "Ite missa est. This Mass is over, Father Scott."

"What?"

Just beyond the altar stood a gentleman draped in shadows. Even a vampire's extraordinary senses could barely detect his presence. He was practically invisible to a normal human.

"Londinium priest Father Alexander Scott . . . In the name of the Father, and of the Son, and of the Holy Spirit, I am placing you under arrest for seven counts of murder and extortion of blood," the stranger said.

"Who the hell are you?"

"I beg your pardon. I come from Rome—"

It was his mistake to afford the vampire any courtesy. Instantly, the knife flew across the distance between them with near-impossible speed. The aim was true, and the knife stabbed the shadowed man squarely in the chest.

"I don't know who you are, but no one interrupts my supper!" the priest said. The elderly vampire laughed so hard, his long white robe rippled as his shoulders shook. White fangs glinted in the darkness.

The priest hadn't been a vampire for more than a month, so two suppers in one night would mark his finest feast.

"It was foolish to sneak up on the living dead, my son."

"Foolish for you to think I would fall so easily," the man replied.

"What the . . . ?" Father Scott couldn't believe his eyes. The knife had sunk deep into the shadowed man's heart, yet there he stood, unaffected.

"I heard one of your sermons once," the stranger murmured regretfully. "You preached that humans are the only beings capable

The moonlight shone through the gorgeous stained glass window, making the blustery winter night seem even darker.

"Amen. This meal I have prepared is my body. On this holy night, I give thanks." The elderly voice was gentle; the man who spoke was reverent of his holy ritual, and his words were eloquent and full of passion.

But the eyes of the nun—her arms and legs bound to the altar and her mouth gagged—were wide with fear. Perhaps she wouldn't have been so afraid if a mere cold-blooded murderer stood before her. After all, a murderer would only kill her. A cold-blooded murderer would at least be *human*.

"Thank you for being so patient, Sister Angelina. It's time for the Last Supper," he said somberly.

The nun gasped.

When the old man turned, moonlight reflected off the silver blade gripped in his wrinkled hand. He had used the knife countless times to slice bread for worshippers, back when he'd been mortal. But now, the knife was ragged and tarnished from his unholy touch.

" 'Take this bread, for it is my flesh.' "

He carefully cut the nun's habit from her head. The sound of the ripping fabric tore through the eerie silence. Slowly, he trailed his fingertips down her pale skin. His touch made the veins in her chest swell. Her pulse raced.

" 'Take this wine, for it is my blood.' " He sighed wistfully. "Oh, Angelina. You will become a part of me. Through my veins, your blood will live in an eternal night."

FLIGH✝ NIGH✝

Therefore, he that made them will not have mercy on them.
He that formed them will show them no favor.
—Isaiah 27:11

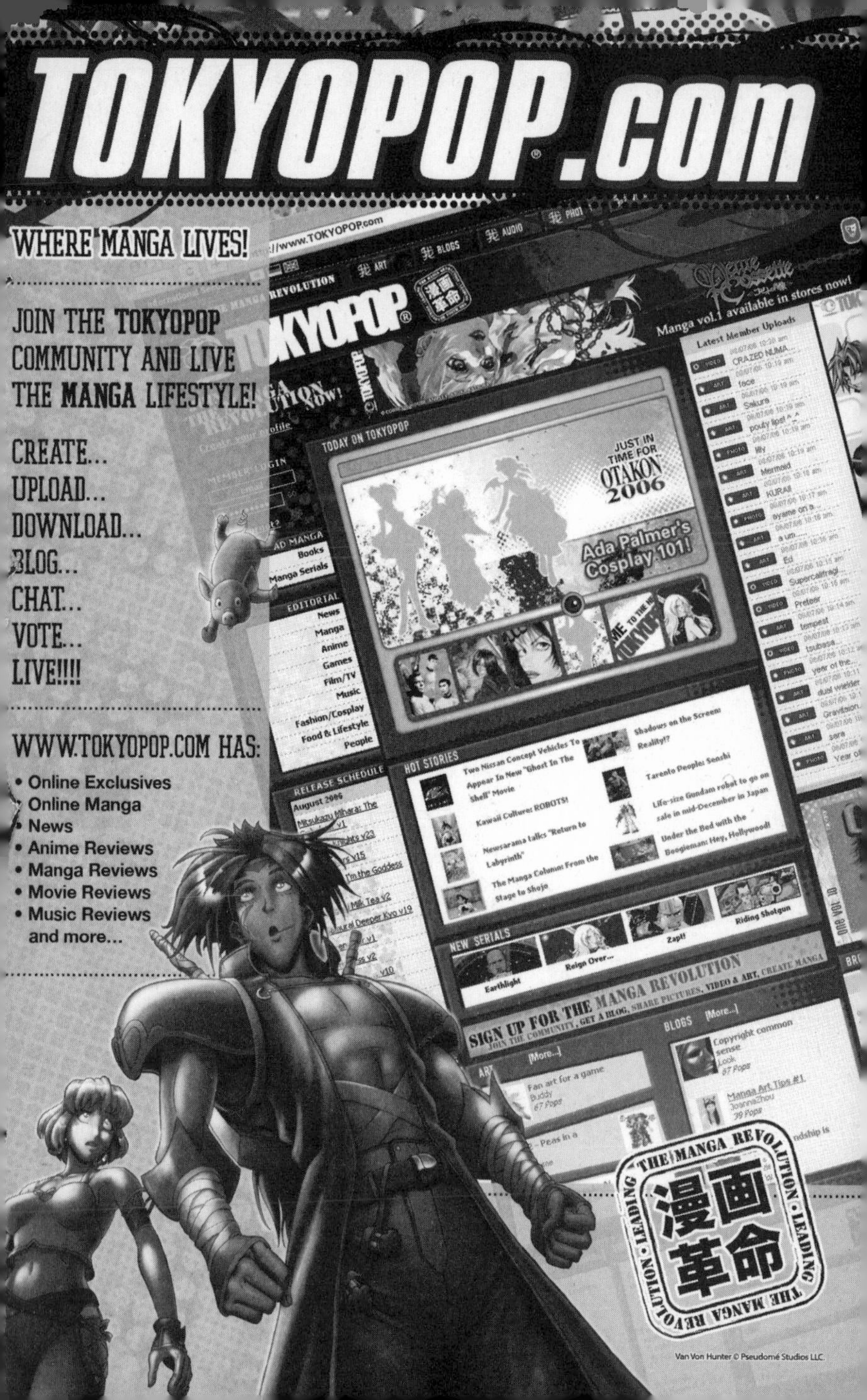
TOKYOPOP.com
WHERE MANGA LIVES!
JOIN THE TOKYOPOP COMMUNITY AND LIVE THE MANGA LIFESTYLE!
CREATE...
UPLOAD...
DOWNLOAD...
BLOG...
CHAT...
VOTE...
LIVE!!!!
WWW.TOKYOPOP.COM HAS:
• Online Exclusives
• Online Manga
• News
• Anime Reviews
• Manga Reviews
• Movie Reviews
• Music Reviews
and more...
THE MANGA REVOLUTION • LEADING • 漫画革命
Van Von Hunter © Pseudomé Studios LLC.

LAUNCHING TOKYOPOP MUSIC

THE NEW SOUND FROM TOKYOPOP!

THE HIGHLY ANTICIPATED LAUNCH OF THE TOKYOPOP MUSIC LABEL IS HERE!

THE MANGA REVOLUTION INFILTRATES MUSIC WITH AN AMAZING ASSORTMENT OF MANGA SOUNDTRACKS AND SONGS FROM PRINCESS AI, INITIAL D, RAVE MASTER, AND MUCH MORE.

HERE IS MUSIC THAT WILL MAKE YOU WANT TO GROOVE, TO RIDE, TO DRIFT, AND TO DREAM...

TOKYOPOP
PRESENTS
ANIME
TRAX
Music by D.J. Milky and b_nCHANt_d

CHECK OUT THE DEBUT ALBUMS NOW

BEATZ 4 RIDERZ
PRODUCED BY D.J. Milky AND b_nCHANt_d
TOKYOPOP
PRESENTS

THIS FALL LOOK OUT FOR MORE NEW RELEASES!

TOKYOPOP
PRESENTS
DRIFT 2 DIE
PRODUCED BY D.J. Milky AND b_nCHANt_d

AVAILABLE ON ITUNES AND WHEREVER DOWNLOADABLE MUSIC IS SOLD

keyword: TOKYOPOP

Music available online only

FOR MORE INFORMATION VISIT: WWW.TOKYOPOP.COM

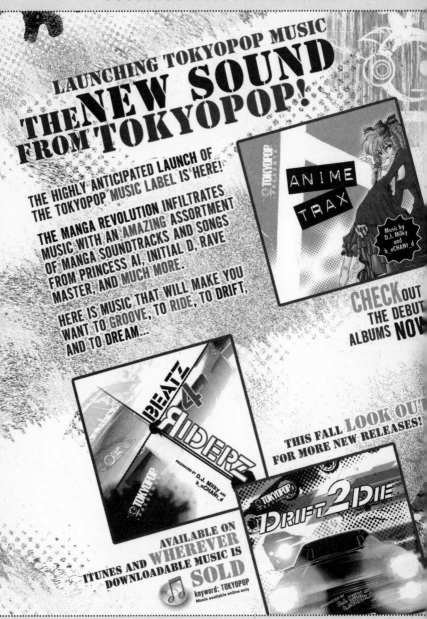

STOP!

This is the back of the book.
You wouldn't want to spoil a great ending!

This book is printed "manga-style," in the authentic Japanese right-to-left format. Since none of the artwork has been flipped or altered, readers get to experience the story just as the creator intended. You've been asking for it, so TOKYOPOP® delivered: authentic, hot-off-the-press, and far more fun!

DIRECTIONS

If this is your first time reading manga-style, here's a quick guide to help you understand how it works.

It's easy... just start in the top right panel and follow the numbers. Have fun, and look for more 100% authentic manga from TOKYOPOP®!